Finding You

Finding You

Agony of Being Me

Explosive Twisting Conclusion

Victoria Valentine
writing as
January Valentine

ISBN-13: 978-0692741535
ISBN-10: 0692741534

Book Design & Cover by Victoria Valentine
Edited by: Phaedra Valentine
Song lyrics by Victoria Valentine

Cover art: © Pyrosky iStockPhoto.com

Water Forest Press Books
PO Box 295, Stormville, NY 12582
waterforestpress.com

January Valentine Books

Love Dreams Contemporary Romance
Michael is in a wheelchair. Sienna has been emotionally damaged. They keep having accidental run-ins, but can they find love?

Sweet Dreams in the Mind of a Serial Killer
He plants roses ... in dead women. A witness says: He doesn't look human.

Fighting For You Steamy Contemporary Romance
Jewelia wants to work for the NYPD. Indigo is a medical student with baggage. They come from two different worlds. Can they beat the odds?

Beautiful Experiment Paranormal Romance Book One of The Island of Defiance Trilogy

Six unruly teens are kidnapped, sent to an uncharted island. Caretaker, Brook, is hot. Father is mysterious. Will they find a way home before the island is overrun with demons?

Wheel Wolf (Werewolf Horror)

Don't stop at the lake! You never know what you'll run into. Jack & Jenny are lovers sharing an unconditional love. Is there an ungodly creature at Hosner Lake? Ask Jack.

Agony of Being Me & Finding You ... Romance Duo

Agony of Being Me. Everyone love Zoe Channing. Everyone other than Zoe. Healing from a brutal attack rockets her to hell. Will she ever return? Ask Jesse Sinclair in *Finding You.*

All titles are available on Amazon Kindle/print, B & N and through other booksellers in paperback. Some are Audio books.

Find all of my books on my Amazon Author pages
http://www.amazon.com/January-Valentine/e/B007Q28DFE/
http://www.amazon.com/Victoria-Valentine/e/B005LYVSTM/

Finding You

Tom, your story had no name, but it was beautiful.

I came with baggage and you welcomed my flaws.

Finding You

"Hanging on to resentment is letting someone you despise live rent-free in your head."– Ann Landers

Finding You

I close my eyes and let the emotions stirring inside me color the canvas. I step back and study the painting: I see fairy wings, butterflies and wildflowers. It's Zoe. Her flowing blonde hair caught by a ray of sun glistens as the wind takes it across the sky. Zoe is the sky.

Finding You

Four Years Ago

The darkness is seductive. The wheels in my head start spinning, which causes my stomach to do all sorts of crazy things. Can a stomach thud, or is it my heart? My chest is aching. Aching like my arms that hang at my sides. My arms that have one purpose tonight. To lead Zoe into a secluded corner, hold her lightly at first, then possessively as my lips crush hers. I want to do so many things with her. To her. Kissing her within the next five minutes is exactly how I plan on starting. If she warms up, that is. Right now Zoe Channing is a big question mark, and if anyone is going to dig for her answer, that guy is me.

After what feels like an eternity, the door flies open. Zoe is wild-eyed. Her skirt is twisted around her hips, the soft fabric of her top is hanging loose around her slender waistline. The stretched neckline bares one creamy white shoulder which is imprinted with red blotches; the result of strong fingers that restrained her. This I notice because with each beat of my heart I am taking in every inch of Zoe. Examining her for damage. Before I can stop her, she bolts past me, sobbing. I'm speechless: a girl half my size almost knocks me off my feet.

My first instinct is to chase after her, make sure she's okay, but when I visualize what he might have done to her, I'm filled with adrenaline I need to work out of my system. Trent is on his knees in the closet, laughing like an idiot.

I don't take the time to think. I react. I grab the collar of his shirt, yank his face up and level with mine, draw back and pound his jaw with my fist. His eyes roll up into his head and he sinks to the floor.

My boot finds his side. "You're not worth my time, douchebag. Zoe better be okay or I'm coming back to finish this." Through gritted teeth I add, "You're lucky I'm in a hurry."

I sprint down the road as fast as my legs will take me, shouting, "Zoe! Zoe, where are you?"

Night mixes with mist, and I see nothing but the outline of trees around me. Ahead of me. Then an outline moves and I believe part of what I thought was a tree could be Zoe. My head is spinning. My chest is heaving.

Taking her by the arms, I gently shake her. But she's a zombie. "Zoe. Zoe, it's me! Jesse!"

When she finally lifts her head, her stare is blank. But her eyes, her big blue eyes are glittering with tears. Nothing I say, nothing I do, seems to be working. She's locked in her own world and won't let me enter.

After finally getting to know her tonight, darkness should bring us closer. I should have the right to reach out to her, pull her into my arms, touch her lips with mine, finish our conversation and begin a relationship. My mind whirls with things to say to this girl who's stealing the breath I've just recovered. I need to reach her; wants and words are just not working. She's slipping further away.

I have no clue why, but I start reciting the words of her song lyrics. Maybe I feel this is something Zoe can identify with. Something she loves. Something that will bring her back to being

Zoe. Instead of a brittle statue standing before me on the darkened road. Cold as ice. Trembling hard enough to break.

Trees not shed
The world needs your splendor
Birds sing sweet and far
So the lost can find shelter

Her eyes widen. She must think I've lost my mind. Correction: we've both lost our minds. Slowly, she starts dancing around me, singing:

If you see a Fae you're forever blessed
She holds the lamp of kindness
An intriguing bit of magic
With a drop of human tears
Once your eyes have brushed her wings
You'll fall in love for years

"Now I know what your future holds, Nightingale." I chuckle, relieved she's broken her silence. "Broadway."

"Nightingale? I like it!" She snatches her jacket from my hand, wraps it around her shoulders, and flaps her arms, singing out, "If I don't fly away, I'll be studying law."

"Ah. Nice to know." In awe, I watch her transform into something unstable, frightening but still beautiful. I know she's not acting right, but I play along. I can't lose her now. Won't let her retreat into her world of silence, even if we have to stand here all night acting like crazies.

"And why is that?" Dancing around me, she's breathless.

"If I ever need a lawyer, I'll know who to call."

"Oh yeah?" She comes to a halt before me. We're almost nose to nose because she's standing on tip toes, attempting to stare me straight in the eye. "If I need an artist, I'll do the same."

Does she know she's doing things to me she might be sorry for? My breath comes faster because I feel like I'm reaching out to touch an angel. Can a guy get this lucky?

She tumbles into my arms, which hungrily fold around her. She's soft, warm, and smells of honey and flowers. I'm balancing on a ledge, feeling lightheaded, ready for a risk.

"Would you want to go to Prom with me?" I whisper into her ear. Then my lips taste her cheek.

She sucks in a breath, but before she can answer …

Headlights come out of nowhere, blinding me. I shield my eyes with one arm, while my other slides around Zoe, pulling her to safety. Dragging her from the path of the maniac who's about to run us over.

"What the fuck?" I yell into the blinding light.

Everything's jumbled. Brakes screech. A car door slams. Some dude is standing before me, hands rolled into fists. Is he threatening me? If my mind wasn't spinning so badly, and my heart wasn't pumping like a damn piston on speed, I'd … I'd.

"What's going on?" My eyes shift to Zoe, who's frozen and distant. "Who is he?"

But Zoe isn't talking to me, she's crying, screaming at the top of her lungs.

"Holy fuck. What's going on?" I turn to the man she calls Dad. "Wait. Let's sort this out, please. Calm down, sir. I didn't touch her."

"Get in the goddamned car, Zoe," he bellows. His eyes catch a reflection of the headlights and they glare; he looks like a fucking demon.

Finding You

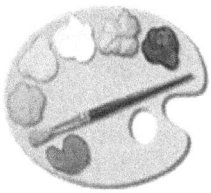

My name is Jesse Sinclair. In my senior year of high school I was in command of my grades, my car, my bike. I made the rules and I broke them. Like a brilliant landscape, I had life painted and framed. I also had my sights set on a girl named Zoe Channing. She was my dream; and like a dream, she vanished. I have no clue what happened to Zoe the night of Trent's party, and it's killing me. The blinding lights in the road, her tortured scream which is forever burned into my brain, will always send a chill down my spine. I'm left in confusion, and I'm haunted. Was I to blame? Did I have a part in causing the car accident that took the lives of her parents and almost killed the girl I was falling helplessly in love with? I can't live with this guilt, can't seem to move on without knowing Zoe's fate. Where is she? Is she safe? Is she as fucked up as I am?

Face it, Jesse, you're addicted and no matter how hard you try, your life is now a nightmare, and Zoe is still just a dream.

Painting is my passion. After graduation, I thought I'd be in art school. But here I am, three years later, still running my dad's service station. After his heart attack, he decided to become a Dallas rancher. There wasn't much to keep him here.

My mom wasted away from cancer when Jamie and I were just kids. Her illness, her death, left an indelible mark; a deep void which might be the reason Jamie is so fucked up. Jamie is my older brother. There are two major differences between my brother and me: Jamie sees his door as half closed. Mine is half open. He's got me by three years, but one would never know it. Staring into a mirror, we look like twins. But that's where the similarities end. Jamie is a man-whore, bagging every chick who shakes her ass at him; wearing down those who don't. I never want to be like Jamie.

I live in New York, played around Jersey, bummed around the country, working odd jobs, drifting, fucking, praying to the powers that I'm not turning into my brother. That I haven't caught the same disease: emotionless, empty, careless sonofabitch. A selfish shitbag like Jamie.

Finding You

Jesse

From the time I was a kid, I hated to see summer end. Early sunsets and bare trees aren't my idea of cheerful. Call me humbug, but winter holidays never did it for me either. Maybe I'm weird, but I don't dig Christmas trees or opening gifts. Maybe it's because I don't like surprises. Jamie took care of that. He pranked me with all kinds of weird shit when we were kids, like frogs in my bed, his outstretched foot when I came around a corner. Jumping me from behind when I was gulping a can of soda. I remember brawling across the living room floor, knocking the Christmas tree over. Mom flew into a frenzy that year. I hated seeing her that way, being part of the cause upsetting her.

So yeah, surprises I can do without. Art is the gift that opens *me* up; so could Zoe. When I first saw her, I felt like I was in the middle of an earthquake. The floor shook. I had nothing to hold onto other than her eyes, and just looking at her cracked me wide open, making me vulnerable to the core. I wasn't sure if I liked it or feared it. But it was fucking amazing. Now that she's gone, I miss that feeling so bad. Zoe's the spring inside me that's stretched my heart so far I'm ready to snap wide open. Sometimes I give in to fantasy. I close my eyes, lose myself in another world that's filled with Zoe. I see her face so clearly, feel the touch of her lips, her skin; it's all so vivid, I sense her standing beside me and I actually believe she'll magically appear and life will be good again.

My cell chirps. It's a text from ... Alana? How the hell did she get my number?

Easy, jerk. You were naked and shitfaced most of the time you were together in Atlantic City. She had access to just about everything on and off your body.

Alana: Where are you?
Me: Why?
Alana: Need a shoulder
ME: What?
Alana: The bastard took my car
Me: Report it stolen
Alana: Not that easy ... please!!!
Me: Where are you?
Alana: Atlantic City

It's Saturday afternoon. If I take the bike I can make it there in about three hours, two and a half if I push it. Unsure of how long I'll be away, I stuff a few things into my pack and stow it in the saddlebag. Just in case. In case what? My mind leaps back in time, and I'm in a hotel room with Alana, and we're rolling around on a king sized bed that didn't seem big enough that night because we ended up on the floor. After another round in the shower, while I stretched out on the bed recovering, she posed before the dresser mirror applying makeup, wearing nothing but a towel wrapped around her hips, making a third round a necessity.

Before leaving the house, I grab a bottle of water from the fridge. On my way to the garage, I keep wondering what Alana might want. The realization of what might be awaiting me in

Atlantic City hits my gut. I may not be thrilled about the actual reason I've been invited to the boardwalk, but I'm feeling good about getting away from this place for a while. Leave work and worries behind. For a single guy who's just reached legal drinking age, I live a fucking boring life. I have no one to blame but myself and the slump I've been in since" Stop it, my brain shouts, so I concentrate on Alana before dwelling on the past brings on a migraine.

With Alana's warm body taking control of my mind, it takes a moment for me to adjust myself on the seat of my bike; my crotch is that tight. My cell sounds again and I glance at the text from my brother, Jamie. I don't reply, just click off the message. Jamie is the last thing I need right now. He's thinking about flying to Dallas and wants me to tag along. Well I'll be damned. There must be a method to his madness. Considering flying to Dallas with Jamie, my hard-on instantly deflates.

Plowing through traffic is a breeze, and just after sunset, I slide to a stop in the parking lot, letting the bike idle as I scan the area for Alana. I figure she'll hop on the back and I'll be driving her home, or, with Alana, who the hell knows what the meaning of *or* could be. We could end up in a room, on the beach, back at her place. That's a joke. I don't know where her place is. Come to think of it, I don't know much about this woman, other than she's hot, horny, and experienced.

The lot is filled with cars, trucks, and safety lights are shining brightly over their gleaming paint. It's been a while since our encounter, so I'm wondering if Alana has changed. Anticipation shoots through me. What does she want? Will I recognize her? It doesn't take me long to find out. I park the bike around the side of the building, fall into a jog on the walkway, then step through the glass entrance doors. After a quick glance around the lobby, my eye catches the corner arrangement of quivering plant life – curious – and that's how I manage to pick out Alana. She's peeking out from behind a wide potted plant that's almost as tall as she is.

When she spots me, half of her body emerges from behind a frilly branch. I have to laugh. She looks like a bad actor trying to imitate a spy in a flop movie. I'm standing in the center of the lobby, and she's barricaded in a corner. What the hell is she up to? My shrugging shoulders instinctively signal her, "And? What's going on?"

Alana shakes her head stubbornly, so I pull my hands from my pockets, throwing them out in front of me, chuckling aloud as I close in. "Hey," I mouth and hitch my head in a confused greeting. "What are you up to, sleuth?"

She isn't decked out in sequins and heels, as I figured she'd be. Maybe tonight isn't going to be a replay of the last time we were together. Thinking I rode all the way out here to receive no reward kind of pisses me off. As I make my way toward her, a long slender leg, covered by snug-fitting blue denim, takes a cautious step. Shaking my head, I watch as the leg is finally followed by the rest of her willowy body. She wears a hooded, unzipped sweatshirt over a black top. Baggy or not, neither garment has a chance in hell of concealing her tantalizing rack.

Grinning and shrugging as I walk, my gaze is intent, taking her in from head to toe. Her hair is longer than I recall, and dark with some light streaks. My eyes rest on her face, or what I can see of it, curious as to why she's wearing enormous sunglasses.

"Jesse," her voice is deep and husky, "thank God."

"After all this time, why'd you text me?" The question that's been bugging me the entire ride is the first thing to pop out of my mouth. "And what's with the shades? Incognito?" My chuckle is forced because this woman asked for my help and is acting gloomy and mysterious, which can mean one of two things. I'll end up in a fight, or jail, by the end of the night. On the bright side, I could end up in bed with her, instead. I'm hoping for the latter. But from the way she's dressed, and her demeanor, hope fades fast.

"Nice to see you too." As I unzip my jacket and let it fall open, my brows crunch. I run my fingers through my mop of hair, which I've decided not to cut in protest of nothing special, which is why I rarely shave anymore as well. "What's up?" I catch my index finger in a loop of her hair and give it a playful tug.

I want to look in her eyes, see if I can read her, so I reach for her shades. Before my fingers can touch the frame, they're swatted away.

"No. Not here."

"I wasn't trying to fuck you," I chuckle, curiosity piquing.

"Follow me," she whispers. "Act natural."

"You're acting anything but natural," I whisper, pulling her to my side.

I study the movement of her lips. Natural pink and plush. Nice.

Alana links her arm through mine and leads me into the lounge. Her perfume is sweet and fruity, filling the air with a sexy essence. Too bad Alana is dark and moody, or this could be the beginning of another memorable night.

When we settle into a corner booth, Alana doesn't remove the big black sunglasses that are masking a third of her face.

"Been a long time," I say as I slip out of my jacket and bundle it on the seat beside me. I push up the arms of my Henley, then rest my hands on the table. "No hello? How've you been?" I grin, but I'm feeling a growing discomfort. I glance around to see if anyone looks as strange as I feel. The stools tucked against the long polished bar are beginning to fill with a variety of bodies, but there are only a few unremarkable couples sitting at tables scattered around the room. The shrub encircled waterfall in the corner masks just about all sound, so Alana has picked the right atmosphere for privacy.

"Hey." My boot nudges her foot beneath the table. "Tell me what's wrong."

Alana is just about to speak when a server appears. One of the chick's rounded hips juts dangerously close to my face. I don't know if she's looking for tips, or just looking, but her eyes are taking bites out of me. She adjusts the waistband of her black trousers, then tugs down the hem of her knit top, exposing bulging cleavage.

"What can I get you folks?" After burning through me, her dark eyes fix on Alana. Her head tilts. "How are you guys tonight?"

It's obvious this girl doesn't give a shit, so why bother asking. Oh yeah, right. Tips. I'm wondering if she's wondering if we're a couple or if Alana is my youthful-looking mother. My sugar mama. Or what. Because she turns back to me with a twinkle in her eye that says she's gained enough experience in this place to analyze faces, places, and situations. I wonder if she's mastered positions as well because that hip and its mate are attached to long legs that could wrap a boy nicely.

"I'll have a draft." I look up into her smoky eyes, then my gaze gets caught in her cleavage.

"Scotch," Alana speaks softly, "straight up." Her clasped hands rest on the table top.

When the server struts off, I can't help but check out her ass before I reach over to grab one of Alana's hands. Her fingers aren't welcoming. They're stiff, cold.

"You're acting like you just escaped from a mental ward. This better be good, Alana."

"Jesse," her lips quiver, "I'm sorry I involved you but I didn't know who else to call. Or what to do."

"You can start by explaining what the hell's going on? What's with the shades at eight p.m.?" This isn't the Alana I knew for one explosive weekend two years ago. I cock my head and tap the table. "It's good to see you too," I'm sarcastic, but when her full bottom lip folds down, I feel bad for being a dick. "Are you okay? Why'd you reach out to me?"

She slowly lifts the sunglasses, revealing a fresh-looking shiner, still red-edged. An irregular gathering of bright red veins surround her navy blue iris.

Finding You

"What the fuck?" I say too loudly. Releasing her hand, I leap to my feet and fall into the seat beside her. I keep shaking my head. Any piece of shit who'd do this to a woman needs to be taught a lesson he'll never forget. "Tell me this was an accident. And not your ex. Because–" My fists are balled and my breath is growing heavy.

"Relax, Jesse. Please don't make a scene."

"Me make a scene?" I recoil. "You get me out here, show me this," I gently run a finger across her bruised cheekbone, "and you want me to relax? Did you have that eye looked at? What the fuck–"

The approach of our server halts us. Alana turns her head to hide her bruises. When the chick leaves, my fist rocks the table, sloshing the beer she just delivered. Alana reaches over to move my mug from the flood of beer, then uses a napkin to mop it up.

"It was Peter." She lifts her drink and gulps like a thirsty dude then slams her almost empty glass down.

"Not that there could be a reason, Alana, but why?" My palm is holding my chin up. Loose-lipped, I stare.

The whites of both of her eyes are pink, watery. She squints. "Did you have to close the station to come out here?"

My palm falls to the table. "What?"

"I'm sorry I bothered you, Jesse." She gathers her purse as if to leave. "It's my mess. I shouldn't expect you to clean it up just because–"

"Just because I fucked your brains out one isolated weekend like a lifetime ago? What the hell, Alana? You get me to come all the way down here and now you're gonna just up and leave? Without telling me what motivated your boyfriend to use your face as a punching bag?"

"Ex," she corrects, rolling a last sip of scotch around her glass. "I shouldn't have involved you." Her tone is not at all convincing.

"Well now that you did." I take her arm, gently urging her back into her seat. "Talk to me. Exactly what's been going on? Is he in the hotel?" My eyes dart around the lounge.

For a moment she rests her head on my shoulder. After a deep breath her head comes up and she pins a lock of hair behind her ear. She looks sheepish, angry, guilty, all rolled into one sick-looking expression. "I blackmailed him," she whispers, chewing her lip.

I recoil, blowing out, "What?"

Her hand lands on my thigh, her fingers squeezing. "Peter took my car, so I told him I would turn him in for dealing drugs."

"He deals?" This night is full of surprises. So is Alana.

She shakes her head, grabs a napkin and furiously shreds it.

"You lost me." I swallow a couple mouthfuls of beer then resume my interrogation. "Why'd he take your car? Why'd you lie?"

"He took my car and gave it to his bitch." She frowns then winces. "With my insurance coverage! I wanted to get even with him." She touches her jaw and as a tear seeps from her duct to her nose, she winces.

My fist comes down on the table and my mug goes flying. "Did he give you more than a black eye?" With the slightest touch, I trace her cheek. "Did you call the cops?"

Her entire face tightens. "I can't."

My palms close around my mug. "You're not making any sense."

Her head snaps up and she glares at me. "My father is running for office in D.C. Can you say scandal?" She buries her face in her hands, then peeks up at me.

"Hey, babe. Don't bite my head off. I'm not–"

She takes my hand. "I'm sorry. I didn't mean to come off that way. It's just that–"

"Your ex is a douchebag." I shake my head and roll my eyes. "So what do you want me to do? Kick Peter's ass? Vote for your father?" My anger erodes to sarcasm.

Alana pulls her hand away to reach into her bag for a clump of tissues. "I just want my car ... my life back. He's threatening me."

"Where is this dude ... right now?"

She lets out an uneven breath. "Outside." Her lids slide closed. "That's why I called you. I can't leave. He's waiting for me." She's distant.

I tip her face to mine. "Look at me, Alana. Let me get this straight. He wants you back? Or use you as a punching bag." My stare is hard. My hands ball up again.

"The suite we stayed in," she looks like a kid awaiting punishment, "I come here a lot."

"Ah. You never mentioned that." My head fills with visions of Alana and *Johns*, and I'm sickened at the possibility of her hanging out here to make money. Maybe Peter's her pimp. The thought makes me cringe. I slide as far from her as I can without falling off the seat.

"Don't look at me like that, Jesse." She sounds crushed. "I never brought anyone here. Not like you think. Not like you and me. I travel for business. I guess you could call this our getaway. My father rents the suite we were in for political reasons. Staff meetings, etc."

"Ah ha." I lift a brow and remove her hand from my thigh.

"He has meetings here, Jesse. He's not cheating on my mother. They're divorced. I came here yesterday to meet clients and–"

I bury my face in my hands then come up for air. "Jesus Christ. You're a hooker. I fucking slept with a hooker." There's not much more separating me from my brother now. My stomach sinks.

"I'm just an escort, for drinks and dinner–"

"Yeah, that's what they all say. So, your father sets you up?" My lips are almost too tight to move.

"Peter likes to keep his clients happy."

"Peter." I shake my head. "He's your pimp. What the fuck did I get myself into?" I scrub my hands over my face and groan. "Who did I get myself into?"

Her cheeks flush. "I'm just an escort, I swear. I don't have sex with men for money. They show me off, tell me their troubles. I cater to them. That's it." She laughs. "I could have practiced law for God's sake. And I wind up in this position. That's the crazy part. I don't know how I ever let him talk me into–"

I stare with disbelief. "So Peter dumped you. You're pissed off. Threaten to ruin his career. Now you want me to–"

"Just get me out of this hotel. Peter has a bad temper sometimes. He'll cool off. We need to keep a low profile. No attention. Sneak me out. That's it." Her eyes look wild. The woman is scared shitless.

Alana drags up her jacket zipper, shoves her glasses back on, pulls her hair over half of her face and we slip out of the bar. Incognito. Just when I thought my life was too boring to live. I almost laugh. Next I'll be hanging out with my brother.

So now that I've fallen into this mess, I know the shit's gonna only get deeper. Because when I get my hands on Petey, I'm gonna make him sorry he ever met a girl named Alana, whatever the hell her last name is. For as serious a matter as this is, the thought of not even knowing her last name is humorous.

We slip out a side door and skulk along the walkway, close to the building. Yeah that's right. Even though there are no floodlights here, we skulk. It's Alana's idea. Mine is to charge out into the parking lot, find this shithead, and knock his brains out.

"You never said how your life is going, Jesse," Alana's whisper is hoarse.

"You never asked. And this isn't the time for small talk. I need to think."

Her arm comes up beside me. "There's my car. Quick. Go the other way." Alana body-slams me away from the lighted parking area.

By the shoulders I spin her. "Wait right over there, behind that stone pillar."

Looking all kinds of innocent, like an average hotel guest, I mosey beneath the floodlights over to the dirtbag wearing a Polo shirt and khakis, leaning against the driver's door of Alana's car. Waiting. A cigarette dangles from his mouth. He looks like a well-dressed douchebag.

I walk right up to him and I'm immediately in his face. "Nice night. You must be Peter." I flash a tight smile inches from his nose.

"Do I know you?" He's got nasty written all over his mug. I'm in his space, so he shifts his stance, moving a few inches away.

"Nope, but you *do* know a friend of mine."

When he cocks his head his jaw tightens. "Says who?"

"The guy who's about to beat your brains out."

Shock grips his face. "What are you talking about?" His eyes shift and return to mine.

"Yeah, I figured a motherfucker like you finds it easier to beat on a woman than confront a man."

I'm so close to his face, I'm sure my breath is slamming him. He inches away; my body moves with his, hugging him as tight as his knit shirt.

"Does Alana ring a bell?" I'm stumped for a last name. My bad. You'd think you'd know the last name of a girl before you screwed her.

Before he can utter another word, the collar of his shirt is gathered in my fists, and his back is pressed to the car. I'm remembering Alana's words. "Keep a low profile." So I throw an undercut to his gut and he grunts and folds.

"Who the fuck are you?" he gags, not attempting to defend himself because his arms are wrapped around his middle.

"I told you. A friend. And unless you want the next fist to bust your face open, I'd suggest you forget you ever knew Alana." Shit, the statement would have been a lot more forceful if I said her last name. "Where's the registration to this car? Her car–"

"Inside," he croaks, still cradling his gut.

I'm enjoying this. My grin is authentic. "Get it."

He stumbles into the car and back out again, then slaps the paperwork into my outstretched hand.

After a quick glance, I shoot him a hard stare. "You don't look like Alana Lundsford to me. So what are you doing with her car?"

He shoots me a blank stare then has the balls to ask, "What are you to Alana? How long have you known her?"

"None of your fucking business." I shove the registration into my pocket. "My advice to you, leave the lady alone. You gave her the car, shithead. It's in her name. Forget you ever knew her. No phone calls. No contact, get me?" Using his collar, I yank his face closer to mine, not only for effect but to make a good enough impression on this sick bastard. "Especially physical contact. Because if you touch her again," I release his shirt and my finger pokes his chest, "I'll hunt you down and kill you. Got it?"

The guy's face is beet red. Nodding, he swats off my hand and attempts to pull away.

I yank his arm and hold out a hand. "Forget something?"

After depositing the car keys into my outstretched palm, he splits, weaving through cars. I stride away, deep in thought: So this is the end of Peter, I hope. For Alana's sake … and mine. I don't want any more emergency phone calls from this chick who has just shown me she can be trouble. Come to think of it, I've never met a girl whose name didn't spell trouble.

Before leaving the lot, I swing my head around, checking to make sure Peter's gone. He could be an occupant of the black Mercedes that's kicking up dust as it tears out of the parking lot. I get a quick glance of the blonde head behind the wheel, wondering if he'll pull this shit on her someday. Dirtbags like him should be shot into space.

I return to find Alana peeking out from behind the pillar. Her face is stone. I slap the keys into her palm. "You look like you need a drink."

"You looked amazing out there." With Peter gone, Alana seems herself.

"Flattery won't get me back up there." Winking, I hitch my head toward the top floor of the hotel.

Alana laughs and hooks her arm through mine. "Let's take that walk on the beach that we started two years ago. The moon's bright. It's a great night." She pulls me to a halt and gazes up at me. "Thank you, Jesse."

I smirk. "Try to stay out of trouble, okay?"

"I really mean it, Jesse. You saved my life."

"Does that mean you'll be following me around until you've repaid me?" I chuckle.

She drops her head on my shoulder and giggles. "Oh Jesse. If only I were ten years younger."

"I'd say age is just a number," I tip her face to mine, "but that would sound like I'm coming on to you."

"I wish." She grins up at me. "You're a good guy. Honest and sweet." She taps my chest. "You've got a good heart. And I think someone owns it." Her eyes dig into mine. "Am I right?"

Is she perceptive or does my loss really show? "Why do you say that?"

"Otherwise we'd be in the elevator, on our way up there." She points to the hotel.

I laugh. "How far would a woman go to get inside a guy's head?"

"Should I try?"

I shake my head and grin. "By the time this night is over, you'll have turned me into an alcoholic."

She laughs. "Come on. I know a good place for a drink. So how have you been, Jesse? Now I can ask. And I really do want to know. I've thought about you … a lot."

"You've just sampled my life. Need I say more?" Linking arms we walk. "So where are you taking me?"

"You'll see."

We end up at a grocery store, and leave with a six of beer and some plastic cups stashed inside Alana's tote bag. Paid for of course.

By the time we reach the beach, all that's visible is the illuminated sand and the outline of dark waves breaking on the shore. We lose our shoes and walk barefoot until we find a cozy spot where we sit and break out the brew.

"You really helped me, Jesse. In more ways than one. I want you to know, I'll never forget what you did for me."

My arm goes lightly around her and I tug her in for a quick hug. "You're not so bad yourself. But damn, woman, find yourself a decent guy next time. Someone who'll treat you right."

"Some women just end up falling for the wrong men."

"Doesn't have to be that way. Hand me another beer."

Moonlight softens Alana's bruises and even in pants and sweatshirt, she's as hot as ever. We sit side by side. Now and then she checks me sideways, her expression growing curious. She runs her fingers from my cheek to my sideburns, then strokes my head. "The ocean air is curling your hair. You let it grow. I like it."

I scrub a hand through her hair. "Yours too. You look like a little poodle."

She bursts out laughing. "I hope that's a compliment."

"Hey, I never said I was perfect." I chuckle. "I guess I'm not that smooth around women, huh?"

"I wouldn't complain about you. How about your girlfriend? What does she think?"

I take a slug of beer, then run a hand over my bearded chin. "My girlfriend. Let me think. Which one to start with."

Alana bursts out laughing, then her face goes serious. She nudges my shoulder with hers. "How are things going with the girl who puts that dreamy look in your eyes every time I ask, 'Do you have a girlfriend?' What's her problem, anyway? Leaving you to run loose on a night like this?"

"This calls for another beer." I brush my fingers through my hair and focus on the stars. "It's complicated."

"The story of my life." She sighs. "Again. If you were a few years older, not that you don't act old enough," she bumps my shoulder with hers, "I'd be all over you."

"Age didn't seem to matter before."

Alana pops open a beer and offers it to me. "Uh uh. Nursing this one. I have to ride home tonight. Work tomorrow."

She takes a slug then lets out a loud sigh. "I knew a guy once. We were a little bit older than you but still, it was young love." Her voice falls so soft I can barely hear her, so I lean in close. "My first real love, if you know what I mean."

Nodding, I study her profile, then full face when she turns to me.

She chews her lip. "Michael and I practically grew up together. Then life took us in different directions. Thank God we found each other again because I thought about him all the time, wondering *what if*. We didn't have much time together, though. He was an Army Ranger, about to deploy. When he came home on leave he popped the question. He was sweet and wonderful. Just like you."

A breeze has kicked up, blowing our hair. I sweep strands from her face, tuck them behind her ears. "What happened? Where is he?"

A flood of tears rolls down her cheeks. "He went back to finish his tour overseas and came home in a box."

"Christ, hon. I'm so sorry." I pull her into my arms and she sobs against my chest.

"Everybody's got a story. Grief or some kind of shit." I circle her back with massaging fingers.

She cups my face with her palms. "My point in telling you this is, don't let life get in the way. If you care about her, go get her."

So then it all spills out. The entire story about me and Zoe and the last night I saw her.

Alana and I are hugging and mourning together. "She was my angel, Alana. No one else ever made me feel the way she did. No one will. There was that connection. Instant and just–"

"Electricity, right?"

"Yeah." I stare at the moon. "Soul mates." My laugh is bitter. "Who'd ever believe it? It was fucked up man. It could have been beautiful."

"It still could be," Alana says. "If she really is your soul mate, then you'll meet again."

"Sure. So what do I do, hire Sherlock to find her?"

"Not a bad idea."

"I'm joking. The way I look at it is, she left without a word. To me that equals, I don't give a shit." I shake my head and run a hand through my hair. "It felt so right."

"I guess you never get over first love, huh Jesse?"

Finding You

Zoe

In high school I had three names: Zoe Channing, Peanut, and Nightingale. In high school I had a life. A loving mother and father. A potential hot boyfriend who named me Nightingale hours before my life ended. Peanut was the name my father came up with. Mom said he called me Peanut from the day I was born, and it was the last word I heard from my father's lips that fucked up night, moments before our car flew off a bridge and plunged into a river, killing both of my parents. Leaving me a fifteen-year-old guilty mess.

I hadn't had a chance to come to terms with the brutal attack at school, which in reality was rape, which I can't admit, so I still call it physical assault. Assault and battery. That's an easier term to cope with. Losing myself to a maniac was impossible to face, so I blocked it. Straight from the hospital, I was sent to live with Aunt Molly, her second husband, Rye McCabe, and my street-wise twin cousins, Nina and Nino Romano. I despised them all, and couldn't believe being inducted into their family would be my fate till I turned eighteen. But something happened during that summer they took me in. Nina and Nino became my family. Molly and Rye, along with falling in with the wrong crowd, tore us apart.

Bubbles to my chin, I soak in the tub, letting hot water engulf me, trying to relax as scenes roll through my head. When my palms run over my smooth, soap coated skin, my breasts and hips tell me the little girl victim has grown up in more ways than one; externally, anyway. Years, months, days sabotage my mind. Self-examination has become a big part of my life. I hang on to some memories, others are conveniently shoved against the back of my skull. Like the accident that is buried in the deepest recesses of my mind, along with the assault. Tragedy never happened, at least not to me. I'm not sure who I am, other than an identity-less senior about to graduate PS 243.

When I think about coming to live here, with my sadistic aunt and unhinged twin cousins, recall the terrifying first week of a new city school, I smile; I ended up walking away from a fight with a bloody nose, split lip, bruises around my eyes and forehead, but most importantly, I walked away with my dignity ... and a reputation. *Thank you girls*, because I'm still enjoying my newfound persona. I'm not a bully, but I can handle myself. I'm respected. No one will fuck with me after word of me taking on three of the toughest girls circulated the school.

Surprisingly, Nina and Nino made it through graduation. School is weird without them, but I'm not looking for new homies. I'm not sure what I'm looking for actually, but one thing for certain, the last thing I need right now is a relationship. Guys hit on me all the time, but I'm a loner. A survivor. And it feels amazing.

Days pass. Nights are most difficult, but I feel the metamorphosis dig deep into my soul. I was the prey; now I'm the predator. I'm not sure if I like this pseudo gangsta chick emerging from the old Zoe, but it's a necessity if I'm going to make it to my eighteenth birthday when I can collect my parents' insurance money and escape this neighborhood. I'll be moving out of PS 243 and Molly's clutches.

Nights when I can't sleep, I write lyrics and music. When bad memories block me, I walk. Sometimes I end up in front of Nolan's house. Nolan must have a sixth sense because when I stare up at his window the blinds move and he peers out. Then the casement window cranks open, and a hand sticks out, signaling me to the front porch. My breathing eases, and in a moment, the tall white front door cracks open and without a word he pulls me inside, then rushes me up the stairs, past his parents' bedroom. I hear his father snoring loudly, so I know the coast is clear.

Our feet move in time, almost as if they're duct taped together. I barely move mine because his are leading from behind. I slam a hand over my lips to stifle a laugh because it's so comical. I feel like a thief in the night. Or a hooker on a call. This is why I like to hang with Nolan. He makes me laugh. Makes life easy.

"Hey," I whisper, tripping over the hallway runner, "stop digging your fist into my back."

"Shush." His breath warms my neck as he shoves me into his room and quietly snaps the door shut behind us.

In the safety of his bedroom, the first thing I take in is the look on his face. Tired, but he's standing here with me chilled from the night air, and him warmed from sleep. That counts for a lot. I check the clock on his nightstand. 11:53 pm, and I'm guilty.

"You're unbelievable. You always know when I'm outside." I shake my head and unzip my sweatshirt. "I don't even have to throw pebbles at the window."

I must still be too loud because his index finger goes over my lips. "You're predictable," he snorts.

"Is that so?" I smack his arm. "Predictable is for fools and bores." I pull my face into a mad scowl. "That's an insult."

"A bore you're definitely not. A fool? Debatable. What are you doing walking around alone at night? Especially in this neighborhood." He untwists the waistband of his obviously hastily pulled on sweat pants.

My lips scrunch and I shrug. "I live on the rough side of town, remember? You're uptown, practically in the suburbs." I remember the real suburbs of Pleasantville where my old house was rented right after hell hit. Someday I might go back. Might is a big word right now. Like Nolan's room. Big and airy, but his room is cozy and safe. My world is still in a tailspin.

Nolan moves his backpack from a chair to his desk that is stacked with papers and expensive books, which will get him through his first year of college.

"Sure, Zoe. I live uptown like about ten blocks from Fordham Road. It's still not the greatest neighborhood. Let me guess. You can't sleep." He tugs my arm toward his bed, then releases me to dig into a dresser drawer and pull out a white t-shirt. "Again, huh? What are we gonna do with you, girl?" The neck band catches his wide bottom lip as he quickly pulls the shirt over his head and down his rounded chest.

"Why do you need all those books, Nolan?" I ask. "You're brilliant. You could probably write them."

"Thanks for the vote of confidence, but I don't think my professors would agree."

By the shoulders, he walks me in reverse, and when the back of my legs hit his mattress, he fluffs a pillow covered by a cornflower blue percale case and presses me down on his navy blue comforter. Before lifting my feet, I kick off my sneakers. The sheets are fresh and fragrant with a mix of Nolan's cologne and meadow-like fabric softener.

"Mmm." Sinking into the mattress, I snuggle in the softness. "Comfy."

"No sleeping," he warns as he plops down beside me. "I have

exams tomorrow. We can't be up all night like we were almost every night last week."

I shift to my side to watch him as he punches his pillow and shoves it behind his head. "What do you do, look out the window all night?" I quirk a brow. "For reals. How'd you know I was outside?"

"I could hear it in your voice before we hung up the phone. You sounded intense tonight. More than usual. I knew you wouldn't be able to sleep."

I run a finger over his cheek. He turns his face. Nolan is self-conscious about his skin. Deliberately, I run my finger over the very slight remnant of adolescent acne no one would even guess was there, if Nolan didn't point it out.

"Your skin is soft. Like you." A genuine smile makes its way across my face, and any negative energy I've been struggling with drains from my body. Nolan and I usually banter. Right now, I'm not horsing around. "I was in need and you came to my rescue. My best friend."

He pulls his mouth to one side in a playful smirk. "Yeah. Right. You're just trying to make me feel good."

"Like you do to me." I look deep into his sleepy eyes, then examine his features. His skin is pure cocoa, setting off gorgeous crystal green eyes. My finger finds its way over a thick black brow, then down the bridge of his straight nose. I focus on his mouth. "Girls get fillers to have lips like yours. Yup. You're beautiful, Nolan." I wink at him and he rolls his eyes.

"Who do you look like? Your mom or dad?" I bite my cheek and scan the room for photos. "Why haven't I ever met your parents?"

"Because you always mysteriously appear at midnight, when they're asleep."

"You don't have any pictures in here. What do they look like?"

"Aliens." His chuckle is soft, then he shrugs. "Like normal people, I guess."

He grabs the remote and clicks the TV on, but mutes the sound.

With the light of the 45 inch screen, we don't need the table lamp, so I reach over and snap it off. "Would they like me?"

"What's not to like?" He yawns out the words.

"We've known each other for what, two years?" My big toe runs up and down his shin.

"I guess." He shakes me off. "Stop, you're tickling me."

Pulling my leg back, I cross my ankles. "I'm sorry."

He leans toward his nightstand and grabs his cell phone, checking that his alarm is set. "Why?"

"I bug you constantly, don't I?" I turn on my side and pinch his bicep.

"Dammit girl. If you don't stop manhandling me." He pulls the cord on my hood. "My girlfriend's gonna be wondering where all these bruises are coming from."

"You have a girlfriend?"

He flashes a cocky grin. "College chicks are hot as hell."

"Hotter than high school?" Although we're just friends, the thought of another girl stealing Nolan away is disturbing. Where would I run to when I couldn't sleep?

"I think I'll keep you around. At least for another year." His chuckle is light.

My curling lip is fake but the dip in my stomach is real. "You'll be going away to a four year. What will I do without you?"

He tucks his leg through mine. "I'll pack you in my suitcase and sneak you into the dorm at UNC. How's that?"

"I'm sure that would go over big with your dorm master."

"You're a breath of fresh air, Zoe. I'm going to feel it too. This place is empty without you."

Wide-eyed, I grab his chin and snap his face around. "Really? What about your family?"

He pins an arm beneath his head and stares at the ceiling. "You know they're busy. Dad with his practice, and my mother with her fundraising and the museum."

"Let's go meet them right now." I'm not serious. I just want to know what he'll say.

His shocked expression tells me he doesn't think waking his parents at midnight on a school night, or any night for that matter, would go over very big. And I agree. I just want to know if he's hiding me from his parents because I'm different.

I punch his pillow. "Would they approve of me?"

"I guess." He pulls the pillow from under my head and slaps it over my face.

I snatch the pillow and whip it across his abs.

"When the time is right." He grabs the pillow and tosses it onto the floor.

"When?" I'm intentionally pestering him because I can see I'm annoying him, which is fun. Nolan is quiet most of the time. Bugging him drags out some emotion.

Pulling myself up, I untangle my hair and lean against the headboard. "Remember the first day we met?" My elbow digs into his side.

"Hey," he complains, rubbing the rib I just poked. "How could I forget? Ah, my senior year at PS 243," he sighs, "your cousin wasn't letting me escape Coney Island." He tries to control his laugh, but pulls the pillow from behind him onto his lap, crunches over, and buries his face. When he surfaces, he's grinning. "Or you."

"You wanted to escape me?" Focusing on the silent TV screen, I whisper. "You stalked me."

"I didn't stalk you. I thought you were cute. Vulnerable I guess. In need of a friend." He leans into me and we're pressed shoulder to shoulder. "Interesting," his voice is reflective. "I thought you were interesting. I didn't realize I was staring ... that much ... that hard."

"Oh, you were." I watch his profile for a reaction.

His full lips spread into a cunning grin. "So why did Nina drag me out with you guys?"

I lace my fingers behind my neck and brood. "She's an asshole."

"Come on. Truth or dare," he presses.

I exaggerate a huff of annoyance. "I thought you looked nice, ok?"

His fingers dig into my rib cage. "I've heard that one before." His grin broadens. "You're not bad yourself. Plus, you're a good study partner."

"And I was right. I knew you'd be good for me. And you have been. If it wasn't for you, I might not be graduating this spring. I was that close to failing just about everything."

"You didn't remember that first day when our paths crossed." His bottom lip folds into a pout.

"Our paths did more than cross." I giggle. "I almost knocked you into a wall." I cover my mouth to quiet a laugh. "Blame your eyes. They threw me into a trance." I remember the way he turned at the stairs for a quick look back before disappearing.

"You looked so forlorn. Like you needed a friend. Like you do now." He tugs a lock of my hair. "I'm proud of how far you've come."

Heat fills my cheeks so I rest my head on his shoulder to hide my face, the tears burning my eyes. "My dad was proud of me too."

Nolan's arm comes around me. "I'm sorry about the accident, Zoe. So sorry for your loss. I can't imagine how you got through it all. I wish there was something I could do for you."

My cheek rests on his chest. I sniff. "There is something you can do."

"Name it." He drags his fingers through the long strands of my hair.

My stomach growls so loud, I slap a hand over it.

Nolan holds his gut, trying to restrain his amusement. "You're hungry," he says inside a bout of laughter. "I should have been prepared for this."

I cradle my tummy and peer up at him. "I'm starving."

"What do you want? A sandwich or something?" He runs a hand over his head, as if trying to decide whether or not he should try to feed me at midnight. With a stern look he sighs, "Only for you," and hops off the bed.

"No sandwich." I scrunch my mouth. "Go make us some popcorn."

Standing at the door, Nolan shoots me a defeated look and shakes his head, then he tiptoes out of his room and I don't hear another sound until he reenters with a big bowl of hot buttered popcorn. The aroma alone could knock me over.

"Wow. That smells so good." I immediately start stuffing my mouth.

"I can hear that." He smirks, motioning to my constantly growling gut. "Didn't you eat tonight?"

I groan. "Molly's been scarce. Nina's with Scott half the time. The other half she's in cosmetology school. So it's me and Nino." Rolling my eyes, I bite my lip. "Neither of us can cook." I giggle. "I had a power bar, though." Digging my hand into the bowl, I munch popcorn non-stop.

Nolan stuffs a fistful of popcorn into his mouth and after he swallows, says, "You're cute when you're yourself. And not trying to be some tough chick."

I drop my head onto his shoulder and laugh. Too loud. This brings the knock on his door. Or maybe it's the wafting aroma of popcorn. Either way, the knock is angry and we both freak out.

"Holy shit. We woke them up." Nolan shoves the bowl into my lap, leaps off the bed and in two strides is gripping the door knob. Still chewing, he opens the door wide enough to stick his head out.

"What's going on in there?" I hear his father's deep voice grumble.

"Nothing. I'm on the phone with a friend." Nolan leans heavily on the door, surely to discourage his father's entry.

"I thought I heard a girl's voice."

"Speaker phone. Sorry. I'll be quiet. Go back to bed."

"I smell …" His father shoves past him and enters the room. When he sees me sitting on the bed, his eyes bulge. "Popcorn?" His gaze washes over the room, landing on me clutching the bowl for dear life. "Speaker phone, huh? Who's this?" He growls. "And what's she doing here at this hour? And in your bed?" His head spins toward Nolan, frozen near the door.

I haven't felt my eyes widen, or my heart race this fast, since watching Richie Santana belt out my lyrics on the stage of the 42nd street Dive, the night his eyes passed right through the girl who had written the words he was singing. Which the crowd loved, by the way.

"This is Zoe, Dad," Nolan's voice vibrates, kind of like every nerve in my body. "A friend from school. We were studying for her finals."

His father's head swings back to me and his eyes burn into mine. The flush on my face is so severe I feel feverish and cold, all at the same time. "Hi Mr. Royce." I try to keep my voice steady. "I was just leaving."

"Doctor Royce," the astute-looking man corrects, "and yes, you're leaving. I'm driving you home." He grumbles to Nolan, "Put her in the car. I'll be right down." On his way out the door, he shakes his head. "What are her parents going to think? What kind of parents would let their daughter stay out this late?" he mutters with disdain.

"My parents are dead," I deadpan to his pajama-clad back as he stalks off. My stomach is churning, my heart breaking. "Put me in the car?" I croak, half furious, half crushed at his father's reaction. "What am I the family pet?" I let out a sob. "The homeless dog going back to its shelter?" I dab my eyes with my sleeve. "You've been hiding me. I knew it. You knew he wouldn't approve. That's why you never invited me over."

Nolan's face is stone, then turns sheepish. His eyes barely meet mine. He tugs at his t-shirt then shoves his hands onto the pockets of his sweats. "I'm sorry, Zoe. He didn't mean to make you feel bad–"

"Bad?" I flare. "He made me feel like garbage."

"He shouldn't have been so harsh. He's worried, that's all. He doesn't want me to make the same mistake my brother did."

"So being my friend is a mistake?" Shoving my feet into my sneakers, I trip across the room, anxious to make my exit before I can be 'put into the car'.

Nolan's strong arms stop me. Steady me. "My brother got a girl pregnant when he was a freshman in college."

"With a father like that, no wonder," shrugging away, I mumble. After zipping my sweatshirt to my neck, I flop on the bed to tie my sneakers. "Did they keep the baby? Is that who's in the picture over there?" I nod to the nightstand and a photo of a curly-haired toddler being hugged by a blonde girl who looks no older than me.

"She did. My brother took off. Left college. Left home. He didn't want to be a dad. I guess he didn't want to be a doctor, either. My father refused to pay for college after that because he was paying child support for Adam instead." Nolan's voice breaks. I sense his heart is breaking too. "My dad wanted his sons to follow in his footsteps."

"My dad wanted things too. Like seeing his daughter graduate law school." As I speak, I remember the night my father acted just as furious as Dr. Royce, when he confronted Jesse on that dark, lonely road. Jesse. Where are you? Where would we be right now if that fucking night never happened?

Harsh wind reaches out to touch a smile
A smile that was lost within a child
Mourning for the home they'll never find
Inside a vacant heart of faded time

Losing me lost me erase me misplace me
Forsake me come take me
I want you to make me
Make me into something fine

Finding You

Jesse

It's barely eight o'clock and the sun is diving into the horizon. Keeping my eyes on the road as I ride is difficult. The colors streaking the sky are amazing. All golds and pinks and purples slashing a dusky blue canvas. I'd love to have a brush in my hand right now. Nope. No more sunset paintings, Jesse, I laugh to myself on my way home from the garage. I think of Kirby's dinner invitation, consider texting her, then I remember her joking, "No dinner. Nothing to hang around for." After confirming I'd stored her number in my cell phone, her parting words before kissing my cheek were, "Keep in touch, Jesse."

My front tire rolls onto my driveway when my phone chimes. Reading the screen, I shake my head. Perfect timing, bro.

Christian texts me: I might show up soon, bro, bearing gifts ... *chuckle face* ... for me, not you.

Me: After flying through eight semesters you're flunking out?

Christian: Met a pre-med named Piper HOT

I hit the call button. This calls for more than texting.

"Hey, dude. What's up?"

He groans, like he's rolling over, stretching out in bed. "I met a rocking chick. Gorgeous, hot, rich."

"What's she want with you?" I laugh.

"Fuck you, asshole."

"Kidding, champ. More power to you. When do we get to meet her?"

"Hopefully for the holidays."

After parking my bike, I head into the house through the back entrance which leads into the kitchen. The refrigerator is wide open and Jamie is leaning in with one hand braced on the door. With his other hand he rummages through the shelves, cursing fuck this, fuck that. I've never known such a miserable soul in my life.

"Yo. What's up?" I say, dropping into a chair to unlace my boots. "Why are you pissed off at the fridge?"

"I'm not," he says without turning to look at me. "I'm pissed off at the vegetable drawer."

"What?" I laugh.

"We don't have any onions." He throws his hands up. "Why don't we have onions?!"

"I'm not even going to ask." I pull off my boots and slide them under the table. "We don't have a vegetable drawer either, dude," I say with sarcasm.

When Jamie faces me, he looks frazzled. "I'm cooking dinner." He's wearing a worn concert t-shirt and even more worn out jeans, which he jams his hands into the pockets of.

Jamie cooking dinner is even funnier than the jackass the real estate agent brought around this afternoon. "Some jamoke offered fifty grand for the garage," I say, peeling off my work shirt which I roll into a ball and aim through the doorway, hoping it lands on top of the washing machine and not the mud-tracked floor.

Jamie huffs out a laugh. "What the fuck?"

"That's what I told him. While you're in there, toss me a

beer."

He reaches into the refrigerator and slams a can on the table. "The sweat we poured into that place is worth fifty K alone. Not to mention everything else inside and out," he says with a sober face.

I'm about ready to bust a gut. "Yeah, right. I told him that too." I pop the can and slug, then go to the sink and wash my hands, face and neck. "I told him my brother Jamie did nothing but leave body fluids in the back room, and your balls are worth way more than fifty K." I reach for a towel, but the rack is empty. "Fetch me a towel, James."

"You're an asshole," he says as a roll of paper towels sails through the air and connects with my head.

Scrubbing off water and grime, I shake my head. "Takes one to know one. So who's the lucky dinner guest?"

He shuts the door, presses his back against the refrigerator, crosses his arms and smirks. "Greshan." He nods a few times. "Oh yeah. In the flesh. And I do mean ... f l e s h."

"Ooh. I finally get to meet Shamie's girl?" I stride to the table to finish my brew.

"She's got a three day layover." He wiggles his brows. "Lay over." He winks and watches me.

"Layover. Yeah, I get it." I slide my hands into my back pockets. "Your uniqueness is amazing. Not."

Ignoring my sarcasm, he says, "I promised her a real Italian dinner. Where are Mom's cookbooks at?"

"You're pathetic," I snort. "Not even cookbooks will help you. You don't even know how to turn the stove on. Why do you want to poison Greshan, anyway?"

He rubs a palm over his stubbly beard and shoots me a sick smile. "She thinks I'm domesticated."

"So are dogs. But they're still dogs," I chuckle.

"Heads up. She also thinks I'm twenty-nine and own a couple

of garages." He stands in the doorway, a hand pressed to each side of the molding, deep in thought. "Yeah. Maybe I'll take her to Fortunatos instead. I'm gonna hit the shower. She'll be here in a few."

I pull a can of meat ravioli in tomato sauce out of a cabinet and toss it at him. "Here's your Italian dinner." I laugh. "If your dick hasn't won her over yet, this should help."

The can hits Jamie's chest. He fumbles, but grabs the can before it falls, and hurls it back at me. This begins the ravioli in a can fight, which is how I end up with a black eye.

"Asshole," I shout. "Ow. Ow. Ow." I slap my hand over half of my face.

"You started it," Jamie chuckles, tossing me a bag of frozen vegetables from the freezer before heading to the shower.

I end up microwaving the ravioli that I spoon from the mangled can, along with some of the vegetables my face thawed out. No sooner do the sounds of the shower stop, there's a knock at the front door. I place my dishes into the sink and run my fingers through my messed up hair. Bare-chested and barefoot, I stride to the living room foyer.

"Greshan's here," I aim my bellowing voice toward the bathroom.

The door flies open and Jamie bounds out, wrapping a towel around his hips. "Entertain her for a few. I'll be right out. And hands off."

"No problem." I laugh. "I've never seen you so nervous to meet a chick, bro. What's she got? Forty-four D's?" I call out, just to embarrass my bro, while holding a hand over my black eye and simultaneously reaching for the doorknob.

"Hey," I say, a breath catching in my throat when my gaze hits the stunning blonde in a stretchy mini dress that wraps her like an elastic bandage. Beside her is one hell of a knockout brunette. Sonofabitch, I think, not one but two. Only these girls aren't cheerleaders. They are beautiful busty ladies. I extend my free hand to the blonde, "You must be Gretchen."

Her shocking blue eyes focus on my hand which is covering my eye. I swear, her eyes gleam for a second, then she lifts a brow. "Accident at work. Just got in." Motioning to my attire, or lack thereof, I grin. "And who is this?" I lower my hand and hitch my head for them to enter.

"You must be Shessie." The words ooze from her hot pink lips.

I hold back a laugh. "That's me. Shessie. Shames will join us in a minute." If this girl wasn't so gorgeous, I'd be on the floor rolling because she sounds nothing like she looks.

She tugs her curvy friend to her side. "This is Nadgia."

Nodding, I smile. "Hello, Nadgia."

"Nadia," the brunette corrects with a wink, her eyes taking in every inch of my bare chest, landing on my fly. Then her chocolate eyes jerk to my face, "Nice to meet you, Shessie."

I laugh. "The name's Jesse. Come on in. Have a seat. I'll get you ladies some drinks."

I smell Jamie before he appears in the doorway. The strong scent of spice wafts through the room, stinging my nose. Gretchen throws her arms out in greeting.

Jamie's hair is slicked back and still damp from the shower. He's wearing what looks like a new blue shirt and not so worn jeans. "Shamie. I miss you so much," Gretchen shrieks, flinging herself at him.

First their arms lock, then their lips. When they come up for air, Jamie says, "Me too, baby girl. So much. You've met my bro, I see." His eyes flash over Nadia and he shoots a questioning glance at Gretchen.

"This is Nadgia, Shames. She is on layover too. She came hoping to see Christian."

Jamie rubs his freshly shaved cheek. "Oh yeah. That's right.

You and Christian," he says, nodding at Nadia. "Christian's not here, but this is Jesse. I hope he'll do." He narrows his eyes at me. "You're hanging around tonight, right?"

"Funny you didn't say that the other night when Claudette was here–" I'm thinking Gretchen is enough to handle all by herself. I shake my head. Bro has met his match. My grin at him broadens. "I wouldn't think of leaving."

Nadia's red lips break into a smile. "It's good to meet you, Jesse. Since you mentioned drinks, I'd like red wine if you have."

"We have it all," Jamie says. "If not, we'll get it."

After handing out drinks, I excuse myself for a shower. When I return, I settle beside Nadia, who is sitting on the sofa, sipping wine. She leans close. "You smell delicious."

"So do you," my eyes scroll her face, dropping to her cleavage, "like vanilla cupcakes." I moisten my lips, wondering if the slide of my tongue is obvious.

She smiles. "Are you in business with Jamie?"

My eyes cut to Jamie and roll. "I help out. Oh, and we're having an epic party for his thirtieth birthday next week. Will you be coming?"

Jamie shoots me a glare and moves Gretchen off his lap long enough to put some music on.

"Dance?" After a few more glasses of wine, Nadia asks.

Nadia and I rock and sway until Jamie calls us to join him and Gretchen up in his room.

Gretchen is sprawled on the bed. Jamie is hovering over her.

"Is this weird to you?" I ask Nadia, who is eager to unzip my fly.

"Having sex?" She squints. "Not in the least."

"I mean, with my brother here. In his room."

Jamie's head pops up from between Gretchen's legs. "She says they do everything together, so shut the fuck up."

"Well we don't." I wrap an arm around Nadia, and as I lead her down the hall, her head rests on my shoulder. While her lips find my neck, my palm finds her ass.

Zoe

I'm not the greatest company, and two girls sharing a room usually know each other's secrets. But I'm like a locked vault Nina constantly tries to pry open. Her questions and nagging finally break the safe.

"You think I'm a nerd. I wasn't always this way. I was violated. I'll never be the same." My jaw sets. I've lifted myself to another plane Nina could never reach because she's never been through what I've faced.

Nina sits beside me on my bed. I believe she's trying to console me but she's more of an annoyance. "So you aren't a virgin. No big deal. Who is these days?" Nina's tone is flat. She draws back and shoots me a smirk. "Don't feel bad if he did you and dumped you. Guys are pigs."

I throw her arm off my shoulder and jump to my feet so quickly I get a head-rush. "It's not like that. I didn't have sex with my boyfriend. I was raped, Nina. Remember?"

Her hands go to her cheeks and she gasps. "Holy shit, Zoe. You never had sex before that?"

My eyes roll. "This is why I don't bother talking to you. You just never understand. We're so different–"

With a shocked stare, Nina groans. "You're not kidding. Holy fucking shit. I would have never guessed."

"Why would you?" I snap. "Didn't you say you were going out?"

Her eyes narrow. "Why? Am I bothering you?"

I walk to the window and watch a taxi pick up a fare. This city is so crowded. I miss the privacy of the town I lived in, the bedroom that made me feel secure. "I just want to be alone," I say, weary but not defeated.

"Suit yourself. I was going to ask if you wanted to hang at the Pizza Palace." Nina shrugs. "I'll leave you alone, but this is my room, just don't forget that."

Sleep refuses to come easy, and while I wait to drop into darkness, I find myself pondering my future. Graduate high school, move back to the old house, which is now rented and being cared for by my parents' estate. I'll inherit everything. Do I want to return to that place? Time will tell. Time feels endless. Time doesn't seem to be healing.

I want to change my name to fit my new personality, so that when the time comes I can escape back into Zoe should I want to. Sylvie Sterling comes to mind. Great rocker name. I can see me now up on stage with Chasing Dinero. Richie would like to nail a Sylvie, I'm sure. I laugh aloud while actually considering this name change; maybe Richie.

I haven't seen Nolan since the night his father barged into his room and threw me out. Nolan texted me a few times, but I guess I'm too hurt to face reality, so I haven't replied. Maybe in time we'll speak again, but right now, well … I have to concentrate on right now, which involves getting out of PS 243 and the McCabe prison.

Finding You

Thanks to budget cuts there's no drama club at this school. I no longer fit the part of a fairy anyway, so who gives a damn about drama club. I've lived through enough of it to last a lifetime. To write a book. I laugh with sarcasm. So the next best thing for after school recreation is to hang out at the pizza place around the corner. Nino landed a job in one of his favorite haunts; a smoke shop downtown. I hang there too. This is where I almost cough my lungs out during my initiation to weed.

Days crawl by. I lie in bed each night, and when I permit myself, I think about home, about my parents, and the knot in my stomach reaches my throat. That's when Zoe Channing seeps back into my soul. The way I miss my mom and dad, my old way of life, is almost unbearable. This is where Nino's bong and Molly's booze ease the pain, not to mention her Xanax.

I curl up on the twin bed designated mine in the room I've been sharing with Nina since I came here, like an eternity ago. The mattress is soft. The sheets softer. Wearing baggy tee and sweats, Nina saunters through the doorway, rosy from the shower. She pauses to check herself in the mirror, then arms crossed, she plops down at the foot of my bed, watching me with a calculating look.

I give her my profile. "What?"

"Scott has this friend…" Nina is normally firm. Tonight she's testing.

I'd rather stare at the blank wall than Nina's interrogating face, so I roll over onto my side. "Forget it." My voice is flat. "You know I hang with Nolan."

"Bullshit. After his old man caught you in his bed, bye bye Nolan."

"That's not true. He's been busy. If he's gonna get into medical school ..." I sigh. "Just forget it, Nina. I'm not in the same place you are."

The mattress heaves with the weight of Nina's body as she leans over me, sticking her face between the wall and mine. Forcing me to roll back onto my other side to avoid her stare.

"No. I won't forget it. Bobby's a nice guy. He's got awesome wheels. We could have such fun. He's got a good job too. So he can pay—" On all fours, Nina's like a puppy, bouncing around the bed to get in my face.

"I don't care about his car or bike or whatever is awesome. And I don't need his money!" I'm appalled at her insinuation that I'd want to date a guy for any reason other than emotion.

"I know it. You're an heiress," she exaggerates, "and a snot, but listen. He saw you, okay?"

"What are you talking about?" I feel every muscle in my body stiffen and hurl my face in her direction. "Saw me when? Doing what?" The concept of being stalked is chilling.

"Relax," she snorts, "he's not a creeper. He was at Destiny's when you got this," she grabs my arm and points to the falcon tattoo on my shoulder. "The one for Nolan, who's not your boyfriend, who you never really dated, just hung with, doing Christ knows what." She scowls. "Ah ha. Whatever. Anyway, Bobby thinks you're hot."

"He should know me," I huff.

She rolls off the bed and onto her feet, but hovers above me. "I know." She flips her head down and ruffles her hair with her fingers to air dry it. "You're an ice cube, which appropriately fits you."

"What are you talking about?" I brush strands of hair from my face.

"Ice cube. Square. Get it?" She chuckles.

I dangle a hand over my face, studying my hot pink manicured fingernails I polished out of boredom. "And you're popular because you're a slut."

"Don't shoot the messenger, okay? I'm just trying to—" When she lifts her head, her thick, maroon waves frame her face. She's come a long way since cosmetology school, going from raggy chopped frizz to healthy long perfectly dyed hair.

"You're interfering. I can handle my own life. Leave so I can get some sleep." I punch my pillow and duck under it.

She snatches the pillow and gets in my face again. Her long black eyelashes flutter with sarcasm. "Gimme a break miss perfect. And this is *my* room, remember?"

"How could I forget? You keep reminding me. This isn't the greatest for me either. I'm either listening to you and Scott phone fuck, or Nino blasting music from across the hall. Then there's Molly and her new boyfriend moaning up a storm on the living room sofa now that she finally drove Rye out. Not that I blame her. But why can't she take that bozo to her room?" My jaw clenches. "He gives me the creeps. As soon as I get my insurance money, I'm outta here."

"But you *will* remember me when you're rich, right? And what a great cousin I've been?" She shoots me an over-stretched grin.

"I'm not gonna be rich. Now leave me alone." Hopping up I shove her out of the way, flounce to the light switch and snap it off. Before I can fall back into bed, Nina snaps the light back on. Her grin shrinks. "Are you into guys?"

I groan and slap a hand over half of my face. "Are you serious?"

She tags my shoulder and we both land on my bed. "Yeah I'm serious."

Face heating, I scowl. "As if it's your biz, but why are you asking me this at almost midnight when I have to get up in less than six hours?" I rub my gritty eyes. "I have tests," I groan, "I want to get out of jail this spring. Please…"

"Just curious." She hops to her feet and pads to the dresser where she snatches a hairbrush. Instead of using it on her coiling hair, she pulls strands from the bristles and lets them float into the trash can she nudges with her foot.

"That stud you almost walked through at the mall last week was fine. You know, the guy who then followed you to Starbucks. The one you snubbed. That's number one." She shoots me a side glance, obviously checking for my reaction. "I could have gone for him myself. But he didn't give me a second glance. He drooled over you." Her normally large round eyes are narrowed.

Damn well remembering Mr. Unforgettable, I play dumb. "What guy?" I turn on my side to face her and prop on an elbow.

"Don't be a smart-ass." She jabs my foot with her big toe. "You could have easily hooked up with him but you didn't. He hawked you for at least forty-five seconds before getting lost in the crowd. You blew him off like a little bitch." She clicks her tongue and tosses me a sour look.

"No I didn't. No he didn't, but ... Not interested." Throwing my legs over the side of the bed, I lift myself and stand beside her where I examine my reflection in the mirror. I smooth my blonde, black streaked bed-head hair, unwrapping long locks that cling to the back of my perspiring neck. My eyes slide from Nina to myself. No family resemblance. I could easily rest my head in her armpit without slouching and her clothes would hang on me since she put hourglass weight on.

I make sure my eye-crawl is obvious. "You're comfortable with Scott."

"What?"

"You gained weight."

She flies to the mirror and spins. "I'm not fat! And stop trying to change the subject." She presses a finger to her chin. "Let me think ... Then there was the tattoo guy you managed to turn off in less than thirty seconds. You know, the hunk who tried to hit on you when you got your first tatt."

"That's not fair. He wanted me to go to a club. You know damn well I can't get into a club."

"Don't give me that crap. We get in clubs all the time. Fake ID?" She swats my thigh with the brush. "It's right inside your purse." Her stare brings me to my satchel hanging on the back of the desk chair. The desktop holds a mountain of books, pads, and my stack of lyrics which is never far from my reach.

"Hey," I snap, "do you get off on beating on me?" I rub my thigh which I'm sure will bruise with an imprint of the brush head.

"Yeah. I'll beat the truth out of you if I have to." She lets out a hearty laugh then persists, "Why aren't you into anyone?" Her breath brushes my neck. "You got a boyfriend hiding in Pleasantville or something? Is that where you disappear to when you go MIA?"

Frowning, I grab a lip balm and smear a thick coating over my parted lips. I avoid Nina's drilling stare. I can't admit I ride the bus some nights just to get away from everyone, everything. I know the drivers better than I know myself; they do the talking, I listen. That's one thing about riding an empty bus; most people are comfortable baring their souls to strangers.

Nina's stare burns, so I scramble to come up with an answer because I know my cousin. She's relentless. And I do have pride; I don't want her thinking I'm a geek without any interests, even if it's true.

"Sure," my tone is breezy, "I have a boyfriend. Had, I mean." I shift my gaze, wanting to bury myself under my bed covers rather than admit how fucked up I am.

I watch Nina through the mirror. She lifts a brow and turns the hairbrush on me, this time using the bristles to run long strokes down the back of my head. "I know you're holding out on me. It's about time I met this mystery stud."

Backed against the dresser, I roll my eyes. "Since when are

you worried about my welfare?"

"Let's talk business, Zoe. This is what I think. You're pretending to be celibate." Her brows crunch. "Either you're uptown every weekend fucking some dude's brains out or there really isn't – or wasn't – any dude in Pleasantville. Which is it?" She lets the brush drop onto the dresser top with a thud.

I spin to face her, shoving her what I feel is a safe distance away. "It's none of your *business*."

She shrugs and smirks. "Just wondering who I've been rooming with all this time and if half the bullshit you talk is true."

Am I an open book? Does all of my personal stuff show? "What does a non-virgin look like, Nina?" I snicker. "You?"

"We're talking about *you*. So, *are* you doing this dude or do you like girls?"

"Oh God," I click my tongue, "sorry to disappoint you, but I'm not into girls either." My hip grazes the edge of the dresser as I retreat. I lift the hair brush and point it at her. "How far have *you* gone with a guy or a girl?"

She laughs. "Where have I *not* gone is a better question."

She's making me remember things I've managed to bury. I see Jesse, feel his arms around me and imagine his unforgettable almost kiss as he gazed down at me in Trent's backyard. I'm sad. Lonely. Longing. What could have been beautiful was destroyed by...

"After all this time, I still miss everyone. Everything." I burst into tears. Under Nina's persuasive dark stare, I'm ready to spill my guts. Tell her Nolan was really just a friend, maybe a tryout for the future to see if I could ever feel anything again. Tell her I can't stop thinking about a guy I had a crush on at my old school. A guy who fit perfectly into my world, my life, my plans, everything that was stolen from me.

"You're stuck in a rut. You've never accepted reality, Cus, so it's like you're stalled in time. You need to flush all the shit out of your system. Move on with your life."

She shoves me onto the bed and throws an arm around my shoulder. Her compassion is not gentle, but at least she acts like she cares. Her words are gruff, honest. "I can't imagine losing everything. Parents, house, boyfriend. It must feel like shit."

"My virginity." My head falls onto her shoulder and I sob. "Not even for love."

"I can't believe this shit." Rhythmically, she taps my back with a clumsy beat. "Cos it's you. Ya know? You've always been the good girl. I mean, always under your mommy and daddy's wings."

Nina's becoming too personal, so I lift my head. She edges away from me; maybe she feels uncomfortable too.

"I still don't understand how that shit could have happened in school." Her face pulls into confusion and her chocolate eyes bore into mine. She's up on her feet, pacing. "And you never told anyone. Never did anything about it. Why the fuck not? I just don't get it. I would've flown to the nearest pork station," her hand goes to a hip, "to tell them I just killed the fuck who tried to rape me, 'cos he wouldn't've gotten very far." She slaps her lifted knee. "Right in the balls, then I'd stomp his skull."

"I *did* fight. He knocked me out with ammonia or..." What's the point of arguing? I'm tired of life. My head feels so heavy, I let it drop and stare at the floor. "I know. I should've fought harder. I was so stupid. Stupid in school. Stupid at home. Stupid with Jesse."

"Jesse?" Her head tilts.

"Yeah, this really nice guy. He liked me, we almost got together, but I ran away–" The words race through my lips.

"Seriously? You ran?" She runs her fingers through her curling hair and grimaces. "Why did you run away?"

"I couldn't face him without telling him what happened to me, which I'd never do," my eyes water and burn, "I had no choice.

I ... I couldn't stop thinking about it. I still can't." I press my palms over my eyes, then scowl. "I've never seen you so sympathetic."

"Cos I feel awful for you. No one can blame you for not wanting to mess with a dude after that, even if he's hot. Especially if he's hot. Not after being raped. Who'd want to look at a dude? Even a hot dude? At least for a couple months, anyway. But it's over two years! Don't you think it's time you get over it or go for some therapy? You've got to let yourself forget the past and move on."

"I can't. And I don't think I can ever be with a guy, Nina. If I tried to do anything, if anyone touched me, I think I'd freak out. When I close my eyes, all I'd see is that horrible man. I have these vivid dreams–"

"Yeah, I hear you moan in your sleep. Cry out – in a good way." She tags me with her shoulder. "At least now I know who Jesse is." She winks.

"Huh?"

"You moan the dude's name in your sleep."

Finding You

Jesse

Kirby is standing beside a coffee shop tucked into a corner of the airport, waving one arm wildly. I have to laugh. Her enthusiasm, and obvious delight at my acceptance of her offer, are evident by her misty green eyes and grinning glossy lips.

She's holding two drink cups nestled in a cardboard tray which she sets down on a table when I'm within a few feet. I brace for the collision as she breaks into a jog, throws her arms around my neck and literally climbs me, straddling my body with her legs wrapped around my hips.

"Well it's about damn time," she squeals. "I thought you'd never make up that cute little mind of yours." Her finger jabs my forehead.

"Little mind?" I let out a rumble of laughter. "Are you calling me small-minded?"

Her chin digs into the base of my neck as her grip around me tightens.

"Hey, Kirby. It's great to see you babe," I choke out as I struggle to balance this chick and my backpack, so we don't crash into the travelers weaving around us.

"Jesse," her moist lips sweep my ear, "Jesse, I'm so happy to see you."

Reluctantly, she slides down my body, but my arms remain around her as she plasters herself against me. Her perfume is overwhelming and I stifle a sneeze. I pluck a clean napkin from my jacket pocket and dab a tear that's made its way from the corner of her eye to her cheek.

"Good to be here, Kirby. And looking forward to this job you've been talking about." I coil a lock of her hair around my finger. "You changed your hair. Looks nice kinda blondish."

"It's called highlights." Her lips take a swipe at my cheek but land on my neck instead. "I can't tell you how thrilled I am to see you," she squeals.

"I think you just did." I chuckle and tap her nose with the pad of my finger. "It was a big decision, for damn sure."

She tips her face. "It took you long enough to decide." She's going for perturbed, but her eyes are a dead giveaway; she's ecstatic.

"As my dad used to say, 'Good things come to he who waits'," I scruff her hair, "in your case, she."

"Absolutely worth the wait," she whispers, running her hands down my chest, possessively.

Warning sign #1.

Her eyes are sparkling. Her complacent expression, and familiar handling of my body, makes me uneasy. I remember the evenings I screwed her at the lake and could kick myself for heading down that road. "You do realize why I came down here, right?"

She purses her lips, green eyes glued to mine.

"This is a noncommittal deal, non-relationship. Are we both clear on this?" My voice is as firm as her grip on my arm.

She grins up at me with fluttering lashes. "Mm-hmm."

"I'm serious, Kirby. You're a nice girl. I don't want to string you along. I know things got out of hand back home–"

"You mean *in hand*. We've got great lakes here, too," she purrs.

"I'm here strictly for a job." I shake my head and run a hand over my bearded chin. "I'm restless. Can't get my shit together. I'm content being single. No responsibility. Just want to set the record straight."

"Yeah, me too. See, I'm still single after all this time." She spins around and holding up her naked ring finger, shoots me a grin. "How was your flight? You're probably tired, huh? Want to stop for lunch? Let's get outta here."

Her eagerness is entertaining. "Which question should I answer first?"

Her head jerks to the side and she snorts out a laugh. "I know. I promised myself I wouldn't bombard you. But you know me and my reporter instincts and procedures."

"Yeah, your mind never stops. Neither does your mouth." Chuckling, I point toward the tall frappe cups sitting on the table. "One for me I hope?"

She pulls me to the table, grabs a cup and shoves it into my hand. "Yup. Figured you'd be thirsty." She lifts her cup and sips.

"Always thoughtful." I raise my cup to toast. "So what do we do first? Check me into a hotel or meet your boss who I hope will be as enthusiastic about hiring me as you are." I drop a light kiss on the tip of her nose, then bring the straw to my mouth.

With pursed lips, she nods, confident. "Don't worry about my boss. I can handle him."

"You can handle him?" Not liking the tone of our conversation, I lift a brow. "I thought it was in the bag. Did I fly down here for a *maybe* interview?" Warning sign #2. "He knows about me, right? I hope you didn't get me down here to be your playmate ... because–"

Her finger seals my lips. "Stop worrying," she says with a

grin. "It's in the bag." She runs a smoothing finger over my forehead. "No wrinkles."

After a trip to the baggage area, we're on our way to the parking lot, me lugging enough *essentials* as Kirby instructed, to last at least a month.

No worries, no wrinkles, no job? I consider hopping on the first flight back to New York, but by the end of the day, I've enjoyed a heat-blasting tour of Miami, cordial lakeside dining, and by dusk Kirby has moved me into a spare room in her apartment. Spare meaning no one inhabits it, however, spare doesn't necessarily mean the room is empty.

I shove my stuff into a corner, alongside a rack of Kirby's clothing that I assume won't fit into her closet. Sitting on a desk beneath a large window is a computer and tons of magazines.

"Kirby, this is your office. I'll check into a hotel." I decide it might be the best idea for more reasons than one, then I joke, "I don't want to put your clothes out."

"Nope. I won't hear of it." Her full lips pin. Plowing into me, she shoves me onto the bed. "We Floridians are very friendly," she coos, straddling my lap. Then her lips trace a line from my neck to my cheek, finally landing on my mouth.

"I can see that," I hum out, because she's prying my mouth open searching for my tongue. I guess one could say I'm your typical red-blooded male. Against my better judgment, and promises to myself, my arms fold around her. We fumble with our clothing, and I'm not sure which body part presses harder, mouths, chests, or crotches. All I know is she's removed my shirt, my jeans are crushing my balls and my dick wants to unzip my fly, all by itself. From Kirby's rate of respiration and enticing grind, I'm sure she's ready to begin a series of orgasms. Thinking back to the lake, I believe I counted three in the water and two on shore.

The ring of my cell breaks the moment and my thoughts. It

also shocks my erection back to reality. *Fool don't lead her on.*

Kirby, flushed as hell, pants, "Oh shit. Don't answer it," and continues to hump my lap.

I unwind her arms and urge her to her feet, breathlessly replying, "I've got to, babe. Since my dad's heart attack, I always answer my phone."

Unlocking her body from mine, she snatches my cell from her desk and tosses it at me, then stares out the window into moonlight. Her turned back tells me she's disappointed, maybe uncomfortable, maybe pissed.

"Don't feel bad, Kirby," I whisper as I slide the answer button on my phone. "I'm getting used to your aggression." I'm playful, hoping I can soothe her ego. After all, she's doing me a favor. The least I can do is thank her, not fuck her.

"You're getting used to what?" The voice on the other end of the phone is an indignant Claudette.

I flop onto the bed, ready for an explosive interrogation. "Hey Claudette."

"Hey, dick. Thanks for cluing me in that you were leaving." The huffing on the other end tells me she's flushed and biting her bottom lip, and if I were there, she'd smack me with the nearest object for not keeping her in the loop.

"Sorry," I say, although I'm not really because she's the one who dropped out of sight with an anonymous companion. "It was a last minute decision. How'd you find out?"

"Delorese, of course. I'm surprised you'd leave your twin. After all, you two have been conjoined for months."

"You should talk." I laugh, although I'm not amused. "Before you split, you girls were the twins."

"That's my business," Claudette's voice oozes with venom. "I won't be the topic of anyone's conversation, which includes you and Delorese."

"Easy killer. You're the one who bailed. Shame on you for

ditching your bestie." I take pleasure in pushing her buttons. "How *is* Dee doing? Last I heard she missed your counseling sessions." I remember the two of them setting up shop in the back room of the garage where they messed with their hair and makeup. Claudette doesn't reply, so I repeat, "Is Dee doing okay without me?" Incredibly stupid and absentminded question to ask one chick in front of another, but the nice guy in me feels like a traitor for leaving Dee in the lurch when she pleaded, "Don't go, Jesse. You're the only one left."

My concern for Dee attracts Kirby's attention, and I catch her glare before she manages to control it.

"When are you coming home?" Claudette's demanding whine in my ear is irritating.

"Not sure. Why?"

"Do you have to ask?"

I know she's referring to the morning I accidentally slipped into her ... or to put it more accurately ... when she intentionally slipped herself onto me while I was still shitfaced and dreaming of Zoe, which is something I'll never forgive myself for; unintentionally screwing Claudette, not dreaming about Zoe.

"Who's taking care of the garage? The house? Jamie?" Claudette sounds hopeful. "Will he be checking in on them ... with you?"

"The house is locked up tight, and the garage has a 'closed for renovations' sign hanging on the door. Dee's feeding Shoo, but—"

She cuts me off indignantly. "You left the cat alone?"

"He's an alley cat. He found me, remember? He refuses to use the litter box. He's an outside guy. So if you're around, check in to make sure he's eating. He hangs at the back of the garage."

"Maybe I'll take him home with me." I visualize her pout.

"Whatever you want, just let Dee know. Listen, I just landed and need to get settled. Talk later." I lie on both counts.

"Talk later?" Kirby spins and mouths as she hikes up the waistband of her shorts and slips her top back on. My eyes catch a fleeting glimpse of her red bra and panties and I begin to realize we may not be strictly business for long.

"Don't you even care where I've been?" Claudette is obviously not about to disconnect. "What I've been doing?" She plays the victim well, but with Jamie as her ex it's understandable. She's had her share of practice.

After a deep inhale I ask, "Sure. I wondered where you jetted to. Figured you finally handcuffed the bro to your bed." The thought of Jamie brings me to my dad, and I make a mental note to call and see how he's doing in Dallas.

"Ha ha. Very funny. And rumor has it you're no stranger to handcuffs either, not that I handcuffed Jamie to my bed. Jamie…" By the sound of her voice, Claudette is on the verge of tears. Jamie can't be the culprit this time. Last I heard he was thirteen hundred miles away and having yet another time of his life with some horny cowgirls.

"Okay. I give up. Where have you been and who have you been with." As I speak, I roll my eyes and shoot funny faces at Kirby who is pacing ... and openly eavesdropping.

"Pittsburgh."

"What?" My gut tightens. I know the answer but ask anyway. "Why Pittsburgh?"

"With Christian." My memory rolls back to the night of Trent's party, when Claudette was so tanked she blacked out in my arms, and Christian wanted to babysit her in an upstairs bedroom. Of course, I stopped him by sitting with her until Jamie finally picked her up, the precursor to my morning after surprise awakening. Later that night, Christian ended up in New Jersey with Jamie where they bagged some flight attendants. I groan. "Oh no. Christian? Why the hell would you do that?" Christian's a dog. Claudette is like a kid sister.

Claudette's attitude changes from weepy to snippy. "Because he invited me for Thanksgiving, duh." I hear her light up, inhale and blow out.

"When did you start smoking?"

"It's not tobacco, and it's better than pills so don't even start on me."

"I thought Christian had a girlfriend? Poppy or whatever?"

"Piper. She's old news. I think he's getting homesick." She giggles. "Speaking of which, I ask again, when are you coming home, Jesse?"

Zoe

Nina, being the relentless witch that she is, finally talks me into a double date: her and Scott, me and Bobby. Against my better judgment, I agree. Deep inside though, I want to know if I can handle it. How would I feel? Would I scream if he tried to hold my hand? Would I slug him? God, suppose he tries to kiss me? I don't have anyone who could shoot me a rescue phone call, but … I could tell him I'm just getting over a stomach virus. That would work. He'd surely keep his distance.

We arrange to meet Scott and Bobby at the pizzeria around the corner. Nina and I are lost in conversation as we walk, but the moment I see the two guys leaning against the brick wall, I begin to feel sorry I accepted the offer. Parked at the curb are two Harleys.

"Great. He's got a bike, which means physical contact. Why didn't you tell me?" With gritted teeth I growl at Nina.

She leans in with a low voice. "Holy shit, Zoe. You're touching his jacket, not his skin."

"Why are you so snippy?" I flare.

Now she's loud, and I hope everyone around us can't hear her rant, so I elbow her and she elbows me right back.

"Because you're a pain in the ass. I'm trying to do you a favor and you're gonna blow it, I just know it." Nina whips out her lip gloss and smears on another coat, offering me some, but tonight I prefer bare lips.

Actually, I decided not to wear makeup at all. I'm going simple and plain; baggy jeans and an oversized shirt topped off with a black hoodie and black boots. My hair is pulled up in a ponytail and I believe I look so underage, I couldn't get into a club, even with my fake ID. So this won't be a booze night unless the guys want to bring beer, which I'll object to. I don't care if Bobby likes me or not.

This is the first time I'll actually be face to face with Scott. Normally, I see him through the apartment window when he picks Nina up for dates. Nina refuses to have him in the house because of Molly. I'm not sure if she's afraid Molly would hit on Scott or throw him out. So she's playing it cool.

Bobby is average height, maybe five ten. Average build, maybe one eighty. He's dressed pretty much like me, except his jacket is leather. His hair is brown and slicked back. Whereas Scott's head is shaved. Scott is uber-muscular. I can see why Nina is into him. They do make a good couple.

Nina pops a piece of gum into her mouth and hands one to me, so we're chewing away frantically as we saunter up to them.

"Hey, baby," Scott greets Nina with a bear hug. I don't look at Bobby because I'm watching Nina and Scott lock lips. When they angle their heads I see his tongue search for hers.

"Hey," Bobby's voice pulls me from my trance, "I'm Bobby." He doesn't stick out a hand or try to hug me. He just stands there, hands in pockets, offering a smile.

"Hey. I'm Zoe." I glance up at him sideways, then acting out of impulse, I kick Nina's leg. "You two are drawing stares." This untangles them. It also lets Bobby know I'm not about making out with him.

Scott's arm is still hooked around Nina's neck, but his chuckle is aimed at me. "Zoe in the flesh." He shakes his head and smirks. "Straight up Zoe from what I hear."

I don't like his use of flesh so I reply, "Yup, Zoe in person." I bite the inside of my cheek. "What did you hear?"

He grins at Nina then gives me the onceover and a couple of head nods. "Yeah, you look about the same as through the window." He gives Nina a squeeze and brushes his chin over her hair. "I didn't hear anything, right babe? I'm a good judge of character."

Caught in the act of peeking at them through the window makes my face heat. Bobby gives a tight chuckle. Nina rolls her eyes at me, mouthing, "Be cool, nerd."

Scott isn't finished insulting me yet. "Yeah, same head, just you're shorter than I figured. What do you stand on a stool or something to reach the window?"

I imagine he notices the flexing of my jaw. Reaching out, he taps my arm. "Teasing. Nice to meet you, Zoe." His smile is really warm; his voice is too. He's not the hardened criminal type I had him figured for. He's actually quite charming.

Bobby inches slightly closer. "What do you have in mind for tonight?"

Nothing you'd probably like to do flashes through my head but I spit out, "A movie would be great."

"How about Coney," Nina chirps in.

I have no idea what her love affair with Coney Island is, but it's safe so, "I'm down with that," I say, gaining confidence this might not be too bad of a night after all.

"Cool. Let's ride," Scott says and lifts Nina into the air to set her down beside his bike. It seems he likes touching her, holding her, handling her like a plaything. He slips her a helmet and slides onto the seat of his bike. Nina hangs onto his shoulder and hops on behind him. While they wait for me and Bobby to get situated, they snuggle.

Bobby tries to instruct me on how to mount his bike but I tell him, "I've got this. I'm fine. Thanks."

"Cool," he shrugs and hands me a helmet, "here," he grunts, "put this on."

After strapping on the helmet I thrust myself onto the back of the seat, hoping I don't slide off the other side.

It's a nice evening. The sun is setting over the cityscape and soon we're cruising down the highway. My heart is in my throat; first, due to the speed I have to hold Bobby tighter; second, because of the speed I'm afraid we'll crash. By the Grace of God, we arrive at Coney safely and quickly. We disembark, stow the helmets, and while Scott and Nina walk with arms around one another, Bobby and I barely brush sleeves.

"I'm hungry," gazing up at Scott, Nina complains. I've never seen this side of my cousin who is normally rough and tumble, calloused and careless.

"Sure babe," Scott pampers her, "let's get my baby some protein." He tugs her in for a cheek-to-cheek squeeze.

"Chili cheese fries," Bobby chants, "rad. I can do that. How about you, Zoe?" With half a grin, he's pretty cute.

"Sure." So far so good. This night is going so much better than I feared. I'm actually falling into a state of relaxation, maybe even fun.

We head to Nathan's where Nina and I share a bench across from the guys.

"You know what we need right now?" Bobby pops a fry into his mouth and pats his stomach.

Munching, we all stare.

"The parachute jump." He bursts out laughing.

"I'll stick with the carousel," I joke.

Scott reaches across the table, taking Nina's hand. "Wanna ride the horse, babe?"

Of course, I blush for Nina, who just giggles and stuffs her mouth with cheese fries.

We eat and continue to banter, then Scott says, "Did you girls bring your ID?"

My stomach lurches because I know Scott apparently has clubbing in mind and I know the effect alcohol can have on people, especially guys; a big fat sloppy horny. I fumble through my bag and when my hand comes up empty I'm ready for the lie. But Nina shoves her hand in and instantly pulls out my fake license. I shoot her a dirty look. "Thanks." I'm sarcastic.

"Never a problem, Cus." She gives me a cutesy smile then turns it on Scott. "Can we do a couple booths first? Maybe shooting? Or wait … the fun house."

I slam her with an *I'm going to kill you* look and fall into shock as we get on line.

The last thing I need is to be squashed in a car in the too dark *tunnel of fun and freaks*.

Bobby isn't what I figured he'd be, though. He's relatively tame and polite.

"Do you have enough room?" he asks as we climb into the fun house car.

I'm plastered against the metal side. "I'm good."

"Good," he says. "I wouldn't want to squash you. I lost almost thirty pounds recently. I wouldn't have fit in this car three months ago. Alone maybe, but not with you."

If this guy is confiding in me like this, he's not into me. Thank God. If he's looking for a friend, he's found one. At this point I turn to him, and with our faces mere inches apart, I say, "That's a hell of an accomplishment. You should be proud."

"I am, but I did it for my girlfriend."

My voice hits a pitch. "You have a girlfriend?"

"Not anymore. I thought losing weight would help keep her, but she … well … she cheated on me and I would've taken her back, but–"

"The grass is always greener," I cut in. Sure, I'm the voice of experience.

He cocks his head. "What do you mean?"

"How long were you dating?"

He sighs and taps the side of the car where his arm hangs. "Three years."

"Wow," I gasp, "Long time. What I meant was, she might wander and then find out what she really wanted is right here under her nose."

He gives me a thoughtful glance and pulls down the bar to lock us into the car. "You think so?"

"Sometimes it takes change, big change to learn you lost the best."

"I hope you're right." I feel him study me and turn. "You're a nice girl," he says.

"Thanks. You're okay too." I force a chuckle as I have no idea where he's going with this.

"Scott told me you saw me at Destiny's and wanted to hook up."

"Hook up?" I'm certain my face is filled with shock.

"Yeah. I don't see you as a hook-up." Bobby's head tilts as he frowns. "I don't want to lead you on so I have to tell you flat out, I'm not looking for a relationship." He pulls on his ear. "Like I said, I'm just getting out of one."

"Phew. You had me scared there for a minute." I burst out laughing so hard his cautioning stare blanks. "Seems like I heard the same story from Nina."

Bobby's mouth pulls to one side. "You've got to be kidding me." He shakes his head. "Those assholes. We'll have to get even with them sometime."

"Yeah." I nod as the car starts rolling on the tracks. I have to get even with Nina for more than this, I muse in silence.

Finding You

Between music and creatures jumping out at us, we don't have much more time to talk, but Bobby slings his arm over the back of the seat, and it doesn't bother me at all.

We spend a few hours at Coney and after a spectacular firework display ride to Deluge. It's a decent club just outside the city. The parking lot is filled with cars, but there's a separate section for bikes. It's pretty late, and we're lucky to find parking. We stow our helmets and head for the door. We haven't taken two steps and my heart trips. Familiar music pulses through the still night air. This makes my heart rate pick up the way I guess Nina had hoped the date with Bobby would.

"I know that sound," I shriek and am instantly the center of attention.

"Yeah?" Scott says, tugging Nina to his side for quick neck-nuzzle. "You come here all the time?"

"Nope. But I believe I know the band." I'm smug. I'm special. I know Chasing Dinero. My hand flies up to inspect my hair, my face, and my bliss is short-lived. I panic. Quickly, I unleash my ponytail and fluff my hair so it covers half my face, fish inside my bag for a lipstick, smear it on thick and pray I'll pass for twenty-one.

It's crowded, it's dark, and the doorman barely looks at us as we amble by. It seems paying the cover charge and flashing an authentic-looking ID guarantees entry into one of the hottest clubs in town. Phew, one hurdle crossed. My sudden brush with anxiety begins to subside.

After moving with the line through the vestibule, we enter Deluge, me more of a lone star than part of the trio lagging behind me. The place is wall to wall people and sound. Chasing Dinero is blasting floor to ceiling ecstasy. I mean, to me they're like a drug and despite the risk of an overdose and heart failure, I can't get enough of them. Immediately, I shoulder my way to the front of the stage. My ears are throbbing. My pulse is racing. All around me bodies are fluid, flowing with the beat. I don't care if I'm squashed or stampeded to death; I'm freaking out as Richie wails.

"Let's get some drinks," Scott yells.

Nina nods and Bobby and I follow. Tonight I need a drink because my nerves are shot. I feel like I'm walking on air. I'm in some distant place, another universe. I'm so detached I'm not me. I want to be up on that stage so bad. I want to be Sylvie Sterling, Chasing Dinero's songwriter, guitarist, backup singer. Hell, I just want to stand here and never go home.

"It's hot," Bobby's voice is flat. He hands me his bottle of beer. "Hold this. I'm gonna throw my jacket into my saddlebag."

"Great idea. Take mine too, okay?"

Bobby holds the drinks while I whip off my hoodie, then I hold the drinks while he stows our stuff.

The dance floor, which is more like a mosh pit, has devoured Scott and Nina, but Bobby finds me when he reenters Deluge. He's got a pretty good build after all. "You work out," I tell him, I don't ask. This pleases him. His face breaks into a grin and he grabs his beer.

My shirt is so baggy, it slips off one shoulder, granting the escape of my cyclone falcon. "Let me see your ink," Bobby says with a hell of a lot of interest. I actually let him touch my bare skin without flinching. This pleases me.

"Excellent art," he says and pushes up the sleeves of his pullover. "What do you think?"

My stare zeroes in on his thick forearms and amazing skull and rose tattoo embedded in his sleeve; then I track the vine wrapping his other arm, coiling into a heart with a center scroll that says: Jeannie. "Wow, Bobby. That's really beautiful. That's her, right? Jeannie?"

He nods then slugs his beer nonstop. The closest physical contact I've had is holding Bobby's jacket when we rode and skimming his tattoos with the tip of my finger. There's zilch chemistry between us; we both know we have to make it through the night and will probably never see each other again. I really want to ditch him and head back to the stage, but he doesn't deserve rude. So we spend an hour sitting at a table we steal when the occupants get up to dance, with Bobby mourning and me holding my head with one hand and sipping drinks with my other. All the while I'm praying I can get back to the stage before the band quits for the night.

The music grinds to a stop and Richie's voice bellows through the speakers announcing they're taking a short break, during which time I decide, rude or not, it's time for me to split.

"I'm gonna get up for a while, Bobby. Catch the beat before the band leaves." Drink in hand I'm on my feet, pushing my chair in.

"Sure. Me too," Bobby agrees and follows. As we make our way through the crowd, I feel the light touch of his arm on my shoulder. "Scott says you're an actress and singer," he says to the side of my face.

My head swings in his direction. "I write lyrics and pick on an acoustic." I roll my eyes. "An actress, not." I laugh with sarcasm. Sadness. Longing. Because I could have been if that day never happened. My sadness is replaced with anger. My teeth clench and I plow through bodies to cram mine right before the stage.

Dinero comes back from break and Richie and his boys start rocking the crowd again. A rumbling intro brings my eyes to drummer, Jonny Champion. Jonny is hot and totally looks it. He's still flushed from the last set. He wears a black wife-beater and I marvel at his glistening mechanic-muscled tatted shoulders, arms and neck. He pauses the roll, flips his drumsticks, then digs in with a steady beat.

I don't know how Bobby feels, but I'm buzzed and want to shake things up.

"I'm gonna get another drink," Bobby nudges me with his shoulder, "how about you?"

"If you can get near the bar, sure." For a moment I watch Bobby elbow through the crowd then he disappears. My head flips back to the stage where I zero in on frontman Richie Santana. Richie wears *dangerous* from the top of his head to his worn out boots. A lock of coal black hair drapes one of his equally dark eyes, twisting down his ink-covered neck. He wears leather straps on his wrists, and he has that mean look girls like me want to steer clear of but are so damn drawn to, regardless of the consequences. Tattoos creep up his arms and around the neck of his ripped t-shirt. His jeans cling to every inch of his lower torso.

"How's it going?" Nina yells in my ear and I spin. Her face is rosy and her hair is curling around her damp face. She's either been making out in a corner or rocking her ass off.

"You mean Bobby?" I yell back, although I don't want to be disturbed. I'm trying to focus on the band.

"No. I mean the elephant over there in the corner." She laughs.

I give her a sour look. "Fine. He's really a nice guy."

"So you're seeing him again?" Her entire face breaks into a hopeful *I knew it and I'm responsible for this* smile.

"No. He's hung up on his Ex." I scowl. "And you know my position on relationships."

She forces her mouth into a phony looking gape. "Ex? You're kidding. But he said…he thought… he told Scott–"

"That I'm hot," I cut in with an eye-roll. "You're such a liar. You and Scott used the same line on both of us. But I don't care. I'm having a good time. As for Bobby, I think he's trying out his wings to see if he can get over her. Kind of like I was trying out my wings with him to see if I could deal within ten personal feet of the opposite sex."

Nina frowns then shrugs. "Oh well. I tried. At least you didn't freak out, right?" She stops for a breath. "Listen. Scott has other friends–"

My body is bumped and shoved, but I manage to glue myself to my cousin's side. "Don't bother, Nina. I have things planned out."

"Like what?" She swipes loose strands of hair from her eyes and squints.

"Right up on that stage. I'm gonna be one of them someday." Although the pointing of my finger is discreet, I try for determined but believe I sound wistful, dammit.

"As if," she yells then laughs.

"As if what?" Scott comes from behind and hooks his arm around her neck. "As if I wanna rock with my baby? Come on, Nina."

Bobby and I end up downing our drinks, and theirs, then we're all rocking out, but my eyes never leave the band. I'm dancing to them, for them. Now and then I'm jabbed by an elbow, stomped by a foot, even feel the bite of a high heel on my jean covered shin, but who gives a damn? I lose myself in Richie's voice, how he strums the strings with grace then with fury. He's a pro. Richie's eyes are half closed. He's belting out "Mess" a song that should be on every radio station, but isn't.

Richie is a talented writer and composer. His love for music shows in the way he moves, holds his guitar like I imagine he would a woman. The thought gives me a chill. Dammit Zoe, clear your gutter mind. What the hell is wrong with you? You're a virgin. Stop. You lost it to a slimy creep. Stop. If not for him, you WOULD be. Therefore, you are. These days, I can talk myself into just about anything. Out of things too, like the guy with the long black ponytail clinging to his back who's owning the stage right now.

The music winds down; they finish the set and hop off the stage; the crowd parts for them, so they make their way to the bar, which has also cleared room for them. Of course, everyone wants to be near Dinero.

My head is like a beacon, stare never letting the guys out of sight. I watch as they slug down shots. Are swarmed by fans, especially the chicks who try to climb all over them. I know one of the guys from school. It's Denny. He graduated a few years ago. A chick hanging around his neck seems to irk him, and when he turns to shake free, our eyes meet. His fill with recognition. Mine aren't even able to blink. A force passes between us – I'm not sure what it is, but it's powerful. Besides recognition, he gives me a huge smile. His eyes that had glared at the hanging fan, soften. He nudges Richie, who is slouching against the bar, and their heads move close. Then Denny grabs two glasses off the bar and heads in my direction. My eyes go from Richie's smirk to Denny, who's grinning as he weaves through the crowd. He's the only non-rocker-looking band member. He wears clean pressed jeans and half unbuttoned khaki sport shirt, and his chest is bare and tatted. The floor almost gives way beneath me. Facing Denny is exciting enough, but talking to him could be embarrassing because I'm falling into shock.

I'm praying Richie doesn't decide to follow, for more reasons than one. His eyes are glazed. He's got *heartbreaker* written all over him, from the top of his messy dark hair down the length of his sleek toned body. There's something scary about Richie Santana. But in a sick way, I'm drawn to him. I convince myself it's his music, his stage presence. The mere fact that he's the frontman of this amazing band.

Denny's breath, and the scent of scotch, slam the side of my face as he lowers his head and leans into me. His nearness hits me like a jolt of electricity and I almost bolt when he touches my arm. "Hey." His voice pours into my ear like warm honey.

"Hey." Tilting my head, I manage a smile. If Denny is coming on to me there's a problem; I'm here with someone. Well, in name only, not in body or heart or mind for that matter.

After a quick glance around, I let out a breath of relief. I haven't seen Nina or Scott or Bobby since the band stopped playing. When my stare reaches the end of the bar, I spot them. Scott has an arm wrapped around Nina's shoulders and Bobby is talking to a blonde standing next to him. They tap glasses in a toast and my relief doubles. Is that Bobby's ex-girlfriend? Please let it be Jeannie!

Denny presses a glass into my hand. When our fingers touch my stomach dips. Those fingers are too talented to be wasted on me, I want to say. Oh but waste them on me, I find myself thinking, then my cheeks begin to burn.

"Zoe, right?" Even with the band on break, Deluge is so chaotic, Denny has no choice but to yell or put his lips up to my ear. His moist lips choose my ear.

Downing the scotch, I nod and stare up at him. "Denny Brisk." I'm shocked at the fact that I'm holding my own, and the bitter scotch that burned a path down my throat. "I guess you don't remember, or even know, but the first time I saw you was in the cafeteria of 243. You and Richie were writing lyrics … I think …" How presumptuous and forward of me. Awkward. Another shockwave ripples through me.

"Don't sell yourself short, little girl. Who could forget you?" Our faces are inches apart. His voice is a soft song; I lip read as well as strain to hear him. The tip of his finger glides lazily down my cheek then his fingers push my hair aside to circle my ear.

Eyeing the empty glass I'm clutching to my chest, he says, "Can I get you a refill?"

I'm dizzy enough. "Um. No, thanks, I'm good." It takes a moment to gain control of my voice, mostly because of his eyes: big, hazel and soulful. "You guys sound great up there. I heard you all the way out in the parking lot – if the bikes weren't so loud, probably would have down the street – when we were walking I heard you." Damn, can I be so idiotic?

"You heard me specifically?" he teases, breaking out in a

triumphant smile. Denny is an above average looking guy, different from Richie, different from Jesse. They're dark. Denny's hair is light brown, with either natural or bottle highlighted strands framing his face. His nose is straight, but not as masculine as Jesse's and his complexion is a bit ruddy, or maybe he's warm from the stage lights.

"I haven't seen you since school. Wait," he runs his fingers through his hair, which is damp and curling around his ears, "you were at the Dive. Like ages ago." His laugh is light, but his voice is deep and hoarse from singing his lungs out. "Where you been hiding?" Distracted, his eyes land on my tattoo and his fingers take a leisurely stroll.

My shirt is exposing my entire shoulder and bra strap. I don't have to look down to see this, his eyes tell me, along with his touch.

"Nice," he says as his gaze crawls over me. "Ink … and shirt." He winks.

"Yours too. Tatts I mean." I motion to the black tribal art and other designs working their way down his sleeve. My tripping voice is cringe-worthy; my cheeks are on fire.

Denny chuckles. I believe he's enjoying our encounter; his strength; my ineptitude. His arm goes around my waist and squeezes, then his grip slackens and his arm falls to my hips. I'm not sure if his attention is alcohol induced or if he … no, he can't possibly be hitting on me.

I'm only five two, and he towers over me. Leaning in close, the tip of his finger finds the edge of my neckline and probes. "What's hidden under here?"

My head snaps up. I'm ready to slam him or hit the road. My expression must display my displeasure at his too intimate touch.

He chuckles, but his fingers linger. "The ink, not your top. Although I wouldn't mind knowing that too."

Ignoring his innuendo, sweeping his fingers aside I point to my clavicle. "It's a cyclone. See how it spreads across my shoulder? Then the falcon is like … falling from a storm … or maybe the cyclone giving birth to the falcon is a better way of describing it," boldly I tug my shirt slightly past my shoulder so the falcon and text is fully exposed, "see it now?"

"Yeah, I dig it." Denny looks genuinely impressed. "Very cool." His finger traces the inked words. "Born from the storm, huh?" He pulls back to analyze me. "Are you stormy?" His half grin is sultry. I can see why girls find him irresistible. But I'm not like other girls. Keeping my distance comes naturally.

"I've been through some rough seas," I toss my hair over a shoulder, "but I guess we all have in one way or another." The toss of my hair has exposed my other tattoos.

"I like your storm … and the bird on your neck. Nightingale. Cool." His eyes sink into mine. "Ahh. Fantasy girl?" He touches the top of my left shoulder, where a fairy spreads her wings just below the nightingale that climbs the side of my neck. "Any other hidden treasures?"

Is he analyzing me? My heart rate increases. "Not yet. Only for special occasions," I twirl a lock of hair around my finger, "you know, meaningful things that leave an impression. That I want to memorialize."

He tugs my shirt up to cover each shoulder. "Sometime you'll have to tell me about your storm and … meaningful things." His lips drop onto the top of my head, into my hair, and I almost faint.

"Gotta run, babe," his eyes hold something special, like maybe he doesn't want to leave but has to, "get my ass back on stage."

"Okay. I'll be here watching." I act as cool as possible, but inside I'm barely holding it together.

"No you won't." His finger taps my chin.

I let out one of my classic responses. "Huh?"

"You'll be up there," I follow the hitch of his head, "with us."

"Holy shit," emerges with a muffled breath. Am I breathing? My heart is pounding so hard I should really be dying.

A slow grin slips across his face. "We're gonna do one of your songs."

"Huh?" With a deep swallow, I croak, "One of my songs? What am I going up there for?"

He quirks a brow. "Hey. I wasn't born yesterday. I know you slipped your lyrics into my locker."

"You saw me?" I lose my breath. My throat almost closes. Goosebumps break out all over my body. How can I deny this? I've been made. I'm mortified.

"Let's say I had spies hanging in the corridors of 243 and leave it at that." He brings a hand up to rub the back of his neck. "Songwriters sing, right? So come on, Nightingale." His arm goes around my waist and he begins to maneuver me forward.

"Don't call me that," I snap, which brings his head around, his brows close together. I don't plan on being a bitch, but only one person has – and can ever call me Nightingale; the one from my deep dark past.

Denny cocks his head and his face turns intense, then his lips melt into a gentle curve. He nods, then whispers directly into my ear, "Something special. I get it. Maybe I'll get you sometime."

It occurs to me, I'm faced with a double entendre. I'd like to interpret his interest as getting to know me, not getting into me. On both counts, captivating as he is, I highly doubt it.

My eyes shoot around the room and everything's a blur. "I don't think I can go up there…" I take a few steps back.

"You just need to get out there and do it." The next thing I feel is Denny's hand as he takes mine and drags me through the crowd and onto the stage. Yes, he drags me because my entire body feels too numb to move.

Finding You

When the rest of the band struts onto the stage the crowd cheers. The guys are pumped and ready to rock us into oblivion. Richie's cradling his guitar. Corky Bastian is plucking the strings of his bass, as though he's tuning it, maybe just messing with it. Jonny tests the audience with a brief drum solo, and they immediately respond with screams and cheers.

Beneath the blinding lights I feel like the same little girl who almost had her moment of stardom at the school play. Nervous yet filled with butterflies. I think of the school I left behind and the play and the handsome stagehand I met there, then peer over at Denny and my emotions go haywire.

Sporting a cocky expression, Richie bumps me. "Well hello there. You must be Doey." His cloudy eyes rake over me and my legs get even weaker. I'm about to crumble right here, right now, in front of the world.

I'm standing straight. Richie is wobbly. This gives me the upper hand is what I tell myself, so I don't make a fool of myself by swooning.

Still, I can't believe I'm sharing the stage with these experienced musicians who I know will be going places. This makes me want to crumble, but Richie's brashness empowers me.

"It's Zoe." I pull off annoyance, but my tongue is stiff. I'm mush. Inside I'm a tug of war; so much for power. I'm out of my element, ready to bolt, till Denny puts himself between me and Richie.

The glaring lights are making me dizzier than the alcohol I've consumed; Richie is making my heart beat faster. Denny's smile and his faith in me as a musician is the only grounding force. "Make Me Fine," he says first to Richie, then the rest of the band.

Denny grabs a mic and addresses the crowd. "Listen up. This is Falcon Channing," his arm winds around me, "and you're in for a thrill."

The audience roars. Beads of sweat gather on my scalp; thank God my hair absorbs my anxiety; the last thing I want is to have stress written all over my face with perspiration.

"You're the first ever to hear Falcon sing one of the songs she wrote and slipped to Dinero," he turns to shoot me a grin, "a long time ago." The audience applauds harder. "Give it up for Falcon Channing!"

Jonny's drum roll is deafening. Involuntarily, my palms cup my ears.

Denny's lips brush my ear, "I hope tonight qualifies for a very special tattoo. I'd love to make a lasting impression." He reaches into a pocket and sticks an earplug in the same ear he just shocked with his words. He presses another plug into my other ear.

I'm too stunned to reply. Denny's charisma is driving me up a wall. Get those lips moving, Zoe, my mind screams. You are about to sing! This is your dream, your future, your ticket to heaven.

Denny is shredding his guitar, swaying beside me, doing all kinds of crazy things to my insides, and the crowd cheers and chants my name. I'm stage-struck beaming and shaking. From somewhere in my brain, through the fog, it occurs to me; how does Denny know my last name? Internal face palm; I brand every piece of music Zoe Channing. So I guess I won't be Sylvie Sterling after all. I like Falcon so much more.

Denny pauses to scream into the mic, "Our next song, Make Me Fine, is Falcon's. She can't be talking about herself," he shakes his head, "no man, Falcon is already fine."

From a side glance, I catch Richie shooting squinty glares at us. He's so wasted; I wonder if it's all from alcohol and hope he's not into drugs.

Denny takes an acoustic from Corky and hands it to me.

Finding You

Is this really me? It's not my guitar but it fits right into my arms and I cradle it like my own. My fingers feel stiff but one touch of the strings bring them to life. The moment I start to strum, the band is on my side, softly at first, then they kick in with a vengeance. Swept away, I'm suddenly unafraid of the staring faces. I'm free and at ease. I'm Falcon Channing.

I play. I sing. I rock out like I used to at home in front of the mirror when no one was looking. But now all eyes are on me and I'm someone, not only someone, I'm someone special.

Forever searching for a place to feel
What exists for others yet for some unreal
Have I been nurtured in a house so full of lies?
For there's no peace inside a restless mind
Harsh wind reaches out to touch a smile
A smile that was lost within a child
Mourning for the home they'll never find
Inside a vacant heart of faded time

Denny is pressed against me, his body rhythmically grazing my side, his rich, mellow voice backing me up for the chorus. We're performing an emotional song … together … and we're sinking into a sea of agony, groaning out anguish.

Where is the lust I miss the most
My skin is stained with me.
Losing me lost me can't face me erase me misplace me
Forsake me come take me I want you to make me
Make me into something fine

I could stay up here and sing all night, but Jonny's beat slows, the guitars fade, and my five minutes of fame ends all too soon. I smile down at the faces staring up at me, cheering for me, and my heart fills with pride. Accomplishment. Hope. I hand the acoustic to Corky, but before I have a chance to exit the stage, Denny pulls me to a halt, almost squeezing the breath from my lungs. His lips slide down my neck. "Zoe, you're amazing, girl."

My confidence blooms, along with the flush I feel hit my cheeks which are already so hot, they feel sunburned. Through my bubblehead haze, I catch the eye of a blonde in the first row who's shooting me lethal looks and a light bulb goes off in my head. Denny's girlfriend?

Richie swaggers over to us, guitar hanging at his hip. By now he's lost his high. He looks a bit shaky which gives me the courage to stand up to him. Stare him straight in the face and say, "Good, huh?"

Richie laughs and shakes his head. "Yeah, kid. You're something else."

With stunned faces, Nina, Scott and Bobby rush the stage. I believe they lost it just watching me perform. Nina is proud, telling everyone within earshot, "That's my cousin up there." She pats me on the back, grabs my arm and pulls me off the stage and back to reality.

Rocking with Dinero was amazing, but the ultimate tease. I've gotten a taste of being with the band and now I want more. But Dinero is off doing their own thing, and I'm trying to do mine. Which is almost impossible because my life is a series of dull days and miserable nights.

Despite my better judgment, Nina's nagging wins; and I'm feeling desperate, so I date Bobby a few more times. We're just companions filling our time by complaining to each other. He moans about Jeannie, who's stringing him along. I talk about music, waiting for graduation to come and go so I can get on with my life. I plan on putting college aside to bury myself in the world of rockers and stardom.

Finding You

Nina and Scott drag Bobby and me along to the movies, we eat out a lot, take long rides, but Bobby and I avoid physical contact. His faithful gym routine is paying off; he looks fantastic. Still, nada. Not only am I frigid, I don't find him attractive in that way, not like I did Jesse. Or Richie for that matter. Or Denny. I think about Nolan, who's dropped out of my life, or did I push him? But Jesse had something over all of them. There was a sweetness about him that made him extra sexy, like when you see a hot guy holding a baby, or a rescue worker saving a kitten, his compassion makes him the most amazing person in the world. Jesse was a combination of all good things that made him unforgettable. He left such an impression I want to ink his name inside a heart on my skin. Jesse was the epitome of *meaningful*. Face it Zoe, who are you saving yourself for? There will never be another Jesse.

Jesse

"Do I need to dress for this party or event or whatever the hell it is you're dragging me to … or what?" I call out from the bedroom, thinking about the crumpled jeans and shirts stuffed into my bag.

Kirby struts through the doorway, decked out in a yellow dress one could mistake for shorts and tube top. The only reason I know it's a dress is because I slide my hand up her leg and snap the strap of her thong. I let out a whistle beneath my breath. "Wow. You're smokin' baby." Spinning her around, I catch her in my arms. "To say you look hot is an understatement … but you look hot." Releasing her with a swat on the ass, I chuckle.

She shoots me a sexy grin, saunters to the closet, and shoves a clothes hanger at me. "So will you." Her peach colored lips blow me a kiss, then she turns to the mirror to mess with her hair. "Today is for you, babe," she says over her shoulder.

"What's this?" My eyes slip over the dress pants and green knit pullover with price tags still attached, dangling from the hanger.

"The big big boss will be there, and we need to make a big big impression so you'll get hired."

I watch the movement of her lips through the mirror, for the first time noticing the slight bump at the tip of her nose that makes it look somewhat crooked.

I toss the clothing onto the bed, stripping down to my shorts for a shower. "Wait a minute. I thought this was an informal meeting, and that you already spoke to him. What's with the dress?" My eyes land on her breasts bulging from the strapless top. "I thought it was business—"

I catch her eyes sweep my bare chest, then she twirls from the mirror to face me with a grin. "It is. Don't worry." She runs a finger over my creasing forehead. "Everything is on track, now that you're here." Her hand slides across my cheek and down my chest where she draws circles across my abs.

"You are so ripped," she murmurs, leaving a lipstick track on a couple ribs.

I'm starting to get a strange feeling Kirby is trying to run my life or something. The something is concerning. I get the feeling she wants something I don't; a serious relationship. She's a sweet girl, but she just doesn't do it for me. And I'm not about settling down anyway.

"Don't worry about my boss or anything for that matter," she insists, arms sliding around my waist, lips sucking my neck. "He'll find you as irresistible as I do."

Unwinding her arms, I grunt, "Let's hope so."

"Get going," she pats my ass, "we're gonna be late." I feel her grip on my crotch. "If I weren't already dressed I'd be joining you." Her tone is matter of fact.

I shoot her a smirk, then I shower and think, dry and think, dress and think. *What are you doing so far from home with someone you barely know?* When are you going to seriously start your life – the art institute – something other than following Kirby around like her booty call?

With Kirby behind the wheel of a leased Corolla, we weave through congested streets until we're cruising through an upscale area with homes and gardens you'd never see in New York. Hollywood maybe. The Florida sun feels good on my arm, which is hanging out the window. Leaning into the breeze, I close my eyes and think about bringing my bike down here.

"This is it," Kirby says, and we stop alongside a wall of trees guarded by an iron fence. Whipping her cell from her purse, she punches out a text. In moments a metallic blue sports car rounds the curve in the driveway, and I realize we're going to be escorted into this tropical paradise lined with palms and exotic plants. I'm about to walk into a millionaire's lifestyle and it feels weird as fuck. I think of my service station, the work I do, and almost laugh. Then I think of the way I paint, and hell, I could decorate this place with my eyes closed.

"What's this party for?" I ask, checking out the pale blonde hair of the jock maneuvering the approaching car.

"Just your everyday get together." She sounds preoccupied.

Her tone brings my head around. "This is some classy joint. Why didn't you tell me–"

Glancing at the gate, she says, "I was afraid you wouldn't come."

I chuckle but recoil. "Why?"

She tucks her hair behind an ear and checks her makeup in the rearview mirror, mumbling as she applies another coat of peach lipstick. "You'll fit in fine." She smacks her lips. "Just chill, baby."

"I never said I was feeling outclass…" I'm unable to finish telling her I'm not about to bow down to her wealthy homies, because Kirby's leaning over me, boobs smashing my face, her voice pitching through the open window.

"Thanks for meeting us Anthony. Hope we didn't miss Leanne."

"Who's Leanne?" I ask, scrutinizing Anthony's finely structured bronzed features, wondering if he's the boss's bitch.

Kirby wriggles back behind the wheel. "She's an amazing singer."

"So this deal includes entertainment?" I ask.

She squeezes my thigh. "This deal includes everything."

Anthony's convertible idles before the extravagant wrought iron fencing; he hits a button and the gate opens. We follow, and at the end of a long, snaking driveway sits a classic white mansion not more than fifty feet from a waterfall leading into a glistening lake.

We park the Corolla in a lot with a couple dozen other cars, most of which are as classy as the surroundings. "I take it this isn't just an employee gig." Hands in pockets, I mumble as we walk on patterned gray pavers. "I have a feeling this isn't a job interview, either. What are we doing here?"

"Rubbing elbows with the crowd but mostly getting in good with the boss. Once he meets you he'll fall for you, like I did."

"The boss. The big boss. Who is the boss anyway?"

"The big boss is Will Wilson."

I laugh. "First name better be William."

Kirby grins. "Wilson. Family history. Don't ask."

I roll my eyes, then pick up vibes from Anthony. I refuse to display my awe of the place as he's studying my reaction, and my pants. "Nice place. Nice lake." My head bobs. I'm so cool, Kirby shoots me an admonishing look. "You do a great job with the landscaping," I grin at Anthony, taking in his sandals and manicured toes, smooth legs leading up to pink walking shorts and white polo shirt.

The toss of his head shows a precision haircut that falls flawlessly back into a wedge shape. "I don't landscape," he drawls, adding, "Nice to see you, Kirby."

I catch Kirby staring at the waterfall. "This makes me miss

our lake," she grins up at me, "maybe we'll take a few laps later." Her fingers grip my butt, which is stuffed into these damn slim-fitting pants she strongly suggested I wear. Without a word, Anthony takes it all in. He doesn't smile, just nods and lifts his chin, occasionally drawing on the vape pen he carries. I'm beginning to think Kirby might not be the little sweetie I figured her to be. They say you don't really know someone until you live with them, so I guess I'll be finding out soon.

Following the pavers, we stroll into the backyard, let me correct that, courtyard is more like it. A stage is set up but music is playing through speakers. I don't see a singer, so I'm guessing we missed Leanne. A variety of guests are dressed like casual clones, which is good, so I won't stand out as the new guy, or the insecure guy, or the guy depending upon a girl he really doesn't know to get him a job he's not really sure he'll like, or even land for that matter. With Kirby by my side, my eyes cautiously skip over the bikini babes.

Drinks in hand, we circle the courtyard, Kirby introducing me to a variety of guest milling around under awnings, some worshipping the sun on loungers.

"Don't bother," I squeeze her hand and whisper. "I'll forget their names the minute we leave. Just take me to the master so we can get the fuck outta here." I'm considering a night on the town, after which Kirby and I peel each other's clothes off and fuck like animals in the shower.

"You'll be working with some of these people." She shoots me a warning glance.

"Oh yeah? Like that jackass over there in the cheap suit?"

"Don't judge a book by its cover. Or suit, which by the way is designer." She's flippant. "He's the finance officer. Come on. I'll intro you."

"David this is Jesse."

Designer suit eyes me coolly. "The man you've told me

about."

Automatically, I extend a hand. "Hey, Dave."

His weak grip weakens. "David." He draws back his hand and slips it into his jacket pocket. "Danbree. David Danbree."

"Ohhkay David."

Then and there I know the guy's a dick, but if he's got a say in my hire, I'll swallow my pride. "Nice to meet you." I can't help but land a jab. "The man Kirby never mentioned."

He ignores me and directs his attention to Kirby. "Nice dress. Where's the rest of it," he says in a flat voice. I'm not sure how to react. Should I be angry? Is he teasing? Ridiculing her? Would her boss talk to her this way? When she elbows him and says, "Jerk" my curiosity jumps into high.

Somehow, these two know each other better than they let on, although David is exercising authority. "Why don't you grab us some more drinks, hon. Jesse and I will be chatting. I'll show him the lake."

I restrain a laugh.

So we walk in silence for a few minutes, passing a tennis court where couples are playing, then David gives me another once over. "I'm the finance officer."

"Should I be impressed?" Hands in pockets, I'm casually mocking him, while enjoying the ass cheeks of the Bobbsey Twins swinging rackets. "Those babes have some strokes."

Ignoring my arrogance, he studies my face. "I guess I was around your age when I started here. Let me think, over ten years ago."

I nod, then shrug.

"It's not easy making your way up the ladder. Especially in a family business." David shoots me a superior look.

My head cocks, trying to figure this guy and his story. "You're family?"

"No. That's my point. You need to be sharp to get it over on the cutthroats who watch you like a hawk."

"This is sounding like a serious bummer." I shrug off his hand which has landed on my shoulder.

David shoves his hand into a pocket. "To be honest, you're not what I was expecting."

Taken aback, I frown. "What did Kirby tell you about me?"

His pale eyes narrow. "More importantly, what did Kirby tell you about this position?"

I'm testy. "That I'd be interviewing for a job in the art department."

"Ah, an artist. Have you exhibited? Anywhere I might know? What are your qualifications?"

"I paint. Sculpt. Run a gas station." I deadpan. "High school diploma."

"I can make you an offer right now, Jesse."

"Which is?" I'm ready to accept the offer on the spot, without discussing salary, although I'm wondering why a financial patsy would be hiring me.

"We have an opening in the finance department. Junior accountant. You'd be working under me."

"Bookkeeper you mean?" I choke, ready to turn heel and walk. "Hey man. I'm an artist, not a mathematician."

His voice remains steady. "It's an opportunity until something you feel more suited for opens up. Let me know by the end of the day whether or not you're interested."

Kirby returns with drinks; I suck down mine and sip the scotch intended for David, who has deserted us to make the rounds. I don't trust this guy. Maybe it's because of the financial angle. I don't trust bankers or brokers either. David huddles with Anthony in what appears to be a deep conversation.

"Seems some serious shit going on over there." I hitch my head toward the two men.

Kirby follows my stare and turns to me, grinning. "They're

talking about you. I think they approve."

I draw back and crunch a brow sarcastically. "Yeah, I noticed the way Anthony kept checking me out. What's his position around here?"

"House boy, friend, adviser, whatever the boss needs." She giggles. "Anthony and I have something in common."

"Oh yeah?" I cock my head. "Sorry babe, but there's no way you're a guy."

"Neither is he." She swats my chest with the back of her hand. "He knows a hunk when he sees one."

"Hey Kirby," I stare deep into her green cat eyes, "David offered me a bookkeeping job. What happened to the art department?"

Her eyes dart from her huddled coworkers to me. "I dunno, but let me work on it."

"I've had it with fucking around with these bozos. Let's split."

Kirby appears disturbed. "Okay, listen. I'll talk to *my* boss. See if we can do some kind of a dual position for you. Shadow me–"

"Fuck, babe, I do that already." I feel heat rise from chest to neck to face.

"Relax, Jesse. I get the news, you get the pictures. Hang here, I'll be right back." She takes my glass and leaves.

"There're a hell of a lot of bosses around here." Hands stuffed into pockets, my head revolves around the courtyard then lands back on Kirby, who returns with more drinks and an intense look. "So ... who's your boss?" I press.

"Steven Wilson. He's head of personnel and just about everything else in the company. He's over there." Her reply seems absent of thought.

"Son of Will Wilson no doubt?" I check out the snarky looking guy who appears to be in his forties.

David approaches and I down the scotch Kirby has handed

me. "Get Jesse another, will you, Kirby?" he says when he steps to her side. "And Steven needs to speak with you."

My head follows Kirby in the direction of Steven Wilson. His brown hair is close-cropped; he's clean shaven and neatly dressed in sport clothes screaming dollar signs. Kirby takes off in his direction and David slings an arm loosely around my shoulders.

Part of my brain says David's intention was to give Kirby the brush-off, but the other part processes the possessive slide of his arm around her hips before sending her off with a pat on the ass.

Kirby and Steven meet and huddle. Their facial expressions might clue me in on the conversation, but their backs are turned.

"Make a decision yet?" David slaps my back.

Shrugging free, I distance myself. "It's not the end of the day yet." I give him a blank stare.

"Per Kirby, you own a service station. You must have run some numbers."

Hand on hip, I scratch my head with the other. "Yeah, but mostly my parents took care of that end. I'm not sure this is right for me, Dave."

"David." He's relentless and begins to sell me on the job. "It's just temporary. Take it to get your foot in the door. As soon as George retires, the ad job is yours."

"Yeah, I guess." I have my reservations but since I'm already here with no one else knocking down the door, other than Kirby at night ... "Yeah, okay. I'll take it." Against my better judgment, I accept David's handshake which seals the deal. "So when's George retiring?"

Drinks in hand, Kirby returns.

"Jesse has accepted our offer." David is beaming.

"Part time accountant, part time photographer according to Mr. Wilson," Kirby chirps.

"You never said part time–" Swiping perspiration from my

forehead, I narrow my eyes at her.

Did Kirby just run her idea by Steven or has this been the case since day one, when she got me down here for a job as an artist? Whoa, we're a long way from home, maybe the truth.

Kirby must sense my dissatisfaction; she hooks her arm through mine. "Let me show you around. It's amazing, isn't it?"

We pass a swimming pool and cabanas and cottages fit for royalty, not to mention the twelve car garage that looks like a mini replica of the mansion. "Christ, this guy must own half the planet to be able to afford all this."

"He might," Kirby sounds serious. "He's a real estate mogul. The paper is just one of his smaller ventures." She smirks. "Gives Steven something to do I guess."

"Fuck that. I'd be somewhere in the Mediterranean if I were him."

"Trust me, Mr. Wilson has a fortune there too."

We tour the mansion and stop in a third floor hallway, isolated and dim. "I need to take a pee," Kirby whispers, pulling me through the doorway of the bathroom that's more like a ballroom with chandeliers, glistening fixtures, peach and ivory granite. "Holy fuck, who lives here, the Pope?"

"Bath?" She points to a jetted tub sized for more than one, "or shower?" She starts leading me to a wall to wall shower. "Steam shower … steamy … nice," she says, shoving me toward the glass doors.

"So I need a steam shower before I can meet the big big Wilsons?"

Kirby shoves me against a granite counter. Throwing a leg up, she begins to climb me. Devour my mouth. Rip my clothes off.

"Hey." I gently shove her off. "What are you doing?"

"I'm horny."

"I don't have any condoms so you're out of luck," I say, but my body is screaming for hers.

"Your turn then." She unzips my fly, and as she drops to her knees, my pants go with her. The granite is cool against my bare ass. Kirby's breath on my dick is hot. So is her tongue.

I'm just about ready to come when she lifts her head, "My turn tonight." Her lips are rosy and swollen.

"Don't stop now," I moan, guiding her head back to finish the job. "You … tonight … okay … yeah …" I groan.

I'm the man with the camera instead of the paintbrush, which is not so cool. I begin my new career doing a few layouts for clothing manufacturers and drug companies. For a small outfit, it's producing a classy magazine. I go right to work, giving it my all.

Tuesdays and Thursdays I stay in the office - at my desk - with a window view of life going on around me. Occasionally, they send me to the bank with a deposit of checks. "No hurry, man," I'm told, so I hang at Wendy's or McDonalds for an hour or two before returning to the office. Nobody says a word. I collect my weekly paychecks and figure hell, I landed a tit job. But I still want to pursue my art career, so I scout the area for galleries, scour the Internet for ads. I figure in my spare time, which is plentiful, I'll paint the portrait that makes me a name.

Between jobs, I hang at Kirby's desk in case something more exciting than accounting comes in. "You know, Kirby. I never figured on medicine bottles as models when I took this job." I shoot her an annoyed look. "Or following you around. No offense."

"None taken." She smiles. "It's a start, babe. You'll work your way up the ladder—"

"Like David?" I shoot her a sour look.

She ignores me and dives right in. "Everyone is thrilled with your layouts. You'll be head of design in no time. Then you get to pick your subjects."

"My subjects are people and nature, not racks of clothing and pill bottles. I dunno if this is gonna work, babe. I'm thinking of heading back to New York ... and school."

Kirby's eyes flash. I swear, they almost cross. "There are schools down here."

"Yeah, I know but, I've always figured I'd fit in best in Manhattan."

"So why'd you come to Florida?" she snaps.

"I didn't exactly invite myself down here, Kirby. Take some responsibility." My eyes harden with my voice. "You fucking hounded me."

"My advice to you. Grow up, Jesse," she hisses. I never saw this nasty side of her before. Sweet horny girl is challenged and flips out.

We're arguing at her desk, drawing attention.

Someone turns up the radio and I hear a voice that sounds so much like Zoe's. Damn, "I swear it's Nightingale," I whisper, shaking my head. But it's wishful thinking. No way can she be on the air. Or can she? I remember some of the words she sang the night of the accident and I'm being propelled back in time ... and back to New York.

Zoe

Time passes and people change, leaving little room for Coney or Pizza Palace or the things the twins and I used to do together, which I now realize, were really fun. Mental note: make the most of every moment of every day 'cos you can't cheat time … or bring back the dead.

Nina's moving on with her life. She's great at color and style and has landed a job in a fancy hair salon. Leave it to Nina. Be it stealing or pushing, she'll attain her goal. One way or another. Legal or illegal. She's rubbing elbows with big shots in Manhattan, she's got potential and might be raking in the bucks … someday. On the other hand, Nino, with little to no incentive, still works at the smoke shop. Me? I'm studying my ass off so I graduate with honors. Whether or not I'll attain my goal remains to be seen.

No matter who I hang with, school is not the same without the twins. I've made a lot of friends but I miss my family. The thought that I now consider the Romanos my family is startling. I've banked some of my monthly support checks and have halfheartedly looked into colleges. My trust fund would pay the tuition, but not extra living expenses, so again halfheartedly, I search for jobs. I've learned to live large, shopping in expensive stores, which eats up my spare cash. Recreation doesn't come cheap, either. But I'm still not ready for the nine-to-five.

In a perpetual slump, I decide to take Nina's advice and start seeing a therapist twice a week. The problem is, on my good days therapy brings me down, when I'm bad I don't feel like digging into my soul. I'd never discourage anyone from seeking help, but after a month I decide it's just not for me. If I'm going to make it, it's got to be at my own pace. I'm waiting for the ultimate test of recovery, however. Although I don't want a relationship, I want to know that if I ever do, I'll be able to feel the like, the joy, the excitement, the desire I felt during the Jesse days, should such a time ever arise. So from time to time I test the waters … with caution.

Paul Gordon isn't an honors student, but he's not like the gang Nino and Nina hung with when they were still trashing the halls of PS 243.

Paul is in my senior English lit class, and I feel his eyes on me often. When I snag him checking me out, he quickly looks away. It's a silly game we've learned to play. I find his shyness empowering. I enjoy flying solo, but since everyone is pairing up for a break-bash at Millie Gerard's house, I accept Paul's stuttering invitation.

We spend the first hour together not being together, roaming around the backyard draining and crushing cans of soda. Millie's parents are home and supervising the party, but now and then we sneak into the woods behind the garage to smoke a bone or two, while some couples sneak other stuff. That's when the music blasts and the real party gets started. After hours of partying, the bash ends with a barbeque and Paul walks me home, leaving me on the front porch without even asking if he can come in, or if I want to see him again.

"Bye," he says politely. "It was fun."

"It was good," I reply. "Laters."

The most Paul and I share are school grades and fantasy. He wants to be a pharmacist. He says I could rock the world as a lawyer, but I'm not sure if I could rock anything right now, other than music.

When I'm with Paul something inside me changes. The old me twists back into shape. I'm torn between wanting to remain a slouch or be an A+ student and become the attorney I've always dreamed of. But being me is painful. So after a few friendly dates, I drop Paul like he's contagious.

The house I was born in has been rented to a family I've never met, and I'll receive the proceeds if it's ever sold. Molly's been my watchdog, checking in on the renters weekly, my bank statements monthly, to *protect my interests.*

Rye is back and he and Molly fight almost constantly.

"Has it always been this way?" I ask Nina, whose ears are covered with fluffy headphones. She's sitting on her bed, polishing her toenails. When she doesn't reply, I slide one cuff aside. "Did they always fight this way? Or is it me being here? Is that why Rye comes and goes like he does?"

She rips the hairy looking earphones off her head and tosses them onto the bed beside her. They look like two curled up kittens. I plop down next to her, scoop up the headphones and fiddle with them, thinking; I've never had a pet. When I'm out on my own I'm getting a cat, maybe a dog. Shelter pets need good homes. So do kids like me. Funny, I'm not really a kid anymore. I take care of myself as if I'm an adult living on my own. We're all on our own actually; the apartment is just our crash pad.

"It's not you. Molly and Rye have been like this since day one," Nina replies unaffectedly while checking her toenails to make sure the polish has dried before hopping to her feet. After several spins before the dresser mirror, she blurts, "Let's get the hell outta here."

"I'm down." I join her, checking my spinning reflection, deciding wherever we go, jeans and hoodie will work just fine. I run a brush through my hair, gloss my lips, cream my hands, slip on a couple silver rings and in seconds I'm standing beside Nina in the hallway.

She lands a few low taps on Nino's closed bedroom door. The lock clicks and the door opens just enough for us to hear rap music and for a stream of smoke to drizzle out. Nino jerks his head, which means he's giving us permission to enter.

"Sup?" He grunts through sealed lips, so the hit he just took doesn't exit his lungs too soon. "Cop a squat." He lowers the music, then pats the bare floor beside him.

So we join him, passing the bong around, which takes the edge off. After that we hear no fighting. We get high and crack jokes.

"Let's hit the trail," Nina says as she stretches, then smoothes laugh-smeared black liner under her lower lids. She's dressed like me, hoodie and jeans, only her hair is tucked in a clip at the top of her head. She wears huge hoop earrings. My ears are bare, but I feel around my neck to make sure my silver Z is hanging between my boobs and the chain is secure. I haven't taken the necklace off since my parents gave it to me for my twelfth birthday, and will be buried with it, which reminds me, I should make a Will consisting of my possessions and wishes. My parents were thoughtful; their Wills covered anything and everything, making my decisions much easier because my decisions were made for me. If I sound bitter, I am. Not with my parents, with life in general.

"Scott's at the Palace." Nina's grin tells me Scott is her salvation. "We can grab some pizza, then decide what to do tonight."

"Cool," I say, repositioning my bag on my shoulder.

"Rad," Nino says and stows his paraphernalia in the back of his closet. He takes a moment to strip off his tee and slip on a clean one, but he wears jeans that are torn at the knee, with shredded cuffs he walks on.

On our way to the door, Rye fires off questions. He's leaning against the kitchen sink, gulping a glass of water. "Where you goin'?"

"Not that it's any of your business … out," Nina snaps. She doesn't look at him for more than ten seconds before turning her back. She bends to re-tie the lace of one sneaker that slapped the tiles when she schlepped through the kitchen.

But I look at Rye, comparing him to my dad. It's no wonder the twins are the way they are. Between Molly and Rye … look at me, I'm proof of what a bad marriage can do … as I'm pretty much the same as the twins. Although I was already fucked up before my arrival to this asylum. Only in a different way.

The thinning hair on Rye's head is graying, so is his facial hair which is always in need of trimming. His shirt is buttoned midway up and his undershirt looks stained and worn. Rye is a carpenter. I imagine him working in a wife-beater when the sun is hot, like the construction guys downtown, then coming home and just throwing an equally grubby looking sport shirt over it, without showering first. It might not be true, but he just has that look about him.

"Come over here so I can smack your face," Rye growls back to Nina.

He sounds so angry, I'm relieved he's using his voice and not his hands.

"As if," Nino says, grabbing a bag of chips from a kitchen cabinet. "Touch her and I'll fuck you up, old man." He stows the chips in the backpack he always carries.

"Any time, punk." Rye slams the glass onto the counter.

"Anytime you wanna step outside I'll show you what this old man can do to a punk."

Nino lunges for Rye, but Nina's body-slam blocks him. Still, this doesn't stop Nino from taking a swing at Rye with his backpack. So Rye makes a move for Nino and Nina gets right up in his face.

"Just try something, Rye, anything," she says through gritted teeth, "and I'll have CPS over here so fast your ugly head will fall off your shoulders."

Rye's neck is red, his face contorts, but without another word he stalks into the living room, while we shuffle out the door.

Regardless of Rye's appearance and behavior, I'm still a bit stunned. "You talk to your father that way?" My lips coil with disbelief.

Leaning close to my ear, she whispers, "Husband number two and not the real deal and probably not the last. Why the hell not?"

She checks my reaction, then bursts into laughter as we head down the stairs and into not so sweet-smelling dusk.

We pile into Nino's car and head for lower Manhattan. Thus begins the routine of Nina and me hanging with Nino. It's taken some time, but he's turned out to be pretty cool. He shares his bong, booze, and drives us places. Since the fight at school, when three girls kicked my ass and he helped me regain my dignity, he's been like a big brother.

Nino offers to bring us with him when he goes out. Offers us the use of his *meds*, as long as he's able to sit on the floor with us. Be part of our secrets. At almost nineteen, he's matured and has lost his sadistic instincts. With me, anyway. I'm not exactly sure of how he behaves outside of the house, with girls, but no longer is he impatient when Nina and I hog the bathroom. No, we don't shower together. The apartment is a tight fit for five, but we manage to maintain privacy.

Is it a combination of Molly's nagging and the twins' drinking? Or maybe it's Molly's mysterious phone calls that have finally gotten to him, but McCabe ditches Molly yet again. One night after a raging argument, she flees to a *friend's* house, and he disappears like the moon behind storm clouds in the dark of night. Taking every dime from their bank account. Every decent piece of jewelry Molly collected over more than twenty years. Needless to say, she's now on a permanent warpath. Where she was a calculating conniver, she's become the world's admittedly worst bitch. She's also broke, so when my monthly support checks arrive, she holds her hand out for my cost of living expenses.

"How about we hit the Dive?" Nino says. I'm jolted back and forth as he hits the gas and brakes in bumper to bumper crawling traffic. Impatient Nino zips out of our lane and almost sideswipes a cab; the driver lays on the horn and curses out the window.

"Christ," Nina screeches, "I'd like to live long enough to see another sunrise."

"It's all good," Nino replies, chuckling as we leapfrog through a line of traffic, and a red light.

"Don't do that," I warn, wondering if Nino is carrying any drugs in his backpack, praying he's not.

I watch his eyes in the rearview mirror. "Do what?"

"Blow through red lights. We'll get pulled over."

"Thank you," Nina grumbles as we park in an alley not far from the Dive.

"Any time, sis." Nino grabs his pack, hops from the car and slams the door.

"You're a horrible driver," I mumble, considering taking a bus home.

The Dive is just that; a dive. We saunter into the dank club like we did the tattoo shop. Only now my shoulders aren't bare. I'm wearing a falcon on one side and a fairy on the other, with a songbird climbing my neck. I slip out of my sweatshirt to unveil my birds, thankful I'm wearing a tank top. I run a hand over my falcon. In my mind, he's my savior, my best friend, my confidant, my one true love.

The Dive is so lax they don't even proof us. It's on the bad side of town. Drugs are sold and used in the back room. I know we shouldn't be here, but I can't help but follow Chasing Dinero. Where they go, we go. It's nothing formal, but thanks to Denny calling me up on stage, I'm forever in their debt. I believe Denny likes having me around. Not sure about Richie. I long for the day they ask me to join the band so I can travel everywhere with them.

We snag a table and sip beers a bouncer-looking guy slams down.

Anxious, I glance around for a wall clock. There is none, so I pull out my cell and check the time. At ten on the dot the band mounts the stage. Girls go berserk and the entire crowd cheers so loud my ears ring. I'm mesmerized by Richie's voice. His music. His moves. Denny is a close second, holding his own. They rock their electric guitars just as good as any band on the radio. And oh yeah, they rock me. The moment they begin to play, we're out of our seats, moshing with the raging audience. Some of the things the therapist told me stuck in my head like: There is life after rape. And I'm living it. It might not be love, but at least it's more than dead.

Denny spots me thrashing around and jerks his head toward the stage, motioning for me to hop up and join them. As always, the extra acoustic is waiting for me.

My fingers move mechanically, caressing the strings during my mental warm-up. I'm playing pro now. I'm glad I let Nino talk me into going to the storage facility where my belongings are housed until I return home. If I return home. I don't know what walking into that house would do to me. I'm just starting to heal. Heal? Bury my sorrow is more like it. I might not have everything I left home with, but at least I have my guitar.

Standing next to Denny, I share the mic. The audience digging our sound is like ten shots of Tequila.

Hook me up hook me up
Throw me some of that heat
Hook me up strap me in
Yeah I'm lovin every zap

Hook me up lock me in
Dancin thru the stratosphere
I'm flying hypnotized
Lobotomized by the look in your eyes

Not only am I thrilled to be with the band, but each time I'm called up on stage brings me closer to becoming one of them.

Savage enemies tearing holes in your brain
You lie in a paralyzed soul of remains
'Cos the dead can't keep pace
With the whole human race
You retreat, you've been beat,
Can't explain, end of game.

Finding You

Jesse

Steven stomps across the room. I'm about to wonder what the fuck's up when he almost collides with my desk. "We have a problem." He slams his fist down and my Coke can goes flying.

I grab my sweatshirt from the back of my chair and sop up soda before it fries my electronics. "What are you talking about?" I hurl him a toxic look. I don't give a crap who he is, no one's going to treat me this way.

"I know you're new, but any idiot can count with a calculator. What's the difference between 850,000 and 8500?"

With arrogance, I tick the total right off and read the numbers aloud like a smart-ass. "841,500."

"Precisely," he snaps, "841,500 dollars and that's exactly how much one of our accounts is overdrawn."

Overdrawn? My gut takes a dive. "What?" My head jerks up. "When did this happen?"

"Apparently this morning," he growls. One hand is on the back of my chair, the other is pressing his temple. He's leaning in so close, I feel his hot coffee breath and believe me, he's making me nervous.

I'm not about to squirm, but my mind is going berserk trying to figure how the hell I made such a huge mistake on a wire transfer. "Yeah, so that must have gone into this pot. No worries. We'll just transfer it back." I log onto my computer and check one of the accounts I transferred money to this morning. When the cash isn't there, I check another. "It's got to be here." I struggle for confident, but now I start sweating. "Maybe the accounts got crossed or something. The money's here. I had to transfer a payment to a vendor. We'll find it." Stop stammering, I tell myself. You can't lose it. But fuck me, I freaking lost thousands of bucks. Staring up at him, my brows crunch. "The account I used isn't here." I run my palm across my forehead. "Neither is the money."

"So the account just disappeared? Along with over eight hundred K?" His arm drags over my shoulder, shoving me aside, and his fingers plug like a demon on my keyboard. "What happened to the rest of the money from *this* account?" His manicured finger points to another set of numbers I swear must have just popped up on my screen like magic.

"What account?" My mouth drops and my breath runs short. "I've never seen this account before. And it's locked." I hit my keyboard only to get a series of error messages. "My login won't work." Now I'm really getting confused.

"Login?" He pounds my keyboard again, bringing up a hidden file of protected passwords. Fuck, the password to the account is there. "This is the locked account you can't access. But as you can see, you do have access to it." His reddening face breaks out in beads of sweat.

"Hold on," I say, "I have no idea what this account is or where it came from. It wasn't here this morning."

He stares into my eyes with a look that tells me he thinks I'm crazy or lying. What he says next sends a chill down my spine.

"Are you fucking with the books, Jesse? Because the missing funds didn't wire themselves to a hidden account." The cursor highlights a balance of almost a mill and a half.

"Hey, man. Don't accuse me." Astounded, I leap to my feet and confront him. "Ask your financial manager how the money got into that account. He has access to everything. I just go to the bank with checks and do wire transfers when he tells me to."

"Somebody's been dipping into the accounts. I checked the books this morning. They don't balance." He shakes his head, his eyes dark with scorn. "And you're the one handling vendor payments. If you fucked up, admit it. One way or another, the truth's going to come out." The veins in his forehead are bulging. I imagine his blood pressure is through the roof.

"I'm only a junior accountant. Why don't you talk to David? Maybe he knows."

Steven's eyelid twitches with a steady beat. Beads of sweat gather at this hairline. I'm not far behind him with stress signals, but my sweat is gathering in my armpits, and I'll die before I let my hands shake.

Before I have a chance to reason things out, David's palms are flat on my desk. His face is too close for comfort, and to make it worse, his eyes are filled with contempt. I can't take the two of them staring at me like I'm shit, so I shift my gaze to the window while my brain tries to sort this out. That's when I see the flashing lights.

"What the fuck, David? I can't believe you called the cops," I groan, running my hands through my hair. "You know I'm no thief."

"I don't know anything." Arms crossed he's unwavering, and I know I'm fucked.

Backed into a corner of the room, I'm percolating; I mean I'm literally boiling and sputtering. "David, call off 5-0. Let's you and me work this out. There has to be a logical explanation … a mistake."

The cops crash through the door and cuff me. "This is fucking bizarre," I shout to no one in particular. Every eye in the office is focused on me. Then Kirby breaks through the circle of my rubbernecking coworkers and I'm relieved.

"This is fucking surreal," I mumble to her as I'm being led away. "Call someone."

"Call who?" Big fat tears run down her cheeks. "What did you do Jesse? I trusted you with every part of my life, even my job. How does this look for me?"

"What the fuck? How does it look for you?" I yell over the voice of the cop who's mirandizing me. "Have you given any thought to the sentence for embezzling? Grand larceny? I'm fucking innocent, Kirby. You know that. You know me." I hate the pleading tone in my voice.

Since my hands are locked behind my back, there's nothing to express my outrage but my mouth. And believe me, I'm using it.

"Do you think I want to spend the next twenty years behind bars for something I didn't do?"

My three accusers huddle, just like that day at the party. "What are you saying, Jesse?" Kirby babbles. "That you didn't–" She turns her head.

"Look at me!" I shout, wondering why she's not defending me. "It's a fucking mistake Kirby or I was…" My guts are twisting and she's … Ding … A light bulb goes off in my head. I was mother fucking set up. Which answers a question that's been bugging me; why the hell was Kirby so insistent to get me down here? Even if it took months. Promising me a job as an artist, instead I'm a fucking bookkeeper.

"Is that what I am? A sucker?" I spit as I shout. "Is this why you got me down here? To pin this on me?" My blood is boiling. I feel so sick I could vomit. The worst part is, there they stand, gawking, and I can't get my hands on them.

As I'm shoved through the door, I glance back at Kirby's eyes. They're so empty, it's chilling.

I'm fingerprinted, booked and tossed into a cell with some redneck degenerates. Just what I need. Assault added to my charges when I kick some dirtbag's ass because he's threatening to kick mine.

"Don't I get to call someone?" I yell at the douche locking my cage.

I don't have a lawyer. Jaime's no help. He'd just laugh it off saying I've belonged behind bars since the day I was born. The last thing I want to do is call Dad. Then it dawns on me. Alana. Her old man has connections. What the hell. I have no choice but to give it a shot.

"One phone call. Five minutes," a detective announces.

"I need a number out of my cell phone," I say as he leads me down the corridor. I assume I'm about to be questioned, and sure enough, I'm pushed into an office, shoved onto a chair, and the dick walks out. I check out my surroundings; I've seen rooms like this before but never imagined I'd ever occupy one. Jamie yes. Me … fuck no. I'm getting hotter and hotter. I want my hands around Kirby's neck; fuck Kirby, give me David. Don't go off on a rampage, I tell myself. I can't help but flip off the corner camera, then start praying I get my life back. *I'll lay off pussy forever, I swear, just get me out of here, God.*

Another plainclothes dick schleps in with my cell, letting me hold it long enough to get Alana's number.

He shoves a desk phone at me. "Here," he grunts. "Make it fast."

"Alana." I refuse to let my voice crack.

"Jesse?"

"Yeah, it's me."

"Jesse!" I imagine her smile. "Long time. How've you–"

"Listen, hon." My voice is tight. "I need your help."

"Sure, Jesse, anything." Her voice tenses. "Where are you, Jesse? Are you okay?"

I cup the receiver with my palm. "Not really."

"What's wrong?" Her panic hits my ear.

"I'm in a Miami jail."

Alana doesn't ask any questions. Her level voice shoots through the phone line. "I'll take the next flight. Be there in a few hours. Try to hold it together."

"Yeah. Right."

"Whatever it is, we'll work it out."

"Did I ever tell you how much I love you?"

She laughs and the line goes dead.

Alana arrives and I give her a full rundown.

"How did you get yourself into this mess?" Her voice is flat, but her eyes say she'd like to fuck me again.

"We should have stayed in Atlantic City." I grin.

"I'll do some nosing around, Jesse. Hang tight." She gives me what I assume is a reassuring smile, but I sense her concern.

"I have no choice," I smirk, "but hanging isn't really my thing." I mug. Seeing Alana, knowing she'll do what she can to help me, lifts my mood, and more, if you know what I mean.

Our eyes meet and hold. "If I weren't in this cell…"

"I'll pull strings if I have to, hon. I'll get you out ASAP."

I'm shitting bricks. She's confident. Thank Christ.

I'm wondering why I haven't heard from Alana, and why she hasn't posted bail. Finally, after three nights on a crappy cot in an even crappier cell, some dick swings the door open and tells me I'm free to go.

"It was a mistake. I knew it." I throw my arms around Alana and smash her lips with mine. I'm so happy to be out, I'd tongue-fuck her, right here, right now, if she wanted. "How can I ever repay you?"

"I'll come up with something," Alana says provocatively. "The mistake came from the top, Jesse."

"What are you, high?" We walk out of the station and into the scorching day. I'm drenched with sweat but I don't give a shit. I'm free and I'm laughing. "Don't tell me the big big boss fucked up?"

She shakes her head and flips her long dark hair over a shoulder. "I hate to break the news to you, but it was a setup, Jesse."

"No shit. But who?" Pulling Alana to a halt, I swing her around to face me. "What are you saying?"

"Your girlfriend Kirby and her boyfriend David planned it all, with the help of Steven Wilson who was literally a dumb fuck, who hates his old man and wants a chunk of the pie before the old man dies, just in case he's not in the Will."

"Let me set the record straight. That bitch is not and never was my girlfriend."

"Just a cute little fuck." Alana smirks. "I understand it's hard for you," her hand brushes my fly, yeah, outside the police station, in front of the world. "But you really need to start vetting your women, hon."

"That's some kind of bullshit." I drag a hand down my face. "Let's get a drink. I'm burning up."

Over drinks, we dissect the scheme. I think about Kirby and how she used me. My teeth clench so tight my jaw pains.

"That's a joke." Unlocking my mouth, I let out a low laugh. "Steven may not be in Will's Will. It's hysterical, isn't it?"

"They were on the right track, but amateurs," Alana pauses for a sip of wine, then explains:

Feasibly, small withdrawals could have been *overlooked* by David, Kirby's accountant accomplice and Steven, the plan's beneficiary. As Alana talks, it all comes together. From that first day, the way David looked at Kirby, touched her, I should have faced the fact that something was going on. But to be honest, I didn't give a shit if she screwed around with other dudes, but I could wring her little neck for playing me for a fool. Were her moans lies too? My manhood nosedives.

Their plan: Keep milking the company in small increments, using me as a wire transfer scapegoat paying money to a fake vendor in an offshore account. Steven fucked around with the bank accounts to confuse me, frame me if anyone found out. But my major fuck up screwed them. Me, being no mathematical whiz, actually fucked up the numbers on a wire transfer and overdrew the payable account. This triggered a warning bell, and the bank manager informed house boy, friend, adviser, Anthony, of the unusual amount of money that had been transferred. Old man Wilson immediately called Steven who then blamed it on the new guy.

They might have gotten away with it, except the account I used to pay vendors was set up the day I started work, and the fake account had been set up months ago. Steven switched the accounts on my computer after the wire transfer and would have gotten away with it except the dumb fuck forgot to unlink the hidden from the payable. Alana discovered this during her investigation.

So, within 72 hours of Alana's arrival, I'm out of jail, charges dropped, and Kirby, David and Steven are cellmates, left to explain things to Wilson. What a fiasco that will be. I want to stick around to enjoy the fireworks, but I'm heading back home with Alana. That's the least I can do to thank her.

Alana and I catch a car to the airport. We drink the entire flight back to New York. When we disembark at JFK, Alana grins up at me. "My flight isn't boarding for another five hours."

"This place is like a zoo," I say, wheels turning, "I guess we should find a quiet place where you can freshen up and we can catch up."

"You read my mind," she says.

So we get a room in at the nearest Marriot.

"How can I ever thank you?" I swipe the door open.

"Stay out of trouble." Her laugh is light as she enters.

"Trust me," I shake my head, take her bag and lay it beside my stuff on the bed. "I'm done with chicks."

"Well that's not good, or healthy." She slips off her jacket, revealing a sleeveless blue dress. Instinctively, my arms go around her. "This is the first chance we've had for a hello hug."

Drawing back, "Hello," she says in a deep voice and we both laugh.

"Awkward moment, huh?" Releasing her, I grab some clean clothes from my pack. "This has been some crazy ordeal. I'm hitting the shower."

Alana pulls jeans and a top from her bag and lays them on the bed. Stepping in front of me, she cocks a brow. "Company?"

She makes no bones about coming on to me. I owe her, and I have to admit she's damn attractive, it's just I'm not in the mood for fucking right now and I also made a promise … no pussy. Or for an affair with an older woman that can't go anywhere because, as she told me on the plane, she has a lawyer boyfriend back in D.C. I've had enough of triangles to last a lifetime.

I must look stupid or frozen or something other than normal.

"What's wrong?" she asks.

"Nothing." I grab a beer from the small fridge.

When I turn around, she's standing in the bathroom doorway wearing bikini panties and pushup bra, striking a mouthwatering pose, crooking a finger at me.

"You're not into this." She frowns. "Is it because I'm older?" Her bottom lip curls down.

"Hell no, babe. You're gorgeous. And age is just a number." I shrug and smirk then suck on my bottle of beer till half of it's in my stomach and the rest is making its way down my throat. "This is just been a hell of a ride, that's all. I feel like I'm still spinning in space. Hard to explain." I slam the empty bottle onto the dresser.

Alana strolls over to me. Runs her fingers through my hair. "Age is more than a number, Jesse." Her lips sweep my ear. "It's seasoning on the pot roast," she grins and slaps my hands on her ass.

Finding You

Zoe

Spring means more than blossoming trees and bare human limbs; there are only a few more weeks of school. We practice for our last walk down the decrepit halls: graduation. Afterwards, my tummy starts grumbling, and since dinner won't be waiting for me at home, actually nothing, no one will be waiting for me, I head to the Pizza Palace. As I pull the door open, Denny Brisk walks by, flashing a wide-eyed smile. "Hey kid, how've you been?" His baritone voice elevates and his step slows to a halt.

I'm suddenly blinded to the world around me. The sidewalk I'm standing on begins to lift. I have to stop myself from fainting while reminding myself I learned how to talk real words before I was toddling. Sound adult, sound adult, my brain screams. Being with Denny in a group is a hell of a lot easier than this shocking one-on-one. From the tone of his voice, I get an inkling he might be feeling it too.

I'm trying to catch my bearings and my mind's fighting me. I'm flying back to the school cafeteria where I first set eyes on this hunk of talent and charm. His last name is Moran, but he earned the name of Brisk because of the way his fingers glide so quickly across the keyboard. Not to mention the strings of his acoustic guitar. That's how I remember him most. Sitting on a bench during lunch, cradling his acoustic, touching the strings like he was in love with that guitar. He drove girls crazy without even opening his mouth, just by being him, and I wonder how brisk his fingers might have been on their bodies. The thought makes me all but overheat and I have to jump into another train of thought.

"I've been." I nod. "You?" For fear of being regarded as a dork, I decide to act smart-ass. Denny was one of the coolest, most popular guys in school. He definitely left an impression and the sight of him has reignited the way I thought I could have felt about him, had I let myself feel. "Haven't seen you since The Dive. Watcha been up to? Still playing?" Of course, I know he's still playing; my only choice is to rely on small talk or I'll go mute. My eyes sweep over his face, lingering on the shadow of a beard he always wears.

"Hell yeah. Richie's been scoring some paying gigs for us. His personality sucks," he chuckles, "but he's got drive, that's for damn sure." One of his hands rests on a hip, the other glides over his chin. I watch his fingers move to a sideburn, my stare caught by his long spiked-up hair, arranged haphazardly, as if a lucky girl dragged her fingers through his hair while he drove her into a state of ecstasy.

"Cool." Breathing while talking to Denny isn't easy. I think of him and Richie on stage and how I envy them. The way they shared the stage at The Dive almost killed me. Remembering how Denny brought me up to sing takes me back to the very moment, and I long to blurt out, "Need a backup singer?" But restrain myself. Still, I have to wangle Falcon Channing into Dinero one way or another. This could be the chance of a lifetime.

Denny waves a hand in front of my face. "Zoe. Ya still with me?" The hoarseness of his chuckle covers my skin with goosebumps. Not only can't I believe I'm standing here ogling Denny Brisk, but he's actually treating me like an old friend.

"Yeah." I giggle. "I was just thinking of those days … and you guys. You had a good thing going."

Denny fakes a cringe. "Don't sound so past tense."

I laugh. "Sorry. I meant in school. You guys rocked it."

"You're thinking *way* back." He makes a smooth glide to my side, and just as smoothly slings an arm over my shoulder, then his face is inches from mine. "Gotta stop talking that past tense." His words ruffle strands of my hair.

I can't move my head but my eyes shift, and I realize his lips are so close, if I puckered mine they'd probably touch. There's something in his eyes, a softness that isn't in his voice. He drops his arm and takes a step back. His head slowly nods as his gaze tracks mine. "You still writing?" He jams his hands into the pockets of his leather jacket that lays wide open with the tug of his arms.

His stare weakens my legs. "Sure am. I have stacks of stuff. New stuff. Different from…"

"Don't say that."

"Say what?"

"Different. I liked your stuff the way it was. When you let us play it."

"Let you play it? God, I prayed you'd want to play it." I've turned groupie and could strangle myself. "I put it in your locker, remember?"

"Yeah, I remember." Denny's entire face breaks into a smile. He laughs and looks so sincere. "Was our pleasure. My pleasure."

"I have tons more stuff like that too, just new stuff." Oh God, Zoe, get a grip girl. Am I mesmerized by Denny? Or freaking out because he's asking about my lyrics. "I've got lyrics and music."

"Yes you do." His index finger glides over my cheek. "Listen, I gotta run, but how about coming to practice tonight?" His brown hair is streaked with sunshine. Not only are his hazel eyes killer in daylight, but so is the muscular contour beneath the tight-fitting turquoise shirt that molds with his chest. His eyes take on the color of the shirt, and I'm drowning in a turbulent ocean.

Barely able to contain Zoe, Falcon, the stormy me, takes over. "And where would that be? More importantly, what would that involve?" I cock my head and flash my dimples.

"Tonight at a bar over on Highland."

"You practice at Shep's?" Hmm. Now I know why he's near my neck of the woods. "I didn't know they had a stage."

"Small but it works. The owner knew we'd bring in a crowd so he had it built." He gives a random chuckle and runs his fingers through the side of his hair again.

"I bet." I could kick myself for not frequenting Shep's on a regular basis.

"We're playing small time." Denny brings a hand to the back of his neck. He has a habit of massaging it. So sexy. "I call that practice. Money paying gigs aren't in local bars." He winks and something deep in my tummy awakens.

I can't let him cop all the attention, so I remind him I've been practicing and have a better sound than he last heard.

His eyes widen with respect. "You playing electric now?"

"Acoustic, but more proficiently." I fight off memories of Jefferson, the stage, the Fae, the boy who used to make my tummy feel even better than this hunk of handsome standing only inches away. For a fleeting second, I let Jesse's face cross my mind. Wonder where he is. What he's up to.

"We keep playing your tunes – doesn't seem fair. You should be with us," Denny says, still rubbing his neck.

I feel the bulge of my eyes and imagine how dumbstruck I must look, not to mention inexperienced. Guilty on both counts.

"No promises, but let me run it by the guys. Give me your number and I'll hit you up later." He pulls out his cell and bingo,

I'm one of his contacts.

"Either way?" My breath is short.

He gives me a cute smirk. "Either way."

Wow, I need to get myself together, so I begin to mentally sort through the newest lyrics stacked on my desk.

"Don't forget your guitar." Denny's deep voice brings me back. "Remind me what you've got."

"You're taking the bus?" Nino asks, then stuffs his mouth with Oreos.

"Sure. It's too far to walk. Unless you want to lend me your wheels?" I tease with a pleading look while snatching an Oreo from the pack.

"Hey." He pulls the bag away and digs out another cookie. "As if I'd let you behind the wheel of my car." He licks the cream center, grips the wafers with his teeth while he folds the flap and tosses the almost empty package onto the counter. "Hold up." He brushes crumbs from his hands into the sink. "Where are you going?"

"Shep's." I beam, thinking I'll never delete Denny's text: WE'RE ON FOR 9.

"Dressed like that?" Nino's eyes wash over my black leather pants and jacket, landing on my face.

"What? I don't look good?"

"Yeah, you look fine, but for that dive?"

I chew the inside of my cheek, suddenly having second thoughts about my black knit tank top which will be exposed when I'm up on stage without my jacket.

"Hold on. I'll drive you." He goes to the sink, wets a paper towel and wipes chocolate from his lips.

I clutch my hands over my heart. "Oh … you're so sweet."

He smirks and taps the top of my head with his palm. "I'm heading out that way anyway. Let's roll."

Before leaving the kitchen he glances down the hallway. "Nina coming?"

"She's out with Scott," I reply. "It's their six month anniversary or whatever." My hair falls to my waist. I fling the sides over my shoulders and the weight anchors it securely.

"Yeah, so they'll probably be over at the Pizza Palace." Nino laughs. "Nina thinks he's the shit, but I'm afraid he's really shit." He grabs a lightweight jacket from a hook on the wall beside the kitchen door.

"What do you mean? From what I've seen, he treats her good."

Zipping his jacket halfway, he frowns. "Her and everyone else."

"You mean he's cheating on her?" My hand freezes on the door knob.

He shrugs and dislodges my fingers with his. "I don't know, maybe, but keep your mouth shut. I'm not getting involved. Neither are you. I know my sister; she won't listen to reason. She needs to learn everything the hard way."

"Like all of us, I guess." My stomach sinks, hoping Nina's not really in for a not so pleasant surprise. "Oh, wait!" My voice hitches. In less than a minute, I'm back at the door, lugging my guitar case. "Okay, I'm ready."

Nino shoves the door open, holding it with his shoulder to let me pass. He's still on the subject of Nina and Scott, and minding our own business. "If it's bullshit rumor, my sister will blame us for ruining her life."

"Yeah," I sigh, "then she'll ruin ours."

"More than usual." Nino laughs, but with affection.

As I skim by, he lets out a low wolf whistle. "Where you going again?"

"Why?" I panic. "Do I look bad and you're just not telling me?" My wide-eyed stare meets his.

"Real bad," he chuckles, "trouble for whoever it is you're looking to reel in."

"I'm not trying to reel anyone in. Just going to meet some friends. And before you crack another joke, yes," strangling my guitar case against my chest, I'm emphatic, "they're just friends." I bring the tip of one of my new high heeled boots up to his shin but don't kick, just nudge.

Outside the apartment, the moon is brighter than streetlights. But once we drive deeper into the city, neon signs and headlights take over as high-rise buildings block nature. I remember going to a park with my parents, so long ago it almost feels like a dream. I was excited about the fireworks we had come to see. We waited in near darkness, but I'll never forget the sky that night. It was pitch black. But the stars. The stars were so bright, so beautiful, so promising.

Staring out the car window, the sky is nothing but a big black void, and I miss the stars.

Anyone who's ever driven through the city knows you can't always be on time for an appointment. Not that I have an appointment, but I can't wait to reach my destination all the same. Rush hours are hell, but even off hours can be filled with traffic jams, and of course we hit every single one. By the time we arrive at Shep's, the band's already playing. I jump out of the car with my bag over a shoulder and grab my guitar case. Music fills my ears, but my body feels the thrum firing through the air.

"Dammit, I'm late," I scowl at Nino then slam the door.

"Um. You're welcome for the ride," he snorts and takes off.

"Thank you," I call out, watching his taillights disappear.

Late is better than early, I tell myself. I won't look too obvious walking in when the band's playing, and definitely not anxious. Hell, with Dinero playing, no one will even know I'm here. Crap, not even Denny.

When I walk through the door, the first thing my eyes land

on is the stage. Richie is controlling it. He's wearing tight jeans and a vest, so all that's covering his chest are silver chains that are dangling over his pecs. The chains swing with his movements, which are killer. I almost fall over. Not only does he look hot, he sounds amazing. His voice is just the right amount of smooth mixed with gravel when needed.

My eyes roll over the stage. The other guys are all dressed pretty ordinary, but who's looking at their clothes, other than me, as I'm feeling more and more self-conscious about my leathers.

Dinero's playing better tonight than at The Dive, which was amateur compared to now; the music, not the club. This place is seedy, but the crowd doesn't seem to care if it's grubby and there isn't enough seating. They're here to groove while this wild band jams. Their instruments are blasting with a mix of alternative and metal.

Denny's engrossed in his music, so I take a seat on a window sill in a corner near the door, set my case on the floor between my boots, and watch. My gaze catches some wild movements, which I trace across the room to a table of four girls thrashing in their seats. Immediately, I recognize the blonde with the blooming boobs and wonder why she's not hogging the stage like the night at Deluge when she shot daggers at me when I sang with Denny.

Sitting emotionally naked and alone could make me uneasy, but tonight I'm determined. I'm strong. I shake off the feeling of being an outsider and ease my shoulder to the wall, comfortable and alert … and expectant.

After a half hour or so the band stops playing. My eyes are glued to the stage. Denny separates himself from the others who rush the bar. He hops down and weaves through the crowd. It doesn't take him long to find me.

"Shove over," he says, dropping onto the chipped wooden ledge beside me. "You're late." His shoulder bumps mine.

I gaze up at him. He's flushed from playing, which enhances

the spice of his cologne. His tousled spiked hair looks amazing. So much so that I want to touch it, but naturally I don't. "Sorry. I needed to wait for a ride."

"You should've said something. I would've picked you up." He palms his forehead. "I should've asked."

"It's fine. I caught a ride with my cousin."

"Is he here?"

"Nope. Just me." I grin at him.

His smile is warm. "So you'll be needing a ride home?"

Denny is close and getting real personal. The immensity of his words could throw me into shock if I let them, but I'm Falcon tonight.

"How about a drink?" He tugs a length of my hair that's draping my shoulder.

"If you can get near the bar," my giggle turns into a chuckle, "I could use a double."

He shifts to face me with a half grin more curious than humorous. "Don't tell me you've developed stage fright." His face relaxes and he chuckles.

"Of course not," I lie. "I worked up a thirst watching you up there." My head hitches toward the stage.

"And?"

"Huh?"

He laughs softly. "Did you like what you saw?"

Oh my God, is he coming on to me?

"Yeah, I loved what I saw," my swallow is deep, "and heard. You guys are the best."

Denny smiles and squeezes my knee till I screech.

"Tickles, huh?"

"That could drive me crazy." I remember my dad pinning me down on the floor when we wrestled and squeezing my knee till I screamed at the top of my lungs for my mom, who would join us, and we'd all laugh hysterically.

"You could drive me crazy," Denny says before walking away.

The band hasn't returned from break, but Richie's onstage, standing in the shadows, tuning up. I get the feeling he's married to any stage he stands on.

Denny takes me by the hand and together we make our way past the bar.

Standing before the stage, his gaze runs over me, making me realize this is the first chance he's had to see my uncurled limbs free of the corner. His eyes tell me he approves, immensely.

"Ready?" He lifts my guitar onto the stage, then reaches for me.

"I can walk–" I object. "You'll hurt your back." Then I notice his biceps and realize he could lift a hell of a lot more than me.

He holds me in his arms a bit longer than necessary before hopping up beside me. "Don't worry. You're light as a feather," he whispers directly into my ear. "You smell good."

A bit frazzled by Denny's attention, I get right down to business; I open the case to replace my guitar with my jacket.

"What the...?" Richie rushes across the stage, eyes darting from Denny to me and back.

Denny leisurely reaches for his guitar. "You remember Zoe. She's playing with us tonight."

"Do I remember Zoe?" Richie's eyes track up and down my body, landing on my chest, and I regret stashing my jacket in my guitar case. My fingers go to the straps of my tank top, ensuring my bra straps are covered, then slip over the curb chain suspending my silver Z.

"This is getting to be a regular thing," Richie complains. His lips tighten, his voice is flat. "No chicks on stage." His cold eyes are like ebony marble.

This makes me wonder if Denny even ran his invitation by them.

"This isn't student driving, dude. I'm trying out new tunes. Not playtime, man," Richie stomps a circle, running his hands through his long hair. He swings around and glares. I watch as he pulls a band from his pocket, slicks his hair back and fastens it at the nape of his neck.

Now I'm certain; Denny never mentioned me to Richie. His dark eyes almost slice me in two and a chill runs down my spine. Fear or desire? Are they one in the same? I have to wonder why he treats me like an enemy.

"Not that I wouldn't like to test drive this little groupie," he slurs.

I watch Denny's jaw tighten, his light eyes darken. But when I catch sight of his flexing fists, I'm convinced Denny and Richie don't play well ... off stage anyway.

"I'm not a groupie," I snap, my eyes cutting from Denny to Richie, "I'm a musician." My chin lifts so high my eyes meet the lights hanging low from the ceiling. "Don't you remember me? From the club? You played my songs?" I've also mastered the act of control: emotions, tears, hurt. So there's no way Richie will ever know I'm literally crushed because he doesn't remember me.

I blink away tinted spots, refocusing on Richie, who is now a silhouette in a spotlight. I hear a chorus of female voices screaming out their phone numbers. Male voices coax, "Come on man, we came here to hear you play. Not to watch you hit on chicks."

A rumble of laughter escapes Richie's mouth, which he twists into a snarl. "Is that so sweet thing? Musician, show us what you got," he says to me before facing the hecklers, "and you shut your mouths before I come down there and out your asses."

His Latin looks are stunning. The tanned skin on his face extends down his neck to his chest and glistens with perspiration. His eyes are so dark they're almost black, almost evil.

My guitar's already strapped over my shoulder, so I step up to the mic, ignoring the stares of the curious audience that's begun to buzz with excitement, or is it curiosity as to why there's suddenly a girl up here.

Instead of focusing on what feels like a thousand faces, I let my eyes fall on Richie's, daring him to a challenge. "Watcha got in mind?"

He bellows out a laugh and shakes his head.

"Name that tune, dude," I chirp.

My cocky attitude seems to tame Richie's. His gaze falls to the guitar slung across his midsection.

"Here's a new one I've been working on." The love of his music fills his voice, his face. He's suddenly dropped into his own zone, appearing unaware of his surroundings. He strums a riff, brings his mouth to the mic and announces, "Mess," and when he begins to sing, my stomach drops to the floor. Holy shit. He's making love to the audience with his voice.

Must be some mistake
The mirror's telling lies
A pale unshaven face
There's a stranger in your place

You dig into a pocket
The hands are not your own
You're reaching for a wallet
But it's already gone

Inside your head the panic winds
You've seen the streets before
Toy soldiers cut across your mind
But you can't turn back no more

The music ends before the last line of lyrics which he grinds out with a bitter tone. Turning to me he grunts, "Your turn."

My first instinct is to move closer to Denny, but Richie's fingers on my forearm hold me in place. I sneak a peek though, and Denny is watching intently. I can't move my body but I can move my head, which I use to signal Denny. I can't forget he's the reason I'm here; besides, Denny is like my security blanket.

Denny moves to my side and I'm sandwiched between him and Richie. We're a trio. Richie takes the mic and introduces me to the crowd as Falcon Channing and they applaud. When guys whistle, my stomach tightens.

Relax, my head instructs my trembling fingers. This might be the last chance you get to stand on stage between two hot rockers and a screaming audience. This is your dream! Or it could be a nightmare if you bomb. You don't want anxiety to erase this memory … ever. Enjoy the ride for as long as it lasts because this bus might never pick you up again. Or could it? Could this be the band's rehearsal and my audition? This makes my fingers scream to tremble more. Don't blow this, Zoe. No, wait. You can do this. You're Falcon … and you're about to fly.

I open with a soft phrase, then my touch grows aggressive. Jonny picks up on my beat, then Richie and Denny come in. It's amazing how they tailor their sound to mine; it's as though we've done this before.

My lips find the mic and I groan out the words with such emotion my eyes tear.

Spit into this world
I'm fumbling for theory

Hurled into panic
I don't wanna know
Who I don't wanna be

Eyes of all the moons
Attacking on me
I'm battling your stars
Slicing scars into my destiny

Zoe Channing might have stood on the stage of Jefferson High, but Falcon Channing is the girl who has taken the first step to stardom. I'm jittery, disoriented … I'm euphoric.

I hang out as backup for the next few songs then Dinero is done for the night. The crowd immediately thins, leaving the guys from the band at the bar. After a few beers, Denny announces it's time to start packing up. It's after one and he's got an early morning. Odd, I never even considered these guys all have day jobs, other than Richie the nomad, living off unemployment.

"I'm gonna bring my stuff out to my car," Denny says as he slips off his bar stool. "Be right back."

I nod and give him a warm smile. "I'll be here."

It's time for a trip to the restroom, so I sling my bag over my shoulder and leave the bar right after Denny.

I feel the presence behind me, and when I turn, Richie is sneaking up behind me. "Hey," I say, ill at ease because he's been drinking heavily and his eyes have the look of a mad dog.

"Hey yourself," he slurs. "Need some help?"

This really puts me on edge because we're in this dim recess at the rear of the building and there's nowhere to run but into the restroom, which Richie seems to want to follow me into.

"You were good out there," his tone softens, "really good."

He blocks my entry and exit, pinning me to the wall, one strong hand subduing my shoulder, fingers of his other hand tracing my jaw line, my cheek, slipping through my hair. "The crowd really liked you. So do I."

His whiskey breath washes the side of my face and I freeze.

His scent is masculine, like a guy who's just finished working out: a combination of perspiration and spice, all things nice. And he has been working out, on the stage.

"I'm glad you liked it, Richie. I think you need to go back to the bar now. I'll be right out." I attempt to push my way toward the door.

"Where've you been, beautiful? Why'd you stop coming around?"

His hand tightens on my shoulder and his fingers take turns digging in and caressing. His thumb begins to play with the side of my face, working its way down to my lips.

"School. I had to hunker down, get my grades up before graduation."

"I never forgot you, babe." His lips brush my hair.

I turn my head to face him. I know he's not going to hurt me, but I'm worried about Denny showing up and a fight breaking out. "What do you mean?"

"I know you didn't think I remembered you." His face draws back and zeros in again. "You were wrong."

I stare into his dark eyes, shining through dim light. Is he playing me, like the girls in the audience, like the strings of his Gibson guitar?

If I try to speak, I'm sure to stutter, but I shoot him an arrogant look. Stubborn, actually. Pissed off. Because I'm pissed off at myself for letting him make me feel this way. I'm not easy, I'm not prey, and it's going to take a lot more than this for him to gain my trust.

I shove him off so hard his back hits the wall. This seems to sober him.

"I've never met anyone like you." His head is tilting; he's rubbing his temples. "There's something between us, Falcon. I think you feel it too. We could do good things together." His hand reaches for mine. "Instead of popping in and disappearing, how'd you feel about becoming a regular?"

"You're asking me to be part of Chasing Dinero?" Breathe Zoe, Breathe, my brain tells the girl who's about to crumble. You can do this Falcon, another voice takes control, so I assume my new identity.

Becoming part of Chasing Dinero begins to fill the emptiness inside me, replacing the home I lost, longed for. Being on stage, watching the fans go wild when we play, dancing in the aisles, cheering us on, snapping pictures with their cell phones, is like a dream come true. Knowing I am part of their enthusiasm is thrilling. I don't possess an array of normal emotions, but at least I can feel excitement, anxiety, anger.

Richie is backstage sneaking a joint. After a few hits he stubs it out and drops it into a plastic bag. He pulls out a package of Rolos and pops one into his mouth, which hasn't stopped moving all night. "I've been seeing different faces in the audience. There's this dude who's always watching us." He's acting schizo. "I have a feeling we'll be going on tour soon."

I've never seen him so wild-eyed, or elated.

He herds us into a tight circle. "Check out the dude in the gray jacket at the end of the bar. He's got his eye on us. I feel it in my bones."

"Ah ha," Denny pacifies with an eye roll to me. "I'll be on the lookout."

I disguise a giggle under a cough. Denny leans into me, whispering behind a hand, "He's delusional."

Richie schedules as many bookings as he can, hoping Dinero will be magically discovered. We manage to get at least one show each weekend. Tonight we're at an east side club we've never played before. The crowd is older, which concerns me. Suppose they don't like us?

I stand on the stage, skin damp from the harsh lighting, or

maybe it's the uncontrollable anxiety I haven't truly been able to conquer. Either way, I need to perform, and fast, because the audience is getting antsy.

Jonny Champion bangs out a drum roll and the crowd breaks into cheers.

I've heard enough of Richie's songs to catch on to the melody and chorus. If one positive of the old Zoe remains, it's her memory for music. When I hear a song, sheet music wraps around my brain. Some people have a photographic memory. I have hi-fi memory chips in my ears.

"Can you handle this, babe?" Richie whispers. I watch perspiration bead his forehead, saturate his sideburns.

"My eardrums are computerized," I return his whisper. "Let's go."

His velvet voice begins and my knees go weak. Too numb to feel any vibrations, I'm flat, dead, almost lifeless. The two of us stand before one microphone, so close, with each quivering breath I inhale the scent of his cologne, salty perspiration, and the booze he slugged before he left his barstool.

Richie captures the crowd with one strong line, then Jonny jumps back in with a drum solo, slow, sexy, transitioning into a mournful dirge. Richie strums his electric guitar, then hits a chord. His music is soft now, his voice heard above all. I'm dreaming, swooning, my fingers working on their own. I hear my voice, pick out phrases, then I instantly catch on to the chorus. I've been here before, and feel it deep inside:

Now you're walking down the stairs
You're heading out to nowhere
Crouching in a corpse disguise
Breathing gauze instead of air

Richie stops singing while Denny comes in with his guitar.

"What are you feeling," Richie pants in my ear. The audience must sense the electricity flowing between us, or maybe it's Denny wailing out his baritone, but they cheer louder.

"I feel it deep in my tummy."

"Then what," Richie rasps.

"I stop it before it can surface."

"That's no fun." He comes up from behind to rub his body against mine and the place erupts. I'm thinking we'll get thrown off the stage because Richie has stopped making love to his guitar and is now focusing on me.

"I'm not in the market," I yell toward his ear. If I were, it wouldn't be with a guy like Richie Santana. He's a make her and break her. Of this I am sure. Traveling with Dinero I have come to know him. I've been broken enough. I need mending, not breaking.

Richie wraps up *Mess* with a lick and signals Jonny with a snap of his head. Jonny hits the drums and Richie shifts into high gear with a song I've never heard. It seems they'll only play their own music tonight, claiming the stage. Capturing the audience. Richie leaves me dumbfounded. Pulling my eyes from his isn't easy, but I do, so I can scan the faces of the crowd.

I see it coming, but stupidly, don't duck. The perfume-infused thong slaps the side of my head. Holy shit. Such an insult. I want to shrink into the floor, better yet, kick the bitch's ass for disrespecting the girl on the stage. I step back, cradling my acoustic, feeling like a fifth wheel while shrinking into the shadows.

One would have to be blind not to notice the change in Richie. His progression from moody to almost upbeat. The attention he shows me, the kindness. After the show, Denny starts to walk offstage then stops, pivots and strides to my side. When he leans in close his masculine scent is overpowering. His eyes are soft but his voice is gruff. "Not bad, noob." He plucks the tip of my nose with a finger. Nodding, he adds, "Clean sound. You're doing good." He narrows his eyes which are like iridescent crystals first green then blue, at times a combination. "Santana isn't known for courtesy, or charm, not to mention," he gazes deep into my unblinking eyes and my knees almost fail me, "the word honor isn't in his vocabulary. Don't fall for it, Zoe." His stare deepens. "Don't say I didn't warn you."

Richie has been watching us, annoyance in his eyes. Denny flips him the bird, hops off the stage in a graceful yet confident manner, and struts to the bar, where screeching girls flock to him. I am able to catch his profile. He looks amused. Slings his right arm around a blonde, his left around a brunette. Another girl brings a shot to his lips.

The crowd is winding up, chanting, Richie! Richie!

Richie moves center stage again. He doesn't come to me but rather beckons me with a crook of his finger. The crowd must pick up on his dominance because the noise is loud enough to blow the roof off the place. "Oh shit," I mumble. I don't want to, but I slowly step to his side.

"Awesome chops, babe. The crowd loves you." He rubs his cheek against mine. "They're calling out to you."

"Good try," I reply. "It's you they want."

"And you?" His lifted brow and the slant of his grin make his intentions known. His actions tell me he believes he has me sitting in his palm. He chuckles and runs his hand down my back, where his fingers linger on my ass. "One last song, then wanna cut outta here?"

Shaking him off, I give him a look that could kill. Thankfully, Jonny comes in with his drums. I could kiss him for saving the moment. The last thing I need is to fight with Richie, get thrown out of the band. Maybe I *am* sitting in the palm of his hand.

Brushing sides with Richie, we share a mic, and I sing my heart out, cutting heads with the leader of the band.

Close your eyes
Just don't dream
Hold those tears
No turning back now

You made your choice
Tomorrow's coming
Won't make sense
You'll never know

Curl up tightly
Hear the music
Desperation
Haunting changes

Can't think
Can't sleep
Take the hit

Close your eyes
Just don't dream

Finding You

Jesse

The sun is fading when we arrive at JFK, with enough time to unwind in the first bar we hit. Repairing the deteriorating garage has made for a hectic couple of weeks. I'm looking forward to some much needed downtime ... and recreation. Something I'm certain to experience while in the presence of my brother. Hanging out the closed for vacation sign wasn't a lie. This is gonna be one hell of a vacation.

At some point, Jamie is supposed to be hooking up with Miranda, a chick he met last trip down. Me? After my stint in Miami, I plan on flying solo for a long time. Tonight's plan is to down as many shots as possible before boarding our flight, and sleeping all the way to Texas.

After sailing through the TSA checkpoint, we head for the nearest watering hole; yup, I plan on arriving in Dallas a purebred Texan. The bar is basically an open counter flanking a mirrored wall.

Post security is mobbed, so we grab some seats in the waiting area, dump our bags, and ask a cool looking blonde to keep an eye on our stuff while we head to the bar.

She makes strong eye contact with Jamie and nods. No words. No smile. Just a nod while lowering her thickly lashed eyelids. She then returns to sipping her tall drink with tempting plush lips. From the look on his face, I have a strong feeling Jamie would love to put that rosy mouth to use. Maybe on the plane.

"First dibs," Jamie aims his voice toward my ear while we wait for the bartender to pour our drinks.

"What's yours is yours, bro," I say, holding up my hands in surrender. "Far be it from me to lay my dick anywhere near your territory. But what makes you think she's yours?" I scratch my head. "Just curious." I say this because I'm glancing over at the girl who looks pretty classy. "I say she's out of your league, dude." I like taunting Jamie. Anything that pisses my brother off makes my day.

Jamie reaches for his wallet. "Bet you fifty bucks she's flying down to see her sugar daddy. He's old and feeble and his dick is limp. She'll be all over me."

"A hundred says she's a cougar, hiding her wedding ring, while flying to a business meeting. Check out the briefcase. And the book sitting on the seat beside her. She looks like an editor to me."

"An editor?" Jamie bursts out laughing. "How boring are you? At least my fantasy women are strippers and hookers."

"Open that wallet and lay down your bet," I say.

Jamie guffaws. "You think I pulled out my wallet for a bet?"

"So, you're buying then," I say as the bartender sets down our Jim Beam.

Jamie's laugh is lost when a crowd of rowdies passes, but I watch humor fill his face.

I pull out some bills to pay for my drink. Jamie shoves his wallet back into his pocket and walks away, so I end up paying for three whiskeys.

A drink in each hand, Jamie flops into his seat. "Hey.

Thanks ... er ...?"

The blonde chick's lips spread for both of us. "Chickie Malone." She crosses one leg over the other, showing off a nice chunk of thigh.

"Chickie?" Acting as if she's not here, my idiot brother chuckles in my ear. And I have to admit, I almost roll up with laughter. "Would an editor call herself Chickie? If it were her real name, wouldn't she change it to something sophisticated like Elizabeth instead of," I spit out droplets of booze with my laugh, "Chickie Malone?"

Leaning back in his seat, Jamie shoots me a devious grin. He slides his thumb over two fingers, making a money sign.

I shake my head and laugh, mouthing, "Hooker."

"Oh yeah." Jamie rocks a heavenly eye roll. "My kind of woman."

"Try collecting," I mumble. Chickie has no idea of what I'm talking about because she's eye-fucking Jamie, while patting the seat next to hers.

Jamie's response to Chickie has been rudely delayed while we joked. But in all fairness, she's been on her cell phone the entire time. "Hello sweetheart. I'm James," he says in a husky voice, handing her a drink. "And this is my little brother, Jesse."

"Jesse James?" She grins. "What were your parents thinking?"

Not another one…

We board the plane and find our seats. Chickie's slick, and I do believe she's got her eye on my brother. What else is new? She manages to score a seat in our row by batting her eyes at some guy who she slips a business card to. He's willing to switch seats with her, so we settle in comfortably, as comfortable as possible given the fact that there's little to no leg room. But who gives a shit when you're talking and drinking. Drinking and talking.

It turns out Chickie's family owns a couple of car dealerships. She does travel on business, but she's not an editor. So we both lose the bet.

I'm not sure who's first to leave their seat, Chickie or Jamie, but who gives a shit about that either. I'm feeling just fine. I let my head drop to the seatback, turn to the window and close my eyes.

The rumble of our pilot's announcement wakes me from a dead sleep, but Jamie is out like a light beside me. Chickie's head is resting on my brother's broad shoulder. Now and then her lips flutter with soft puffs of air. Yep, they're both still sleeping off the five-hour flight and endless rounds of booze.

We break through the layer of gray marbled clouds and as our plane descends, rain-washed streets and lighted runways come into view. It's almost midnight and I'm wondering if they have an IHOP here where I can feast on an early breakfast. Yeah, pancakes, eggs, bacon, load me up, baby. If Dad were meeting us at Dallas/Fort Worth, I know his first suggestion would be, "Come on boys. Let's put the feedbag on."

My grin goes sappy; it's been a while since I've seen my dad and I miss him. Jamie, on the other hand, has been taking full advantage of Dad's ranch, bouncing back and forth from New York to Dallas whenever the spirit moves him.

I sink my elbow into Jamie's ribs. "Yo. We're here. Wake up."

His leg slams into mine, "Cut the shit. Can't you see I'm sleeping?"

"Open your eyes, asshole, and you'll see you're on a jet and if you don't get your ass up, you'll find it back in New York on the return flight."

"No shit," he grumbles. "What the–" His head spins toward me and he points to Chickie, who hasn't stirred. "Did I get lucky?"

"How the fuck should I know." I stifle a laugh. "But maybe

she'll clue you in. Better wake her up so you can find out if you wore a condom."

"I don't know." Jamie yawns and rubs his eyes. "Those shitters are pretty fucking small. I doubt if–"

"You're such an asswipe." The jet banks and I face the window. We're about to set down.

Jamie stretches and his jerky movements wake Chickie, who also stretches, then gazes up at him. "Hey, baby. How'd you sleep?"

Christ, these two act like they spent the night in a hotel instead of squashed into economy seats.

Chickie and Jamie shuffle in front of me as we disembark, and alongside me as we pick up our gear from the baggage carousel. Jamie unslings his arm from Chickie's shoulder and surprises me by lugging her overnight bag with his. Girls usually end up shouldering his backpack. Something must have happened during the flight. I laugh to myself.

This airport is twice the size of JFK, but Jamie decides to fuck with Chickie. "Damn, this airport is small," he says. "I thought everything in Texas was big." His lips pucker into a fake pout.

"Don't sound so disappointed, baby. I've got some big things I'd be happy to show you later," Chickie drawls, hanging on his shoulder. I'm not sure who is holding up who. Maybe they're holding each other up. "Do you fellas have plans?"

I answer first. "We're heading to our–"

Jamie elbows me. "Not for a few days, sweet thing."

"I thought you had to meet Miranda?" I try to sound innocent, but my sides are about to burst with laughter.

"Miranda is our sister," he lies.

"Well invite her too. I have a couple of brothers I can invite to the party." She winks at me.

The air outside the terminal could char a lung. "It's freaking hot. The first thing I need is a shower."

"The heat can melt the skin right off your body," Chickie says, "clothing first." Her laugh is throaty.

I don't get my shower because Chickie says "I'll throw up if I don't get something into my stomach soon."

We end up in a cafe chowing down on burgers and fries, which has a sobering effect on all of us.

"Ahh. With full belly. Man needs drink. Get me to the nearest watering hole." Jamie plants a kiss on Chickie's cheek.

"I'm ready to call it a night. You two have fun."

"No way," Chickie's fingers clasp my arm and she holds me in place. "You're coming with. Tomorrow I'll take you for a ride in a new car of your choice."

"How about a ride tonight?" Jamie mugs.

Chickie pulls on his cheek. "You're a wild one."

Something tells me my brother has met his match, in the form of a curvy blonde car rep divorcee from Texas.

From the cafe, we head straight to a bar. Weathered letters spell out *House*. Where the hell are you taking us, Chickie? "Keep it in your pants, little bro. This is the best bar this side of paradise."

Before entering the stone and clapboard building resembling a ginormous barn, I hear the music. I like the melody – the band is rocking out okay – but the girl belting out lyrics is amazing. Her style kicks my brain into high gear.

Paradise. Chickie isn't kidding. I have a feeling I'm about to find Zoe Channing inside. Singing her lungs out.

Losing sense of where I am, who I'm with, back in time I float. I must follow them into the bar because I don't even remember walking through the door. I'm back at Jefferson. In the assembly hall, and I'm backstage, drooling over Zoe Channing who is center stage, singing her heart out at the school play. I fall into reverie.

"Yo," Jamie's yodel snaps me to the present.

"Earth to Jess - dig this place. Check it out," he motions to a table in a far corner, where four girls sit sharing a pitcher of beer. Cowgirl boots, hats and boobs overflow.

"Two for each of us. Follow me. I'll show you how it's done."

"Hey." Chickie elbows him. "Don't forget about me."

"Never. But as they say, the more the merrier."

"Cheers," she salutes with a fist.

"You don't have to show me anything." I'm distracted by the girl on the stage. "Holy shit. Don't tell me."

"Tell you what bro?"

"That's Zoe Channing up there."

"Who?"

My brusque reply, "Never mind. Come on." is lost somewhere in the dimness behind me. Maybe going right over Jamie's head. Because I'm alone, hopping up onto the stage, drawing boos from the crowd. The singer is petite and wears a western outfit. A plaid shirt is tied at the waist almost in line with the top of her short skirt.

The lead guitar is thanking the audience, and the band starts packing up to leave the stage.

Perfect timing.

My hands find her shoulders. I spin her around. Her eyes are wide and she gasps.

To my horror, it's not Zoe. Not even close. What the fuck is wrong with me? My arms drop to my sides. Someone comes up behind me. A thick arm goes around my neck; I can barely breathe.

My body goes numb. Yep, I've fallen into shock. Immediately, the air to my lungs is cut off by what feels like a flesh and bone noose. My mind spins struggling between embarrassment and survival because I think I'm about to get my ass kicked big time or maybe shot.

It's a bouncer - races through my head. Maybe one of the band. Either way, I meant her no harm. But this I cannot tell him because I'm gasping for air.

I'm about to throw my weight to the right, throw him off guard, take both of us down to the floor, when I'm suddenly released by Jamie, who's tackling what looks like a grizzly bear wearing jeans and tee.

The girl I spooked is screaming. The crowd is cheering. And Jamie and I are throwing down with the entire band. Fists are flying, bodies lurching back and forth with spring-like activation, dropping and leaping to their feet.

I knock out my opponent, a full bearded long haired dude. "Buddy," I manage to say, "I have nothing against you," before dropping him to the floor with a left hook.

I spin to see Jamie pinned by two others, grab a rope that's hanging from the ceiling and sail across the stage like Tarzan. Unfortunately, Jamie is in the middle – and is a victim of circumstance. The three are knocked out cold.

I drag Jamie to his feet, slapping him awake, half carry him backstage where the cowgirl singer stands with Chickie. I can't fucking believe they're laughing their pretty little asses off.

"Fight the good fight, cowboy," the girl says, sending me off with a shove.

Apparently Chickie explained we're from New York.

"New York is known for its pizza and street fighters." Chickie grins then grimaces. "Look out!"

I spin to see a diesel steam toward me. I feel his fist, stumble, then dropkick a shitbag who has appeared out of nowhere.

Licking my lips, I taste blood. My hand rushes to my mouth, checking my teeth. I took a few hard blows to the jaw. Thank God my teeth aren't loose.

I feel the impact of my boot against some chump's muscular thigh, throwing him off balance. The guitar he holds - intended for Jamie, now back in the fight - is slammed against the chump's head and he drops heavily to the floor.

Time ramps up; I'm amped up and the adrenaline that kicked in earlier is running out.

My movements aren't calculated - they're reactive; reminiscent of every fight my brother and I ever had. But we aren't playing now - we're just trying to survive. Fists and feet fly in every direction. I'm lightheaded but alert. Unstoppable. Defending myself and my asshole brother.

These dudes have a thing for my neck; I fall into the chokehold of another arm. With my air cut off, I have no chance to diffuse the situation. I want to tell him, "Listen chief, it was a mistake. I meant her no harm." But I don't have a chance. The stage that held a band now holds a bunch of brawling assholes. I'm not sure how long this goes on, maybe seconds, maybe minutes, but bouncers rush the stage. Before they get a chance at us, I pull Jamie out of a pileup of bodies and hold up a hand. "Hey, I got this one."

Without looking back, I shove Jamie through the door. Even in moonlight, I can see his right eye is half closed, already turning red and blue.

Chickie's arm comes around him. She's shouldering his weight. "I'll take him to my place. You're welcome to come along." She lets out a sigh. "You two put up one hell of a fight."

A small tug of my arm urges me to turn, and I'm being grinned up at by the cowgirl in the band.

"I'm sorry if I scared you," I mutter. "I thought you were –"

"Someone else," she nods, "I get that a lot."

"It's not a pickup line. I really did. You sound so much like a girl I used to know."

She squints up at me, her green eyes flirty. "Your eyes tell me you're truthful." Her tempting lips purse. "Do I still look like her? I can try to be her for you ... at least for tonight."

Does she see longing in my eyes?

"Come on cowboy. Come home with me," she persists,

running her hand up my thigh. When it reaches my crotch, my decision is made.

So much has happened in such a short time. We walked in leaving midnight and walk out leaving chaos.

The girl's name is Twilight. Her hair is dark, eyes slanted and emerald green. How did I ever think she was a blue-eyed blonde I called Nightingale?

I'm not sure if her name really is Twilight nor do I care; I'm figuring on waking up with Twilight in dawn. Which is exactly what I do.

Sunlight flooding the room awakens me. Opening my swollen eyes isn't easy, but when my lids manage to roll up, I squint until I've adjusted to daylight.

"Holy fuck," I moan. What a night it must have been. I touch my jaw, drag a hand down my face. My head turns to the left. Twilight is a sleeping angel, her perfect naked body plastered against my side, which is moist with her warmth. I unhook my legs, untangle my arms and turn to the right. My eyes skip over the top of the table filled with empty cans and glass bottles turned on their sides.

"Thank Christ," I mumble when I spot the condom wrappers on the floor.

My eyes crawl to a dead stop when they focus on Jamie and Chickie, sacked out in the next bed.

"Fuck, we shared a room?" I mumble and creep off the mattress, pull on the shorts I discarded at the foot of the bed.

I fling my socks at Jamie's face. He swats them away but I've woken him.

Chickie is on her back, the sheet covering her from the waist down. My eyes widen. She wasn't kidding when she said she had some big things to show Jamie. She moans, and turning onto her side, slings an arm over Jamie's bare chest. Propped on an elbow, he grins at me. "Did you enjoy your night?"

In an attempt to refresh my memory, I shake my head. Nothing outstanding, other than a headache hits me. "What I can remember," I grunt, rubbing my cheek. "We were in a fight."

"Yeah, and you got a concussion." He points to Twilight, breathing softly on her back.

My eyes flick over her. "That I do remember. But, what the fuck, bro? We shared a room?" I scratch my head. "I don't remember agreeing to that."

Jamie chuckles. "Share and share alike little brother."

"I slept with Chickie? Christ, tell me we didn't all sleep together."

"Count the wrappers on the floor." He smirks.

My head snaps around and I feel a rush. Everything I drank last night rises to my throat. I run to the bathroom and hang my head over the bowl.

Jamie's laughter is drowned by an annoying banging.

"What the fuck are you up to?" I yell. "Knock it off, shithead. My head's spinning."

I run the shower, step in and spread my lips wide, letting the water cleanse my mouth, then my body. It feels great. I exit the bathroom wrapped in a towel, about to ask Chickie for aspirins.

"Let me in," a hoarse voice hollers while a fist pounds on the door.

Jamie is out of bed, hopping on one foot, trying to get his hairy legs into his jeans.

Chickie, sheeted like a mummy, is still in bed, back to the headboard, finger combing her tousled hair.

"Who's out there?" Unaffected, she yawns.

"Don't open the door!" Twilight leaps from bed, stark naked.

Jamie all but loses his eyeballs. "Wow, babe, you look even better this morning than you did last night."

To me, this confirms we played switcheroo. I shoot Chickie a startled look. She returns a huge nodding smile. "It was great, babe. We need to do this more often." With a contented yawn, her arms stretch to the ceiling.

"Who the fuck is breaking down the door?" Jamie howls. "Shut the fuck up out there. My head…"

Twilight races around the room, stuffing herself into her bra and panties, hissing, "Don't open the door till I get my clothes on."

She runs to the bathroom, leaving the door ajar. The faucet runs full blast. She rushes out with a damp face and messy hair and presses her body against the motel door. "Baby doll?" she murmurs. "Don't be mad at Mommy."

"Mommy?" I gag, sucking in a breath.

Jamie shrugs.

"Let me in Twilight. I'm gonna kill 'em for draggin' you here." The dude bellows.

"No one drug me honey. I'm with my sis. You know, I told you I had family in town." Her head jerks to Chickie. "Get dressed," she hisses. "Quick."

Jamie and I brace for another brawl. I haul in a breath of anticipation. Our fists are balled and shoulder to shoulder we stand like toreadors waiting for the bull to break through the door.

"Let me at him," Jamie taunts, "I've never run from a fight and I'm not about to start now."

"No," Twilight is harsh, "he's real good with his six-guns."

Guns? Maniac knocking down the door? I'm ready to bail through a window. By the look on Jamie's face, he's also changed his tune.

"I know cowboys like him." Chickie nods. "Take it from me, boys. You want no part of a cheating wife and angry old man." She herds us into the bathroom.

Our ears pressed to the door, we strain to hear muffled voices.

"Where's my wife?" he says.

"You must be…"

"Buck!" Twilight's voice sings across the room. "Honey, where you been?"

"Who are you?" Buck's voice calms. I imagine Chickie is pouring on the charm.

"I'm Chickie, Twilight's big sis. Where you been darlin'? We been waiting here all night for you. You forgot your anniversary?" Her tongue clicks. "Well shame on you, cowboy."

"Anniversary?" His voice hitches. "Where's my Twilight? She's some kinda pissed at me I imagine."

Wife? I look at Jamie and I'm ready to throw my head over the bowl again.

"Baby," Buck drawls, "Come to Daddy."

"I couldn't find you after the fight last night." Twilight sniffs. "I was worried sick. Don't you remember we had a rendezvous, babe? We were sneaking off to celebrate the–"

"Rendezvous? Must have slipped my mind, but if you say so bunny cup."

"Where are the boys?" Twilight soothes.

"She's got kids?" My choking whisper is hoarse. "OMG. I fucked a mother?"

Holding his sides, Jamie folds. I slap my hand over his mouth to stifle his laughter. "I always said you're a mother fucker." His lips jerk under my palm.

"The boys are packing up, we're ready to hit the road. Can't leave without my little sugarplum singing canary now, can we?"

"They're leaving. Thank Christ." I sink against the wall. "I can't believe she's married."

"Look at it this way," Jamie's hand comes down on my shoulder, "you did the guy a favor. He missed their anniversary, and we were here."

"You are such an asshole." I stare with disbelief. "Doesn't anything matter to you?"

With half a grin he shrugs.

Chickie taps at the door. "Come on out, fellas."

I shove Jamie through the door.

Chickie's hands go to her rosy cheeks. Her eyes wide. "He sure was a big one, with two black eyes." She elbows Jamie. Her laugh is so loud, my eardrums vibrate.

"I can't believe this," I groan, rubbing my temples. "First night here and I…" I shake my throbbing head. "I can't believe my luck."

"Your stupidity is more like it. Thinking you knew that chick." Jamie shakes his head. "Why the hell do you think I never get tangled up with any broads? No ties. No responsibility. I'm a free spirit. No kid's ever gonna call *me* daddy.

Finding You

Zoe

It's a rainy summer day. I'm home alone, finishing up packing books and other useless stuff from school into a box which I shove on the top shelf of my closet. I've collected yearbooks for every year of high school, other than my freshman year, which I never completed. But diploma in hand, I'm out and free.

My cell buzzes and I'm shocked to see Denny's text. He never texts or calls, he doesn't have to, we spend so much time together. I think back to the day he did text me and get a lump in my throat. If not for Denny saying it was okay to join Dinero at Shep's, I most likely wouldn't be with them now. What path would I be on?

Denny: Issues on this end.

Me: What? *My heart trips; am I the issue? Are they dumping me?*

Denny: Richie

Me: Is that all? *Richie's like a two year old, throwing tantrums when he can't get his own way so now I'm not too worried.*

Denny: Pack your bags

Me: Why?

Denny: We're heading to Sag Harbor.

Me: Sag Harbor?

Denny: Where are you?

Me: The apartment.

Denny: Meet me at the Palace.

Minutes later I'm face to face with Denny. He's not in the van. He's driving his own car.

I stand by his open window. "What's up?" I pop a bubble with the gum I'm chewing.

"I told you. We're hitting up Sag Harbor." His arm hangs from the window, fingers tapping a beat. "You coming or what?"

"I'm not sure. I mean, I have obligations."

"What, like cashing your monthly checks?" His brow shoots up. "Come on Zoe, you're part of the band plus listen," reaching to the dash he lowers the radio. His fingers stop drumming the side of the car, "if I don't bring you back with me Richie's gonna have a shit fit."

"What are you talking about? Richie's always having shit fits." I giggle.

"You have a calming effect on the beast. You've got to come. Have you eaten yet?"

I shake my head, feeling another rumble hit my stomach.

"Come on, let's get a couple slices."

We sit at a corner table in front of the window where I watch traffic crawl by the Pizza Palace. Denny's slugging soda from a paper cup. I start munching pizza, intermittently swiping my mouth with a napkin and talking between bites.

"So what's in Sag Harbor?"

"An audition. Richie wants more of your lyrics," he says in a flat voice like *he's* not happy about it.

"Okay, I can do that."

"I don't like him taking advantage of you … not giving you enough credit."

"Listen, Denny, I don't care. Whether you realize or not, you guys are giving me a humongous break."

"So you'll come?

"An audition?" Goosebumps cover my skin. "When do we leave?"

Although everyone tells Richie the band isn't ready to go pro, he's been on the phone, leaving messages for a dude named Billy Hawkins. Hawkins travels the world looking for new talent and he'll be at a club in Sag Harbor in a week, giving us little time to get our asses down there and into a recording studio to make a demo for our audition. If we're lucky and can score a gig, we might not need the CD – he'll hear us live – but that's a big IF.

We pile into the van with Richie behind the wheel – big mistake. Within an hour we're pulled over for speeding. When Richie produces his license, a bag of weed falls from his pocket. *Great.* So, along with a speeding ticket, he gets a UPM (unlawful possession of marijuana). After the cop pulls away, Richie flies into one of his rants. "Great way to ruin my night, Mr. Dick." He shakes his head. "If I was that guy in the Mercedes," he's referring to a black convertible that just passed us doing at least ninety, "I wouldn't even have been stopped," he grumbles. "Takes money to get anywhere in this world." He swings his head around and says, "Which is why we're gonna make this happen. Tonight's the night. I feel it in my bones."

Richie's eyes are demonic.

"You're in no condition to drive," Denny says. "Let me take over."

No one tells Richie Santana what to do, but at this moment, he doesn't argue. He hops over the seat, willingly, which surprises me. But he has plans in the back seat. No, not with me. With his cell.

He bounces down beside me and starts punching the numbers of his cell pad so hard I feel sorry for the phone.

"Who do you keep texting?" I ask watching out the window as city streets turn to beaches.

"Studios. The club. Hawkins." He squeezes my thigh.

Between phone calls, he grills me. "You got your music with you?"

"Yup."

"Acoustic?"

"In the back."

"Still writing new stuff?"

"Yup."

"Shut up, I can't think," he tells me, although he's the one talking. Half the time he acts like he hates me; the other half he's falling all over me. During our drive, he's tense and lethal.

"Is this Billy Hawkins?" Richie's bellow overtakes road noise. "THE Billy Hawkins?" He elbows me, nodding. "Hey man, I didn't think I'd ever reach you. Listen, my New York band is on the way out there right now. We're looking to get an audition. Chasing Dinero. Brooklyn. Right."

Pause.

"Tonight?" His voice pitches then settles. "Dock Tavern? Vine Street. Shelter Island, got it." He makes swoony faces and his head jerks. "Ten. We'll be there. Thank you, Mr. Hawkins. Okay, Billy."

Richie swipes his phone off and throws it into the air. It lands on my head.

"Thanks for that." Shooting him an annoyed look, I rub the sore spot.

For the first time since I met him, Richie is wearing a continuous smile.

We arrive at the Hamptons, take a Ferry and we're at the Dock with an hour to spare, so of course, we hit the nearest bar other than Dock Tavern. Richie, and all of us actually, don't think it's a good idea for Billy to see us at the bar, no less walk in tanked, so we hold Richie to a minimum.

When we bust into the tavern, Hawkins sits at a table. I believe every single knee of Chasing Dinero is as weak as mine, but our performance comes off flawlessly.

We're not the only ones here, and after playing, we listen to some other bands, realizing we're up against some stiff competition. After Billy leaves, we decide to hang around, hoping for good news.

Richie has convinced himself we bombed because Billy doesn't call within the next two hours. So we party, celebrating the fact that we were able to pull this off at all. Even if we don't get signed, we're more organized now and can keep looking for a manager. We drink and get looks because our table is louder than the others, no doubt. No one cares. Music flows from speakers and while everyone knocks down Tequila, Denny and I dance.

"Look at this place," Denny breathes into my ear during a slow dance. "I can't believe the shithead got us this gig."

After celebrating and closing the bar, there's no way we can drive home, so we check into a hotel.

Exhausted but too excited to sleep, I search the Internet on my phone, looking for outfits and boots. If Dinero's going pro on the road, I need to dress the part of a real rocker chick with more than one leather outfit.

While imagining myself capturing the crowd like Richie, I must doze off because the ring of my phone that has fallen onto my chest startles me. I fumble, catching my cell before it slides off my body; the first thing I do is check the time: Three a.m. The next thing I do is stare at Richie's name, then his text.

DREAM GIRL. MY ROOM. NOW. URGENT

I drag my body from a warm bed because I'm too psyched to sleep. No, I hop to my feet and quickly dress because Richie Santana wants me.

I creep down the hall and tap on his door, which cracks open wide enough for me to spot Richie standing beside the bed, a pawing girl on either side of him. They're doing shots. Must be Tequila; following each shot, they lick something off their hands.

"Baby," he calls when he sees me, shooing the other girls away. Daggers fly in my direction; not knives, murderous looks threatening to kill me all the same.

Pushing past the girl who's hanging on the door, I stomp into the smoke-filled room. "What's urgent?" I ask, my eyes darting from face to face. What am I looking for? More women, I guess. The slamming door grabs my attention, and when the three girls stand together, I'm unable to distinguish the one who let me in from the two who were drinking with Richie. They're all brunettes wearing cutoffs and halter tops; triplets runs through my mind.

His lips brush my cheek, then he pulls my hair free of a clip that's been fastening the mass of waves on the back of my head. I shake it free and it glides down my back, over my shoulders. Richie's fingers run through, loosening snarls, then he curls a lock around a finger.

"Pack your axe, baby. We're going on tour." Richie's grin is lopsided.

I let out a screech loud enough to wake the entire floor, suddenly unaware of the time and the fact that Richie has had the audacity to yank me out of bed, displaying his harem to me.

Richie silences me with his palm over my mouth. "Sssh." He hisses. "There'll be plenty of time for that later." Bringing his face around, he winks at me.

I pull free to stare at him, my fingers closing around the drink one of the girls has shoved into my hand. "What? What do you mean? Billy called you?" I down the shot that dives straight into my bloodstream. Warmth spreads across my chest, down the length of my arms. I drop the glass onto the nightstand and Richie motions to the girl to keep pouring.

"Remember that Stan guy who kept dropping by when we played Deluge? He's a road manager."

Everything in the room is blurry, including Richie's face. "Do you think he's really interested?"

"Interested?" His laugh sounds robotic. "We're signed, baby." His arms come around me and I get nauseous when he twirls me around and around. He finally stops when we crash into the wall and onto the floor. I land on my back, with Richie on top of me, gazing down at me with an intense look on his face. I know that look. I've seen it before, but it was worn by someone I wanted to be with. Someone sober, not a shitfaced fickle rock star. Before I can turn my head away, his lips drop onto mine. For a moment I permit mine to go soft, then I tense. After all these months of close encounters, this is our first actual kiss. I guess we're no longer friends. Will we be lovers is the question? When I turn my head I spot the triplets watching with envy. This seals the deal. If Richie wants me, they have to go.

Jesse

"Dad's gonna be so pissed," I say holding my hand out to Chickie who drops two extra strength aspirins into my palm. "He expected us two days ago." I pop them into my mouth and drink water from the faucet to flush them down.

"Don't worry. I'll handle him." Jamie shoots off his mouth like a bigshot for Chickie's benefit. I think both our manhoods have nosedived. "I told him we got hung up. Had to help a friend out we met on the plane." He smirks. "Dad knows me."

"He doesn't know me that way." I'm annoyed. "He's pissed. He's not picking us up."

"He's not pissed."

"So where is he?"

"Hmm. I don't see him," Jamie grunts. "Did you give him the right info?"

"I did. I gave him this address." My stare weaves around heads and bodies, but no familiar face. It's not like Dad to forget us. Well, there was the one time he forgot to pick us up from daycare, and Mom didn't talk to him for a week.

"I've got to grab a coffee," I duck into a cafe across the street.

Chickie and Jamie follow.

The three of us walk from the air conditioned cafe out into immediate moisture. Yeah, it's hot and humid and I'm drinking steaming hot coffee. I glance over at Jamie and Chickie, drinking sweating bottles of ice cold water, thinking, jerk, you should have…

"Colton," Jamie's bellow crosses the street. "Where's the old man?"

I follow Jamie's wave to a mountain of a dude with coarse graying hair busting out from beneath his Stetson.

"Who's that?" I ask, dumping my coffee into a trash can.

Colton hauls ass through traffic and comes up beside us, bringing Jamie in for a shoulder tag. "How was your flight?"

Jamie's completely disheveled. He runs a hand through his hair and grins. "I believe it might have been delightful." He pulls Chickie against him. "This here's Chickie Malone."

Colton whips up his dark sunglasses. "Nice to meet you, ma'am." He tips his hat.

"Likewise." Chickie has the same twang in her voice as Colton. She extends a hand to shake, but after giving her the onceover, Colton takes her hand and brushes it with his lips.

Did we land in France?

"How ya doing, sweet thing?"

"I'm just fine, big boy." She beams up at him, offering her other hand to his lips. We all laugh, but Colton smacks his mouth over that one too, removes his hat, brings it to his chest and nods. "Who does this lovely lady belong to?" The creases around his eyes deepen.

Jamie lifts a hand and grins. "Me I guess?"

"What am I? Livestock?" Chickie grimaces, then chuckles.

"You must be Jesse." Colton's leathered fingers close around my hand. "How are ya? I'm Colton Thomas. Luke's … your dad's roundup boss."

"Roundup boss?"

Jamie grins. "You'll see."

"Where is my father?" I ask, annoyed this stranger knows more about my dad than I do.

"Luke is back at the ranch, waltzing Matilda." His stare ricochets from me to Jamie and back. "Looks like you had yourselves one helluva time. Bit off more than you could chew?" When he grins, the toothpick he's chewing shifts sides.

Matilda? What the fuck? I know we don't talk often now that Dad's in Texas, but damn, he could have told me he's been seeing someone.

I shoot a heated glance at Jamie, who's got an arm around Chickie, whispering into her ear. She's giggling, so I have a feeling she'll be coming with us or vice versa.

"Dad's back at the ranch with Geraldine." Jamie's mouth cocks a grin.

Matilda? Geraldine? Okay, one could be the housekeeper … but two? Thinking of Dad with another woman makes my stomach churn. I know Mom's been gone for years, but I always figured him for a one woman guy. I recall Mom's laughing comments, "Your brother is just like your father," and suddenly lose my appetite.

"Who's Matilda," leaning into Jamie, I ask. "And Geraldine?" I'm blown away.

Colton gives me a poker face. Great. They're all in on this and no one wants to tell me because they figure I'll explode.

"It's his life," Jamie shrugs, "more power to him."

We pile into Colton's oversized pickup; I'm shotgun, with Jamie and Chickie sharing the back seat. Now and then I glance in the side mirror. Correction; Chickie is sharing Jamie's lap and they're going at it. Unreal.

We drive until heavy traffic fades into a one lane highway flanked by rolling fields as far as the eye can see. In the distance are shadowy mountains, but flatlands are dominant. My window is open, and I'm gulping warm air that smells something like I imagine a farm would: fresh cut grass and cow shit. Up ahead is a post; the hanging sign reads: Sinclair & Sons.

"Holy shit," I mumble as we make a right onto the dirt road. "Dad's got one hell of a spread here."

Dust billows up from our tires, so to avoid coughing up a lung, I roll up my window.

Colton must notice my discomfort. "We've done a lot around this place, but still got a heap of work facing us."

"Like paving this runway, I hope."

Jamie pokes his head over the seat. "Watcha think, bro? The shit, huh?"

"Smells like it," I remark, gazing out over a meadow with countless heads of steer. "You never told me Dad was so into this ranch thing—"

"You never asked," Jamie says, "you were so wrapped up with your Miami—"

"Spare me," I yell over the seat, vowing never to tell my brother or father about Kirby or the setup which resulted in my arrest. Thank Christ for Alana. "I was job hunting in Florida," I snap.

"Job hunting." Jamie spits out a laugh behind my head. "Yeah. Okay. Right. I really believe you."

I swipe my hand over the back of my head. "Thanks for the shower, jerk."

"What kind of job?" Chickie asks and I groan, wanting to avoid a Pandora's Box containing my personal affairs and stupidity.

"Art, Chickie."

"Yeah, bros a pretty decent artist," Jamie says, and I'm shocked at the rare compliment. "You should see some of his work. He's really got tits and pussies down to a science."

"You're an asshole," I bellow over my shoulder. "Fine art, Chickie. Abstract actually."

"Fine ass." Jamie bursts out a howl.

"You'll have to show me your art sometime, Jesse. I might be able to put you in touch with some dealers."

At this, I perk up, ignoring my growling stomach and the strong smell of manure entering the cab through the rear window Jamie insists on opening, claiming the crosswinds will work better than air conditioning.

Colton parks the truck in front of a massive barn and we pile out. Through the open doors I spot all kinds of gear, some of which I couldn't name. What I do know is there's a hell of a lot of hay in there, rakes, pitchforks, stalls.

"There's your dad." Colton's flannel-clad arm slides past my face as he points toward the field. "He's out and working early, before the heat hits."

"It gets worse than this?" I swipe my forehead.

"You'll get used to it." He puts the same arm around me, leading me to a post and rail fence where he flags down my dad, who's riding a monster tractor like a pro. The moment he sees us, he revs the engine, covering the field in less than three minutes.

"Jesse James," waving, he bellows. Another Jesse James? I frown. This is getting to be a constant annoyance, not only from strangers, but my dad?

Colton drags the gate open and Dad drives through, hopping off like a twenty year old, well maybe like a forty year old. I stare in awe. He looks amazing. Pale and gaunt has been replaced by tan, husky and healthy. No wonder some woman snatched him up. He's handsome, owns a cool ranch, with a few bucks in the bank.

He wears authentic cowboy garb: jeans, plaid shirt, ten-gallon hat and boots. One would never mistake him for a native New Yorker.

"Yo, Dad," Jamie dives in for a hug before I jump in for a tackle.

"You look great, Dad," I shout, dodging Jamie's head which is blocking most of Dad's face.

"He looks like an outlaw." Drawing back, Jamie laughs. Jamie and outlaw, yep, he's into Dad's appearance alright.

"He looks damn good to me," Chickie purrs.

Jamie slings a controlling arm around her. "Off limits, little lady. He's taken."

His remark brings me back to brooding over Dad dating someone, then I'm stricken by the thought: don't tell me he got married and never told me.

Jamie steps back so I can jump in for Dad's bear hug. He smells fresh and every bit a farmer, or rancher, grass and hay. No cologne, but I detect the scent of Irish Spring.

Thumbs hooked in a thick leather belt, Colton has been keeping his distance, permitting us our private time. When Dad releases me, Colton's brows crunch. "How's Matilda?"

Hawkeyed, Jamie watches me. "I was just thinking about asking him that myself." Jamie's grin is plastered all over his face. Diabolical comes to mind. He's got something up the rolled up sleeve of his t-shirt.

"She's just fine." Dad nods.

"When do I get to meet her?" I ask, bracing myself for a coronary.

"You two are inseparable," Jamie says. "I figured she'd be out here with you, waiting to meet the rest of the fam." He slaps my back and my body moves forward an inch.

Colton jumps in. "We've been keeping her in shade as much as possible. Being she's with–"

"Pregnant," Jamie says. Nodding, he seals his lips.

Holy shit. I'm about to faint or shit myself. "Dad?" I watch in horror as the conversation continues. I can't believe the old man still has it in him.

"Doc says any day now," he says with pride. "Come on, Jess. I'll show you my gal." He shoots me a wink. I remember when he built our fort in a backyard tree. He stood back and winked, anticipating our reaction. Kind of like now.

Dragging in a breath, my sneakers follow his boots. What I don't understand is why we're not walking toward the sprawling ranch house, not far from the barn, which we're walking around.

"Where are we going?" I ask.

"You'll see." Jamie creeps up behind me, hands pouncing on my shoulders.

Turning, I swat him away. "Can I have some alone time with *our* father?"

While Jamie and I start sparring, Dad leads us to a fenced in pasture. The grass is lush and green, and this part of the ranch could be mistaken for Ireland.

"Here she is." Dad turns to me anxiously. "What do you think, Jess?"

My eyes work slowly over the gorgeous grazing mare with the shiny black and white coat. I let out a laugh of relief. "You've got yourself a filly. She's beautiful." I tilt my head. "And Geraldine?"

Dad gives me a bewildered look. "She's in the house. Why?"

I swallow hard. "Dad, you didn't go and get–"

Dad's laugh bellows through the air. "Hitched?" He slaps my shoulder. "Come on. I'll introduce you to Geraldine, my border collie." As we walk he chuckles. "What did those fools go telling you?"

"You know Jamie." I shake my head.

"Too well. And between your brother and Colton, let's just say I have my hands full. In a good way. I was fading fast back in that tomb."

I know he's referring to our house and his loneliness since

Mom passed. "It's good for you, Dad. I'm happy you decided to make the move, but sorry you're stuck with Jamie." My smile is sarcastic.

We laugh, we shower, we eat the grits Colton prepares, and most of all we catch up. Chickie fits right in with the Sinclairs. She's a hell-raiser. I know Colton has his eye on her, but her sparkling hazel eyes see nothing but Jamie.

Zoe

We kick off our tour with a celebration at the place it all started: Deluge. None of us can believe we'll be playing other cities now, spending a lot of time on the road together. Despite the fact that we're feeling like we own the world, this deal could prove difficult with five unique personalities crammed into a utility van; the biggest problem being Richie and his explosive temperament. His booze. His insatiable need for women.

While we travel, Richie and I fall into a routine of bouncing lyrics off one another. Apart we're good. Together we're great.

He seems to have formed an unhealthy attachment to me, or is it the other way around? He's all I have and it seems I'm all he has, during working hours that is.

"Lighten up, Richie. You're wearing yourself out," I tell him, concerned by dark circles forming beneath his even darker eyes. "Like my mother would say, burning the candle at both ends." A terrible thought strikes me and my hand goes over my mouth. "Ohmagod. Your appearance ticket! You never showed up at court."

His head jerks. "So now you're my mother?"

"I'm just saying." I feel the rise of a flush and my cheeks tingle.

"I'll admit it. I'm worried." He sighs.

"Don't worry. We'll call the court and tell them you've been away. Explain that…"

His face curls up with a sour look. "I don't give a shit about court. I'm worried I might get writer's block." He tries to grin but I read him well.

"That'll never happen. You're too talented to ever run dry."

"Yeah, my well is deep," he jokes and taps my shoulder. "That's why I keep you around."

"I can't believe you openly admit you're using me for my music." The least he could do would be to fake it. I shake my head. I'm not sure what I feel for Richie, or why I even said what I just did. Maybe I want the bad boy rocker who doesn't give a damn about anyone but himself and just won't admit it? Am I envious of his fan girls? My stomach churns.

His sharp features contort. "What? You think we have a thing going?" His laugh is cruel. "Some kind of celibate relationship?"

"I…I thought you…we," pull yourself together, Zoe, "I figured we were at least friends."

When his arms come around me, I wriggle away.

"See," he says, "you're no good for anything but music."

I've never used the words, "Fuck you," so much in my life.

Denny is another problem; he's growing distant. I catch him watching me and Richie working songs together, his face lined with frustration. The closest Denny comes to me these days is to drum, "Be careful, Zoe. You don't want to end up Richie's faithful backstage pass, if you know what I mean."

"That's not ever going to happen, Den. I'm all about music, that's it."

"Tell me about it," he grunts and walks away.

Now that Denny realizes Richie rocks my world more than

he does, musically speaking, he leaves every show with his arms around a different girl, making sure he parades them in front of me before taking them to the van.

All I do is write. It keeps me sane. The guys use what they want. But some stuff I keep private, like my emotions when Richie staggers into a room with one of his half-naked fans tagging along. Sometimes he's followed by two and three. No wonder he's burning out.

Wrapped up in my whirlwind existence, I forget that I have a semblance of a family in New York. I keep reminding myself to text Nina, but never do, and if she tries to reach me, well, good luck, I rarely check for messages. Everything I need, anyone I'd want to receive a message from, is right here with me.

Still, my emotions are locked up tighter than a drum. In a drum. In my heart. In my head. In some dark place I can't find my way out of. Concentration has never been this difficult. To think I might have to live this way indefinitely is enough to blow my mind.

I've been struggling to write with the passion I used to. But after our final night in Boston, a song finally emerges. Thanks to Richie. The sight of him towing two girls behind him on his way to his dressing room, one under each arm while they reach for his fly, I'm filled with anger; especially when Richie deliberately moons me before they have the courtesy of closing the door.

"You're disgusting," I mumble, although I know he can't hear me.

I'm sick. I'm falling. I'm desperate. I'm longing. I'm everything negative. Of this, I am positive. I think of Denny's warning: Richie's not known for his charm, courtesy, or honor. I'm learning this the hard way and turn it into a song.

Wake up little girl
He played you for a fool

Finding You

He has better things to do
Than mess around with you

He did the least to get by with
Someday he'll cry with

Crazy that he threw you away

Here comes the rain
Yeah I know you feel the pain
Tonight you hate him
But you're cravin to make him

See the light of day
Just see things my way

Tonight he set you free
Tomorrow he's a memory

Denny's been off doing his own thing. He's got girls climbing all over him, literally. He'll be at the bar and they'll hop up onto his lap and make out in public. He seems to have the keys to paradise, so who could blame him for spending less and less off time with us. With me. I push everyone away.

We're earning a name, so we land a road manager with a bus more ample than our van which is packed and attached to a tow hitch.

In each town there's a hotel, a dressing room, a stage. I take the stage and stay in a hotel room, but wouldn't be caught dead in the guys' dressing rooms in the clubs we play. Since our songs have made it onto the air, more and more groupies follow us. Guys hit on me, but groupie dudes aren't my thing.

My time is spent writing and traveling with Dinero from town to town, city to city. We're drawing larger crowds. Everywhere we go lightbulbs flash, and we've even been interviewed by a couple of Internet tabloids.

Being on stage no longer makes my legs feel like jelly. If ever I do falter, I close my eyes, clear my mind, and focus on my mom's words: "You sound so much like Norah Jones, Zoe." Can Mom see me now? Would she be proud? I grind out the song, the audience breaks into applause, and when I try to leave the stage they scream for more.

As weeks fly by, Richie gets hooked on pills; he was born hooked on women, so now he's totally occupied or high all the time. We all worry the band will start suffering from his neglect. We're making money, but Richie relies on me when his share runs out. I hesitate to front him because what's draining my bank account isn't helping anyone.

The tour bus we travel in is old, but at least our road manager, Stan Kozoki, has provided transportation. It's a sixty-five-thirty-five split, in Billy Hawkin's favor, but we have to do what's necessary. We want to make a splash. And Billy and Stan could be our ticket to the future. What better way to be discovered than a nationwide tour? Well, almost nationwide. We'll be hitting over a dozen big cities. Needless to say, we're all going psycho with joy.

We work our way up the East Coast, almost to the Canadian border. From there we hit the West Coast. By the time we reach Seattle, I'm exhausted. My throat is sore from singing almost nonstop every single weekend. Practicing almost every day during the week.

Richie and I are writing furiously. The fact that the band is actually relying on some of the pieces I compose is blowing my mind. When the audience reacts to the tunes I've created, my confidence grows.

But Richie. Richie is a different story. He's clashing with every member of the band, including Stan. Richie wants a bigger cut. Needs, actually.

Occasionally, I catch Denny checking me out, but he hasn't approached me since the night he brought me into all of this. He parades an array of screeching whores before me every night. I'm getting sick of crossing paths with half naked bodies; watching asses grabbed, naked boobs signed by guys I have to work with, practically room with.

There's never enough downtime. We're either writing, practicing, playing or traveling. Richie grows tenser by the day. His desire to be a famous rock star is so strong it's affecting his life in a negative way.

The five of us are in a hotel room in Tennessee, bouncing ideas off one another. The guys are drinking beer; I'm drinking iced tea.

"Richie. Be happy," I tell him, crossing the room to open a window because they're smoking me out. "We've got a lot going for us."

"Yeah, ride the wave, man," Denny chimes in, hopping up from the sofa. He grabs a beer from the small fridge.

While we've been bouncing, Richie has been stalking from bedroom to sitting room, running his hands through his unleashed hair. "Fuck you and your wave Brisk," he snarls, tossing his beer bottle into the trash can filled with empty bottles.

The moment the bottle leaves his fingers, he turns to me. Why me? I have no clue. "I'm going out for a while."

"I'm not your keeper," I snap, sick of his attitude. "Just your banker," I mumble on my way back to the window to stare out at hotel guests lazing around the pool.

"Do you want to come?" His sarcasm follows me across the room.

I wrap my hair beneath a barrette and snap it shut. "Nope."

Our exchange brings Denny back into the conversation. "Where are you going, man?"

Richie's reply spins my head around. "I'm outta weed."

"Uh oh," I mumble under my breath as I watch Denny hop off the sofa and drop his guitar on a cushion.

"Who do you know in Seattle?" Denny reaches over his head, threads his fingers and stretches; a wide arc brings his hands to his sides.

Richie retreats to the bedroom doorway, a shoulder against the frame. I'm assuming he's going in to get a shirt, as his chest is bare.

"Don't worry about who I know in Seattle or anywhere else." He's like a spoiled brat too big to spank, but Denny's tensing fists tell me he's had it with Richie's moods.

I desert my window scene to stand beside Denny. "You can't tell him anything." I shake my head. "Want to work on You Said?"

Denny turns to me, and his jaw stops working. "Sure. Why not." He shrugs.

Richie struts out of the bedroom, t-shirt slung over a shoulder.

"One step closer to dressing, I see," my eyes rake over him, "now all you need is something to cover your big ugly toes."

The room erupts in laughter.

Richie slips his feet into rubber thongs he left on the floor when he came in this morning, ties his hair back and yanks the door open.

"Hey," Corky calls across the room, "bring back a pizza, will ya?"

Richie mumbles something like, "Fuck off," before the door slams shut.

I pull out a sheet of my lyrics and hand it to Denny. I don't need to read my own words; they're embedded in my brain.

Denny's eyes sweep over the paper. He nods a few times,

saying, "Nice," like he really means it.

We sit in chairs across from each other, knees touching. While Corky dozes on the sofa, Denny and I pluck out a tune on our acoustics. Jonny listens for a bit then drums a beat on the table beside him; no drumsticks, he uses his hands.

Denny's head is down; he's watching his fingers bring his guitar strings to life, but I'm watching the way his hair falls around his face, suntanned from outdoor shows in Texas.

He lifts his head when I say, "You Said."

"Alternate lyrics?" He replies, eyes filled with respect.

I nod. "You first?"

"No. More like yours, Falcon." His grin reminds me of old times.

So I begin.

I have something to tell you
That's been burning inside
Life's not easy answers
This may be a surprise

"Yours," I tap my guitar's blonde body, and lyrics begin to pour from Denny's lips; it's as if he's living every word.

I stopped breathing for a while
Let fear control my days
Guess I knew I'd lose
Sooner or later anyway

"Go." He nods.

So I lived myself a lie
Thinking on my own
Couldn't face the fact
That you'd already gone

"You," I say.

Seems only yesterday
I was on the inside
Now you're further than a stranger

Who has passed me by
"Go, Zoe..."
And if I saw those eyes
Pass in my direction
It would be...
It would be like the first time.

"This is mine," he whispers, his eyes so soft, I'm about to melt.

I swallowed you whole
You were in my blood
I couldn't stand without you
Even after what you said

Singing together, so intimate, so softly, takes its toll on my emotions; bridges the gap that's grown between us. Butterflies fill my tummy. If I sink into Denny's eyes I'll faint, or end up on his lap. And I don't want to be a lap dancing groupie, so I bolster my courage and dare to look him straight in the eye. "So... watcha think, Den?"

He clears his throat and his head jerks, as though he's coming out of someplace so deep, he's been drowning. For a moment our eyes lock, then he's up and out of the chair so fast, I have to crane my neck to see his face.

"Yeah," he says, "cool, Zoe. We'll have to do this one soon." His cheeks are pink. His voice almost breaking. "I'm gonna take a shower."

Denny disappears into the bedroom, while I continue writing music.

The door flies open and Richie crashes into the room, carrying a crushed pizza box, which I'm surprised survived the abuse he obviously inflicted.

"I'm back," he yells.

This revives Corky who makes an instant dash for the pizza.

Denny emerges from the bathroom, hair damp and curling. He wears only jeans, and with bare feet he pads to the sofa. "What else did you pick up?" He stares at Richie. His reply seems to interest Jonny as well.

We pig out on pizza. We drink and smoke pot.

Richie stands up, pulls a bag from his jeans and dangles it under our noses. He swats the pizza box off the cocktail table and onto the rug, then proceeds to set up lines of coke. Without hesitation, he presses one nostril closed and snorts through a rolled up bill.

Lifting his head, he gives his nose a good snort. "Ah. Straight to the brain. Ladies first." His stare lands on me.

Feeling Denny's eyes on me, I turn to watch them narrow. I'm surprised he thinks he has to warn me. No one speaks. I believe we're all too shocked. We're all into weed but have never touched the hard stuff.

Gawking, Richie spreads out his arms. "What?"

"Don't do it, man." Denny shakes his head. I know he wants to blast Richie, but his lips do little more than tighten.

"Mind your business," Richie snarls and does another line, coming up crowing, "Fucking amazing."

"It *is* my business," Denny fires back. "It's everyone's business." Pausing he glances around the room, his eyes targeting each of us. "You'll fuck things up for everyone if you start using this shit. You're bad enough when you drink."

Corky pulls out an electric cigarette, possibly to break the tension, and Jonny cracks up. I just stare.

Frustrated, Denny storms out of the hotel room.

I don't want to, but I yell after him, "Where are you going, Denny?"

His reply is the slam of the door.

Denny is right. Between stress of possible failure and an

addictive nature, Richie has turned into a perpetually nasty prick.

By the time we circle back to the East Coast, Richie is using heroine. He's up. He's down. Mostly, he's as unstable as a lunatic.

I work out the chorus of *You Said*:

It's run its course
We're over now
We can still be friends
Loving you is not for me
It don't feel right
I'm too unsure
Can't give you what you want
Can you live with it this way?

Richie will have to live with it this way.

Finding You

Jesse

We've spent two weeks at Dad's ranch. Half the time Jamie is God knows where. Half the time I'm a handyman. It's been an enriching visit, but I'm getting antsy.

Dad's in the shower. I'm hanging in the kitchen with Colton who's getting ready for a barbeque. I offer to help, so he sticks me with shucking corn and walks across the room laughing.

Listening to the radio, I shuck and slug beer. I'm in a decent mood, singing along when a chick song starts playing. The voice hits me like a ton of bricks, as does the acoustic guitar. This brings me to tears.

It feels like an eternity ago that Zoe Channing sang to me on a dark road. A tragic night. I still see her plain as day onstage, strumming her acoustic. I palm my forehead. Plain and simple: I don't know how to forget her, therefore, I never will forget her. I'm fucking doomed to live out my life a miserable fuck.

My revelation must show on my face. Colton shoots me a typical dude expression. "What's wrong, Jesse? You look like you just saw a ghost. Who is she?" He dials the radio down, ready for a mentoring. I swat his hand away and raise the volume.

"What the hell is your problem, boy?"

"Shush."

Lost in surprise and confusion, I swear it's Zoe's voice, most definitely her style of lyrics. I get that old familiar feeling; butterflies are tearing through the knots in my stomach. How the hell did this band get Zoe's lyrics? Did they steal them? Holy fuck. Is Zoe with a band?

"I'm sorry, Colton." I cradle my head which is whipping from side to side. "I didn't mean to come off a dick. But ... I think that's someone I know."

"You know somebody on the radio?" Setting down a bowl of lettuce he's washing, he cocks his head, impressed.

"Just a sec." Turning my back on him I listen intently.

After the set of songs, the DJ spouts off the usual rundown of the music he's played. When he says Falcon, I don't flinch, but when he says Channing, my heart wants to leap from my chest.

"Did you hear what he just said?" I ask Colton, who is now peeling cucumbers, for confirmation.

"Who said what?" He methodically dices the cukes on a cutting board.

"The guy on the radio," I'm feeling desperate, impatient, "did you hear what he just said? Were you listening?" I want to shake him. I drop the ear of corn I've shucked into a pot of water with a splash.

Colton wipes his hands on a towel and brings his brows together. "Something about a falcon?" He shakes his head. "You on something, kid?"

"Did you hear the name Channing?"

"Like the actor? Yeah. I think so."

"Falcon Channing." That's all I need to hear. "Thanks," I say and rush out of the kitchen.

I grab my cell and search social media sites, like I've done countless times before. Still no Zoe Channing. I grip my phone like it's a lifeline, hit the google button, and search for Falcon Channing.

New York indie band hitting the big time is the headline. I fall into a chair in the living room, my eyeballs straining to consume the entire article faster than my brain dissects the type. It's a short article, and I want more details! There's a thumbnail picture of the band. I pinch the screen to expand the pic and sonofabitch, it is Zoe. Falcon? I struggle to understand how, when, where.

She's standing in front of a mic beside a dude, as though they're both singing. Three other dudes fade in the background. Zoe looks fantastic. Hot. Her hair looks longer than I remember, sides hanging in beaded braids. I can't believe my fucking eyes. She's making her dream come true. My emotions split in half. Of course, I'm happy she's making it big, but my heart is sinking in my chest. Zoe is gone for good.

What to do. What to do. I pace. I drink beer. I eat barbeque without tasting. Dad asks, "What's wrong, Jess? You're quiet. Something I should know?"

Colton's voice rings out through the silence. "Girl trouble."

"Want to talk about it, son?" Dad leaves his seat on the picnic bench and comes to my side and puts his arm around my shoulder, ready to deliver a pep talk.

"An old friend is in North Carolina," I try to sound as casual as possible, keeping my composure while not jumping up and down like a lunatic. "I might take off tomorrow. Stop off and see her on my way back to New York," I say, thinking: I'm leaving. I have to find her.

The final symphony
You slipped away from me
Ice cold in mourning
Words bleeding agony

Help me to understand
Did you have it all planned?
To turn away from me
To split and set me free

Can I walk on alone?
Along this road you chose
Recalling flawless past
While you dwell on the rest

Lies in your own closed eyes
Hiding from where you've been
Tearing my soul again
And again I'd let you in

Yesterday's love a mystery
My mind still stained with history
So easy for you to let me go
How can you turn your back on me?

Did I matter in all this time
Were you ever on my side?
Do I sometimes cross your mind?
Are you sorry that we failed?

You slipped away from me
Helpless I watched you play
The final symphony
And walk away from me

Falcon Channing. The Final Symphony.

My head spins. My temples pound. Called back from Texas by a song?

I sure as fuck identify with the lyrics. I can't believe this. Is it fate that keeps reminding me of her? Or is Zoe lodged in some dark part of my brain. A place where all my emotion is stored. Because I'm sure as hell not capable of emotion with any other girl. I have sex, but I don't have love.

Leaving Colton with a gaping mouth, Dad with an understanding smile, and Jamie whoring around Dallas, I hop a flight back to New York. There's no way I can coincidentally pop into one of Zoe's gigs. How fucked up would that be? When I'm at home I'll be able to think more clearly. Maybe toss the idea around with Dee.

On the way home, I stop by the garage. I'm hashing things out. Take a flight down to North Carolina? Spy on her? What have you been reduced to? Fuck it. No way. Fuck her. She's with her own kind now, which doesn't include me. I don't see her trying to find me. What am I, stupid or insane?

Glancing around the walls covered with posters and aging calendar girls, I'm smothered by a flood of emotions. I left so abruptly, I should have hung around longer. Seeing Dad was great, now I miss him more than ever. So I permit myself the luxury of one last walk down memory lane.

Like a ghost, Dad is standing beside me. His heavy hand rests on my shoulder, and he's telling me and Jamie, "This is the first day of the rest of our lives, boys." He's glowing, not because he's the ghost of my undead father, but because the garage has just opened for business.

Jamie and I were little kids when Dad built this place. We were so proud of him, thrilled that at the ages of seven and ten, *we* were business owners. We even shook on our deal to help out with customers and hold signs on the corner to build business. *Five free gallons of gas with every oil change.* Jamie was way different back in the days when we devised our plans; when we acted like brothers.

I remember jumping up and down, skipping across the very room I'm packing up now, but I wasn't wearing worn work boots and grimy jeans. I skipped across the floor in shorts and sneakers, begging my father to let me work the register. In later years, arguing with Jamie over who got to cash out customers versus who had to do oil changes. Being the oldest, and the loudest, Jamie usually won.

I'm not sure if this place is what made the Sinclair brothers top dogs in school. *Garages are an awesome hangout for friends who need a lift and the right tools to work on their cars and bikes.* Or if it was Jamie's bizarre behavior, and I was his brother, so naturally I was just as crazy and cool as the dude who could bag any girl he wanted.

In the slatted desk chair that's serviced two generations, sorting through a stack of receipts I stashed in the top drawer before leaving for Texas, but I don't tally. I slide the calculator aside and run my hand over the scratched top of the oak desk; this is where Mom dropped grocery bags to stock the backroom fridge; lunch when we ran out without or brown bags and thermoses. I think of the days of McDonald's. Doing homework at this desk. Jamie and I hung out here after school and every weekend. Dad would call home and put in his order. An hour or so later, Mom would walk through the door, waving bags of burgers and fries under our noses. Smiling. Mom smiled a lot in those days. Come to think of it, so did Dad. Life is unpredictable. Can be cruel. Gotta move on. That's what Dad said the day she passed. But from the way he lived from that moment on, I knew he wasn't about to practice what he preached.

Coming back down to earth, I sigh. Can I really transfer this place over to a new owner? This place has been my life for as long as I can remember. Hands shoved deep in my pockets, I wander around the office, kicking a gum wrapper aside, the sole of my boot scraping a couple of bottle caps along the concrete floor. This calls for a broom.

The surface is pretty much litter free, but I decide to do another sweep of the back room, where our after hour parties rocked the place. In dim light. Shades closed. Doors bolted. Radio low. Jamie brought girls here. Lots of girls. On my sixteenth birthday, he delivered my *gift*. I shake my head and laugh, reliving the moments when my brother wasn't such a big dick. Just an asshole.

It's after ten. I'm in the washroom, drying my hands and face. Dad's been gone since six, leaving me to pump gas. Of course, Jamie went missing the minute Dad left. I'm going through my checklist: Pumps are locked. Register cashed out. Money sack is in the safe. I even take care of the bank deposit Mom will come by for when the station opens at six am. Ready to change, I slip out of my work clothes. No sooner do I step out of the can, Jamie comes bouncing through the door with two hot blondes in tow.

"Happy birthday, bro," he sings out, slamming a bottle of Southern Comfort down on the desk. "Pull the shades, dude. We are about to party." Then he laughs because he notices I'm only wearing boxers and a t-shirt. "Expecting company?"

He's hyper. He bops to a cabinet, grabs some paper cups, and proceeds to pour shots into the cups he's lined up. The next thing he grabs is one of the girls. She's wearing low rise shorts and a halter top. This I notice first. Then my eyes grip the rest of her. Her soft hair hangs loose, framing her pretty face, covering her shoulders and part of her braless breasts. After lingering on her nipple buds, I remember checking out her legs: so long, smooth, and I contemplate the length of time it will take for Jamie to wrap them around his hips. Wondering how they'd feel wrapped around mine.

"Look what I found at Smileys, little bro." He grins the way he does when he believes he's the most brilliant rocket scientist on earth. "This is Amelia. Amelia this is my boring, half naked brother."

All the while, my stomach is knotting. Not only because I'm standing in my underwear gawked at by six pairs of eyes, but because I know what he has in mind, and having sex in the same tight quarters as my brother feels perverted.

As if to deliberately escalate my discomfort, he snatches the shorter girl's hand, twirls her around to the front of his body and pulls her into him, like they're about to dance, but instead, he spins her back out and slams her palm onto mine. "This is Gracie. Your treat for the night. Teach him some moves, sweetheart. You know, like the ones you did on the stage tonight." When she giggles, he winks at me.

"What do you think, slick?" His head does a slow rock.

"Think?" I think I'm about to be gifted with a lay. That's what I think. The look on my face, or maybe it's the bulge in my shorts that tells Jamie I appreciate my surprise because he folds with laughter, then lifts his girl onto the counter and pulls her gorgeous legs around his hips.

What a night it was indeed. It was safe, it was wild, it was *memorable*, that's for sure.

With Dad gone, and Jamie out of town more than he's here, this place is too much for me to handle. If we sell, Jamie and I will split the proceeds. He'll go his way. I'll go mine. He might permanently relocate to Texas. What will I do? I have no fucking idea.

I have the rest of my life ahead of me. I have my own dreams, none of which involve ranches and cowgirls. I want to be an artist, a painter, a sculptor. I want it all. I want to mold clay with my hands, paint with a brush, not fingers spreading auto grease for the rest of my life, like my Dad did.

I'm just about ready to close down for the night when two of my bros crash through the door. Christian's away at college, but Tim and Finch have stayed in town and are attending a local community college. They're here to drag me to a local dive called Smileys, which won't take much dragging. The thought of a lap dance hits the bliss spot. Or will soon. Just what I need to end a depressing week. I can feel myself sinking back in a chair, as a warm ass settles onto my wood. A pair of bare double D's pressed to my chest. Yeah, I'm so ready to be dragged to Smileys.

"You couldn't have showed at a better time. Give me ten," I say to Tim. "I have a few more things to do before I lock up. Maybe thirty." I sniff my armpit. "I need a shower. I'll meet you over there."

"Don't hang us up, man. It's your party."

"How so?"

Finch doubles over with laughter. "You're buying, bro."

"After the week I've had, even the chick waiting for me in the back room won't keep me."

Their eyes bulge.

I wink. "See you in thirty." Let them wonder. I laugh to myself as they leave the garage, cackling like hens.

There isn't a girl waiting for me in the back room, but we make a habit of keeping a change of clothes back there, so our cars don't stink from gasoline when we drive home. With every intention of joining my boys, I anxiously strip out of my grimy clothes and hop into the shower, letting suds and hot water run over me. Just thinking about Smileys, my dick is already semi-hard. Keeping it in check is difficult.

As I envision the pair of tits I'm about to nuzzle, the shower curtain ripples. Thinking it's the force of the shower, I ignore it, until something forms a lump and scoots across the vinyl. A hand? "What the fuck?" My heart jumps in my chest. My first thought is my boys have come back to check out the girl I have stashed. "Finch?" I poke my head out of the curtain and holler.

No reply. But I do see a shadow slide across the doorway. Naked and unarmed, I'm at a definite disadvantage and prime target for a robbery. Not to mention, a joke. Fuck me.

In a quick move, without turning off the shower, I whip back the curtain and throw up my fists.

"Shit…" I draw the curtain over my dick. "Claudette. What the hell are you doing here? You're lucky I didn't …"

"Nail me?" She giggles, tugging on the curtain. "I like your vinyl." She frowns. "Thanks for letting me know you were back in town. Turning into Jamie?"

"No such luck for you, babe. What are you doing here?" I say, without any intention of inviting her in.

Her full mouth puffs into a pout. "Come on, Jesse. Nail me. Right here. Right now. In the shower." The curtain slips from her fingers and she begins to unbutton her jeans. "We could have such fun."

"Bring your face over here," I say.

"Gladly." She leans in close and puckers for a kiss but all I want is to smell her breath.

"You've been drinking." I frown.

"And?" Drawing back, she continues to undress, slowly, moving like a stripper.

I'm wide eyed, tracing her movements, her bulging breasts beneath her halter top, her smooth flat tummy. As she peels the fabric away, my eyes dart to the leaf-wrapped peacock tattooed on her hip. Sexy as hell. I'd love to stroke its feathers with my tongue.

"Dare me?" she purrs.

"Dare you?" I emit a sarcastic chuckle. "I don't put anything past you, Claudette. But let me clue you in. I'm not Jamie. And I'm not about to let you use me to make him jealous or …"

Finding You

On tiptoes, she strains to reach me, and her lips press firmly against mine, then slide to my ear where her whisper is husky. "He's not around is he? So how would fucking *you* have any effect on *him*?" Her tongue runs the length of my neck, lingering on my collar bone, which she wraps with her tongue and sucks.

Claudette has been hanging out a lot lately. I figure she's been hoping to recapture Jamie's interest as she perches at the edge of the desk. Wearing short skirts which, in the poses she strikes, doesn't leave anything to the imagination. I'm not Jaime, but Christ, I'm human.

That's easy enough to ignore, but this is different. She's stripping. I'm naked and wet. And she's in my face, pulling the curtain aside. Pressing her heavenly tits against my chest.

Her arm comes around behind me. Slides across my back. I feel her fingers wind through my soggy hair.

"I was hoping to catch you in your jeans and sweaty tee," she says in her most seductive voice, "Mmm. But I like you so much more like this. Nice and naked."

She reaches deeper into the shower and grabs my nuts, giggling at my straining erection. I want her badly, but I know I'd be doing the walk of shame afterward. Kicking myself in the ass.

It takes every fucking ounce of self-control, but my fingers lock around her wrist and I squeeze. "You're sick, you know that?" I roll my eyes then turn the knob and the water stops. I finger comb my hair and slick it back. Still water rolls over my face, meeting the stream dripping off my skin. "Listen. We're friends. Friends don't shower together."

She wrenches her hand away, and with her other, rubs her wrist. "Ouch. That hurt. I thought we were family."

"Family doesn't fuck either. At least not mine," I snap.

Backing up she fires back at me, "Come on Jesse. You're the poster child for sexy. And I'm so damn down it isn't even funny."

"And I'm your upper? No thanks."

After being fucked around by Jamie for so long, I assume she can handle rejection, but she breaks into sobs. Between gasps, she says, "Jamie and I go way back, Jesse. Remember the old days? I liked being with your family. I liked your dad and your mom. We had fun. Remember?"

Now she's getting to me. "Yeah. I remember." I grab a towel from the rack and tie it around my hips. "Wait in the office, I'll be right out."

Remember? Of course, I remember. Her mood is rubbing off on me. My throat tightens. My voice softens. "I'll be right out, okay? I'll make you a cup of coffee ... before we both hit the road."

My dick is throbbing. In the back of my mind, I'm thinking about the lap dance I'm missing. Half expecting my bros to pop back in or for my cell to chime.

I leave the back room zipping my fly, tucking my shirt into my jeans. When I enter the office, Claudette is leaning back in the chair with her bare feet up on the desk. A bottle of Jack Daniels and two glasses are strategically centered on the top. She's got my cell phone in her hand.

"Hey, are you going through my phone?" I snatch it. "Did somebody just call?"

"Yeah," she says idly, "Finch."

"I'm supposed to meet them." I check the time. It's been almost an hour since they were here. "I'm late."

"Not anymore," she coos, grinning up at me.

"What?"

"I told them you had better things to do."

I suck in my bottom lip and shake my head. "Nothing's happening tonight, Claudette. Come on, off the desk," I grab her ankles and tug, "other than you're about to hit the road, and I'm going to Smileys."

She turns scary serious, leans forward in the chair, hugging herself. "Jesse. Not yet. Just have a drink with me. I don't want to be alone."

"What's wrong?" Immediately, I figure Jamie's to blame for something she doesn't want to tell me.

"Everything's changing. Everything but me. Jamie's gone. You're thinking of closing this place. I don't know what I'm gonna do without ... this." She swings an arm around the room. "What will I do?" She pours Jack into the glasses. "If you sell this place and go away to college?" She takes a gulp and makes a face. "Are you going away?"

I shrug. "I hope to. What about you? Do you have plans?"

"I'm a creature of the moment," she winks, handing me a glass brimming with booze. Squinting, she studies me. "You on the other hand are a faithful fuck."

"Wow. Where's that coming from?"

"Whoever she is, she's a lucky bitch."

My eyes sweep her face. Cagey looking. Conniving. If not for the Jack, her expression would send a chill down my spine. But right now I'm numb.

"Remember the girl we knew in high school?"

"We knew a lot of girls."

She presses a finger to her lips. "Oh yeah, Zoe, that's her name."

"What about her?"

"Zoe AKA Falcon Channing," she smirks. "Did you see her video on YouTube? Her and her boyfriend, I think his name is Santana." Pausing, she gauges me. "Have you seen it?"

"Yeah, I heard when I was in Texas." I slug a drink. "I was thinking of stopping off to catch a show on my way home."

Claudette shoots me a look of shock. "Are you crazy? Do you want to be the world's biggest asshole, Jesse?"

"What the fuck?" I flare.

"You can't go chasing after her. She's with her boys, in a

band, and I've seen some of them. They are hot hot hot. She's out of your league now."

"Says who?" I'm indignant. I'm crushed. I'm every fucking negative emotion in the dictionary, plus I could strangle Claudette for making me feel this way.

She won't let up. She paces and chants, "Do you really think you'd have a chance with her? She's got a rocker boyfriend, why would she want a grease–"

My furious face or balled up fists stop her dead in her tracks. "Don't even go there."

"I'm sorry, Jess," her arms go around my neck. She stares up at me. "I'm looking out for you. That's all."

I unhook her arms and back away. "I've always looked out for you with compassion, Claudette. Not humiliation."

"Forgive me?" She pouts, and dangles the Jack in front of me.

"I'm crushed," I tease, "but I forgive you."

We drink. We drink and I get so wasted I can barely see straight.

I catch her watching me watching her and immediately shift my gaze.

She wrinkles her nose at me. "I missed you."

I think of being with Zoe and wonder if this is how Jamie feels, or doesn't.

Each time I empty my glass, Claudette pours another. Deep in conversation, we knock off the bottle.

"Yeah. Jamie wasn't always this way. I don't know what happened to him."

"I do. He never grew up. Never got over losing your mom."

This starts the conversation with me focusing on my parents, Claudette whining about Jamie, and the next thing I know she's in my arms and I'm offering comfort.

With a bit of squinting, Claudette's face comes into focus,

then her body. She's a sensual chick. The thin fabric of her top does little to disguise the outline of her breasts. Her legs are long and sleek, her skin naturally tan. I want to sink my teeth into her and if not for Jamie, I probably would.

Claudette's eyes are liquid silver and taunting. Gazing into them, I can see the hurt. This makes me angry with Jamie. I don't understand him. This girl is decent and she obviously cares a lot for the shithead. Why is he throwing years of love away? Claudette is not my type, but the look in her eyes softens me. Emotionally and physically, because her fingers are brushing rhythmically across my dick.

Her lips are soft on my neck. The Jack Daniels clouds my brain, lowers my defenses. I feel no guilt, just lust. The perfume she's wearing adds to my desire. I'm dizzy. Fucking horny. My mouth covers hers and I'm mindless. Acting on instinct, I free the ties of her halter. My tongue gets lost in her cleavage, wrapping her nipples. She undoes my jeans and her fingers graze my wood with long, slow strokes. With a swipe of my arm, the desk is clear and Claudette is sprawled out on her back. Her legs part. My fingers trace up and down her thighs. Her wriggling hips, her moans, make my fingers work faster. I tug her against me, a leg on either side of my hips and we grind. My tongue tastes her sweet neck, then her ear, settling inside her mouth. I yank her off the desk and spin her. Bend her over the desk, and drag her panties to her ankles. When my finger slides inside her, she groans.

My breath comes fast. Panting, Claudette reaches from behind, guiding me into her. "I want you, right now, but." Stopping isn't easy. My whisper is hoarse, "I need to wrap this wood first."

"No," she's breathless. "I'm safe. I'm on the pill, and I don't have any STD's or anything. I promise."

She's writhing against me, pulling me into her. My cock, pressed against her ass, is pulsing. Temptation is overwhelming, but in the heat of the moment, I could fuck up the rest of my life;

this I realize, drunk or sober.

My hands stop cupping her breasts and move to her face, massaging her cheeks, stroking her hair, and I find my resolve. One by one, I slide the desk drawers open and dig; thank you, Jamie. I pull out a wrapped condom.

"Jamie never used condoms," she pants, "I promise, it's okay."

By the time she finishes complaining, I've torn the package open with my teeth and slid the condom over my bulging cock. "Yeah, it's okay," I assure as I slide into her.

She gasps and rolls her hips; I pound and groan until I know she's come, and my cock twitches in time with her tightening muscles.

"Holy shit, Claudette." I gasp. What the fuck?" I'm dizzy from the booze, but even dizzier as a result of what she's done to me. "Jamie's a freaking ass."

She spins and buries herself in my arms. "I really like you, Jesse. I always have."

I sober up in the garage. Sprawled on the cot. Claudette is gone. The last I remember, she was in my arms.

The sun hasn't yet risen as I slowly ride home. The air is damp, maybe it rained. Maybe it will. I park my bike and stare. My house is a shadow and the windows are blank. It doesn't look like anyone lives here. They don't. I just stay here. Live? What's live anyway? By the time I crawl up the stairs to my room, I'm sick with a hangover and remorse. And I'm worried. How old was that condom? Condoms have been known to break. Don't go there, Jesse. You haven't suffered OCD since you were a kid jacking off to vintage Hustler mags in your old man's garage.

I drag myself to my room, taking the narrow pathway from the door to my bed. The walls are lined with paintings. So many paintings. Rewind … I do live here. I have a life. Painting.

Two tables hold my sketch pads, paint and brushes, pens and

photos. I've set up my easel before one of the windows, my headboard near the other.

I'm not sure how I should feel after last night with Claudette. Relaxed? Not really. Satisfied? Eh. I would never have expected for things to go this way, and I don't plan on it ever happening again. It was a drunken mistake I can't forget fast enough.

Filled with agitation, my best stress relief is to paint. So I pick up a brush, dip the tip, close my eyes and the brush finds its way across a blank canvas.

If I were a writer, I wouldn't use outlines. I'd write by the seat of my pants, as I paint, with nothing particular in mind. If I set out to paint a forest, I might end up with the moon fading into storm clouds. I'm not into portraits, or one to precisely capture nature in landscapes.

When I'm in one of these moods, I start with a canvas as blank as my mind, but my veins are bubbling with emotion. This is what fuels my desire to paint. Not the final outcome. I could give a shit what the finished product looks like. If it describes my feelings tonight, it will look like the gates of hell. Locked. Chained. Swallowed by orange and red flames.

A sliver of moonlight squeezes through my window blinds. I feel as random as the base color I choose. I dip a brush and close my eyes. Yeah, I could end up painting the walls an endless eternity, but I focus on the blank space before me. And I vent. Through the brush, my fingers send signals, mine. Agitation, frustration, fury. I dip and zap, swiping like a swordsman, through the air, tip to jar, brush to air. Exhausted I step back. Studying. Totally emotionless. What is this piece of shit I just wasted the past hour on? I ask myself then I laugh. Yeah, Sinclair, you'll make it big in the art world with crap like this.

The painting, if you can call it that, is basic black. Streaked. Striated. Dotted. By the time I've finished abusing the terms, art and study, the strokes come into focus. Take shape, explaining to my eyes what to tell my mind. The gates of hell. They're winged. And set in the center of a boiling ocean of red and orange flame. Behind the bars is a floating cloud, and inside the cloud is an eye. Staring straight ahead. At me. In defiance. Accusing, because it's ugly. But I feel no guilt for the misery I've just created. It equals mine.

I drop onto my bed, spread eagle, stare at the ceiling, and in the shadows, now that is art. Satanic tongues licking flames swipe the ceiling. Swirling wings. Static. I'm digging the static. So I hop out of bed, grab a sketch pad and pencil, and proceed to coat the white page with gray static. This is what I do until I've penciled every clean sheet of paper, and my eyes pain from straining through darkness.

Finding You

Zoe

It's been a long day, even longer night, but I'm not sleepy. I'm wired. I get this way after a show. It takes time to unwind.

I climb into the front of the bus, resting my head on the back of the seat. Tonight we're moving out of Tennessee, heading for North Carolina, so I don't bother staring through the windshield; there's not much to see other than reflective highway signs. Instead, my eyes flash over guardrails. Now and then a passing vehicle blasts a horn; we're the snail hogging the right lane and wouldn't move for an earthquake.

The sound of tires on blacktop is annoying, but mind clearing. Our road manager, Stan, is driving Big Blooper, as he calls our third-rate transportation; a big blue mistake often in need of jump starts. It's not much of a bus. It's pretty bare; most of the seats have been torn out to be replaced by a row of benches with attached tabletops and mini fridge. The rear crash pad contains a chemical toilet and twin bed bolted to the floor, and is cordoned off with a curtain decorated with air balloons. The guys roll dice for dibs on the bed; sometimes they win the mattress with a coin toss.

I think about where we've been, where we might be headed. I'm sad and relieved all at the same time; a few more stops and we'll be back in New York. It's been crazy. I'm not sure how I'll feel when the tour ends. Will there be another? Would I want there to be?

Stan's Yankees cap is on backwards and he's hunched over the steering wheel, smoking up a storm.

"That's so bad for your health, dude." I exaggerate a cough, but my lungs are starting to burn.

"What?"

"Cigarettes. Even secondhand smoke." Hint. Hint. "Especially if you're overweight." Muttering, I add, "heart attack in the making."

He takes a second to face me with a blend of shock and sarcasm, then his head whips back to the road, and he separates his gut from the wheel by sitting up straight.

I roll my window way down, inhaling fresh air instead of his cigarette, trying to drown out animal sounds I'd rather not hear from Blooper's rear end.

"Radio?" I say to Stan. Although he's concentrating on the dark road ahead, I point to the dash.

"Not fixed yet." His voice is void of emotion.

"But I thought you were–"

"Not fixed yet." His tone, now firm, suggests he doesn't want to be bothered talking. Bothered period. Maybe I insulted him? Maybe he's had it with us…

A chilly breeze ruffles my hair, but I still hear the guys at the rear of our big blue mistake; they're drinking and playing cards. Placing bets on who gets laid first at the next stop.

Stan flips his cigarette out the window and the air clears. The air rushing in my window is fresh and smells like rain. I pull the zipper of my sweatshirt to my chin and hunker down in the seat. My head falls to the side. Drifting off I laugh to myself, thinking these guys are cool to be with as musicians, not bad as friends, but I'd never take one for a lover.

A scream wakes me. When I hear the rhythmic slapping of windshield wipers, my mind spins. Wet roads. Old bus. An accident? Did we drive off a bridge? Another scream and I realize the bus is moving ... slowly, but moving. Half asleep, feeling drugged, I pull myself into an erect position, climb out of the seat and charge toward the back of the bus. *Something's wrong. Someone is hurt.* The interior is dim, so I place one foot carefully in front of the other as I investigate. You never know what, or who, you could trip over on the floor of a rocker bus. Not that we're rockstars, but the guys are adapting to their new environment like they were born into it.

Jonny's crashed on a bench; I watch the rise and fall of the thermal covering his chest. Richie's hunched over a table, a beer a fingertip away. Carefully I check his breathing; yep, he's alive. I pass Corky, also comatose on a bench.

Against my better judgment, I creep to Blooper's rear where my retinas almost burn out. Gaping, I freeze. I don't want to look, but I can't tear my eyes from the brutal view of a fan girl impaling herself on Denny's lap. He must feel my stare because his head comes over her shoulder and he stares back at me with goo-goo eyes and a sloppy grin. He lifts a hand and crooks a finger.

Christ, Denny, what are you doing? You were the only one I could... God knows what you might catch... I mouth, "What the fuck?" and his eyelids lower.

The girl grabs handfuls of his hair, which has grown past his shoulders, and she's pulling. Gyrating. Moaning. She throws her head back and groans, then tosses it to the side, her hair whipping over her shoulder. I watch a butterfly tattoo dance across the rippling muscles of her toned back as she moves. When she screams Denny's name, I'm freed from my trance.

My hands drop to my hips, while my voice fills with disgust.

"You could have the decency to pull the curtain closed. And you might want to muzzle her with your mouth, or…" my glare drops to her bare ass dancing on his lap, "or something."

"You have an open invite, babe." Denny chuckles deep and devious. His hands grip her hips. He lifts her ass and rams her back down onto his lap. *Sadist.* This is not the guy I met on stage like an eternity ago. His warning about Richie must extend to every member of the band, himself included.

"Come-back-here-Falcon," he pants each word because he's giving her, or she's giving him, one hell of a workout.

"I'd rather ingest rat poison."

"You callin' me a rat? You wanna ingest me, baby?" His slur controls half of his mouth.

The girl frees a hand and jerks his head back to the place she wants it; aligned with hers. I believe she's devouring his lips because they both fall silent while their bodies thrust wildly. I rip the curtain closed and return to my seat, but not to sleep. I'm tiring of this life. Longing for something else. What, I'm still not sure. Just not this.

Richie is out of control. Sinking deeper and deeper into his own private darkness. He's a Jekyll and Hyde look alike, disappearing for hours at a time. The quality of the band is sacrificed. The guys are all for fun and games, but not at the expense of their careers.

"Where's Richie?" Corky runs a soft cloth up the neck of his bass guitar as we impatiently wait for our leader who's a half hour late for practice.

"Dunno, man." Denny paces across the stage of the North Carolina bar we'll play tonight, sets his guitar down, and runs his fingers over the keyboard to his right, playing a glissando and the first few bars of *London Bridge is Falling Down.*

I stand on the stage, hugging my acoustic, watching Jonny

twirl his drumsticks, smack his thigh, twirl, smack, again and again.

I break the silence. "I have a new song and I need feedback." I strum and sing a verse of *Comatose*:

Inside this coma I hide from your eyes
Your lies and hurt that I despise
You're not the peace I thought I'd find
Trapped inside my mind
My mind's not mine....
I sacrificed my sanity
Just before you abandoned me

No one seems to care ... or to be listening. They're all pissed and showing it.

"Have you got any idea where he is, Zoe?" Denny's eyes capture mine.

"How would I know?" Dimpling the side of my cheek, I shrug.

His eyes harden, he smirks and shakes his head. "Fuck it. We'll start without him."

"Start without who?" Richie swaggers into the club where just a few people line the bar at noon. His hair isn't smooth and shining, it's stringy. His arm is slung around the shoulders of a redhead in short shorts who appears to be supporting his weight. She's wearing black patent Stilettos and I'm wondering who will cave first.

"Christ," Corky mutters under his breath. "We've gotta do something with him. He never came back last night. Now this." He throws his hands up.

"No shit," Jonny grunts, banging out a satirical drum roll.

"Come on babe," Richie says, smearing his lips up and down the girl's neck until she belts out an obnoxious giggle. "Up we go–"

"Not on the stage." Denny's voice rings out louder than Jonny's drum roll. "This is practice. No chicks."

Richie lifts his chin like a sun-worshiper, only the sun is the stage. His squinting eyes are calculating. "Seems to me I said that to *you* once, Brisk."

He proceeds to pat the girl's ass, then swings in front of her to crush her mouth with his.

"Come on." Groans ripple across the stage. "This is bullshit."

"We got an awesome break, Richie." If I didn't know Jonny better I'd swear he was pleading. "Clean up your act, dude. You're fucking the gig for all of us."

Patrons at the bar are watching. I'm afraid the manager will come over any minute and toss us all out on our asses.

Richie pulls his mouth from the girl's. "This is my band," he snarls, "I know what I'm doing. We're a sellout. Stop worrying."

"We're a sellout," Jonny, sitting at his drums, mumbles, "and you're a fucking burnout."

You finally did it, Richie. Exactly what you worried about. You're burned out to the soul.

"Fuck you," Richie says and stumbles out of the club, hanging onto the girl with ass-cheeks bulging from her shorts.

I heave a sigh of relief because the watching heads return to their drinks, and no manager has appeared. I also heave a sigh because I no longer have to watch Richie paw all over this half-naked girl.

"We can do this without him," Denny says, giving me a warm smile.

For the first time ever, Chasing Dinero rocks a practice without Richie Santana, and we sound pretty damn good. We jam for a couple hours, focusing on my new song which the guys seem to dig.

"Let's call it a day," Denny announces to everyone, but walks to my side. "I worked up an appetite. How about you?"

My head snaps back. "You're talking to me?"

"Get over it, Zoe. Stop acting like..."

I stare up at him, ready to mouth off. But the softness of his eyes stops me.

"Truce, okay?" He sticks a hand out.

Instead of shaking his hand, I slap him five. "Shower first, okay?"

"I'm down," he grins, "your room or mine?"

I elbow his abs and he laughs.

He lowers his face to mine, speaking softly. "I missed you." The faint scent of cologne is too much to be disregarded; the cologne and lips on my cheek.

I gaze up and our eyes lock. "I'm not the one who left." My brow shoots up.

He presses it back down with the tip of his finger. "Meet you in an hour?"

"Give me two. I want to work out a few kinks I picked up in the music."

He smiles and taps the tip of my nose. "You really are all about music."

I tilt my head and give him a dimpled grin, turn my back and walk away.

Denny and I end up leaving three hours later.

"I've got an idea," he says, as we walk from the hotel lobby out into afternoon sun.

"Shock me," I tease, breathing deeply.

As we walk, he takes my hand. "How about pizza and a flick? I noticed this theater when we drove into town. A cool zombie flick was playing. Hopefully it's still there."

I roll my eyes. "Ugh."

He strides ahead of me and proceeds to walk backward. "What, you don't like zombies?"

Victoria January Valentine

"Come here before you crash into that little old lady..." I tug him back to my side, where he pretends to take a bite out of my neck. "Okay. Pizza and zombies it is."

On our way out of the theater, "That was disgusting," I remark.

"I agree," Denny dumps our tub of uneaten popcorn into a trash can, "it tasted like crap," he brushes his hands off. "Fake butter."

"I was talking about the movie." I giggle.

"Oh, I thought you were referring to the popcorn." He hooks his arm around mine and we cross the street.

"The popcorn was disgusting too," I reply, watching the sun highlight his hair that bounces as we dodge oncoming traffic and horns.

Our feet land on the sidewalk and he tweaks my nose. "Which is a good thing."

I gaze up at him and tug his earlobe. "It is?"

When he jams his hands into the pockets of his pants, he looks so damn cute. "Yep. It leaves plenty of room for dinner." His brows lift. "Interested?"

"I'm down with that. Watcha got in mind?" Bringing up a hand I block the sun which is hell bent on blinding me.

Denny's chuckle is evil. He drapes an arm around my shoulders and leans in close. His breath holds a hint of the cherry soda we shared during the movie. "You don't ever want to ask a guy that question."

I take a swipe at his jaw. "You're just full of warnings."

"Yes I am."

"You think you know what's best for me?"

"Yes I do."

As we banter, we decide on an outdoor restaurant with entertainment and dancing.

Strings of colorful lanterns hanging around the perimeter

sway with the breeze, casting multicolored light across white wrought iron tables and carpeted dance floor. My antenna springs up. This place is very romantic, especially when I glance down at the sundress I'm wearing.

My eyes flick over Denny, noticing he's freshly shaved. He smells like ocean and pine or maybe oriental musk? Regardless, he smells delicious. He's ditched his jeans and tee for a sport shirt and khakis, reminding me of how he looked the first time we met. I remember thinking he didn't look like the other guys; one would never figure him to be part of a crazy rock band.

Denny orders steak and I opt for lobster. We even share a bottle of wine.

Denny lifts his glass. "To us," he says, tapping my goblet with his.

When I reply, "And Dinero," I watch a frown crease his face.

The air is fresh. I breathe in deeply. "This is amazing, Denny. It's great to relax for a change."

"We need to do this more often." He pours more wine.

"Relax?" I tease.

"Sneak off together." His smile turns thoughtful. "And Comatose sounds promising." He nods. "Really good, Zoe. Or should I continue to call you Falcon?" He wiggles his brows and grins.

I roll my eyes. "Zoe is just fine."

"Yes she is."

I can't help but laugh. "We can work it out together, okay?"

His head tilts. "Work it out?"

"Comatose," I say.

"Ah. Comatose." He nods. "Absolutely." He hitches his head toward the dance floor. "Dance?"

I've never been in Denny's arms before, and it feels warm and safe. My hands slide up his chest and hook at the wrists behind his neck. His arms tighten around my waist and we sway.

"This is nice," he says, his lips pressed against my cheek.

"Mmm." I agree. "What do you think about Richie pulling that crap?"

"I don't want to talk about Richie," Denny groans. "Tonight's for us. Let's not let him bring us down."

"You're right. I'm just surprised. He worked so hard to get us where we are. Why?"

"Drugs'll do that to you."

"You're not speaking from experience, right?"

He draws back and studies me. "No, I've never been there, thank God."

I snuggle close.

"You feeling good?" he whispers into my ear.

I sigh. "Happy we've called a truce."

"Me too, babe, and I hope you're finished with him."

"I've never been with him."

"You should be with someone who appreciates you."

"Like?" I gaze up at him.

"I'd never pull that shit on you."

"You do a good job in the back of the bus," I tease, but inside I'm not joking. Seeing Denny act that way with groupies bothers me.

"That's only because I don't have someone like you with me."

"You're a nice guy," I smirk, "when you're not screwing groupies. But honestly, Denny, right now, I can't even commit to myself. No less to some guy."

"Is that all I am? Some guy?" His pulls his mouth into a pout.

"You know what I mean." I bury my face against his chest.

The music stops and I move to slide from our embrace.

Denny pulls me closer. "One last dance before you break my heart?"

212

"Sure." I smile.

He takes me in his arms and we sway back and forth without moving our feet. When my body begins to react, I freeze.

Denny must feel me tense. "What's wrong?" he asks.

I stare up into his crystal eyes, glistening in darkness. His lids lower. He pulls me closer. I lay my head on his chest and sigh. "If only I could, Denny. It would be you. But I can't."

Against the side of my face, he softly sings, *Get Outta My Head*

You took me to heaven
Then sent me to hell

Twisted control
Stepped into my soul

Laid me on this spinnin ride
Lovin landslide

Promised to catch me
Then we'd have it all

Get outta my head
Get outta my head

"Sounds like a hit, Denny." I lift my face for a sweet kiss; my lips are sealed. So is my heart.

Phase Three Coming Together

Jesse

My family is scattered. My friends practically non-existent. Dee drops in and out of my life. My stupidity comes back to haunt me. In the back of my mind, I'm becoming more and more paranoid about the night Claudette and I slept together. *Condoms have been known to break* is a nagging mantra. I begin to sweat out my big mistake.

My cell chimes with a text from Dee.

Dee: Hey.

Me: Hey yourself STRANGER

Dee: Opening a shop. Artist NEEDED. Interested?

Dee: Meet me at Moon café.

Me: Half hour.

I haven't been to Moon's in ages. School is out. The street and sidewalks are eerily still. When I walk through the door I'm slammed with memories of better days.

Dee is at a corner table. Private. Serious. Dark hair hanging in a thick braid over one shoulder. She's eagerly digging into a box of donuts. Watching her, I chuckle.

Napkins are set on either side of the table, obviously serving as paper plates, and two cups of unlidded coffee are venting steam. Other than the hum of machines, the air is quiet, but heavy with the aroma of coffee and baked goods.

I slide onto the seat across from Dee. "Hey. I was starting to think you left town," I grin, "or maybe are pissed at me?" I shoot her a cutesy face.

"Why should I be pissed?" Her teeth dig into a chocolate frosted donut.

"Uh oh." I know that look. I lift a brow, and a jelly donut from the box. "You *are* pissed. What did I do now?" I shake my head. "Seems every woman I've ever known ends up pissed at me or missing." I bite soft dough and lick raspberry jelly from my lips.

"You been hanging with Claudette?" I'm not sure which is more prominent, Dee's full arched brows or their fall when her inquisitive eyes squint.

"No. Why?" My gut threatens to reject the donut I'm attempting to swallow. "She hasn't been around in a while," I mumble under a napkin.

Dee's eyes burn into mine. "She's been shooting her mouth off via texts."

I hold my breath. "About what?"

Elbows on tabletop, her palms cradle her cheeks. "That you and her been happening. That you're a shit. That you're as bad as Jamie."

"What the fuck?" My donut drops and I grab another napkin to wipe my hands.

"That she might be pregnant." Dee's voice is flat, her strong gaze accusing.

Panic sets in. I shove my chair from the table, ready to lunge for the door. "What the fuck? That's totally impossible."

"Sit down, Jesse. I don't believe her and I told her so. Has she been stalking you again?"

"She drops by the garage, but it's just casual. And like I said, I haven't seen her in a while." Sinking

in the seat, I poke my mangled donut with a coffee stirrer. "Last I heard she was heading for PA."

"Christian, ugh." Dee scowls. "Why don't you tell Christian to keep her? Or better yet, tell your brother to take her off your hands. I don't know what the hell happened to her. She used to be cool. I mean," Dee's eyes grow sad, "we used to be tight. You know?"

"Tell me about it. You turned my garage into a beauty shop." I can't chuckle. OCD is clawing at my insides. "Jamie treats her like shit. I think she'll turn to any guy who'll–"

"She's going off the deep end." Dee shakes her head.

"I don't know what to say. I'll support her if she comes to me with a problem, but I'm not about to nose around, especially if she's claiming to be pregnant."

Dee's forehead creases. "Did you fuck her?"

I bring my cup to my lips and take long sips of coffee, stalling for time. For an answer. For lies. I decide the safest thing is to dodge the question.

I cock my head with interest. "So what kind of shop are we talking about?"

"Don't leave me hanging, Jesse. I had a big ass fight with her defending you."

Reaching across the table, I take her hand. "I'd never leave you hanging."

"God." She pulls her hand away. "No wonder chicks throw themselves at you. Those eyes."

"What about my eyes?"

"Bedroom, baby." She bites her lip. "Sometimes it's hard to look at you."

I hunch over laughing.

"I think you did her. Dumped her. Watch out, she'll put a curse on you."

"You can see right through me." In an offhanded way, I admit to my transgression.

"Spare me the sordid details," she says wryly as her hand comes down on the tabletop. "Back to business. The shop," her eyes light with excitement, "tattoos. You know me, ink and bad boys." She grins and grabs another donut.

"You want me to help out?"

"Yeah. You're the best artist I know. And you know how to handle a machine, right?"

"Yeah. I got my license a while ago when I hung at the shop that did mine." I take the risk and ask, "You haven't heard from Zoe, have you?"

The tip of her tongue licks chocolate from her lips. "Talk about coming out of left field." Her head tilts. "Why are you asking me?"

I shrug. "Just thinking about her lately, I guess." My eyes lower to my coffee. My fingers tap the cup. "Figured you might have heard her. Heard from her."

"You haven't moved on yet." I lift my eyes to watch Dee's bottom lip turn down. "I'm the last one she'd ... I doubt she'll ever talk to me again," she says, folding her hands on the table, twisting a silver ring on her finger.

"I'd love to know what happened that night. What I did." I hate my wistful tone.

"You didn't fuck her over, Jesse. It had nothing to do with you." She drops her donut and sighs. "She hates me."

I lean forward, abs pressed to table. "What are you talking about? You were her bestie."

Dee bites the inside of her cheek. "I let her down. I wasn't there when she needed me. I gave her the wrong advice. I was selfish. Things are different now. Could be different."

"I don't know what went on between you two, and apparently you'll never tell me," my eyes narrow, "right?" My pause is hopeful, but Dee just nods. "I'm still trying to handle my own demons."

I stare out the window. The school we attended hasn't changed. I remember hanging at Moon's before class. Watching Zoe run across the street, dodging hecklers and horn-blowing cars. This is where it all began. This is where I met the biggest challenge of my life. My heart sinks. I harden my voice. "She's living her dream, so I guess it doesn't matter now, for either of us." Carelessly, I shrug.

"Why didn't you ever get with her? She was nuts about you." Dee frowns.

Her words send a rush of adrenaline through me. "Are you kidding? She kept to herself. Locked in her own place. I figured she had no desire to be with me, or any guy, but it seems she's with some dude now. So..."

"I don't know where she is or who she's with, but she *was* into you." Dee is solemn.

"I feel like a jerk stalking the Internet," my lips pull tight, "waiting for her band to play our town. I watch their videos. She's got *star* written all over her. She's writing. Touring with a band. Living life on a stage like she always wanted. I'm happy for her." Happy for her. Bitter for me.

"Now that she's found her dream, I hope she finds herself." Dee's mouth pulls to the side. Her shoulders jerk.

I wonder what the misty-eyed girl sitting across from me means by her comment and cryptic expression.

Finding You

Zoe

In just about a year, Richie Santana has brought the band down. He's lost his music, his heart, every emotion he ever had is contained in a syringe.

Our show tonight is in a pub; a hole in one of North Carolina's walls. I check myself in the mirror. The braided sides of my hair are beaded and wrapped around my head. I smooth my brown suede vest over my boobs, pull the hem of my pink tank top down to meet the waistband of my jeans so only a sliver of skin shows. I check the clasp on the chain I entrust with my silver Z, to make sure it won't fall off when I thrash around the stage. Before leaving my room, I slip on the black leather boots I always wear. So far they've brought me good luck. I hope they never wear out.

I lock my door and am on my way down to the lobby to meet the guys. When I near their room, loud voices stop me, so I pause to listen. "Zoe's off limits." I'm certain this growl belongs to Denny.

I press my ear to the door. *What the fuck?* I try the handle and it clicks, so I crack the door open and peer through. Denny and Richie are facing off in the center of the room. They appear to be alone. Jonny and Corky must be waiting in the lobby.

"You're bringing us down," Denny's voice strains. *This is a hell of a way to start a show.* His fists are balled. I notice veins bulging along the sides of his thick neck.

"It's my band," Richie isn't as angry, he's high and his usual arrogant. "You can't write music," he condescends. "How far do you think you'll get on your own?" He laughs and reaches into a pocket for a bone.

"You're bringing us down, Richie." Denny runs a hand through his hair, frustrated. "And before you ruin us," he works his jaw, "Corky and Jonny … we've all been talking. Before you ruin us, we're gone. We're so close now," passion fills his voice. "If we go down in flames with you, we'll never have another chance." One hand is on his hip, the other massaging his temples. "We've decided to make a clean break."

Richie's laugh is bitter yet careless. "Whatever," he shrugs, "but I'm keeping Zoe."

I can't stand here and listen to myself being a rope in this tug of war. I push through the door and stomp into the room. "Keeping Zoe?" I snap. "Does Zoe have a say in this matter?"

Their heads whip around. Denny's cheeks are beginning to redden. Richie narrows his eyes at me as if daring me to challenge him. He stalks a circle, grumbling and pulling smoke through his joint.

Denny comes to my side, shaking his head. His hand goes to the back of his neck and he massages. "I'm sorry you had to hear this Zoe."

I throw my hands up. "It would have been nice if you'd have clued me in."

"It wasn't definite until tonight."

"What happened tonight?"

"Richie started in on Stan again–"

"About money you mean?"

Denny frowns. "You got it, and this time Stan walked out."

"Great. So what do we do now? No manager. No bus. Who's going to handle bookings?" I talk myself short of breath. "And everything else Stan does."

"Ask the rocket scientist over there." He jerks his head at Richie, who's popping one Rolo after another into his mouth, greedily chewing before lighting another bone.

"Should I talk to him?" My lips tighten.

"Nah. Leave him alone," Denny sighs with resignation. "Hopefully he'll come out of his mood. We'll hash it out after the show." His fingers slip down the side of my hair and for a moment his eyes reach out to mine. "You look nice."

"Richie," Denny's voice crosses the room to where Richie now sinks into a chair, sulking. "We have a show in an hour. Come on, man."

Richie pulls himself out of the chair and drags his boots deliberately to the door ... and me. I've seen his surly side before, but tonight he outdoes himself. "Yeah, we'll finish this later." He grips a button on my vest and tugs it aside. "Nice threads, babe. That's another reason I keep you around, you're irresistible eye candy."

Regardless of the fact that Richie is stoned half out of his mind, the minute his boots hit the stage he springs into action and we rock a full house.

We've had some enthusiastic crowds before, but this pack goes ballistic, cheering, dancing, lifting cells phone high in the air snapping pics and videos. Three girls leap onto the stage for a crazy bashment battle.

This show better end up on YouTube, as it's proved to be one of our best performances, despite the discourse that kicked off the evening.

The crowd applauded Richie's solos, but they totally freaked when I sang with him.

I'm feeling invincible.

The flip side of the coin is; everything revolves around Richie, and the fact that our lives depend upon his roller coaster existence is disconcerting. Although Dinero is his band, he's the loose cannon that could completely blow us out of the water. I'm beginning to agree more and more with Denny.

I leave Richie and Denny hashing things out backstage after the show, and walk through the night exhaling deeply, slowly. My shoulder finds the fender of the van, and I wait in the parking area while Corky and Jonny load some gear. Imagining what's going down with Richie and Denny, my raw nerves send an adrenaline rush through my body.

The buzz of voices calls my attention to the front of the pub where laughter and chatter disturb the warm, otherwise tranquil night. We could be partially responsible for their exuberance. I wish Richie wasn't such a dick. This could be a good life. What will I do if the band breaks up? I'm not ready to go back to my old life, to reality. Being introduced as Falcon Channing is like my second skin I don't want to shed.

The side door of the pub flies open and Richie shuffles out, momentarily pausing beneath the overhead light. The sag of his face and his stature confirm he's beat. He lights up a cig and after a few long drags flips the butt in an arc across the darkness.

A few minutes later, Denny follows, a busty brunette hanging on his arm, making it appear as though he's dragging her with him. That's how bad she's throwing herself at him. But I believe he's leading her to her car.

"Den," Richie shouts, "Leave the load here and come with us, bro."

I snicker, imagining him to be referring to the girl.

Denny ignores him, but shoots me a sheepish look, as though he's concerned I've caught him screwing around with a groupie.

222

Finding You

"Life is good," Richie's voice rings out before he slides behind the wheel, leaving me to wonder if he and Denny came to an amicable agreement.

Although my side door is open, and I'm about to climb in, Richie leans across the seat and yanks me up by an arm. "You're not getting away my little sugarplum." He's behaving quite erratic; I'm not sure how to interpret his comment or his tone. I know he had a few drinks, and I'm hesitant to surrender my body to his care.

"Let me drive." I shake off his arm and level my butt on the seat. "Come on, Rich, slide over here and change places with me. I'll get out and run around–"

His eyes gleam; demonic. "Slide on this," he says, attempting to drag my hand onto his fly.

The moment I yank my arm away, he reaches for my door handle and slams the door shut. "Stay put."

The van rocks and the springs squeak when the rest of the guys jam themselves and their instruments into the back. Corky must hear me tell Richie to fuck off because his head pops up from the dimness like a groundhog from a hole. "Who's getting fucked?"

"Last call," Richie swings around and shoves Corky back onto his seat, "this ship is about to sail." He starts the engine and we tear out of the parking lot. We bounce, we jerk. The interior of the van sounds like Grand Central at rush hour.

"Shut up back there," Richie yells and cranks the radio. He starts singing to a metal song while his palms beat the steering wheel.

From the sounds in the rear, the guys have gifted a couple of the many girls who flooded them after the show with a ride home, or who knows what.

Richie is pounding the wheel with a vengeance, which is unusual, even for him. He's letting off steam, I tell myself. He's so damn unpredictable, and I'm on edge. I'm not sure if he's on something other than weed and a couple shots of Jim Beam, and not liking this ride at all.

"Slow down, Richie," I warn, uncomfortable because the van has no seatbelts in the back, and the clasp on mine feels as insecure as me.

The van swerves and shouts of "Slow the fuck down," holler above the radio.

We're in a nine passenger utility vehicle with a large cargo area in the rear. Tonight the van is packed. I swing my head around to see Corky chugging a soda. Jonny has a girl on his lap and they're making out as if there is no one else around. When he strips off her bra, I whip around and stare at the path of illumination ahead of us. A light rain begins to fall. Richie doesn't use the wipers. He's still belting out someone else's lyrics, and the noise is almost unbearable.

The one thing I'm thankful for; it's almost two a.m., and ours is the only vehicle on the road. Our headlights wash over the yellow dividing line and the blacktop gleams with a steadier rain that drums the roof louder than Richie.

"You're driving too fast," I complain to Richie, who ignores me, so I reach over and lower the radio. "Slow down! The roads are slick. And put the damn wipers on." I shake my head, mumbling to the window, "This is my last ride in this van."

He swats my hand away and turns up the radio, but he also engages the windshield wipers. "I can't hear myself think with those animals in the back."

Our headlights display the heavy rain bouncing off the road. As if this isn't frightening enough, I watch the tail end of a car widen as we approach a straightaway.

Richie lays on the horn.

"What are you doing?" My heart is in my throat, fear reflected in my voice.

"Giving the pussface a little goose." His snicker turns into a grumble and his grip on the wheel tightens. "A little rain and they panic. Pussies don't belong on the road if you don't know how to drive."

Petrified, I press deep into the seat. My foot instinctively pumps the floor as if hitting the brakes. Every muscle in my body tenses.

Richie blows the horn once more before the solid yellow line breaks into a passing lane. Jerking the wheel, he whips out from behind the car; we're instantly racing down the wrong side of the road. This might work in daylight when you can see what's up ahead. And it would work even better if Richie wasn't a lunatic, and the car we're passing didn't try to race us. I wonder if the driver is someone who just left the pub; maybe he's tanked.

My head turns to my window in time to see the guy with a death grip on his steering wheel. His head swings to mine then forward again.

"Why won't he let us pass?" We're riding side by side. Our headlights reach a bend in the road before our van does. The broken line turns solid.

"Richie" I scream, "drop back. He's not letting us pass. You're gonna kill us all!"

The approach of oncoming headlights blinds me. Someone lays on their horn, or maybe all three of us do, because the sound is almost deafening. The van careens across the road, picking up momentum. My heart is pounding, my brain is in overdrive. I know we're going to crash, so I grab the door handle and console, bracing myself for the imminent collision.

I feel the impact, then a sense of acceleration. I'm reliving the night my parents' car dove off the bridge. Only I don't think we're driving over a bridge. There's no water to break my fall after I break through the windshield; a sharp pain grips my head, my mouth fills with the taste of blood, then I'm sailing through the air. The last thing I remember is a second impact and a thud as my body hits the pavement, followed by what must be my skull because everything goes black.

When I finally awaken, I'm filled with the same dread I had after the accident that took my parents' lives, leaving me with nothing but guilt and loneliness. But this time, I'm in a hell of a lot more pain, physically that is. Emotionally, I'm dead. Sensing someone beside me, I struggle to hold my eyelids up. *You're heavily sedated* says my mind.

"Mom? Dad?" I moan, wondering why they're not holding me. I remember seeing them right after Richie lost control of the van. Everything was vivid. Mom wore a pastel smock, like at the pediatric office. Dad had on his work uniform. They looked just like they did when they came home from work, only now they were radiant. Dad wasn't furious, and Mom wasn't crying out in a panicked voice like the night we went over the bridge. I threw my arms around them, refusing to let go. We hugged. We cried. We laughed. This can't be heaven, I remember thinking. Because I don't hear harps, and there aren't any angels or Jesus. Everything in my past must have been one big nightmare, and now I'm finally awake. I began to rejoice then it hit me. My parents are my angels, and everything is true.

"I can't believe we're together," I cried. "I never want to leave you."

"You can't stay, Zoe," Mom's voice still fills my head like a song. "You have to go back."

My mind asked, "Why?"

"A beautiful life is awaiting you." I still see her brilliant smile.

"Peanut," Dad's voice was soft, and like Mom's, in my head, not my ears. "You have great things to do, remember what we talked about?"

I feel so ashamed because I disappointed them. I haven't been good. I've been horrible. I'm not in law school. I've been screwing around with a rock band and a lunatic. Wasting my life.

"Zoe," a gentle voice fills my ears. "Honey."

I'm floating on a cloud, maybe in an ocean, still struggling to awaken. When my eyes are able to focus, I see Denny. He stands close to the bed, hovering over me, his face drawn tight with concern. "I'm sorry, Zoe. You deserve more than this. Someone who'll take care of you. Not put you in the hospital." I watch his jaw clench.

He's got a black eye and some cuts on his face, but he's standing, so he must be okay. Alive.

"Richie?" My whisper is hoarse because my throat is so dry.

Denny holds a cup of ice chips and presses a few into my mouth. I let them melt, which feels good. Soothing.

Denny smiles. "He's okay, babe. By some kind of a miracle, we're all okay. But I'm worried about you. You got it the worst."

"When I was ejected?" I manage a dumb grin.

He touches my shoulder, carefully, like he's afraid I'll break, although I'm already broken. "You remember?"

"Who could forget hitting the road with their entire body?" I try to laugh but bandages, and the pain in my ribs, restrain me. "Did I die?"

I watch the tilt of Denny's head, the twitch of his bottom lip. "You had a rough time in the ambulance, babe. I think they had to restart your heart."

"What day is it? How long have I been here?"

"It's Friday. You were unconscious for five days." He frowns.

"Holy shit, Denny. I think I saw my parents."

He pats my arm, whispering, "You were out like a light dreaming, babe. Just rest."

I try to move my head and it feels like a knife is piercing my skull. "So what's wrong with me? Will I make it? Do I even give a shit?"

"Don't talk that way." His frown deepens. "You have a

concussion, and your face…"

His expression, and the fact that he's talking about my face sends a shockwave of fear through every nerve in my body. A chill races down my spine to my feet that don't want to move when I try to kick free.

"I'm paralyzed!" I try to yell but all that emerges from my dry lips is a sick sounding squeal that Denny interprets.

"No, you're not paralyzed. You had a spinal. They had to do another surgery on you this morning. It'll wear off soon." His fingers sift the edge of the sheet that's covering my body.

"So it's affecting my face? Which isn't numb, as I'm able to move my mouth."

"You have some bad cuts, scrapes …" His voice is so soothing I freak.

My hand flies to my cheek, which is bandaged. I run my fingers over my face and am horrified to feel almost every inch of skin covered with bandages. "Did my face drag across the road? Am I gonna be scarred?" An eerie calm overtakes panic. *Now the outside will match the inside*, is the first thing to hit me.

"No, a plastic surgeon, he took good care of you. You're bruised and stitched, but you'll heal. Maybe have a few war wounds," he tries to joke, "you can cover with war paint you girls wear." I watch sorrow in his eyes turn to anger. This makes my stomach twist.

"Will I ever be the same again?" I croak, with the sudden realization that I don't want to die. I don't want to be here, in this bed, with these injuries, or with Richie, even Denny. I want to be home, with my parents, in my mother's arms. But even Nina and Nino would do right now. "I wanna go home, Denny," I sob, "I wanna go home so bad."

"Soon, love." I feel his lips on my hand. "We'll be back on tour and this will all be in the past."

"No, I mean home home. Back to New York."

"You want to leave the band?"

"Uh huh. My nose is so clogged I can't breathe through it. I sound nasal."

"That's because ..." he pauses to watch me, maybe he's wondering how much bad news I can handle at one time.

"Because why? What's all wrong with me, Denny?" I want to shriek, but I can't.

"Broken ribs, facial lacerations, broken nose, ruptured spleen, which they removed, and a few other things, like–"

"Like what?" My eyes want to bulge but my head hurts too much to make the movement.

"Bruised liver, you had a bleed inside, but they fixed it all and you'll be as good as new ... soon babe. Just hang in there."

My fingers test the thick, hard cone covering my nose. "How good was this surgeon? Will I look the same?"

"Even better, if that's possible." He grins and ever so lightly taps the tip of my bandaged nose. "You can't improve perfection."

Denny steps closer to the bed, as though he's about to climb in beside me, but instead he leans over me. His eyes are watering.

"I'm sorry, Zoe. I could kill Richie for doing this to you. You deserve more than this. Someone who—"

I stop him to object. "I don't need anyone." My words are as defiant as possible through lips that want to tremble.

I stare deep into his unblinking eyes, seeing a lost lonely soul: seeing myself. I lift a hand, run two fingers lightly over the side of his stubbly face.

"I know that look, Den. You're struggling with something."

"Life I guess. The band's fucked up. Richie ..."

"Richie is the most fucked up person I've ever known ... worse than me." I groan.

"Don't say that. You're solid."

"I guess this is what I get for hanging with animals, huh?" I try to return his smile.

"You're strong Zoe. I know you can stand on your own, but it wouldn't hurt to share yourself with someone." His gaze shifts across the room. "With the right person." His eyes glide back to mine. "You're closed tighter than a book with so many different chapters of emotions locked inside. Someone's done a hell of a job writing your story, Zoe, you just need to edit it." He looks so sad. "Unfortunately, not any of us, honey." His voice holds resignation, his eyes pain.

"You care for me. I wish things were different."

"Yeah I care but I'm still tuning in. You're in the lead, Zoe. I'm just learning how to walk."

Jesse

Dee and I kick ideas around, trying to come up with the perfect name for her tattoo shop. It doesn't take long for me to hit on a winner because the name has always been just beneath the surface of my skin, my brain. "How about Nightingale?"

"Oh my God, Jesse. That's freaking perfect! How did you come up with that?"

I shrug, thinking; just something that stuck with me since the night of Trent's party, singing in the middle of the road with Zoe when I called her my Nightingale. Those were moments I'll remember if I live to be a hundred. I'll never forget Zoe Channing.

"Before I paint the sign, are you sure you don't want it to be DeesInk?"

"Why wouldn't I want Nightingale?"

"Women are fickle." I chuckle.

"Wise ass." Dee smacks my arm and points to my box of paints and opening day banner. "Get to work. I'm going to run out and bring back lunch. Pizza or–"

"Burgers," I say. "Loaded. You're kicking my ass. I need beef."

Dee bursts out laughing. "You're a real joy, you know that?"

"Stop busting my balls and bring me some food, boss."

Raindrops dot the banner hanging above Nightingale Tattoo Salon. I check it out from across the street, up the street, down the street, from every possible angle, studying to make sure the wings holding the letters are offset, as intended. One wing is folded like a bat's. The other tips up to the sky, like an eagle taking flight. Each letter is a talon. It's my personal touch which I've painted for the grand opening of Dee's new tattoo salon.

I walk back into the shop shaking off raindrops. Dee is stacking a cabinet with medical supplies and countless plastic bottles of ink. "I'm in love with the sign, Jesse," she sings out.

"Aww. I thought it was my eyes." I pack my supplies.

Dee comes up behind me with a sucker punch. "Smart-ass."

I laugh. "I think I'll let you ink something like that on my shoulder."

"You want me to ink Nightingale Tattoo Salon?" She giggles. "I can, you know. I've got my license." Her face lights up with a smile. "Which means, we're both ready for business. I wish I was as great at art as you are, though."

"Don't sell yourself short, boss. You rock a needle." Holding up a hand, I grin. "I volunteer to be your first victim."

A truck pulls up and furniture is delivered and placed. After the delivery men leave, I stand in a corner, my eyes traveling the room, amazed at how the shop has been transformed from a musty box into a classy salon reeking of incense.

"I think you should raise the prices. This place looks like a million bucks."

"Let's hope it makes us a million bucks."

"Us?"

"We're partners, right?" She tilts her head and gives me a

duckface. "We've been since school, right?"

"Yeah," I say idly, absorbing the atmosphere. "Go you. I knew you could do it. Where'd you get the money for a place like this?" I fall into one of the soft leather recliners. Dee is behind the counter, hanging pictures for advertising. "You have yourself a sugar daddy?" I chuckle.

"Nope." Suddenly she's lost her humor. "Get to work, Jesse. We're opening soon."

"Talk about cracking the whip." I stock some shelves, then scrutinize some pictures in my sketch pad. "If not a sugar daddy, then a rich uncle, huh? Must be nice."

She shrugs, apparently unaffected by the fact that not everyone can be set up this way. Or so I think.

"Family stuff." She's thoughtful. "I do have an uncle who owns an art gallery, though. So if you have anything, he'll show it."

"Are you shittin' me? My own gig?"

"Yours and a couple others. He's planning something in a few weeks."

"Where's his place? I know just about every gallery around here."

"It's downtown. Avocados Mullins. Ever hear of it?"

"Hear of it? Holy shit. That's upscale all the way. Hell, I'm interested. I have paintings lining almost every wall in my house. I'd be grateful for anything you can do."

"I can do it all." She smirks.

I laugh. Dee is something else. Strong and motivated.

"I know you like your ink, but I never knew you were interested in fine art, Dee."

"Me either." She chuckles. "He was looking for investments, and I suggested a bar." She rolls her eyes. "He likes my tatts and suggested a salon for me and a gallery for him," her face shadows. "We decided a long time ago that he'd invest in me. When I was a kid."

I don't question her solemn tone because I'm wrapped up in myself. "This is like a dream, Dee. Thank you ... and your uncle. When do I get to meet him?"

"Not sure. He travels a lot." Her eyes cloud.

"The country?" I'm wondering why Dee has never mentioned this life-altering benefactor, or why I've never seen them together during the time we set up shop.

"International," she says. "Mostly Central America. Doesn't show up here much. Which is fine with me. I'll take his cash. Leave him ... wherever." Her laugh is caustic.

The glass door flies open and Claudette struts into the shop. "Surprise, surprise," she's droll. Dee gives me a sour look.

"What the hell is she doing here, Jesse? Did you invite her?"

"Hell no."

"Stalkers have radar." Dee is deadpan.

Since the night we spent together at the garage, when we screwed for two hours, she hasn't been her unshakable shadow self.

"Hey," Claudette says, strolling into the room. "I had to find out about this place in the news. Thanks for cluing me in." She swings her head and her long dark hair, now highlighted mahogany, wraps her neck, falls over one shoulder.

"That's what you get for fucking her." Dee turns on me angrily.

"That's what I get for knuckling under to you and that sexy stare of yours, Delorese."

"Smart-ass." Brushing past, she shoulders me.

"Is this conversation private?" Claudette stands in the middle of the room, hands on hips. Her narrowing eyes ricochet from Dee to me. "Nothing like being talked about not behind my back. I don't appreciate your candor." She flicks a piece of lint from the shoulder of her mint green sweater. "Especially when I'm standing right here listening to you two rip me up the back."

"I hope you're satisfied, Jess. She's like an alley cat. You fed her, now you'll never get rid of her," Dee whispers, then smirks.

Jesse satisfied? No. I come away empty. Alana, Claudette, Nadia, to name a few. I've never felt an attachment to any of the girls I've been with.

"Alley cat?" Claudette's screech claws my eardrums. "Fuck you both. I won't refer anyone to this place." On her way to the door she lifts her chin. "In fact, I'll bad mouth your *salon* to everyone I know. And you," she shoots me a toxic look, "I need to talk to you ... alone, so I suggest you be home tonight when I drop by."

Mirroring her personality, Claudette's hair is on fire with sunlight. I watch her through the window as she struts away.

"What the fuck was that all about?" With a sinking stomach, I watch Claudette disappear around the corner.

Dee's hands drop to her hips. "Have you been messing around with her? For reals, Jesse."

Shaking my head, I try to hide my guilt.

Dee's amber eyes narrow. She frowns. "What did she do, drug you?"

"We drank too much and she ... she's one persuasive..."

"Bitch. What do you think she wants to talk to you about?"

"Knowing Claudette, her pet hamster died. Who the fuck knows. I won't be home tonight anyway." I chuckle. "If she wants me, she'll have to text me."

"Where you going tonight?"

"To bed. With the doors locked and lights out."

"You know how to handle her, don't you." Dee bursts out laughing. "How do you feel about redheads?"

"You watched her too, huh?" I shake my head. "Did you see the sun on her hair? Amazing what strobes of sunlight can do."

"Those eyes of yours." Dee shoots me an incredulous look

and laughs. "You see everything as art. And I'm not talking about Claudette. I'm talking about redheads."

"Meow," I tease.

"I'm not catty." She rolls her eyes. "Geeze, I'm just asking your opinion. I'm thinking of doing something different with my hair." She pauses. "Like making it green."

"I'm partial to blondes." Zoe comes to mind and I sigh.

"What's wrong with you? You're not listening." Dee's brows crunch. "Don't get bipolar on me."

"Sorry. I zoned out for a minute. I like your hair the way it is."

"Where are you, Jesse?" Dee waves a hand in front of my face. "You sure as hell aren't here."

Raking my fingers through my hair, I pace. I think. I'm angry, bitter, feeling things I'm not even sure there's a name for. "I ask myself why? Why did I wait so long? Why did I let her go back to the party alone? Why did I follow her out into the road? Maybe her parents would be alive right now. She'd be here."

"What the hell are you talking about?"

I fall into a reminiscing rant.

"Don't blame yourself, Jesse." Dee's eyes narrow and she bites her lip. I know that look. She has something on her mind or she's hiding something, like when she swore up and down to our high school art history teacher, "I would never cheat on a test!"

"You want to tell me something, don't you? What do you know about Zoe? About that night?"

Dee does a flash freeze and I know I'm not about to get anything from her. But that doesn't stop me from wondering, or trying.

After unloading my emotions for Zoe on Dee, I return home, grab an ice cold bottle of Sam's from the fridge, and flop onto the sofa. I'm a boiling kettle, and I need to vent. "Nothing a few drinks won't cure," I mumble on the way to the kitchen. The house is dark; other than the creaking floor, silent; so freaking empty without Dad and I hate to admit, my brother. I yank a bottle of Jim Beam from a cabinet, grab a glass, and dive right in. After a few shots and the eleven o'clock news, I'm ready to call it a night. No I'm not. "Paint," I mumble. "You need to paint." So my bottle and I stagger up the stairs to my bedroom. Bottle on dresser. Jesse on bed. Jesse on feet. Jesse pacing. Jesse with paintbrush in hand.

By now I'm so mellow I'm dreamy. My head spins with should haves. What ifs. Maybes. When I finish my portrait I stand back and damn, I don't have to study. My mind has stamped her image onto the canvas. My hands have had nothing to do with it.

Rising from a blue ocean of green forest is the bust of a fairy. Her shoulders are soft hills, her breast gentle knolls. Her long blonde hair is the branch of every tree. Her wings reach to heaven and I imagine them fluttering as her eyelids did the night she gazed up at me, questioning, fragile, pleading for understanding. I imagine she wanted my kiss. Which is why she readied her lips with that irresistible pout. The one I branded with mine.

I just start to fall asleep and my doorbell rings. "No," I groan, burying my head under my pillow. The irritating doorbell turns into an angering pounding.

I open the door to Claudette, who barges past me and finds a seat in the dark living room. I snap on a table lamp.

"What's up?"

"I'm pregnant." She lets out a long breath.

"Whose is it?" My voice is flat.

Her silver eyes flash in lamplight. "That's a fucking shit question to ask me." She falls into a chair, determined to make herself at home.

I drop onto a chair across the room. "What do you want me to do?"

"Marry me." She's blunt.

"Are you out of your mind?"

She buries her face, breaks into sobs, then comes up sniffling. "I have no one, Jesse. No place to go. When I start showing, my parents will either kill me or throw me out."

"Is it Christian's?"

Her shoulders lift. "I was with you last."

Her words, the intensity of her stare, cause the cold sweat that coats my skin.

"Can't be mine. My package was wrapped, hon." My jaw clenches.

"Condoms have been known to break."

I'm becoming more and more paranoid. She's right, condoms do break. I drop my head and cradle it with my hands.

"Jesse," her whisper is soft. "Christian's a dick. I don't want any part of him. I don't want him to be the father of my baby. I haven't been with him that way in months."

"You said you're on the pill, right?"

"Was."

I slap my forehead. "Have you been with Jamie?"

"Jamie?" She looks to the ceiling. "Jamie and I were together right before you left for Texas. So it's his or yours."

"It can't be mine." I have nothing against kids, but staring into Claudette's eyes, I see my life flushing down the toilet.

I feel a wash of relief when she concedes. "Then it must be Jamie's."

Blood pulses at my temples. I know how I feel; Christ knows how Jamie will take this news. "Did you tell him?"

The breath she blows out is accompanied by a groan.

"Well did you?" I hiss. Harsh.

My head is spinning. Both of us slept with the same girl, one before Texas and one after. Only one wore a rubber. Logic tells me it's my bro's baby.

I rush up the stairs, grab my cell, and slide to a halt at Claudette's side.

I hit my call button, Jamie doesn't answer, so I text: Yo, Daddy.

A few minutes later, my cell vibrates in my pocket.

"Who's this?" His gritty voice hits my ear.

If he thinks he's annoyed now, just wait, James. "It's your brother, jerk."

"You dialed the wrong number asshole." He's groggy, but music blares in the background, so I figure he's at a bar, in what state remains to be seen. "Dad's home. Probably sleeping." He laughs. "You haven't called him Daddy since you were five."

"Nope. I dialed you, Dad."

"Are you fucking high? I'm out. Dad's not here." His tone deepens.

"I have someone here who needs to talk to you."

Claudette's face fills with panic. Shaking her head, she mouths, "No. No."

"Stop shit-talking. I'm busy. What do you want, Jesse?"

"You'll see, Daddy."

Payback time, bro.

I drop the phone in Claudette's lap. "You can stay here until you two sort this out," I whisper. "Be diplomatic. Be strong. Don't let him blow you off."

Taking the stairs two at a time, I head for my bedroom and slam the door. Before hopping into bed, I do something I haven't done since I was ten years old. Yep, I lock my door.

I know my brother is a horny bastard, but I'm praying he's honorable.

Phase Four Full Circle

Zoe

My flight is scheduled for ten pm. My bags are packed and by noon, I've finished saying my final goodbyes because I know I'll never see the guys of Dinero again. I don't want to. Regardless of the tenderness Denny showed, he'd be too much of a reminder of the whirlwind year I spent with the band, and of Richie. Maniac Richie who isn't even around to bid me farewell.

I'm sitting in a fourth row window seat, watching the runway, fighting vertigo because I'm reliving the way the road looked the night the van tipped over and my head, followed by my body, broke through the windshield. I have to clear my mind or I'll vomit. I'm so nauseous. I tap my pocket and feel the bottle of Oxy the doctor gave me for pain, but there's no way. No drugs, booze, craziness.

For over a year I watched, first hand, the rise and fall of Chasing Dinero. Watched them graduate from changing in bathrooms and back rooms, to screwing around in real dressing rooms. Watched the groupies come and go. Sat in chairs in hotel rooms, writing my heart out, passed their rooms where naked girls fell all over Richie and Jonny. Denny treated me cordially most of the time, but didn't hesitate to let me see him fool around with the brunette that hung around constantly.

From this moment on I'm straight. I survived two near-fatal accidents. That must mean something. I'm here for a reason, Mom said. Which hopefully I'll find out, this time the easy way. I'll move back into my old house, register for college, and start the rest of my life. I think of that morning when Dad joked about me cleaning up the environment. As I gaze out the window, watching the runway disappear, I smile. "I'll make you proud, Dad," I whisper to the air.

An attendant brings me a container of juice, and I ease back into the seat and close my eyes. That's when I feel the presence beside me. The movement as another body crushes the seat next to mine.

The plane's been in the air for a good fifteen minutes, and everyone's been seated, so what the hell is going on? My nose picks up the familiar scent of spice cologne, the kind Richie always wore after his long hot showers.

My eyes pop open and I slowly turn my head. "Richie? What the hell are you doing on this plane?"

His hand covers mine. "I wanted to make sure you're okay, that you got home safe. And to tell you I'm sorry."

"Sorry you didn't visit me in the hospital?" I spit out, "or sorry you almost killed me?"

His eyes shift from mine. His cheeks flush. I believe he's frightened or ashamed. Maybe both.

"I'm fine Richie. I don't need an escort."

"I want to talk to you." His elbow is on the armrest and he leans too close.

I turn to the window. "There's nothing to talk about."

"I want another chance to prove myself."

"You're full of shit," I huff, "you just want me to write lyrics for you to sing," I speak with venom in my voice. "I'm done with you and everything else."

"That's my point. So am I. We can help each other."

"I don't need your help. You're giving me a migraine. Go back to your own seat," my eyes drill his, "please."

"I'll see you when we land," he says. His body lifts slowly, like an old man. He looks weary, defeated.

"Not if I see you first," I mumble, returning to my state of cloud-watching and daydreaming.

I can't wait to get back home. Start my life over again. Things are going to be different now. I've had my run. Thrilled at the audience and media reception. Will I miss it? Not sure. But right now all I need is to heal.

We land and disembark, and I don't see Richie until I reach for my luggage. His big hand grabs the handle of my bag before I can.

"I told you I don't need your help."

His other hand grips my arm. "Come on. I've got a ride waiting. I'll see you home, then leave you alone."

We're interrupted by the whine of the redhead who flounces over and plasters herself to Richie's side. I recognize her as the one he tried to bring onstage in North Carolina. "Where'd you disappear to baby? I came out of the ladies room and you weren't there." Her eyes rake over me. "Who's she?"

Her indignant stare pisses me off. "Who are you?" I snap, yanking my arm from Richie's grasp.

"Ivonna." She slings the strap of her handbag over a shoulder and drops her hands on her hips.

"This is Zoe. My backup singer." Richie tries to slide his arm around my waist, but I sidestep him.

"Backup?" I hiss. "I wrote most of the lyrics *we* sang on the tour. And I do remember you backing *me* up on occasion." My eyes flash from Richie to Ivonna.

"I'm the girl Richie writes songs about." Ivonna glares at me. "Didn't know it at the time, did ya, your boyfriend was singing for me."

"I guess you were too fucked up to remember me singing *my* songs with your boyfriend." I roll my eyes so hard they hurt. "He's so not my boyfriend. He's all yours. Enjoy." I shoot her a sarcastic smile and snatch my bag from Richie.

"We'll talk again. I didn't want you to think you were sneaking away without saying goodbye." Richie tugs my earlobe.

My head jerks up. "I don't need to sneak. Goodbye, Richie."

"I'll call you, Zoe," he sings out as Ivonna drags him away.

I grab an airport cab, anxious to return to the apartment, expecting to be met by Molly and chaos. Chaos being the twins. That's odd. My key doesn't fit the lock. After a few rhythmic taps, Nina comes to the door wearing a cotton nightie. Her hair is pulled back and a long thick braid dangles over a shoulder. Her face is scrubbed clean. I don't remember her without makeup. She looks different: Young. Healthy. Tired.

"Hey cous, you clean up pretty decent. But, what's with the old lady threads? I thought I taught you better than that at VS." I shoot her a crooked grin.

Nina's jaw drops. She doesn't move from the doorway, so I brush past her, pulling my overnight bag behind me. There I stand, splayed fingers of one hand lifted in a dramatic wave. This gets her attention. Her drooping lids snap up like bungee cords, then her drowsy eyes narrow.

"What are you doing here, Zoe?"

I glance around the living room and into the kitchen, nodding like a bobble head doll. "Hey. Did you hire a cleaning lady? Or is Molly on uppers? Phew. The place is spotless."

Her arms cross her chest. "What the hell? It's almost three

am."

"Sorry. My flight was delayed and I had to catch a cab and all. I figured you'd be up and out partying." I let out a laugh. "To tell you the truth, I expected a houseful, like in the old days." I belt out the chorus of *You Said*, reflective of my last encounter with Denny.

It's run its course
We're over now
We can still be friends
Loving you is not for me.
It don't feel right
I'm too unsure
Can't give you what you want
Can you live with it this way?

Nina does not appreciate this. "Sssh. The baby."

"Baby?" I gasp. "Whose?" I gasp again. "Molly? Holy shit."

I track her eyes toward Molly's room, watching her face curl up with an impish grin. "Not Molly's." She shakes her head. Her gaze fixes on the lanky guy stumbling into the living room, rubbing his eyes with one hand. The fingers of his other hand are yanking up his jeans.

"What's going on?" he says, his voice seductively hoarse.

With a flip of her wrist, Nina shoos him. "Go back to bed, honey."

His eyes flash over me. I must look a wreck because he grimaces. "Hey. Why don't you sit down? You look about to fall over. This must be the family secret." He chuckles. "The long lost rocker girl."

"Alive and kicking," I reply, turning to Nina. "Where's Molly?"

"She moved out a while ago. Struck gold with husband

number three. Need I say more?"

My gaze sweeps from his sleepy look to her concerned face. They have that *settled* look; something tells me they're more than a one night fling. "Please don't tell me you took the plunge?"

He moves to her side to wrap a toned arm around her waist, pulling her to his chest, grinning the entire time. Yep, gotta be hitched.

Nina holds up her left hand, wiggling her ring finger which glistens with a thin band of gold.

I shake my head as though the jarring motion will make everything I'm experiencing make sense. "Wow, Nina. I know you move fast. But marriage? A baby?"

"Yup. This is Lance."

My eyes roll over her husband. *Husband.* Never expecting to be met with this news, I almost choke.

Lance is a pretty good looking dude. Buzzed head, lean but built. A few tattoos slither across his smooth chest.

I cock my head and quip, "You're into snakes and lizards, huh?" But he responds with a frown. Maybe he doesn't realize I'm referring to his ink and thinks I'm ragging on Nina.

After a tense moment, while they stare and I yawn, I drop the bomb Nina must be expecting. "So. You gonna let me crash here or what?" I emit another yawn.

Glancing up at Lance, she gathers her cheek, then her eyes return to mine. "Sure. For a little while. You can use Nino's old room."

"Old room?"

"Yeah. Nino's gone."

"Where?"

"Someplace in the Middle East, I guess. It's the army's decision."

"Holy shit. I never figured Nino for a patriot."

"You remember the losers he was hanging with, right?"

I nod, thinking, we're all losers. "The world is full of them. So what makes Nino or his bros different?"

"Right after you left, he was caught carrying. Third offense. It was army or jail."

"That sucks." I shrug. "Well. Night then. I'm beat." I shoot them a mocking smile.

After they disappear into Molly's old room, I kick off my boots and pad to the doorway of the room Nina and I used to share. I peer into dim lighting. "Never looked like this when we slept here," I mumble. The room is neat and freshly painted. The one window is covered with a frilly curtain. I stare at the window I used to watch Nina and Scott from. It seems like a lifetime ago. I wonder what happened to Scott.

In the cozy corner stands a white crib. On tiptoes, I pad across the carpet to gaze at the newest member of the family.

The room smells like baby, and everything is pink, which tells me the sleeping angel is a girl. Tiny fists curled above her head, plump cherry red lips, she's an adorable little bundle wrapped in a bunny sleeper. "Oh, my ..." I murmur, gripped with memories of holding a sweet warm baby I minded for neighbors. "Hello, new addition to the family."

Family. For a split second, I can't believe I'm actually referring to the people in this apartment, the ones past, the ones present, as family.

When the little one stirs, I can't control the urge. "Wake up. Wake up," I whisper, scooping her up into my arms. Her barely open eyes immediately close and she falls back to sleep without even making a peep. "Don't you cry little one?" I whisper. "Nope. Aunt Zoe is never going to let you cry." I press her close, careful not to squeeze too hard. Her skin holds the fragrance of baby powder. From her fuzzy little head wafts a hint of shampoo. "And you're the one your mom said she'd never get stretch marks for."

I bring her to my shoulder. "Come here you little burger."

For what must be half an hour, I rest in the easy chair in the corner, nuzzling her sweetness, pressing her to my heart. I wonder what her name is. She looks like an Angela. No, Angelina. This little beauty is going to have class. Not like Mommy. I hold back a giggle. Then tears try to gather, but I don't want to risk them falling onto her face, waking her. Wetting her perfect newness. So with burning eyes, I place her down like china, gently tucking, drowning in a prolonged gaze.

Other than a twin bed, which is neatly made, Nino's room is wall to wall sealed cartons. Nina must be getting ready to evict him too, when he returns, of course. I can't say I blame her. She's cleaned up her act and is trying to make a good life for herself and her family.

I'm good at feeling *presence* of living or dead. I glance up to find Nina standing at the doorway, arms crossing her chest. "Zoe. I know it's been a rough ride for you and all, but," she unlocks her arms, appearing hesitant to extend them. "It's good to see you Cus." After a quick hug, she draws back. "I've got a good man now. A decent life. I can't let anything interfere with what I've worked hard for. You know?" She frowns. "You've been gone over a year. You didn't call. Write."

"Neither did you."

"I didn't have to call," she says, smirking, "all I needed to do was google your name and there you were on the Internet. You and your boys had some wild times so I've read ... Falcon." She shakes her head. "Come on in the kitchen so we don't wake Rosey."

I follow her, and she laughs. "Falcon. Who came up with that?"

I bare my tattooed shoulder. "It's a long story, Nina."

"I love you, Zoe but ..." she looks sheepish, "I know you don't have anyone but ... you've been mixed up with drugs and lunatics. You can't stay here forever."

"To set the record straight, I never did drugs. I smoked more pot with you and Nino than with the band. I just need a few days." My heart goes to my throat. All I can do is to croak, "I won't fuck anything up for you, hon. I'll be out of your hair and make my own way. I can take care of myself. I get monthly checks in the mail, remember?"

Her hand flies to her mouth. "Oh my God. I've been saving the envelopes, Zoe." She rushes to a small desk tucked into an alcove and opens a drawer. With a smile, she hands me a stack of mail sent by the trustee. "Here. I hope they're still good and not expired or anything. I would have expected you to have them forwarded."

While thumbing through the envelopes, I count the months I've been away. "I wasn't in one place long enough. Plus, I made money from gigs. This is going straight into the bank."

The first thing I do the next morning is call the estate attorney.

"I'm back in New York and ready to move into my house. I don't have any place to stay. What's in the contract? How fast can you get the renters out?"

"The contract requires a ninety day notice." His voice is crisp.

"Wow, that's a long time for me to stay in a hotel."

"I was going to contact you, Zoe. The tenants want to buy the house."

"What? No way. I'm not selling." My jaw sets.

"They really like the area. Their kids are settled in school. They're offering above market value hoping you'll consider selling."

"An offer I can't refuse." I sigh. "Let me think about it."

Feeling out of place, I check into a hotel the next day. After settling in, I call Denny to see how he's doing. Okay, I admit I really miss him.

"Zoe," his voice rings with pleasure. I imagine his sexy smile.

"How are you? Where are you?"

"In New York."

"With your cousin?"

"Nah. I decided to crash in a hotel till I sort things out. How about you? Still in North Carolina?"

"Yeah. Working out a deal with Stan." His tone drops. "Richie's gone."

"I know. He's here."

"With you?" He hits a pitch.

"No. I ran into him at the airport with his redhead."

Denny laughs, then cautions, "Keep your distance."

"Still with the warnings, huh? You really do think you know what's best for me, don't you." I giggle.

"I know I miss you." By the sound of his voice, I visualize the sad look on his face. "We're starting a new band. Stan's going to manage us. It's gonna work out Zoe."

"Wow. That's awesome, Denny."

"Fly back to us Falcon," he chuckles, "The Next Life needs you."

"Is that the name of your band? The Next Life?"

"Yeah. Like it?"

"Love it. It rocks."

"Now that we're done with small talk. Come with us. I really miss you."

"God, I miss you too." I can barely speak through the lump in my throat. "I can't, Den. I need to get my shit together before even thinking about moving on."

"We never finished Comatose," he says quietly.

"You have the sheet music and lyrics, you can do it, Den. I have confidence in you."

"Hey thanks, but none of us are songwriters. That was yours and Richie's thing."

"So you want Richie back?" My stomach knots.

He laughs. "I'd rather shoot myself in the foot than deal with that asshole." His deep breath fills my ear. "I want you back," he whispers.

"I've been with you long enough, listened to words from your heart." I think of the night we had dinner, the things he said, how he held me when we danced. "You're phenomenal, Denny. You've got it in you. You just need to get out there and do it."

"You sound like me now, when I dragged you on stage that first night at Deluge." His voice is soft.

"Denny, don't, you'll make me cry," I pause and hold the phone from my lips so he doesn't hear the swallow that's being difficult, "I miss you," I whisper.

"Miss you more babe. Keep in touch, okay?" he says, his voice threatening to crack.

"Good luck with The Next Life. I know I'll be reading about you," my throat strains, "hearing you on the radio. Who knows? I might just show up at one of your gigs."

"Please, his voice breaks, "please do."

"Bye Denny."

"Love ya, Zoe." Click.

Finding You

Zoe

I hang around the hotel room, contemplating, listening to music, watching TV. I guess you could say I'm suffering from an extended case of jet lag, better yet, band burnout. A few days into my sojourn, I get a text from Richie.

Richie: Help

Me: What's wrong?

Richie: Ivonnas crashing

Me: Call 911

Richie: Can't. I'll get busted.

Me: You want ME to get busted?

Richie: Just help me get her right. Please. Wouldn't ask if I didn't need you.

Me: Gimme your address.

Against my better judgment, I take a cab to Richie's apartment. It's in a worn out building in an equally worn neighborhood. Grudgingly, my feet deliver me up the stairs to the third floor. But for the scrunch of my sneakers on the sticky floor, the paint-peeling corridor is silent. I glance from left to right, then rap on the door marked 339. Richie greets me with a devious grin, grabs my arm and yanks me into the small entrance foyer.

"What are you doing?" I take back my arm and wander into the disheveled living room where I almost have a coronary.

There sits Ivonna, waning like the sunlight trickling through the closed blinds. She's cross-legged on a sectional sofa, blanket hanging over one of her bare shoulders, staring at the screen of a blasting, flat screen TV. Her fingers idly twist a hank of long red hair.

Grinding my teeth, I reel. "What's this?" I throw an arm out, longing to pull every stubble off Richie's unshaven face. He's shirtless and barefoot. His jeans are unbuttoned and only half zipped. He's so smug I want to polish his teeth with my fist.

What did I just walk into? I'm still a fool, letting him trick me into coming here. Dammit! I can't believe I fell for this!

"What are *you* doing here?" Ivonna unwinds her limbs, leans into the coffee table, face perched over a line of coke. The blanket slips, baring one of her naked breasts.

"I thought she was crashing?" I glare at Richie. "You dragged me down here for this?"

Ivonna's head comes up. She sniffs through a white nostril. "I was what?"

I point to Richie, who's now slouched against the kitchen door frame slugging a can of beer. Eyes swinging from Ivonna to me, he appears to be enjoying himself.

"He told me you were overdosing," I snap, unable to ignore the slide of her blanket onto the floor.

She smirks at me, calls him an asshole and shuts the TV off. "As you can see, I'm fine," she licks her fingertip and shoos me off like an annoying cat, "you can leave."

"No shit." I flip her off and spin to the door.

"Wait," the damp grip of Richie's hand stops me, "okay, so I lied. But she *is* doing coke. And I got a bench warrant out for me." He scratches his head and shrugs. "Remember that appearance ticket?" The smile that once made me melt now turns my stomach. "I could use some financial assistance. I'm losing this place," his arm fans around the room, "and I could use some notes to relocate."

"You're pathetic." I curl my lips into one of Richie's classic snarls. Right now I'm as heartless as he was … is.

His lined forehead glistens. Palms extended, his fingers strain toward me, like his imploring words. "It's not just the cash, I needed to see you."

"What the fuck?" Ivonna's screech nearly pierces my eardrums.

"Shut the fuck up." Richie's voice sails across the room.

"At least stay for a drink, Zoe," he pleads, his head jerking back to mine.

Ivonna cuts in. "He just wants to bleed you for drug money. Like he did to me."

"No way. The well is dry." When I attempt to leave, Richie's body blocks the door. But he doesn't scare me anymore. His molded chest is now kind of gaunt, and ribs replace the firm abs I once found attractive. The creases on Richie's sallow skin are a blueprint of the life he lived and a warning sign that his health is suffering or failing.

"Fuck off, whore," he snaps at Ivonna, who's doing another line. "You're nothing but trouble."

"Look who's talking you sadistic sonofabitch." Shaking my head, I reach for the door knob.

His dark eyes sink into mine. "She's turning into a junkie."

"The company she's been keeping is bringing her down." At the sight of her, my lips pin tight. "I know the feeling."

"And you know this why?" Richie says, tossing his empty beer can across the room.

"Cos I know you, Santana, and what happens to the people you destroy."

"Guess I'll have to take her out and sell her if you don't come through." He grabs my ponytail and tugs.

"Like hell you will," I shout, plowing through him. "You're an evil bastard. Give the girl a break and send her on her way before she really does crash."

Richie's lost a lot of weight. His face is lined and he's gaunt. "You want her?" He offers a weak grin. "It'll cost you."

I feel the onset of a killer migraine. My heart is racing. Blood is swirling through my brain, making me dizzy, so I brace myself against the wall.

"What's the matter with you?" Richie's stare narrows.

"My head." I hold my temples. "You have any aspirins? I need some water too."

"Is that the effect I have on you?"

"Since the accident I'm plagued with visual migraines, so yeah, I guess it's your fault." I frown.

Richie relinquishes his hold on the door, goes to the kitchen and returns with a bottle of water. He removes the cap and says, "Open your mouth."

I snatch the pills from his hand and examine the small white tablets to make sure they're aspirins. My head is pounding so hard, without further thought, I pop them into my mouth and choke them down.

For a moment, Richie's face softens with concern. "Sit down till you feel better," he says, leading me to the sofa.

I sit and wait for the aspirins to take effect but instead of relieving the pain in my head, the room tilts.

"What did you give me?" I slur.

Concern dissipates, the sound of Richie's laugh is chilling. His face distant.

I'm going in and out of a dream. From the corner of my eye I sense movement, but I'm not walking toward Ivonna. I'm floating. I think she's slumped on the sofa, but I'm not really sure. Everything's so blurry.

I stagger across the room.

"Where you going?" Richie sounds a million miles away.

I glimpse the ghost of Richie standing in the middle of the floor, raking his hands through his hair.

"What did you give me?" The room is bright, its contents fuzzy. Mixed with my migraine aura, I'm more than tripping.

"Just a little bit of sunshine, babe. That's all I had. It's good for a headache."

I literally stagger out the door and down the stairs. Out in fresh air, my vision begins to normalize and my head starts to clear. I sit on the curb, watching rush hour traffic. What do I do now? I pull my cell from my pocket and call a cab. My next call is to 911. "There's a girl overdosing in an apartment ..." I give the address but not my name. "And there's a bench warrant out for the owner of the place. You might want to check out Richie Santana."

The cab pulls up and when the driver asks, "Where to?" I give him Nolan's address. Why? I don't really know, other than the fact that he was the only stabilizing factor in the life I tried to recover, and right now I'm still feeling unsteady.

The cab pulls up in front of Nolan's house. My stare tracks up the front of the looming brownstone, and I think about the last time I was here when his father all but threw me out. Butterflies fill my stomach. Is it because I don't want to confront Dr. Royce? Or is it Nolan I'm worried about facing.

I wonder if his parents are home. The entire house is dark. Is Nolan even here? There's only one way to find out. No, I don't throw pebbles at his window. I text him. In seconds the room lights, the blinds whip open, and with a look of shock, Nolan stares down at me, the lost girl standing beneath the streetlight. Lifting a hand for a small wave, I grin.

When Nolan opens the door, he does a double take. I must look like hell itself. "Zoe. Are you okay? What are you doing here?" His face scrunches with confusion as he pulls me into the house, past the staircase and into the living room.

We sit on the sofa drinking coffee, and I fill him in on what just occurred.

Nolan shakes his head, grumbling, "What were you doing with that piece of shit?" He's calm, his voice gentle, yet his jaw is tense.

"I figured I could help Ivonna before Richie ends up killing her. I know what being under his spell can be like." My teeth close over my bottom lip. "It's the cops' worry now. They'll find Richie with more than a system full of drugs, the apartment must be overflowing with crap. Hopefully he and Ivonna will both get the help they need."

The moment Nolan's arm goes around me, my head finds his shoulder and I burst into tears. "I'm sorry, Nolan. Of all people, I didn't want you dragged into this mess."

"Of all people?" Drawing back, he gives me a puzzled look.

"I just mean, you're good. Clean." My face is wet with tumbling tears, so he grabs some tissues from a box on the table.

"Zoe. Zoe. Where have you been, girl?" He dabs my face but the tears keep flowing. "You just like dropped out."

"I know. And I'm about to drop back in," I sniff, "I've been traveling, trying to find myself, but all I wanted was to come home and be me again. The real me."

His embrace tightens. My face buries in his chest and I feel the beat of his heart. I continue to sob, pouring out everything that's happened during the past year. Nolan keeps patting my shoulder. Rocking me in his arms like I'm a baby.

"Just being with you calms me," I whisper.

He tips my chin up and drops a kiss on my forehead. "You know I'd do anything for you." He runs a finger over my lips ever so gently. "Polish up that face with a smile."

"I'm trying." I attempt a grin but my lips won't cooperate. "But I don't know what to do. I can't stay at Nina's anymore, 'cos she's married," my voice shudders, "and I can't go home till the renters move out. The lawyer says they have ninety days, so I got a hotel room–" I blurt out everything that's bringing back my migraine.

"Not with that asshole stalking you. No way." He shakes his head with determination.

Just thinking about the possibility of seeing Richie again trips my heart. "He's on the way to jail by now," I whisper.

"Ever hear of bail?" His eyes widen. "He doesn't know where you live, does he?"

I shake my head. "Nope. Not the apartment ... definitely not the house."

"Ah, the house. You're a homeowner." He chuckles. "What are you going to do in that big house all by yourself?"

"That's another thing." I stare at the fireplace where family photos line the polished mantel." The tenants want to buy the house. I don't know what to do."

"It's late, and you don't have to decide anything right now. Sleep on it." He hitches his head toward the staircase.

"Here?"

His every feature breaks into a smile. "Sure, why not?"

I blow out a "Phew," and bite the inside of my cheek. "What will your parents say?" The thought hits me. "Ohmagod. Are they home?"

"Despite your first impression, my parents don't bite." Nolan chuckles. "And they're at a medical convention, which gives us about twenty-four hours for you to get some rest. We can talk in the morning. I'll help in any way I can."

"You're wonderful, you know that?"

"You're nuts, do you know that?"

"Thanks for being here for me." I smile. "For letting me stay."

"You can start with a shower," Nolan says, his eyes taking in my curb-dusted jeans and tear-stained shirt.

"I'm a wreck, huh?"

"Yeah," he says soberly, then winks, "but still beautiful."

Nolan and I get along so well, it's like the past year never happened. It's as though we haven't been separated at all. We order a pizza and watch a movie.

The next morning, I play video games while Nolan makes breakfast.

"I guess I should be heading out. Your parents will be home soon."

"Not till tonight," he says, and I get the feeling he doesn't want me to leave.

"Let's test the waters," he sounds uncertain, "see if we can keep you here, at least over the weekend. The thought of you alone in a hotel–" He gives me a look of concern. "Are you sure that e-tard doesn't know where you live?"

I shake my head. "Ah ah. In fact, I barely remember where I used to live." Then it hits me, the thought of walking into my own house, after all this time, carrying such heavy memories with me. "Nolan. I don't know if I can do it."

"Do what, hon?"

"Face that house."

"You don't have to face it alone. I'll go with you."

Nolan and I cuddle in the family room watching a comedy flick. His arm is slung around the back of the sofa.

I run a hand over his smooth skin, staring deeply into eyes as green as Irish meadows. "You're beautiful, Nolan. Inside and out."

"Stop." He elbows me.

"Aww. You're embarrassed," I tease, shaking my head. "You have no idea of true beauty, do you?"

He tugs my hair. "I'm looking at it."

I don't believe either of us realize what's happening, but one minute we're joking, and the next our lips are touching, softly at first then harder.

"Make love to me," I pant, pressing so close I'm smashed against his abs.

Nolan's breath also comes fast. His lips brush through my hair. "Do you love me?"

This stops me dead in my tracks. I fall into thought, reasoning why I just said what I did. Since the attack, I've wondered if I could ever be with a guy, and since I'm so close to Nolan, why not him? I didn't scream when he just kissed me. I don't think I'd scream if he touched me. Or would I?

The clasp of his arms loosens. "If you have to think about it, you don't."

I gaze into his eyes, absorbing the intensity of emotion, realizing Nolan really cares for me, more than a friend.

"I do Nolan, but not in that way." I feel my cheeks heat. "I love who you are, how you treat me. I love knowing you, watching you..."

He unlocks my arms and eases away.

"Nah ah, not like this, Zoe."

I take a deep breath and blurt out the truth. "I want to know if I can be with a man without screaming."

The low laugh escaping Nolan's lips isn't from humor. "That's not a good enough reason, Zoe, and for that I'm not your man."

"I'm sorry, Nolan. I shouldn't have–"

"Unless you can look me in the eye, tell me you love me. Like I..."

I lower my eyes. How can I face him?

He tips my face up, his eyes filled with understanding. "It's okay, Zoe girl, I understand where you're coming from. The right guy will come along and you'll know it's right, he's right, and you won't scream. Believe me, you've moved beyond that." He smooths my hair from my face. "I've watched you grow into someone so special, so strong. No matter what you might think of yourself, you're one of the most wonderful women I know, other than my mom, of course." He taps the tip of my nose and grins. "And brave."

"Don't cry, Zoe." Nolan runs a finger across my cheek, dabbing a tear. "There's a lot of life waiting out there for you. And you have decisions to make." He tilts his head. "What are you going to do about the house?"

"I'm still undecided." I go to the window and watch the mail truck stop at Nolan's mailbox. "Maybe I need to see the place." I whip around and stare.

"An old fashioned drive-by?" He grins. "We can take my dad's car."

My fingers twist the hem of my shirt. "What do you think I should do?"

"That's your call, Zoe."

I give Nolan directions and we drive up the Taconic Parkway. When the sign says, Pleasantville, my stomach churns. "Turn here." My voice echoes in my ears, shaky, weak.

We approach my street and I begin to panic. "Maybe this isn't such a good idea."

"You have to face it, girl. The longer you wait, the worse it will get."

"I guess you're right."

"So can I have the house number now?" he says, smirking comically.

We troll the old neighborhood, and I'm filled with mixed emotions. Four years is a long time. We don't see any faces, but the houses look the same.

"Turn here," I point to a side road lined with evergreens. Passing Dee's house, I squint, wondering if she still lives here, half of me wanting to see her, the other half wanting to slink down in the seat in case she's outside. But the only signs of life are the neighborhood dogs penned in their yards.

"There it is," I pull a deep breath. "That's my house, over

there on the right." My heart rate picks up. "Keep driving!"

So we circle the block a few times, until my insides don't feel like they'll eject from my throat.

"Okay, Nolan. I'm ready. Pull over and park for a minute … so I can look … think."

The house still wears the same cream color siding and brown shutters. The lawn is green and velvety and new shrubs and flowers have been planted in the gardens I used to help my mother weed.

"What do you think?" Nolan, who sits patiently beside me, breaks the silence.

"Wow. They've really kept the place up. I almost expected it to be overgrown and broken down, but," reaching over I turn the key to shut off the engine. "Let's just watch for a bit, okay?"

Nolan checks the rearview mirror. "Whatever, but I hope we don't get pinched for staking out the house." He chuckles, and I breathe through my hand which is covering my mouth.

"I want to get out and peer through the windows, see what kind of people they are. I really want to peer through my old bedroom window."

"You could knock on the door and say you're a Jehovah's Witness. That would be one way to meet them." Nolan shrugs.

I burst out laughing, then I begin to cry. "I feel so bipolar, Nolan."

Memories hit my brain so hard, I feel dizzy: the rape, the accident, Dee, Jesse. The year I spent with Chasing Dinero. It's all catching up with me and I'm not sure I can handle it.

"I could have been better. I fucked up Nolan."

"You did fine, Zoe. You're back in one piece. Give yourself some credit, girl, and some time to find the real you under all that history."

I sigh. "What would be worse, walking through that front door or selling the place?"

I crane my neck, checking the backyard where I spot a jungle gym that's replaced my old rusted swing set. The one Dad refused to take down.

The front door opens and a man and woman emerge, followed by a girl and boy.

"Ooh look." I strain to take in every ounce of them while hunching down in the seat so they don't see me gawking. "They do look nice. What grade do you think the kids are in?"

Nolan is hunched in his seat, trying to be discreet. "Eh. Elementary for sure. Fourth or fifth maybe?" He curls his lips and shakes his head. "I don't know. But I do feel like a stalker. Can we leave before someone calls the cops?"

"Give me another minute," I whisper. "I can't uproot them. They look so settled, so happy," I mutter. "They look like such a nice family."

"So you made your decision?" His fingers grip the keys, prepared to start the engine.

I pull out my cell phone and call the estate attorney. "It's Zoe Channing. They can have the house."

As we drive back to the hotel, we talk about thinks in the past, things to come.

"I'm leaving for NC soon." I watch Nolan's grip tighten on the wheel.

"North Carolina." I sigh. "That brings back a lot of memories."

He turns to me for a curious glance. "Good?"

"Yeah, good and bad but mostly frightening. It was a real learning experience."

"Are you going to be okay?" He pulls to the curb and cuts the engine.

Softly, I breathe, "Yeah. I'll be fine." Reaching over I tap his thigh. "My wingman."

Before I leave the car, he draws me close for a bear hug.

"Keep in touch, Zoe. And no more disappearing."

I kiss his cheek. "I promise."

Finding You

Zoe

I can't live in a hotel room forever, so I spend the next two weeks apartment hunting. I find a pretty nice place not far from Nolan's neighborhood and the school I'd like to attend; the only problem is, it's over a bar. I'm used to noise, and being surrounded by people is better than being alone, so I sign the lease. Then I pour over job search sites. I don't want to blow through the insurance money my parents left me, or the proceeds from the sale of the house. So I pretend I don't have a bank account, and decide I must earn my own way, keeping the bank bucks for emergencies, the future, and college. I'll also need the backing when I go into private practice. I plan on doing a lot of pro bono work. I'm not going into law for the money, but for the rights of the planet.

Sipping tea and eating muffins, I scrutinize the scrolling pages on my computer, eyes like magnets ready to lock on a job. It needn't be perfect. Becoming a productive college student is my way of assimilating back into the world. I'll roll my sleeves up, bury myself in work. Someday, something will bring a feeling of happiness. Happiness comes to those who have struggled. Happiness comes to she who appreciates raindrops, lacy branches swaying in a sweet breeze. Baby birds singing in treetops. The most beauty I've ever seen is in the earth. And it's free.

"Hmm, interesting," I mumble, spotting the advertisement: Receptionist wanted for new tattoo salon. Flexible hours. Apply in person. Nightingale. Nightingale? Beautiful name. Reminding me of a boy named Jesse Sinclair. A bird on the back of my neck. Bittersweet memories. I wonder where he is. What he's doing.

The ad gives the address, and I'm thrilled it's within walking distance from my apartment. *I absolutely have to land this job.*

I slip my fingers under the neckline of my shirt, run them over my shoulder. Without looking, I can feel the magic of my fairy tattoo. I lift my pant leg to check the hummingbird on my ankle. The spray of roses on a vine creeping up my abs. Yup, this is MY kind of job. So I call the number, unprepared, yet ready to convince the owner I'm the best person for the job.

A deep voice answers on the third ring. "Nightingale. Check us out. Hours to suit."

He sounds young, smooth, and so cute, I almost giggle. "That's quite a sales pitch."

He clears his throat. "How can I help you?" He's much more sedate.

"I'm calling about the receptionist job."

His voice is musical. "Ah. Can you tell me a bit about yourself? Experience?"

"Life experience?" I giggle, then palm my forehead and pull my phone from my lips so he can't hear my groan. *Why didn't I come up with experience before I called? And stop stress giggling, fool!* "I can fax or email a resume if you'd like." *As soon as I make one up.*

"We're seeing applicants in person. From your voice, you

sound about ... twenty?" He teases.

"Nineteen and in college." Or will be. The pep in my voice should be impressive and persuasive. I hope.

"Can you work full time?"

"I can work between classes."

"Hmm. College, huh? How flexible can you be?"

"Hours you mean?"

He chuckles. "Yeah, I'm not looking for a gymnast."

My laugh is breezy. We're already hitting it off.

"Why don't you come over and we can interview. I've gotten a lot of calls and need to make a decision. I have an opening this afternoon. Better come over quick if you're interested." He's flirty. "A job like this won't be open for long."

By his tone, I can almost visualize his eye-crinkling smile. I think he'd be an awesome person to work for.

"Well in that case," I pause to let him think I'm checking my calendar, "is two okay?"

"Sounds good."

"See you then."

As I hang up, I believe he says, "What's your name?" But I've already disconnected and not about to call him back.

My life is as unpredictable as the weather. It's August and summer is already fading. I refuse to give up my shorts and tank tops for long sleeves and jeans. I look in the mirror at my cutoffs. No way. You cannot wear these shorts to a job interview. But I want to show off my tattoos. If Nightingale is anything like Destiny's, the staff will be inked from top to bottom.

I need to fit in. Showing off my ink is the best way. So I choose a black tank top, roll it up to just beneath my bust and my ab tatts look amazing. No, my mind screams. I slip into a short skirt, roll down the hem of my shirt so it rides just above the waist, displaying a slice of tummy ink. I consider a ponytail, but brush my hair till it shines, braid one side, and tuck the other behind an ear. I apply a bit of makeup, twirl before my full length mirror, and off I go.

.

I stand before the glass front tattoo salon called Nightingale. Never having been on a job interview, I breathe and flow with the feeling of panic that tries to overtake me. You can do this, Zoe. He's going to be nice. He's going to hire you. You're going to be an amazing employee. You're going to jumpstart your life, right here, right now.

Golden sunlight warms my bare shoulders as I pause before the entrance. I lift my face to a soft blue sky and take a deep breath. A steady breeze unleashes the long lock of hair I've tucked behind my left ear to show off my sparkling ear climber.

For a brief moment, I stare at my reflection in the sparkling clear glass doors, which look new or just scrubbed. Why do silly thoughts cram your mind at the oddest times? Like, I wonder who cares enough about this building to keep this glass so spotless. Mom used to clean the windows of our house like this. Not even a fingerprint or smudge remained. #homesick #missingfamily #lovesick #lostgirl

Stop it Zoe! You're here for a job interview, not social media. Shape up girl! My eye roll catches the artwork scrolling across the emerald green canopy. #incredibletalent #wishIcouldpaintlikethat #whopaintedthis?

My gaze follows a dragon's fiery tongue to the sign on the window: *Nightingale* is painted in fancy script. The name is cleverly embedded within the figure of a bird. My first thought: Wow, these dudes are some phenomenal artists.

When I finally curb my revolving thoughts, I cautiously grip the door handle, pull, and force my feet to cross the threshold. While I admire the interior, the exterior images still bounce across my mind. My gaze wanders the room. Big place. Nice. New, which I guess accounts for the clean doors. Pale lavender walls, white tile floor. Like Destiny's, photos and drawings are strategically hung on the walls.

Four black leather-like recliners in a perfect row. Massage tables. Empty. Still life. No life. Who decorated? Some ebony painted tables nest in the corner, squared off by benches with tan seats. Not yet broken in. Binders on the table: someone's artwork, I assume. Not homework, although the binders could appear to be left there by a high school student. Samples, I guess. Artwork. Someone's mind, heart, soul. Tattoos, of course. That's why people come here.

Deliberately relaxing my limbs, I'm on my way across the floor to flip through some pages of this great book of art, when a figure emerges from a doorway to my right. My peripheral tells me it's a guy: tall, lanky but with nice shoulders. Hmm. His dark hair is blurry. I feel the need to spin around, and although I try to stop myself from looking like a startled doe, or idiot, I stare.

I watch him watch me, then his mouth drops. A t-shirt pulls across rippling abs when his chest heaves. My eyes can't help but catch the twist of his hips wrapped by tight jeans, the flex of thigh muscles beneath the indigo fabric as he takes a step toward me.

"Zoe?" He breathes my name as though in disbelief, and I almost lose consciousness.

Say something! Move your lips! Can you blink? No. My eyes instantly dry.

A long moment of silence passes, yet it's not awkward. Magical comes to mind. It's Jesse. The boy I was hooked on what feels like a lifetime ago.

My blood pumps faster, unfreezing my body, and my head bursts with memories.

There's someone out there for everyone, Mom would insist when I doubted my future. *Your heart will whisper.* Whisper? It's like a racehorse. My mind is screaming right now! If only I could tell her.

"Jesse? Oh my God, I can't believe it's you." My hand goes to my forehead. "Is it really you?"

"It's me … and you. You're here." I watch his lips struggle to open and close. Listen to the sound of his mellow voice which I've never heard crack this way before.

I remember he loved to paint. I remember more than that. "Is this your salon?"

His eyes haven't left my face. His stare is warm. Curious. Astonished.

"How are you?" His brows crease. Half of his mouth tries to smile.

I know he's thinking, what happened to you? But is too polite to probe.

I've been through so much, Jesse, but I'm okay … now. I feel at home with Jesse, but must admit, my heart is thudding so hard I fight to normalize my breathing. "I'm good. How about you?" My tone isn't much stronger than his. "How have you been?"

My straining eyes water. From staring in shock, or emotion? I think I feel my mascara begin to run as I study him. Speechless. Both of us. He is a gorgeous, frozen statue, all his life is in his eyes. Soft warm brown eyes. He's slamming me with that same intense look as the last time I saw him, that night on the dark road during Trent's party. When he tried to put his arms around me. When I freaked out. Adrenaline courses through my body as my mind paints the past.

We're surrounded by the outlines of trees, ghosts, like the ones that still haunt me. If I let them. Which I tell myself, I don't. For a moment I'm back there, but I halt the flood of memories. I can't go there. I closed that book a long time ago. But Jesse. I could never close the book on Jesse. He's been on every page of my life since the first day my gaze swept his.

I remember how he looked when I caught him checking me

out. I want to smile, but cannot. Even though I've been through so much, I think unconsciously, Jesse has always been with me. No one could ever measure up to him. Is that why things didn't work out with Nolan or Denny? No; Denny was unstable. Nolan was an innocent bystander tending to the needs of a fragile, damaged girl. These thoughts are all attacking my mind while I stare at Jesse, waiting for him to move. To speak.

He's got that questioning look on his beautiful face, as though he's trying to decide: *Is this girl still crazy?* He looks confused, as though he's wondering: *What's she doing here?* But there's something else in his eyes besides intensity and confusion. Is his brain shuffling through memories like mine? Or is he just stunned by encountering a girl he once knew.

Standing face to face with Jesse, I'm hit with a rush of emotion. Memories: good, bad, torturous. Loving. My mouth is dry, my lips stiff. I might stutter if I try to speak, so I continue to stare. My legs are wobbly, so I let my shoulder sink against the nearest wall.

"Zoe?" Is he questioning or stating? "Are you okay?" He must be as blown away as I am because his voice strains. He runs a hand over his wavy hair, the same way I remember. This masculine touch is an innocent gesture a guy does without realizing his movements could drive a girl out of her mind. Drive her into his arms. Where I'd like to be ... at this very moment. This is all too sudden. All too much.

"I'm just a little … shocked," manages to dribble from my lips, which I'm now biting, dammit. "Jesse. It's really you." I laugh.

You look exactly the same, my mind says. Time has been almost nonexistent. Have you been through nothing? A lot? As much as I have? I'm suddenly angry ... at him. Why? Because he hasn't suffered as I have? Or is it because he's looking at me this way, making my legs go so weak, I feel like my blood sugar level has dropped to ZERO!

I can't pull my gaze from his. It feels like an eternity: Since I knew him. Since we were *almost* together. Since I walked into this place and back into my past.

Moody tilted his head, his eyes filled with recognition. "Under that blonde hair and all that hussy makeup, I remember you. I saw you sing on the stage with that filthy band. Did they have you too? I knew you way back, once, maybe three or four times."

This is what my mind is doing to me. I can't breathe. The sense of the same putrid chemical rag being stuffed down my throat is choking me. I smell ammonia, the dank room, stale boiling water steam, the odor of his body.

I manage to shake free of darkness, concentrating on the goodness before me.

"What are *you* doing here?" I manage.

His eyes smile, then narrow. "I work here." His gaze unlocks from mine to sweep across my face, progressing slowly, as though he is ingesting every inch of me from head to toe. "You look as beautiful as I remember." I watch his swallow, deep, difficult.

The way he looks at me makes every part of my body tingle. Oh God, how much more can I stand? Am I standing? I think I'm sinking to the floor. I also think I should turn and run. Yup, head for those sparkling clean doors, girl. Make the great escape, because there's no way you can rekindle with Jesse without settling the past, which you now realize has only been simmering on a red hot burner. You've blocked it. You're great at that. Sometimes the only way to survive is by blocking out good, along with the bad.

Then it hits me. "You painted the art outside?" My unstable hand points to the canopy visible through the glass. "It's beautiful, Jesse."

Finding You

Jesse

Crushing is for high school kids, I tell myself. But I've always caved to my emotions. "What are you doing here?" A grin controls every muscle of the expression *I'm* trying to control. I run a hand over my chin. "I don't mean to sound rude. I'm ... I can't believe it's you, Zoe." Am I dreaming, or did Zoe Channing just walk back into my life?

I study her. "You look gorgeous, as I remember but ... there's something slightly different." I say, unable to tear my stare from hers.

"I had an involuntary nose job." A grin slides across her tempting lips. "Only an artist could detect, I guess." She giggles.

"Yeah, your hair is longer too. Maybe your nose is a bit different, but your eyes, nah, those eyes will never change." Zoe is exquisitely-crafted. She's been the object of every piece of art I've painted since the first day I set eyes on her.

"What happ ..." I begin to ask then remember how fragile she was that night. Give her time, Jesse. Give yourself time.

I shove my hands into the pockets of my jeans. "How's life been treating you?"

"I've been good," her smile is small, her voice soft, "and not so good." She shrugs. "That's life, I guess. It's really good to see you, Jesse." Her stare devours me and every nerve in my body screams. The butterflies in my stomach are killing me.

There's so much going on behind those killer blue eyes. *What is it, Zoe? Talk to me.*

There's something intimate about her tone when she says my name, and I fight off a tremble. Like a jolt of electricity, realization hits me again; holy shit, it's Zoe Channing.

Does she notice? Chill, bro. You haven't acted ... felt this way since you were a dumbass kid. You've been through your share of girls, hot girls, older women, but what's different here? It's Zoe. She's the difference. Different. Holy Christ ... it's Zoe!

"Yep. Still painting. Exhibiting now." My heart is in my throat, throbbing; it's difficult to concentrate, no less speak. I want to forget the world, take her in my arms, finish what we started, but is she the same girl? Would she knee me in the balls if I approached?

"In a gallery?" Surprise in her voice reaches her eyes.

Nodding, I pull my hands from my pockets and cross my arms over my chest.

"That's amazing." She blinks a few times and kind of stammers. "No. I don't mean amazing as in surprised you did it. I mean, I always knew you were a terrific artist…" her voice trails off. Her cheeks get pink; she bites her bottom lip. Thank you, Universe, she hasn't changed. Warmth floods my body, confirming I'm still hung up on this girl. She's magic and doesn't even know it, that's the best part.

"Yep. Avacados Mullins will host my first show."

She looks unsettled, so I motion to the sitting area. "Want to sit down? How about a cup of coffee? I have a Keurig in the back. Or would you prefer something cold?" Her lack of response is unsettling, bringing me crashing to earth. "So you never answered me." I'm casual, backing up I curl a shoulder against the wall. Look cool, idiot.

Crap, my freaking confusion has confused her. "What?" she says. When she tilts her head, her glistening hair floods her shoulders. One side is tucked behind an ear, the other is braided, kind of like she wore onstage. In sunlight, her earring sparkles, like her eyes.

"What are you doing here?" I chuckle. "Tattoo?" I motion to one of the recliners stationed across the room. "If it's your first time," I say this as though it has a double meaning. I'm such a jerk sometimes. "Don't worry. It doesn't hurt." I give her a goofy grin.

She looks arrogant now, and lifts the strap of her top, exposing what looks like the tail of a bird. "You wouldn't be my first," she quips. "And I didn't come for a tatt, I came about the job." She lifts her chin. "Are you the boss?"

I belt out a laugh. "Kind of. More like the all-around everything, stock the shelves, meet and greet, schedule appointments, tattoo artist dude."

"Like in school," she cuts in, then looks remorseful. "Artist dude, I mean," she giggles the words.

"Actually–" I'm interrupted by the ringtone of my cell. "Excuse me. I have to take this." The last thing I want to do is pull my eyes away, but Dee is calling, asking how the day is going. "Okay. No problem. Nope. No more appointments today. I can close up. Oh, and there's someone here for the reception job. Yeah, very qualified. Sure, I can handle it."

She looks at me questioningly. "Is that your boss? Should I fill out an application?"

"Zoe, you don't need to fill out anything. You've got the job." Neither of us have moved, other than Zoe who is twisting a lock of hair around her finger. I stifle a laugh because we're so stiff, tossing our voices across the room, each afraid to approach or offend.

"We have a lot of catching up to do," I check the wall clock, "over dinner?" I cock my head, hoping she's unattached.

Zoe

"Nothing fancy," I reply to Jesse when he asks where I'd like to have dinner. "I had a late lunch." I don't mention I doubt my stomach could hold much food with all the twists and turns it's doing around the horde of butterflies on the rise. I'm not thinking anything along the lines of this being a date. It's strictly business. Omagosh, I can't believe I'm with Jesse!

"Plus, I'm not really dressed..." I add, clicking my tongue. "Maybe just a slice of pizza–"

"You'd dress up any place, just the way you are," he says and I almost melt on the spot. "No pizza. This is a celebration."

He wants to catch up. Celebrate? My heart thunders. What would be the possibility of picking up where we left off? Is he with someone? Would he ask me to dinner if he was? My head is spinning with questions, possibilities, concerns.

I sit on the tan bench, perfectly poised, pretending to flip through the book of artwork as Jesse rushes around preparing to close the salon. But my mind isn't on the art, it's on Jesse, and I watch his every move.

"Sorry for the wait. There's a great pub not too far from here."

Standing beside me, hands on hips he gazes down at me expectantly. "The best steak blackened with Cajun spices. Are you up for a walk?"

I'm up for anything. "Sure," I say, gracefully lifting my body, following him across the room. "Sounds yummy."

He holds the door and tugs my braid as I slip by.

"I couldn't resist that," as he locks the door he smiles, "your hair got so long. It's been so long…"

"You let yours grow too, and you've got a bit of a beard thing going," I scrunch my mouth, a movement I know deepens my dimples, and let the tip of my finger tap his chin.

Crossing the street, he takes my hand. "Beautiful sunset."

"Let me guess. You'll paint it the minute you get home," I tease.

Our locked hands swing, and he lifts his face to the sky, laughing. "I could wallpaper my entire house with my sunsets."

He frees my hand to hook his arm through mine as we stroll along the sidewalk.

"Feels a bit warmer tonight. I was thinking summer was over. I'm not looking forward to winter." I frown.

His arm slides around my waist and he tugs me close. "Me either. Ever hear of SAD?"

"I've experienced it." Watching the precise timing of our footsteps, I think of my envy the day he guided Claudette across the street on their way to school, so close and intimate; never dreaming one day the girl would be me.

He's the same Jesse, every bit as handsome, polite, compassionate, not to mention charming.

"Nightingale is pretty classy. Artsy. You decorated inside and out." I smile up at him, heady by his ocean scent. My arm winds around his hips, aligning with his.

"How do you know that?" He gives me a tantalizing grin; teeth so white, eyes rich with brown and gold.

"I remember the magic you worked on the school stage." I'm mesmerized, but my words flow easily.

His arm tightens. "You were the magic. Not me."

Jesse stops before Toddy's Pub. He holds the door and we enter.

A girl escorts us to a booth. We sit. We stare. Sitting face to face, without much space between us, threatens our intimacy with awkwardness. I have a feeling we struggle with similar emotions; we'd rather be sharing one bench, side by side, rather than sitting across from each other, hands folded in our laps.

After ordering, Jesse reaches over to clutch my hand. His thumb runs up and down from my fingers to my wrist.

"Before we discuss the job, there are some things we should talk about." He shoots me a questioning look. "Personal things."

I have a feeling I know where this is going and for a moment want to get up and run, but I don't. I fall into his eyes.

I nod. "What did you have in mind?"

When he chuckles, his grin is so sexy. "You don't ever want to ask a guy that question."

I think of Denny Brisk who once said that to me. I miss him. But not as much as I missed Jesse, and certainly not in the same way.

I inhale a deep breath and exhale a sigh.

Jesse tilts his head, caressing my fingers. "Did I say something wrong?"

"No. Someone else once said that to me," I whisper and his grin fades. Releasing my hand, he clears his throat as though to indicate: *let's get down to business.*

But a moment later, my hand is back in his, his grip firmer.

"What happened that night, Zoe? It's been haunting me forever–" Leaning forward, his abs press the table.

I lower my eyes, tighten my lips. My eyes avoid his.

"If you don't want to talk about it, I understand, but." When

I raise my head, he looks pained. "Why did you disappear without a word?"

He looks shy, hesitant to be gushing emotion but doing it anyway. I'm starting to think I'm not the only one about to lose control.

I blink my eyes that burn. "No one showed at the hospital except Dee, right before I was discharged. I didn't think anyone knew I was missing." Liar. You didn't care, and if someone showed up, you'd have sent him or her away. Even Jesse.

"And you haven't spoken to her since." He frowns.

I shake my head.

"I tried to find you."

"You did?"

He nods. "I called every hospital within a fifty mile radius, Zoe." Jesse's eyes cloud. "And when I finally found you, security wouldn't let me up to see you. I almost had a fight with a guard." He's breathless. His grip tightens on my fingers.

With my free hand, I push my hair behind my ear, avoiding his eyes. "I'm sorry if I upset everyone."

"Don't be sorry. I'm sure you did nothing wrong."

He should know ... I blow out a sigh.

"It's been a long time. It's so good to see you." His hands fondle mine.

My gaze seeks his. "I never figured we'd meet up again."

"I never thought I'd be this lucky." His eyes reveal sincerity. "So what has Falcon Channing been up to?" He smiles.

I touch one heated cheek. "How do you know about that?" The thought he might have seen the other side of me makes me shudder.

"You've been all over the Internet, the radio. I heard you, Zoe. Singing with your band. You got what you wanted." He draws a breath. "Right?

I take my hands back, running my palms up and down my

bare arms.

"I thought I did, for a while. But sometimes dreams turn out to be nightmares."

"Ouch," he grimaces, "was being a rock star that bad?"

"No. Yeah, not really what one might wish for, or expect." I sip the wine our waiter has set down. "It wasn't my band. I ... we ... It belonged to this guy, Richie Santana, but it's a long story." I shiver. "Maybe I'll write a book some day."

"I'd like to read it." His gaze intensifies.

"I can tell you this. Chasing Dinero is no more. But the other guys started another band. The Next Life."

He lifts his goblet of wine, emptying it. "You didn't want to stay with them?"

"I'm starting college soon." I'm vague. Less is best, I tell myself.

"Yeah. You said on the phone." His nod says he expects me to elaborate.

My bridged fingers support my chin. "I'll be studying law."

"Aww. No singing?" He makes a fake pout and fills his goblet with wine. When he lifts the bottle, I watch the definition of muscles in his forearm.

"Maybe in the shower." I shrug.

"Or in the rain."

We both laugh

"How about you? Did you finish art school?" When I strain toward him, my ribs hit the table's edge.

Actually, he clears his throat. "Dee cornered me to sign up with her. Sign in blood is more like it." He chuckles.

At the sound of Dee's name, I feel every muscle in my body tighten. "What do you mean?"

"She owns Nightingale." He cuts into his steak.

"I thought it was yours." My head jerks back.

"We're partners I guess ... on her dime." He frowns. "You

still want the job, right? I think you'd be perfect—"

"Who named it?" I reach for his arm, running a finger up his coiling artwork. "No bird tattoos. Love your Aztec designs, though."

His grin spreads. "Guilty," he says. I swear his cheeks turn pink.

"Dinner was delicious. Thank you," I say, sliding from the booth.

"The company made the meal." Jesse stands and stretches; his t-shirt molds to his muscular chest. He reaches into the back pocket of his perfectly fitting jeans, removing bills from his wallet.

"I'm happy we connected again," he says, and after a long pause, he runs a hand through his hair, while his other lands on his hip. "I know we can't pick up where we left off, but I'd like to see you again," he jams his hands into his pockets, "outside of work."

The expression on his face, electricity spilling from the warmth of his earthy eyes, surrounds me like an embrace. The past comes tumbling back and my legs feel like jelly. Standing before me is the one and only guy I've ever cared about. Truly cared about. I want to run to him, fall into his arms. Tell him how many times I've thought about him over the years. But I freeze. I feel naked, unable to bare my soul.

Finding You

Jesse

I suggest Toddy's Pub and Zoe agrees. She's as easygoing as I remember. Sweet. Gentle. Accommodating. Although I have a feeling her mood can change on a dime if provoked, which I am determined will never happen.

Over a dinner of steaks and wine, we begin to catch up.

"Not that it's my business, but what went on between you and Dee? You were tight in school," I say between mouthfuls.

Dropping her fork, Zoe bites her lip and frowns. "Nothing really."

I'm ready for the silent treatment, but after a moment, she continues speaking as she pushes food around her plate.

"It was mostly my fault. You know about the accident, right? That my parents died?" The sorrow in her eyes and voice break my heart.

"Yes I heard. I'm so sorry, Zoe." I push my plate aside.

"Dee waited so long to come and see me, and then all she talked about was Trent's party and Zack Benefield. She was wearing his ring. And I was grief-stricken. Upset that no one else cared enough to want to see me."

I watch emotion seize her eyes, ranging from accusatory to resignation. Then her lids lower to mask it all. She plays with the edge of her napkin, folding it into a triangle.

"And neither of you tried to contact the other after that?"

"No." Her sigh seems to carry the weight of the world. What the hell happened to this girl? What horror has she been through?

I almost leap across the table trying to console her, to explain. "I tried to find you. I called every hospital until I located you. And I came the next day, Zoe. I came to see you but security wouldn't let me up to your room." Reliving that day, my jaw tightens. "They said family only."

Her eyes soften. Unless I'm mistaken, they fill with satisfaction, maybe relief.

I reach for her hand, massage it with mine. When I roll her fingers, I notice the scar creeping from her wrist up her forearm. *Don't tell me.*

"What's this?" Controlling my voice isn't easy. At the thought she might have tried to take her own life, my heart sinks.

She arches her lips into a scowl. "Another one of my mistakes."

My brows lift. "Mistakes aren't all that bad, Zoe, as long as we learn from them." Hoping for some sort of explanation, I study her.

"Learn maybe, but can we learn to live with them?" There's something behind her whisper, a guardedness, remorse maybe.

I let my eyes narrow, but only slightly. "You didn't try to … you didn't cut–"

She recoils, her voice escalates. "God, no. I'd never try to kill myself, not intentionally anyway." Her chuckle hangs in her throat. "I *do* want to see my parents again someday."

"That's heavy." I shake my head, feeling inadequate. "I don't know what to say."

"You don't have to say anything." Her hand comes down on

mine and she smiles. "I survived two near fatal accidents, Jesse." Her lips purse. "And the only scar I have is this. Amazing, isn't it? I guess there's a reason I'm still here, you think?" She runs a finger over my Aztec ink sleeve.

I squeeze her hand. "I know." I study her eyes, wishing they'd sparkle softly. "I hate to bring this up again, but if you're going to work at Nightingale, you need to hash things out with Dee."

"Why?" Perturbed, she gives me a shoulder jerk and tosses her hair back.

"She's the owner." For as sweet as she is, Zoe is stubborn as hell. I want to wrap that hair around my fist, drag her over the table, and kiss her pouting lips until neither one of us can breathe, or move because we're paralyzed with lust and love and every fucking beautiful emotion I've felt since she walked back into my life.

"Thank you for dinner," she says, dismissing me. The evening. I hope not us.

Her mouth is drawn to one side, as if she's chewing the inside of her cheek. My mouth is taut. She's blown ever erotic image from my brain and I'm worried. We slide from the booth, and as she walks slightly ahead of me, my eyes coast over her. Her tattooed shoulders are killer, her ass is perfect, her legs athletic. Christ, she's amazing.

We pause on the sidewalk, Zoe intentionally glancing across the street; me thinking of how to cautiously end this night, not wanting to end this night.

My hand makes a smooth move to her shoulder. "It's early. Would you like to grab a drink?"

She bites her lip. Her eyes search mine. I get the feeling she's struggling too.

Flashing her dimples, she gazes up at me. "There's a comedy at the Alto."

"I'm down for that."

A movie was a fantastic idea; it's a reprieve from talking. We sit in the theatre, my arm goes around the seatback, we watch the movie and we laugh.

"How about some popcorn?" I ask, halfway through.

Her lips touch my ear and my body responds with a jolt I hope she hasn't felt; let's put it this way; I hope she feels her own jolts and not mine. "A soda?" she says.

"The Cajun, huh?" I chuckle. "Me too. I'll be back in a flash."

The movie ends and I'm no closer to holding her, kissing her the way I've been dying to.

"My car's parked at the salon." We begin to walk, and our clutched hands swing loosely. "I'll drive you home."

"No, that's okay," she says all too quickly.

To me, this raises a red flag; she doesn't want me to know where she lives. Is some dude waiting for her at her place? Some innocent guy who doesn't know his girl is out with an old flame. Am I an old flame? Or just the one who offered her a job. It's been years; she must have hooked up with other dudes. Come on, Jesse. What makes you think she's all yours? My gut tightens. My animal side wants to kick ass clear across the country.

"Look. If you're afraid your boyfriend will be pissed, you can tell him I'm just an old friend doing you a favor by giving you a job and buying you dinner to seal the deal."

"How dare you?" Her head snaps back. "Is that what you think I'm doing? Cheating on my boyfriend? Using you?" She yanks her hand from mine. Before I can reply, she turns on her heels and is heading down the street, double-time.

No, not again, my mind screams. "Hold up," I call out, jogging before her to slow her pace. "I'm sorry. I didn't mean … I think only the best of you, Zoe. You have to understand my position. I feel like we're back there … but we're not. I knew you then, do I know you now?" I'm so confused, I'm stammering.

I've made a dent in her hard stare, but she continues to walk. At least at a slower pace.

"It's been so long. So much has happened. I'm raw, Jesse."

"Come on Zoe." Heart in throat, I walk in reverse to face her. "Do you want to talk about it?"

Mouth grim, she shakes her head. Her lips are sealed, indignant, determined.

"Let me drive you home." My palm levels on her shoulder, attempting to draw her to a halt.

She shakes me off, which pisses me off. Her words are curt, cutting. "Really, it's okay. I'd rather take the bus. I need time, Jesse."

Wow, rather take the bus? Did I just get slammed? Should I be the one to turn on heel and get the fuck outta here while there's still time?

"I understand," I say, not truly understanding. Now that we've reconnected, I don't want to risk losing her again, so these fucking heels are firmly implanted on this fucking sidewalk. "I really *don't* understand, Zoe." Coming to an abrupt halt before her, our bodies collide. "We're not kids anymore."

"I know that." She attempts to circumvent my embrace. "What's there to say?"

"We need to talk." My harshness is not intentional, but Zoe is driving me to the edge.

Without another thought, I trap her in my arms and back her against the brick wall beside us. With a grunt she releases a breath. I'm not sure if it's a result of me imposing my will or pure exasperation on her part because I'm physically stronger. Physically is the keyword. Emotionally? I'm not sure.

The sun has set and there's pale light where we stand. A breeze ruffles her hair, blowing strands across her face, flooding me with her floral essence. With the appearance of a mad woman, yes a very angry young woman, she's frightening. Can I restrain her long enough to break through this wall she's built between us?

I crush her to my chest and four years are erased. We're at Trent's party. She's in my arms. We're struggling to find ourselves. And I'm no closer to figuring out what's tearing this beautiful girl apart now as I was then. It's taken what feels like an eternity, but she's here and I'm not giving up.

For a moment she struggles, reversing herself while trying to wiggle from my hold, but this time I refuse to release her. "Zoe. Stop it, Zoe. I don't want to hurt you. I just want to help."

"Let me go," she growls.

"No." I rasp. "I won't let you go. Not again. You have to stop running. Face whatever it is. I'm here. I want you ... I want to help you."

My words have no impact. The more she struggles, the tighter my arms fold. The back of her head slams my chest, again and again, and I feel the hitch of her breath. My chin rests on the top of her head; her sweet fragrance is overpowering. "Zoe," I whisper into her hair, desperate to reach her. "Please, babe. Don't go. Not this way."

I hear a gasp, her body goes limp, and her arms reach up to hook behind my neck. Her face lifts, tilts, bringing us cheek to cheek. He blue eyes stare, as though waiting to capture my next move. I'm mindless, I'm craving, I'm taking a risk I've never thought I was capable of. I spin her, pin her so she can't escape my arms, the wall behind us, and when my lips sink onto hers, my eyes remain open. I want to capture this moment, her face during the onset of bliss, the warmth of her body yielding shamelessly to mine.

I run my fingers through her hair: soft, honey, flowers. The tips of our tongues meet, then in a frenzied reaction, we're locked in passion. I touch, she claws. I groan, she moans. Her lips are mine; my breath is hers. We're no longer separated by our past, our bodies, or our souls. We're one hungry entity indulging in the lust of silver moonlight.

Zoe

My mind races. My first impulse is to rip his heart out. Jesse has accused me of being a slut, not in so many words, but that's how I feel. I want to hit him, hurt him as he's just done to me. Doesn't he realize I have scars? I yank my hand from his and I bolt.

His voice echoes from behind. His breath is fast, his words muffled from his pace. "Hold on Zoe," he attempts to pull me to his side, but my feet keep moving. He stumbles into a frenzied backward step, trying to face me, reason with me. But there's no reasoning with a wild woman.

I'm outraged, crushed, ready to tear into him. But the look on his face is nothing short of heartrending. So is his tone. "Talk to me," he pleads. "Don't leave like this."

What am I doing to him? I stop dead in my tracks and I stare, ready to explain. Before I can utter a word, he yanks me into his arms, backs me toward the building behind us. I panic; attempting to free myself, I whirl, but his arms, his arms around my waist are like steel. He's panting, his breath warming the back of my neck. I feel his lips touch my hair. I think he's kissing my hair. Dear God, what am I doing?

Moonlight is silver; the night is pitch black; shadows dance around us. No, the shadows don't dance, my heart is in my eyes when I look at Jesse. Here we stand and the years roll back. Jesse's touch is no longer gentle, he's demanding. His strong arms pin me to the wall, his face so close I'm suddenly trapped inside one of my wildest dreams.

I like his dominance; my freedom to accept or reject. Every element needed for a passionate bond is right here flowing like electricity between us: attraction, compassion, torturous lust. He's everything a girl could want and the thought that he truly wants *me*, turns me into a mindless, fragile wreck.

I tip my face up to his so I can see him, taste his breath on my cheek, watch desire flood his eyes. Pain; pain and desire, so sensual. He's driving me crazier than a human mind can stand and I'm about to break in two. My head spinning, my body falling, I go limp in his arms.

"I'm sorry," I whisper. But my words are lost as I'm spun in his arms, dragged into his chest, wrapped so tightly I can barely breathe. Or am I suffocating with the need for him. I want you, Jesse. I want to tell him, but my lips are sealed by his, and I can't stop the moan that escapes from my mouth into his.

Finding You

Jesse

My hands on her back are greedy, longing to roam. If we don't stop now, I might not be able to. And making love on a dimly lit street on the outskirts of town is enticing, but wouldn't go over big with passersby, or the cops, should they happen by. "Let's go someplace," I whisper, then bury my lips in the hollow behind her ear.

"To do what?" she pants, her lips sliding to my neck.

"We need to talk. Nothing else. I wouldn't expect…" Short of breath, my heart is pounding.

"Where?" she rasps, and I feel her tremble against my chest.

I've caused the hoarseness in her voice and the reality of tasting every inch of Zoe is enough to make me lose my mind. My fingers tighten, exploring every muscle in her back, her shoulders, her arms, her abs. My touch pauses just beneath the curve of her breasts. "My place," I moan, entirely disoriented. Then it hits me. We can't. Claudette. Fuck.

"Your house?" Zoe stiffens in my arms.

"We can sit in my car." I tilt her face, kiss the tip of her nose. The setting couldn't be more beautiful if I'd painted it from is a patchwork of shadows.

Dangerously, my palms skim her breasts, land on her shoulders. She sucks in a breath. My fingers slide to her wrists, which I bring up and around my neck, locking them tightly.

My palms coast down her body, feeling every curve, lingering on her hips. Then hungrily, my arms encircle her waist, and she buries her face in my chest.

There's no way I can stop the rapid pace of my heart, which is a dead giveaway that I'm falling hard into a place from which I'll never be able to escape. Not after our past. Certainly not after tonight. Every part of my body needs her. I want her … in my life. Forever.

Her hands coast from my neck, travel up and down my back, caressing; she tips her face up, her gaze so persuasive I can barely swallow, no less breathe.

My lips test hers slowly, gently. I draw back to watch a smile form on the beautiful place I have just touched. Her smile fades, her lips part, and our mouths are greedy, tongues wrapping. The burst of adrenaline is distressing, for in a moment it's over, and Zoe moans as our lips peel apart.

My body's responding so wildly, it's painful to stand. "Let's go." I kiss the words into her ear.

In moonlight, hand in hand we walk back to the salon. My car is parked behind the building. The atmosphere is colorless: Dark. Isolated. Tempting.

I unlock the Stang and open the door for her.

Zoe's hand skates over the smooth red paint, then she tucks herself into the bucket seat, stashing her bag on the floor.

I climb onto the driver's seat, and Zoe draws her legs to the side, angling her body toward me.

I slide the key into the ignition. "Radio?"

She shakes her head. "Unless you want to."

My fingers leave the keys to rest on the wheel, where they tap.

The moon either hides behind clouds or surrounding buildings. But for one lamppost across the yard, our surroundings are ashen.

I stare through the static-gray interior, where Zoe is little more than a silhouette, enticing nonetheless.

My mind's on high alert. There's so much I want to know, say, do.

"I didn't mean to upset you, Zoe. I just don't understand you. You have to admit, we have chemistry. History. Why do you keep putting distance between us?" I feel the rise of the threatening wall I had hoped to break through. I refuse to let her silence, or the wall, separate us.

She's small, but even shaded, not at all a child. The slope of her breasts are accented by the top she wears, and the cleavage I tried to avoid over dinner, my eyes can now devour. I long to touch her, bury my lips between the softness of her breasts, permit my fingers to graze every inch of her creamy skin. I want to undress her. Make love to her like no other man ever could. Christ, this is torture.

The movement of her hand tells me she's twisting a lock of her hair. I want to take her in my arms. Let my lips warm hers that had earlier trembled.

I hit a button and a soft interior light brightens her face.

"I don't understand me either," she sighs the words, snapping me from my dream-state. Her eyes glisten with tears. "That's been the problem since..."

Her full pink lips open, then close.

"Don't shut me out," I whisper. "What's going on inside here?" I reach toward her chest, but only a finger brushes her heart. "Is this the place your secrets hide?" My finger goes to her forehead. "Or are they here?" I gently swipe.

Taking my hand, she latches on to my fingers. "I've never felt so shut out of life," she groans. "And my heart? My heart feels broken, Jesse."

She's breaking mine. Here we sit, so close, so far. "I want you in my life. How can I get through to you? Make you believe that you can trust me. I won't hurt you," my soft touch combs through her hair and I take her face in my palms, "I … I wouldn't ever do anything to hurt you, baby."

"I believe you," she whispers. "It's just not easy for me to trust."

"There's something very wrong." My tone is hushed.

"What?" she breathes the question with alarm.

I roll my seat back as far as it will go on the tracks. "You're too far away. Come here." Gripping her arm, I urge her closer, lift her up and over the console and set her onto my lap. Big mistake. I haven't even recovered and I'm instantly reignited.

Her arms go around my neck; my arms wind around her waist. Our legs slide, tangle, settle.

Straining against me, she buries her lips at the base of my neck, murmuring, "I'm sorry."

I free her hair from the side of her face. Run a fingertip around her ear. "Don't keep apologizing." My lips trace the places my finger has skimmed. "You're flawless. Faultless. Whatever it is, babe, you have to let it go."

When she lifts her head, her cheek brushes mine. "I'm trying, but some things latch on … get buried inside like a sickness. Do you know what I mean?"

Talk about latching on and sickness, I think back to the days of Kirby and ending up in the slammer, and pregnant Claudette; my life has been one calamity after another, which causes an involuntary chuckle.

"What's so funny?" she's indignant. "I was serious–"

For a soothing moment, I capture her lips with mine, then

explain, "I know, Zoe. So am I." My fingers sift through her hair, and the fragrance of flowers and honey engulfs me. "I was just thinking of something very stupid I did once. We all have our moments. Our demons to fight. Our mistakes."

"I can't picture you making mistakes." Her blue eyes sparkle with interest.

I laugh. "You'd be surprised." I think of Claudette, who is home waiting for me, ready to complain about 24/7 morning sickness as she does each time I walk through the door. I know the time will come when I drag Zoe home with me. Yes, the caveman inside has spoken. Presumptuous, right? Inevitable, definitely. Do I tell her about Claudette?

"You're quiet all of a sudden." She presses a finger to my forehead. "What's going on in there?"

"Eh, I'm just thinking about airing dirty laundry."

She laughs and presses a fist to my abs.

"I'm serious," I chuckle, moving her fist to my lips. Opening her hand, I nibble each finger. "I promised to do the sheets and towels for the salon. Which reminds me, it's getting late. Not that I ever want this evening to end, but…"

She massages my shoulders and her hands on my body feel so damn good. "We should get going then." She sighs.

Growling, I nibble her ear. "Do you plan on working tomorrow?"

She giggles and squirms. The giggle is cute. The squirm could set off something I've been trying to restrain since I pulled her onto my lap.

"What time?" She stifles a yawn.

I graze her neck with my teeth. "See. You're tired just thinking about it. Don't worry. We won't chase your cute little butt around. That honor is reserved for me."

"She cracks the whip, huh? Like backstage at school?" In dimness, her eyes flash.

"Yeah," I sigh, "those were the days, huh? The play sucked without you."

She groans and buries her face in my shoulder, where her words are muffled. "Oh God, Jesse. It was a terrible time."

"I dropped by school to set things up, but honestly, I split almost immediately because there was no way I could watch that play without you."

When she lifts her face, her cheeks are wet. "I had no idea at the time. Maybe ... maybe things could have been different." As though someone's flipped a switch, her mood changes; she giggles. "I had such a crush on you."

"Had?" I lift her chin.

Her eyes lower; her palms sweep circles on my chest. "We were talking about work, remember?"

"Sure. Cut me off just when it's getting good." I dig my fingers into her ribcage and her screech hits my ear while her ass grazes my wood. I stare at her with awe. "I guess you don't realize you're killing me."

She rubs my ear. "Oh, I screamed in your ear. Sorry." Her bottom lip turns down.

"Yeah, my ear, right." I chuckle. "We open at nine, but you can come in at ten."

"No preferential treatment for this employee," she's smug, "I'll be there at nine, and don't tell Dee. I want to see her jaw-dropping holy shit I just saw a ghost expression when I walk through the door."

As she climbs back into her own seat, I can't help but notice how the curve of her butt fits perfectly into my palms.

I start the engine and reach for the gearshift. "I'll drive you home."

"Uh uh. I'll take the bus," she says, adjusting her skirt, which has managed to slide almost to her hips, making my cool not easy to keep.

"Geeze, I thought we'd gotten past that." I sigh and shift into reverse. "Okay. You win. I respect your wishes because I'm a gentleman."

"Yes you are." She taps my hand and flips the radio on.

"But can I at least drive you to the bus stop?"

"You never give up, do you?" The shake of her head tosses her hair.

"Nope."

What I don't say is, fuck the bus stop, I want to take you home with me.

Zoe

I love being in Jesse's arms. I could stay here forever. His breath on my neck is seductive, comforting. When the time comes, I want to die in his arms, if this makes sense. Being so close to Jesse is like some kind of miracle, promising there could be life after death.

After the movie, after what could have been a horrible end to a beautiful evening, we sit in Jesse's car, where he pulls me onto his lap. My arms encircle his thick, muscular neck. The scent of his cologne could send me into orbit. Clean, fresh outdoors.

I brush his cheek with mine. I want his lips, his mind, I want everything.

"What's going on inside there?" His finger gently taps my chest, where he mistakes my breast for my heart. His accidental brush sends a thrill careening through me. Talk Zoe. Give him what his eyes have been searching for all night.

"To set the record straight, Jesse, I don't live with anyone. I don't have a boyfriend. I left all thoughts of that behind. That night."

"Why did you leave without word? Not come back to school?" When he asks, he holds me protectively.

"After the accident, I had no one. I had to move. I have no family, just an aunt and cousins." My laugh is the old me, harsh, and Jesse's head snaps back.

"Was it that bad? Not the comfort you needed?" His voice hardens. "Christ. I wish I'd have known. I wanted to be there for you."

I drop my lips onto his cheek. "Don't feel bad. You had no way of knowing."

My laugh is hollow. "My cousins," I roll my eyes, "they were misfits. It was a crazy couple of years, but I made it."

He squeezes me so hard, he forces the air from my lungs.

"Life has a way of taking you places you'd never thought you'd end up," he says. "But you're in the right place now. Here in my arms. In my heart."

"Oh Jesse," I whisper. "You settle the anguish inside me."

I feel the crush of his lips on my neck. "You brought me home."

Jesse

I leave my house lugging a plastic bag overstuffed with linens, bleached, dried and folded. My body aches from lack of sleep, aches with the want of Zoe. Last night was amazing. So amazing, I laid awake for hours after my head finally hit the pillow, remembering, imagining. By the time my lids slid down, stars were falling from the sky. This I saw as I gazed out the window, with dawn approaching, while thinking of Zoe. It's always been Zoe. Why did I even bother to wander these past few years? Had I known she'd return, I'd have stayed asleep, sparing myself the agony, headaches, my brother, Jamie.

I hoist the bag of laundry onto the back seat of the Stang and drive through early morning traffic to Nightingale. I consider stopping for donuts, then check the time. No donuts and coffee this morning. I park behind the building, in my usual space, wondering … hoping Zoe will show. Exactly how she'll arrive … I shrug, figuring she'll take the bus. I shake my head, struggling to figure her fascination with the public transportation.

Passing through the alley to the entrance, I check out the sky. A cloudless, glorious blue. The sun is rising, but has not yet reached the rooftops. Still, its warmth is evidence of a late summer day I could spend at the lake: fishing, lazing, jogging. All with Zoe at my side, of course. We'll do so much together, make up for lost time. The world is ours.

I shift the bag to my pitched hip, reaching for the door handle imprinted by Zoe's delicate fingers. The brass she'll touch again today. Adrenaline rushes through my body with a tingling heat.

"You're late," Dee's rasp rings out the moment my feet hit the floor. Either she's coming down with a cold, or she's been up most of the night smoking and her throat is scratchy. The latter is most probable.

Dropping the bag on a recliner, I check the wall clock, then my phone. "Your clock is wrong. I'm early." I tote the linens to the back room and slam them onto Dee's desk. "You're welcome," I yell because she hasn't followed me from her place behind the counter, checking our schedules on the computer as she does every morning.

After a moment or two, she pokes her head around the doorway. "For what?" She sounds like a grouchy old drunk.

Pointing to her desk, I smirk. "There's your clean laundry. Where's my coffee?"

"No Keurig today. It's on the fritz," she grunts, covering her blue-jeaned thighs with a yank of her loose-fitting top.

"If you weren't such a horrible boss, I would've stopped off for donuts. You should have texted me the Keurig was down and I could have brought some coffee."

"Eh. I'll run to the deli later." She stifles a yawn. Her hair hangs loose, thick and wavy, down to her waist.

"Rushed morning, huh?" I grin. "No braids."

She rolls her eyes, turns and backs into me. "I can barely lift my arms. Do it for me."

"What's wrong with your arms?"

"Painting the apartment. My muscles are sore as a

mothafucker."

"So braid and massage?" I say, wrapping long skeins of hair into a loose braid.

"Clip." I hold my hand out. "There, you're done."

"What about my massage?"

"What about the laundry?"

She ruffles my hair. "Thanks, Jesse. You saved me a trip to the laundromat. Being without a washing machine is hell, you know that?"

"When's the repairman coming–"

The entry door chimes, interrupting our conversation. My heart speeds up. Not only can't I wait to see Zoe again, I'm dying to see Dee's *jaw-dropping* reaction.

I run a hand through my hair which Dee has just tousled. "I'll get it."

As I whiz past, she says, "Must be some important client. I've never seen you move so fast. Or look so neat." She refers to my pressed button-down and wrinkle-free jeans.

Zoe stands in the middle of the room, wearing cutoffs and a pink, rhinestone embellished tank top, stealing my breath before I can reach her.

"Hey," she says, her smile bright. Her lips are as pink as her top, and enticingly glossy.

I recover enough to hitch my head in the direction of the back room, where Dee is putting towels and sheets into cabinets, I assume. "She's in her office," I mouth. Striding up to her, I drop a kiss on her forehead. "Right on time." I grin. "I'm happy to see you." I can't resist teasing, "That bus keeps a mean schedule."

Pulling her lips to one side, she rolls her eyes. "Yup. My ride is righteous." Her jaw clenches. "I'm nervous, Jesse." Her deep inhale lifts her chest. She still wears her silver Z suspended on a chain.

I give her an encouraging, one-arm hug. I'd rather not have

Dee walk in and find us in a passionate embrace. It might kill her, I muse. "No worries, Zoe. It'll all work out." My fingers glide down a shank of her gleaming hair. Looks like satin, feels like silk. This girl is killing me. "Dee hasn't really changed. She's still the same grumpy know-it-all." I wink. After devouring her cleavage, my gaze sticks to her lips. "Nice lipstick." I grin. "I'd love to taste it."

Giggling, Zoe stands on her toes and purses her lips, offering me her amazing mouth. Before my lips have a chance to drop, we're rudely interrupted.

From somewhere behind me a scream erupts, followed by Dee's bellow, "What? Oh my God. No way. Zoe?"

For a moment I watch Zoe's jaw go slack, and whip around in time to see Dee give her the 'holy shit jaw-dropping I just saw a ghost expression' or whatever it was Zoe had eluded to last night, in my car, in my arms. I can't shake the feeling of Zoe crushed to my chest. My inability to drag last night into this morning is killing me.

How we'll work together, keep our hands off one another, isn't going to be easy. "I'll taste it later," I whisper into her ear before Dee flies across the room.

The phone rings, and I jump behind the counter, leaving the girls to do their thing. One ear listens to a client, while the other tunes in to the shock in Dee's voice.

"I think I'm going to faint." In her classic display of drama, Dee throws an arm over her forehead before launching herself at Zoe.

"Don't do it until you give me a hug," Zoe says, spreading her arms in welcome.

Concentrating on booking appointments isn't easy. I hope I haven't overbooked, or deleted, or did Christ knows what. I want to throw the damn phone out the window. As soon as it stops ringing, I turn my full attention on the girls.

They're glued together, petite Zoe dwarfed by Dee's generous frame. I hear muffled words, a few sobs, chattering, finally giggling.

"Jesse!" Dee shrieks. "Look who's here for the job!"

Coming out from behind the counter, I throw my arms out for a three-way pile-up. "Look who hired her."

Dee lifts her head, her eyes swimming with tears. "You shit. When did this happen? Why didn't you tell me?" She slams my gut with a fist. "Jerk."

When Zoe giggles her entire face smiles. "It's my fault. I wanted to surprise you."

"Surprise me? You almost gave me a heart attack." Dee's arms flail as she talks. "I just about gave up on ever hearing from you again. If not for YouTube, I would've freaked out months ago."

Zoe's lips twitch, then she smiles.

"This calls for a celebration," Dee says. "How booked are we, Jess? Maybe close early. Get some dinner. Booze."

"We celebrated last night," Zoe replies to Dee, but she shoots me a dimpled grin.

"You?" Dee's gaze swings from Zoe to me. "And Jesse? You two finally got together? Without me?" Her pout is interrupted when she sputters, "You forgive me, right Zoe? Hold no grudges." She shoots her a tooth-clenching smile. "I didn't mean to act coldhearted."

"It's all in the past. This is a new day. A new beginning." Zoe beams. I beam. Dee covers her face with her hands and breaks into sobs.

Zoe and I spend the next ten minutes consoling her. When our first clients arrive, we're forced into an abrupt one-eighty. Dee and I get to work, while Zoe takes charge of bookings and cashing clients out. We don't break for lunch, but during a lull, I guide Zoe to a table.

"Lay down," I instruct, my gazes running over every smooth-skinned part of her not covered by fabric.

Her brows arch. Her lips form a perfect O. "What?"

My palms slide up her arms to land on her shoulders. "Trust me."

Her head swings to the counter. "What about the phone?"

I cock my head and smirk. "The whip cracker ... over there ... behind the counter ... flirting with that dude who just walked in."

"He doesn't look like he's got room left for anymore tattoos," Zoe chuckles, "he's total body inked, I bet."

"Maybe he's the repairman. Stop changing the subject. And stop staring at them ... him." Taking her head in my hands, I bring her face to mine. "Before someone walks in, get on the table, Zoe." I blow out an exasperated sigh.

"Are you gonna tattoo me?" She gasps.

I pull her in for a quick hug. "I'm gonna try."

Zoe appears bewildered, motionless, so I lift her in my arms, set her down on a table, and slip a soft pillow beneath her head, all before she can object.

"Give me that arm." I hold my hand out.

Delight grips her face. "You can cover this? Really?" Her finger runs over the scar.

"Close your eyes. Let me work my magic." Cradling her arm, I examine the damage done by, "Was this from glass?"

She frowns then bites her lip. "Windshield."

I lay a trail of kisses up and down her arm. "Oh baby, I'm sorry. But, whoever sewed you up did a good job." I run my finger over the well healed but pink wound. "You use scar cream?"

She stares at the ceiling. "Ah ha."

I hold my face directly over hers. "You're not at the dentist, Zoe. You can move your head and mouth."

She laughs and reaches a hand up to stroke my cheek. "I

think I'm going to love this job."

As I work, I explain. "Scar tissue is different from regular skin. So I need to treat this area a special way." My eyes climb from her forearm to her shoulder. I tap the killer falcon stretching its wings. "Where'd you get this amazing work?"

"Destiny's. In the city."

"Yeah, I've heard of them. Do you like color or all black? Let me see your other work."

She rolls onto her hip, grabs a fistful of hair and whips it aside, just missing my face.

"Whoa. You could flog somebody with that head of hair." I tease.

"Do you think I should cut it?" She appears alarmed.

"Never, babe. I was just joking."

She gives me a smile of satisfaction. "So was I."

"What do we have here?" When I see not only the fairy, but the nightingale riding up the back of her neck, I get a lump in my throat; I swear I almost cry. I ease her onto her back and drop my lips onto hers to steal a kiss. "Mmm. Sweet lips."

Her fingers work at the back of my neck, bringing me closer for a deep kiss; a real kiss. I come up for air with a, "Phew. Honey, keep that up and you might get off this table with an X-rated piece of art on your arm."

She laughs, but her eyes sink into mine, saying things that make me wish we were alone, in the dark, in the light, who gives a shit day or night, I just want to be alone with her.

I lift my head and clear my throat, considering a trip to the restroom to readjust myself. Yeah, my crotch is that tight.

"In that case, I'll let you concentrate." She pulls her lips into a sexy grin.

As I work, I explain. "I'm using a flesh color first, as a concealer." For a moment I pause. "Tell me if it hurts."

"I've been through worse, Jesse." She smirks. "Like glass."

She reaches up and runs a finger over my lips. "Thanks for asking, but as you can see, I've done this before."

I wonder what else she's done before. Yeah, I know I've whored around, but you have to realize how a guy thinks when he finally finds his dream girl; me Tarzan you Jane type of thing. Maybe all men aren't this way, but Zoe's turning me into a territorial caveman.

When I finish stage one, I stand back and study her arm. "Hmm. Not bad, if I say so myself. Check it out, babe."

Her head and arm lift simultaneously and she stares. "Wow. I can barely see that ugly scar." She sings the words like a happy song.

"Nothing on you could ever be ugly." I tap her nose.

She sits up to leave. I push her back down. "Not finished yet."

Her eyes pop. She bites her bottom lip. "More?"

"Yep, lots more."

With black ink, I weave a braided vine back and forth over the now less obvious snaking scar, then slash the vine with thorns. Between the thorns I etch some leaves. "I think this is my best work to date." My head rocks, and I'm feeling pretty damn great.

Zoe's eyes have been closed the entire time. I believe she wants me to concentrate, so she hasn't said a single word other than, "Wow," after one quick peek.

When I finish, my lips land on her forehead. "Done."

Zoe pulls herself to a sit, gives me a sleepy gaze, then stares at her new tattoo.

"It's a miracle, Jesse. It's perfect. I couldn't imagine … I don't even see the scar."

"You're a miracle." My lips roll into a smile that says, *You've been through some bad shit, babe, but better days are coming.*

"Let me dress it and you'll be all set. You know how to care for it, so I won't give you the spiel."

Dee finishes with a client and saunters over. "Wow that rocks," she nods. "Great placement, Jess. Cool work." Her head rocks.

I tug her braid. "I also do hair." I bat my lashes at Zoe.

"You're just amazing," Zoe indulges with a grin. She hops to her feet and stretches, then shakes out her mane of hair.

We stand in a tight circle, eyes jumping from face to face until Dee lets out a screech. "Would you look at the three of us? Come on. Bring it in." She pulls us into a huddle. "I cannot believe this. The trio's together again."

Zoe

Days fly, weeks gather into ... "I can't believe I've been working at Nightingale for two months," I marvel over dinner.

"And acing your first semester. Go you, Wonder Woman," Jesse says, raising his bottle of beer.

I burst out laughing and almost spit out my mouthful of salad. After washing down lettuce with wine, I can speak. "Who fails community college?" I'm wry.

"I can give you a couple of examples," he grins, sarcastic, "the first being my brother." He pulls a dinner roll apart. "You never met him, huh."

"No. But I've heard of him, back in the day, I mean."

"The legend of Jamie Sinclair." Jesse rolls his eyes. "Don't believe a word of any level of goodness my brother might have been credited with. He's a selfish shithead."

"If you don't stop making me laugh, I'll be spitting my dinner all over Toddy's floor." I giggle. "Change of subject so I can finish eating." Another few gulps of wine and I'm a bit heady. "You're going to have your debut show at the end of the month," I sing to him. "I can't believe your show and Halloween … all in the same week. Exciting, isn't it?"

"There's something more exciting." He reaches across the table for my hand. "Don't forget. It's also our anniversary."

I roll my bottom lip down. "Never. Never. Never."

"I take it you've just confirmed you'll treasure tonight for the rest of your life?" Again he lifts his beer in toast. "And me?" He squints at me.

I've noticed Jesse hides behind jokes, but tonight his eyes are a dead giveaway. He means every word. "Absolutely. Who else will cover the scars from my next accident?"

"Bite your tongue." He winces. "Seriously, Zoe. Don't ever say that."

"You know what they say. Things come in threes." I give my brows a shrug.

He tugs my hand. "Consider me your third and final accident then." He tugs my hand and nuzzles my fingers.

"You've done so much for me, Jesse. It's payback time. Need help bringing your art to the gallery?" Flexing my bicep, I give him a cutesy smile. "I'm available."

"Very impressive muscles, and forearm ink I might add." He finishes his beer and orders another. "That would be seriously great. I have so much stuff at the house, I could use help picking out my best pieces." He winks. "You have a good eye for beauty."

"Aww. Everything you do is best … and beautiful. Look at my arm." I shove it closer to his face.

He gives me a thoughtful look, somewhat testing, I believe. "Speaking of beauty, we have a cabin at Lake George. I was thinking about shooting some change of season photos up there. Maybe do some sketching." His stare pierces mine and my stomach sinks. We've grown so close, I knew we'd be heading toward overnights sooner or later. "We have five acres on a lake," he entices. "Just you and me," he caresses my hand, "and nature.

How about it?"

Just you and me …my mind warns … that's what I'm afraid of.

"Next weekend?" At the thought, my heart lunges for my throat. I mentally calculate my classes and papers that are due. "For how long?"

"Just the weekend. We can ride up on my bike after work on Friday. Are you in?" This is all one sentence he says without breaking for air.

"Sounds great." I bite my bottom lip. "Yeah, I could use a change of scene."

"You have Friday classes though," he runs a hand across his trimmed beard and blows out an ebbing whistle. "How about I pick you up … at your place … after work." Jesse isn't asking, he's stating.

I emit a "Phew. I guess."

"What? Do you never intend for me to see where you live?" He takes a drink and gags out a laugh. "You're starting to make me think you're homeless … or maybe you live at the zoo."

I cover my laugh with my hand.

"Maybe the aquarium. Do you have gills? Maybe a mermaid tail you're hiding under those sexy shorts and skirts of yours?"

By now, I'm in a state of hysteria. We're drawing stares.

"We better get out of here before men in white coats come in with strait jackets."

"Or animal control," I roar.

We laugh all the way out of the pub and are still laughing when we practically fall into his car.

We reserve Saturday for selecting paintings. I've never been to Jesse's house, and wonder if we'll run into family there. When I arrive at Nightingale, Jesse is on his bike, waiting at the curb.

"Will your dad be home?" I ask, slipping on a helmet.

"He's in Texas."

"Your brother?"

"Invading Texas."

"Uh oh. Sounds serious." Before sliding onto the back, I ask, "How are we going to carry paintings on your bike? I figured you'd have a truck or–"

"Dad's old work van is at the house. We'll deliver the stuff, drive back and … how about dinner then?"

"One of these days I'll have to cook for you." I don't really mean I'll cook; just order a pizza; but realize that would mean inviting him up to my tiny apartment.

Jesse's head whips around. "If it's lasagna and cheesecake, you've got a deal."

"I'll keep that in mind." I slide on behind him and hug him tighter than necessary to hold myself in place.

Jesse lives not far from my old house. Mine was a ranch, his is a two-story with a porch in the front and sunroom off the kitchen.

Jesse gives me the full tour, lingering in his room where we decide what to take. My eyes linger on his desk, his bed, his pillow, thinking, this is where Jesse sleeps. I've wondered so many things about Jesse over the years and can't believe I'm learning that he's greater than I could have imagined.

We head down the stairs and land in the kitchen where he offers me a soda. "It's a nice house, Jesse. Big for one person."

"A place to call home." He shrugs and grabs two Cokes from the refrigerator.

"You." I elbow him. "So serious. Unassuming."

"You." He sets the cans on the table and pulls me in for a kiss. "So beautiful. So brilliant."

When our lips part, I'm breathless.

"Now that you've seen my inventory, what do you think? I should bring at least a couple dozen. Help me make up my mind." He holds his head. "So many choices."

Finding You

Climbing up and down the stairs, we select, carry carefully, and load his dad's van till it's full.

I'm in the process of catching my breath and enjoying a breeze, when a small import takes the turn into the driveway like a racecar then skids to a stop. For a moment the car idles, the engine revs, then it rumbles into silence.

"Oh great," Jesse groans, "perfect timing." Sunshine streams across his face, lighting the gold in his eyes. He's tan, and the tips of his hair and some strands are the color of gold. As though just delivered bad news, his mood changes.

At his reaction to the car, or its driver, my antenna shoots up. Shielding my eyes from the sun, I watch as drama unfolds.

The car door is flung open, and to my shock, a very pregnant Claudette slides clumsily from behind the wheel. Hands on hips her eyes claw over me, then dart to Jesse, who has just closed the van doors and is brushing dust off his hands.

"What's all this?" She over emphasizes.

"I have a show in a couple weeks," Jesse says, slinging an arm around my shoulders. "I'm not sure you ever met Zoe Channing. We were–"

"In high school together. Well," she drawls, "if I remember correctly, which I usually do, not for long." Her gaze reaches the sky which since her arrival has begun to cloud. "She was a freshman and you were a senior." She looks to Jesse for confirmation, but he shoots her a warning glare. Ignoring him, she continues, "For a semester or two, then from what I recall, she disappeared." She levels her gaze on me. "So you're back. For how long?"

"Permanently." Seething, I hiss. This girl was my arch nemesis then and apparently still is. I also know she adored Jesse, and from her reaction to me, she still does.

"Have you heard back from Jamie yet?" Jesse cuts in.

"Nope." Her reply is cool.

"Is she living here?" I whisper close to Jesse's ear. "With you? Alone? Just the two of you?" I suck in a breath. "She … she's pregnant."

Claudette obviously hears me because she snaps, "Very observant. And yes to all your questions."

"Pregnant is the worst part," he says under his breath. "Unfortunately for my brother." He drags a hand down his cheek. "I'll fill you in later."

"Fill her in on what?" Claudette takes a step closer.

"On how you're going to buy a one way ticket to Dallas within the next week or two."

Her much in need of waxing brows arch like half-moons. "I am?"

"You are. Dudes sometimes respond to shock therapy. Even assholes like Jamie." He gives me a squeeze. "Thanks for the help, babe. I have to lock up. Be right back." His eyes cut from me to Claudette, and he seems to be considering something, then drops a kiss on my cheek, takes the porch steps two at a time, and the screen door slams.

Since Jesse has left Claudette and me to face each other with cold stares, I figure we might be friendly enemies for his sake, and amble toward her. "So you're moving to Dallas soon."

She shrugs and purses her pale lips. "That remains to be seen." She wears no makeup and could still be considered gorgeous.

Jesse need not explain the situation to me. Once she confronts Jamie, he has no choice but to accept the fact that he's the father of her child. I hope he's the father of her child.

My eyes travel to her tummy.

"How many months?"

"Almost five."

"You have the glow they talk about." I'm honest.

"Bullshit." The last time I saw a snarl like hers was on a dog in a meme. I Eat Burgers & Burglars.

"I meant it." I frown. In a way I envy her. She'll be giving birth to the baby of the man she's loved for so long. They'll be a family. But will Jamie be enough? Does she want to drag Jesse along with her?

She closes the space between us and gets right up in my face. "You're a lucky girl," she says with eyes so narrow I'm surprised she can see.

"So are you," I reply, letting my gaze drop to her tummy. "Is this your first?" I needle.

"Don't worry about how many times I've been knocked up. Jesse obviously still likes you. So I'm gonna give you a little advice."

"Still?" I don't know why I expect juicy girl talk because she's shooting daggers at my heart.

"You better treat him right or I'll kick your ass," she says through gritted teeth.

My chuckle is caustic. "You're lucky you're pregnant," my fists instinctively ball, "or you'd be laid out on this driveway … right now … with paramedics en route."

This is what Jesse hears as he jogs from the house to my side, with eyes bulging wider than hers.

"Later, Claudette." His voice is flat.

"Get in the car, Zoe."

Before we pull away, he faces me. "What the hell was that all about?"

"She threatened me." I shoot him a warning glance that could start a fire. "You wouldn't ever lie to me, right Jesse?"

"Of course not. What are you getting at?"

"Claudette has always been protective of you. She's downright territorial now."

"Eh." He shrugs. With both hands on the wheel, his knuckles are bloodless. "Claudette's been like part of the family forever."

"How big a part?"

"She's Jamie's ex."

"You're sure the baby isn't yours, right?"

"What?" he recoils, his eyes leaving the road long enough to display a look of disbelief.

The gallery where Jesse's art will be showcased is located in the Village. The used brick exterior doesn't prepare one for the spell they fall under when they walk through the towering doors. It's a huge renovated warehouse, all new, all white. Exposed pipes line the ceilings and a decorator's choice of hanging chandeliers amazingly coincide with the flair. It's a big cold building yet warm with talent, art, lives. Workmen are putting a final coat of chaste white paint on the walls.

Others are hanging their work. Jesse and I begin to carry his art, and helpful hands join in. In no time at all, he's got his own private corner of this aged palace brought to life by Jesse and several other artists.

I sit on a bench watching as he lovingly levels a frame then stands back, arms crossed, and analyzes. I always knew he was amazing, but never realized exactly how much of a professional Jesse Sinclair truly is. Goosebumps spread over my skin.

Before we leave, someone erects an easel at our section, and on it they place a board with his name and brief bio, including an introduction to his art. Abstract. Oils. Charcoal sketches.

As we leave the gallery, I link my arm through his. "I'm so proud of you, Jesse."

Finding You

Jesse

Leaving Zoe standing at the bus stop is getting old. I feel like an idiot, a deserter. I worry about her riding the loop late at night. Being with her, and leaving her at all, has been giving me anxiety attacks. Or, it might be due to the fact that my fucked up life is finally falling into a beautiful place, and I'm becoming a superstitious asshole. How can I be so lucky? With fate on my side these days, something is bound to go wrong. That's how I can suddenly become unlucky.

I'm psyched about my upcoming show, but nervous at the same time. Most of all, I'm seriously anticipating this weekend alone with Zoe, where I hope to take our relationship to the next level.

Sure, we see each other at work, have dinners, watch movies, make out in my car, but I'm craving more intimacy. Admit it Jesse. You're craving her naked body pressed to yours.

I've been counting the days since Saturday, when we set up the gallery. Friday's finally arrived.

Zoe's address is stored in my phone. Yes, my girl finally gave me her address. Go me. I pack an overnight bag, shower, change into jeans and a sweater, and hop on the bike by late afternoon.

"Something's wrong," I say to no one in particular, as I'm riding alone. "She must have given you the wrong address. Was it an error? No way could she have sent me to the wrong house intentionally. House? What house? I'm not all that familiar with the suburbs of Valhalla, but know my way around enough to realize I'm not riding through suburbs. There are no houses on these roads, just stores and bars and sonofabitch, the address she gave me matches this place called Darios Tavern.

I park at the curb and hit her number on auto dial. While the phone rings, my eyes rake over the brown shake building, which looks a bit decrepit. It's a two story, and yep, when my gaze hits the second floor I notice windows with curtains. An apartment? Zoe lives above a bar? I let out a laugh and shake my head. So this is the big mystery? Wait till I get my hands on her. Tickle torture time.

When her phone goes to voicemail, I send out a text. No response, so I hop off my bike, ready to walk to the side staircase and surprise her. Surprise her? I hope to hell this is her place, and my second hope is that she's home. *You still don't trust her, do you Jess?*

While I'm still considering, the window flies open and her head pops out. "I'll be right down," she yells at the top of her lungs.

Her hair takes off in the wind. She pulls it away from her face and stares down at me, kind of like she's in shock or something. This girl is a never-ending puzzle of missing pieces.

A smile breaks my tight lips apart and I heave the biggest fucking sigh of my life. She's home.

"Be right down," she yells, restraining her windblown mane.

"Be right here," I yell back, laughing because she looks so damn adorable up there. Like Rapunzel in her tower.

Arms crossed, I rest on my bike and as I wait I scope out the area. Clean sidewalks. No drunks filing out of Darios, which is a good thing, considering this is Happy Hour. About a block away is a sign: Bus Stop.

For the hell of it, I mosey around the side of the building and almost bump into Zoe who's into a strong jog.

"Hey," I laugh, gripping her shoulders. "You almost knocked me off my feet."

"Sorry," she says. But this sorry comes with a grin.

I grin back. "We have to break you of that habit."

Squinting, she tilts her head. "Knocking you off your feet?"

"Wise guy." I pluck her nose. "No more sorrys."

"Hope it's okay that I brought my guitar?" She spins a three-sixty, showing me the acoustic strapped across her back.

"Impressive." My head bobs. "You can rock me anytime."

She giggles. "I might rock you to sleep."

"Don't sell yourself short, babe. I've heard you." I wink and take her arm. "Let's hit the road. We have a long ride. Would you like to eat something first?"

Her brows arch and she pats her tummy. "Nope. Already ate." She draws in a deep breath. "And I'm ready for some clean country air."

I angle my head and bring her in for a quick kiss. "You're adorable, you know that?"

One side of her mouth lifts and there's that dimple.

Zoe

This week has been torture. Seeing Jesse at work, trying to act casual, sneaking split-second kisses in the back room between clients is cute, safe, but it's been like T-6 and counting; with the clock running down and stress winding up. Since Sunday, I've been freaking out about this weekend.

Rushing around the apartment, I huff and puff, and my breath is not short from rushing. I sing, I dance, I have great lungs and diaphragm. Nope, I'm breathless because Jesse is picking me up for a weekend alone. In the woods. A chill runs down my spine. I rub my arms to stave off goosebumps, and imagine.

What's going to happen this weekend when we're alone in a cabin? Holy shit. The woods. Animals? Wolves? Jesse? I laugh at the analogy. I believe Jesse could become a lusting animal if he so desired, with surging testosterone and insatiable demands. Heaven help me. The scenario would be amazing for someone experienced. Someone without baggage. Someone craving a sensual getaway with her boyfriend. Did I mention, her very romantic boyfriend? My internal thermometer is going haywire, turning chills into hot flashes.

"Phew. Phew. Phew." Stop it, girl! I slap my cheek. Pull yourself together! Xanax. I need Xanax. The problem is, Xanax went out with Chasing Dinero. You forgot the band so forget the drugs. Back to the weekend.

I don't plan on having sex. I won't be a saint, but I'm not going all the way, if you get my drift. I've lived so long with the fear of freaking out if a guy laid a hand on me, no less on top of me ... I just can't. I won't. I refuse to drive Jesse away by turning totally psycho. I'll take the chaste school girl approach. Technically, I haven't slept with any guys. "Phew." My fingers work across my damp forehead.

In anticipation of using the hot tub Jesse mentioned, casually might I add, I waxed every last piece of hair from my body, so nothing will peek from my swimsuit. Along with a retro black and white polka dot two piece with a plunging push-up top and high-waisted bikini bottom, promising to make me look like Marilyn Monroe, I bought a sensible terry cover up and robe. Nothing tempting, other than the two piece. A string bikini? For the beach, sure. Definitely not for a cabin on a first getaway. A one piece? I laugh. No. I want to keep him, not scare him away by portraying a nun. I think of the swimsuits people wore in the forties and choke. Imagine if I showed up in one of those. I roll into a belly laugh ... until my phone rings, jarring me back to reality, but by the time I pull it from my bag, which at the moment is hidden beneath a mound of clothes on my bed, the phone has gone silent. I check my messages. Yup, missed call & text from Jesse.

I trip over my sneakers on my way to the window, yank the curtain aside and watch the street below. Living over a bar isn't my greatest joy, but it's a working neighborhood, close to the bus, close to school. I watch people walking in and out of Darios, coming and going at all hours. Funny, none stumble, which is good. Seems the patrons of this place either know how to hold their liquor or when to stop. Either way, having people around is a comfort.

Jesse has parked his bike and is walking toward the building. Holy crap!

I throw the window open and stick my head out, followed by a frantically waving arm. "I'll be right down," I yell into the breeze whipping my hair across my face. The last thing I want is for Jesse to come upstairs, so I hold up a 'one minute' finger.

I take comfort in his smile, the sound of his voice as he yells, "Okay," and the curtain slides from my death grip. My momentary reprieve has ended and my tension escalates.

After knotting my hair at the top of my head, I check my makeup and do a quick spin before the mirror. My jeans fit just right. And my blue sweater deepens the color of my eyes. I've applied blush, so I don't look bloodless and sleepless. I slip into my jacket, sling my backpack over a shoulder, my guitar over my back, and fly down the wooden stairs attached to the side of the building, almost running headlong into Jesse who is heading in my direction.

"Hey," he's smiling. "I was just on my way up."

"Well, I'm here, so … I guess we should get going? Or," I fall into his eyes and they're so warm, so soft, I just about melt. "Did you want to go upstairs like to use the bathroom or something?" My eyes feel too wide. My pointing finger too stiff. Oh God, I'm such a loser. Pull yourself together Zoe!

Jesse laughs. "No thanks. I'm good to go. All set?" He's talking fast. Maybe he's as nervous as I am.

I nod. Half my mouth smiles. He pokes a gentle fingertip into the dimple my habit has permanently creased into my cheek. "Nice," he says.

"Huh?"

"Dimples. I like your dimples." His eyes skate over me approvingly. "You look pretty." He reaches for the strap of my bag. "Need a hand with your stuff?"

"Nope. I'm balanced."

He laughs. "You're balanced?"

"Yes. The weight is evenly distributed. I … I'm fine." What are you doing, Zoe?

"To the lake, then?" His brows arch. His eyes smile more than his lips.

"Yup. It's a great day. Look at the sky. Not a cloud. So blue."

His fingers brush the side of my face. "Like your eyes … electric blue."

I'm usually good with comebacks, but Jesse's stares sink deep into my soul. For a moment I'm tongue-tied, then I nod. "The artist in you. Electric blue. I like it."

The chemistry between us feels combustible. We're two beakers on a flame and if we add the wrong ingredients, the explosion could be fatal. I feel like I'm walking on eggshells, no, clouds, because I think this is the end of hell and the beginning of all things awaiting us in heaven.

We reach his bike and Jesse says, "I don't want to unbalance you, but I have to stow your gear." He looks so serious, my face flames. Then he chuckles.

"I meant, I was–"

"Perfectly balanced. I know," he teases, stowing my bag. When he hands me a helmet he's all business and very gentlemanly, helping me slide on behind him.

He turns to ask, "Ever ride one of these?"

With a broad grin, I nod.

"Of course you have." He smirks. "Silly of me." Then he draws my arms tight around him. So tight, I have to turn my head or I'll crush my nose on his back. And we ride. We ride for hours watching city streets turn into highways, buildings into trees. I'm thankful my lunch was light, and I didn't drink much, because by the time the bike pulls down a dirt road my bladder is about to burst.

The cabin is a rustic, redwood A-frame, aging and modest, choked by an overwhelming forest of evergreens. Where there are no trees, tall grass and bushes form impenetrable barriers. There's nothing getting in here on two legs or four, I tell myself … or out for that matter, which feels a bit creepy.

Jesse helps me off the bike and grabs our bags. The first thing I do is whip off my helmet. It makes me feel so unbecoming. I rip out the band holding my hair and I feel it cascade over my shoulders. When Jesse turns, he does a wide-eyed double take. I must look good. I feel good.

Leaning in, he drops his lips on mine. When we come up for air, he says, "I'm really happy you came."

"Me too." I grin up at him.

"I've never seen so many evergreens." My head twists in every direction.

"Yep. Plenty of privacy."

"Your cabin is awesome." I scrunch my lips. "It reminds me of a gingerbread house, only red velvet and chocolate." I refer to the redwood siding and brown stained trim.

Jesse laughs. "No one's ever described the old place quite like that, but hey, it sounds delicious. There's a beautiful lake over there." His arms are full, so he hitches his head toward a narrow path snaking between the trees. "We can settle in and take a walk unless we run out of sunlight."

"Sounds good. It's really beautiful here. The forest is so dark though, it's hard to see the sky. It almost feels like dusk."

"You'll get used to it." Jesse smiles. "Come on, I'll show you around."

We hike up to the porch. Jesse drops the bags to unlock the door, which he holds with a shoulder so I can enter first. I take a few steps and pause, awed by one big yet cozy room. A fieldstone fireplace is the focal point, and on the mantle are some picture frames. I'll check out the pictures later because right now, "Where's the bathroom?" I ask, dropping my guitar on a chair near a window overlooking the front path which is lined with brush and ferns.

"A long ride it was," he chuckles. "Right through that doorway, down the hall and hang a right."

After a pee that felt never ending, I wash my hands and check my face in the mirror. My lip gloss was bitten off during my first five minutes with Jesse, but my lips are full and naturally pink; I moisten them with the tip of my tongue. My blush has been lost in the wind or on the back of Jesse's jacket, but my cheeks glow with excitement. I run a hand over my tummy, hoping dinner will calm the flutters. This is going to be a wonderful weekend. Hopefully a breakthrough. Before exiting, I toss my head a few times and finger comb my hair.

When I return to the great room, Jesse is loading wood into the fireplace.

"This is really cool, Jesse. Everything's pine, the floor, walls. This place is fantastic." Something unusual catches my eye. "What's that hanging over the fireplace?"

"You know," he stands, runs a hand through his hair, and says, "it's some kind of a horn."

"Obviously." I'm droll.

His hands drop to his hips. "It was here when we bought the place. You're the musician. You tell me."

I close in to examine the wood and metal instrument strung on a cord. "It's a horn." I nod with confirmation and clasp my hands behind my back. "I was hoping for some kind of history, you know, like Igor used it when he snuck out at night and played for the villagers." I chew my lip. "Or was it for the monster?"

Jesse cracks up. "Should I take it down so you can play it?"

I giggle. "No, I'll stick with that." I point to my guitar.

I walk around checking things out. My fingers run over some

folded quilts lying over the arm of the sofa. "It's very cozy here."

"I know." His arms go around me and we spend at least five minutes standing before the fireplace kissing, our embrace broken only by the growl of my stomach.

"Hungry?" Jesse asks, running his palms up and down my back.

I smirk. "As you can hear, yes."

"I'll fire up the grill. We have burgers in the freezer. We also have a microwave in the kitchen, if you'd prefer a frozen lasagna." He drops to a squat, stacking the rest of the wood from a bin into the fireplace. His movements mold his sweater to his broad back, and I watch the flex of well-defined muscles in his arms. My gaze slips to his jeans, and the exposed skin on his lower back when his stretch lifts his sweater. I've never seen him shirtless, and wonder where the trail of black ink on the tip of his spine begins. He stands and brushes dust from his hands before pulling down his sweater. I believe he's caught me at a rapturous disadvantage because a brow lifts, and his lips purse ever so slightly to one side, then he winks. "I'll light this later."

I kick off my boots and pad to a triangle shaped window where I see only my reflection.

"No lake, I guess." I sigh. "We missed dusk. It went from light to pitch black." My fingertip taps the glass. "Well, there's always tomorrow," I mutter to myself because Jesse has disappeared into the kitchen.

His voice wafts into my ears. "I'm going through the freezer. Want to shop or is–"

"Lasagna is fine," I call out, still mesmerized by the forest, and the fact that I'm up here with Jesse and still able to function.

Strolling to the chair, I replace the guitar with my butt, position my fingers, and begin to play. I've written a new song, dedicated to finding Jesse again. Maybe I'll sing it to him someday.

Jesse enters the room, an astonished look on his face. "You

have really improved your skills."

I stop playing, hug my guitar, and stare at him. Does he realize how gorgeous he is?

He finishes drying his hands with a towel he slings over a shoulder, and runs his fingers through his tousled hair. "I mean you've really honed in on your technique. Sing for me?"

I feel the rise of heat, wondering what he'd say if he knew I'd written a romantic song for him.

"Maybe later," I say, returning my gaze, and fingers, to the strings.

Jesse lights the fire, and candles on the table, heats our meals and we crack open a bottle of wine.

After dinner, we remain at the table. Jesse's wine glass is full. Head resting on his palm, he stares into space then his dreamy gaze shifts to me.

I sit across from him, sipping wine, anticipating his next move.

He lifts his glass and all the while his eyes are on mine. They're smiling. Soulful. Questioning. All kinds of sparks are flying between us.

My butterflies are acting up, so I gulp … too much wine. I take a deep breath and slowly exhale.

"Don't worry. I won't let you get bored," he says and drains his glass, then rolls it in his palms.

My explosion of butterflies scream for release. The look in his eyes tells me he's serious. He leaves his chair, goes to a cabinet, and pulls out a carton which he sets down before me.

"Let's see what we have here." He rifles through an assortment of games. "What's your choice? Checkers, Monopoly, Scrabble."

I let out chuckle of relief. "Monopoly. I haven't played it in years."

Jesse must sense my tension; he's ultra-sensitive tonight.

I wonder if he's brought girls here before. Of course, dingbat, do you think you're his first?

"Do you always keep the cabin stocked?" Innocently, I pry.

"Jamie comes up here a lot." He frowns.

I glance around the romantic atmosphere, thinking of the rumors, or truths I've heard about his brother. "Ah ha. I can see why."

"If these walls could talk," Jesse says with a laugh that doesn't hold humor.

"And you? You don't come here often?"

He comes from his chair to mine, stands behind me and massages my shoulders. Then his face leans close to mine. "You're wondering if I bring every girl I meet here." I taste the wine on his breath as it brushes my cheek.

My arched brows aid the lift of my eyes as I strain to see him. "I guess."

He leaves me and moves around the table, beginning to gather things. "You're not just any girl." His side-glance is sexy.

"Thank you," I mumble.

"You don't have to thank me." His chuckle is soft. "At least you're not apologizing."

"You're making fun of me." I pout.

"You're irresistible. And I'm trying to make you smile."

Together we clear the table. I wash the dishes, he dries. Then we listen to music and set up Monopoly.

We drink, we joke. Now and then a gust of wind slams the house, but I know wind when I hear it. And the lift of tiny hairs on my neck isn't the result of Jesse, or the wind. Our game is interrupted by a different kind of noise beyond the safety of the glass which sounds threatening.

My gaze cuts from the game board to the window. "What's that?"

"The wind," Jesse assures, studying his properties.

I listen to the click of my token hitting the board. "I thought I heard a howl."

He rolls his dice and moves his battleship past go. "I doubt that." He sticks out his palm. "Dole out the cash, banker."

I count out fake money, but my concentration is no longer on the game. "Okay, now that was a howl," I object. "And there's rustling going on out there."

He chuckles. "The only howl could be the neighbor's dog, and they keep him locked up in a pen. There are animals here, small and harmless, that like to root around the bushes. And let's hope it's not a skunk because I'd hate to close the windows." His voice turns persuasive. "I love sleeping with a cool breeze washing over my body."

I jump to my feet, cross the room and stare out the window, certain we'll be attacked by a prowler, or worse.

Jesse is on his feet beside me. "Don't worry, Zoe, it's nothing but wind, tree branches and little critters." He pinches my cheek and teases, "If this is a ruse because I'm winning the game…"

He flips a wall switch and the outdoor floodlights cast an eerie glow over a chunk of the perimeter.

I rub my arms, suddenly cold, wishing I was back in my apartment.

I feel his presence behind me before his breath hits my neck, before his hands massage my shoulders, before his lips run a chain of kisses across my shoulders. He unclasps my arms, lifting them up and around his neck, and his hands slide around my waist.

"There aren't any wolves," his voice becomes gritty, "just the one standing behind you."

His body molds to mine. I feel the nudge of his excitement, the graze of his teeth on my neck. The hitch of his breath is a final warning.

"Zoe," Jesse's hoarse voice enters my ear, along with a moan.

His arms wrap me tightly, then the palm of his hand presses my tummy.

Goosebumps prickle my skin. His touch is setting me on fire and I long to be completely engulfed.

His hands move like lightning, exploring, caressing. He finds my breasts and his cupping fingers knead. His thumb teases a nipple, and my body reacts with a shiver.

My hands rush to his, fully intending to peel his fingers away, but I can't. And so I cover his hands with mine and we move together. I don't know who this girl is, it's certainly not me. I've never been so uninhibited, not in real life, nor in my wildest dreams of Jesse Sinclair. But here I am, urging him to make love to me.

Jesse has stirred something inside me, sweet yet wild, and the passion is escalating. My ass feels the pressure of his bulge and I strain to move closer. My cheek burrows into his shoulder. I lift my face, hungry for his lips.

I feel his strong arms move me, step by step, heartbeat by heartbeat, until we're standing before the crackling fire. My face is flushed, not only from the blood gushing through my veins, but from the flame.

I'm lifted and spun, crushed to his chest, and I'm facing a man whose features are altered by desire, or are my eyes glazed by the effect of too much wine.

We don't speak. This is no time for words. I don't think I could speak if I tried. My body tingles and throbs. Adrenaline mixes with alcohol and I'm lightheaded.

I watch a pulse in his neck, which seems to be racing like mine. His touch intensifies, and the movement of his hips triggers mine.

"No. Not here. Not near the windows," I rasp. "Someone could see." A mere fragment of my brain is registering reality.

I'm lifted in his arms, kissed as I'm cradled and carried to another room where I'm positioned on a bed. Jesse lies beside me, propped on an elbow. The only light comes from the great room, and Jesse's features are shadowed, but I face the ceiling and close my eyes. You can do this, my heart pumps but my brain won't listen. It's Jesse, I keep telling myself. It's Jesse. You're safe. He's brought you to life. He's opened the door, all you need to do is walk through. Jesse, Jesse, Jesse.

I feel the tip of his finger graze my throat, coast to my belly, where his fingertip teases circular patterns, close, so close to the yearning inside me. I shiver. I moan. I turn my head to the side, eyes still shut tight. It's Jesse; It's Jesse, my stuttering brain insists. The boy you've loved forever. With each pounding thought, my head tosses.

Jesse's breath elevates, his hand searches beneath me, sweeps under my sweater where he unhooks the clasp of my bra. His palm is as hot as the fire inside me, skating across my ribcage to capture a breast.

"Jesse," I pant. "Jesse."

He must believe I'm in the throes of passion and smoothly straddles my hips. What he doesn't realize is my passion has turned to fear, and my moans which grow louder, more desperate … are not from desire.

Everything slams me at once: the day, the night, the present, the past. And suddenly, I'm mindless.

Things are happening faster than I can process. Jesse's body blankets mine, and he's kissing me with such ferocity, my head won't stop spinning. He's so wrought with passion, I panic.

Darkness rushes back and I'm staring at the devil. I'm in the boiler room. His hands are all over me, his mouth sealing mine. I'm trying to scream but I can't! My mouth is stuffed with that chemical rag and I feel myself losing consciousness.

It's said insanity provides a body of one with the strength of ten. Well I must be bat shit insane because I throw Jesse off me like he's weightless, then leap to my feet. My arms flail, disoriented, in circles I spin, and I bolt. From the bedroom, I stumble to the great room, clutching my head with my hands. What to do! Where to hide! Through a blur, I see the door, and out I rush, into the forest, into the night.

Now and then a sliver of moon slices through the towering canopy of evergreens that are now ashen. I can barely see my hand in front of my face, no less where my stumbling feet are taking me. But I run. I run until my heart threatens to burst through my chest.

What are you doing here Zoe? A voice inside me screams. Why did you come here? Why are you running? You've waited so long for him. But you're not ready, a conflicting voice takes charge. Jesse will understand. He'll wait. Talk to him. Tell him…

The growl of an animal cuts the flow of blood to my brain. But I can't pass out. I scream like the demon from hell that has chased me for almost four years.

"Jesse," his name rips from my throat like a gale wind, "a wolf. It's a wolf." The more I scream the more the animal growls and circles. In darkness, its threatening eyes shine. The shadow looms larger than the tree I cower beside. The forest is silent but for the blood in my ears, the crunch of leaves as it stalks me.

The pines glow with a sudden flash of lightning which illuminates the animal, but only for a split-second, so I'm not certain what I'm facing. Still, I am able to glimpse the gaping jaws, razor teeth, drawn back ears. A crack of thunder in the distance is no match for the fear drumming my ears.

So this is how it's going to end, flashes through my head while another streak of lightning zaps the trees. Three years of misery: torn apart by a monster, now devoured by a wolf. "At the brink of my return to being me," I whisper, resigned to the fact I'm about to die.

Finding You

Jesse

When Zoe's dazzling blue eyes stare up at me, I'm a goner. My legs go weak, and that army of butterflies shoots electricity down my spine. Nah, not the butterflies. Zoe is firing the delectable tingle down my spine. My arms tighten around her waist, and I bury my lips in her throat. She flattens against me and my instinct is to squeeze tighter. I feel the release of a soft breath. Maybe a gasp. I want her to be part of me, and her body tells me she feels the same. My lips travel up her neck, trail to her cheek and find her lips. She melts into me and I feel the gentle vibration of her sigh against my chest. Her tongue finds mine, lashes and locks.

Mindless, I back her toward the center of the room, bracing her spine with my palms. She's pressed so tight against me, I think we'll never part. We'll mold this way for the rest of our lives. I want her so bad, more than any other woman, but differently. Not in an animal sense. Of course the crotch of my jeans is unbearably tight, but I want her with love, not lust. Holy shit. Love? Hell yeah. I love this girl. Our kiss breaks and I nibble her ear, whispering, "I want you, Zoe, but only if you feel the same." I'm literally panting. "Tell me, babe. What do you feel?"

When she moans, I lift her in my arms, kiss her all the way to the bedroom, place her on the bed, and lie down beside her. My finger traces her neck, followed by my lips. Her head tosses, she moans. I take this as a "Yes Jesse, I want you too." So I reach under her sweater to unhook her bra. My hand finds her ribs, clutches a firm but soft as hell breast, which I knead. This seems to make her go wild. Hey, I'm a red-blooded male with a killer hard-on, so I straddle her, jack up her hips, and begin to grind. Instead of her wrapping her legs around me, she makes a choking sound and wriggles beneath me.

I have no idea what just happened. One minute our tongues are buried in each other's throats, our bodies convulsing, and the next she's screaming at the top of her lungs, throwing punches like she's fighting for her life, hurling me off her.

"Christ, Zoe. Did I do something wrong?" I gasp as she leaps off the bed and heads for the door. "Where are you going?" I'm so breathless I can barely get the words out. "Are you okay?"

What the fuck is going on? I need to get my shit together, so I sit at the edge of the bed, cradling my head with my hands. Trying to figure out what the hell went wrong as my hard-on deflates enough for me to move. I'm starting to think this girl isn't right in the head, which scares me. Not because I wouldn't love someone who has issues, but because she may choose not to stay.

I take a painful walk across the room, my balls screaming for relief, and pause in the doorway, calling her name. "Zoe," I say forcing patience so I don't spook her any more than she obviously is. "Babe?" I call louder, surveying the great room. I pop into the kitchen, tap on the bathroom door, but Zoe's not here. A gust of wind blows the front door against the jamb and I realize it's been left open. What the fuck? Don't tell me she's outside…

On my way out the door, I grab a flashlight and baseball bat.

Ready for anything, I sprint down the path leading to the lake, screaming her name.

Owls call out, but I hear nothing from Zoe until a blood-curdling screech pierces my ears. "Jesse!" She screeches my name over and over. Her screams grow more urgent until she's shouting her voice raw, telling me she's cornered by a wolf. What the fuck?

Reason tells me the neighbor's shepherd got loose again, but I ready the bat, just in case.

A sweat breaks out, clinging to my hairline. Nah, we can't possibly have wolves around here.

"I'm coming," I shout through the darkness, thankful I had the presence of mind to grab a flashlight. "Zoe," I yell at the top of my lungs, "where are you?"

Her strangled screams are chilling. Imagining some fucking creep with his hands around her throat, adrenaline kicks me into a runner's high. Frantically, I dash around trees, crash through bushes. Finally, the beam of light finds her, backed against a massive tree trunk. She's sobbing, "Get away from me. Get away from me."

She's not making sense. She hasn't made sense all night.

The light shows me no mugger, just a panic-stricken girl and the dog she's scaring the crap out of. I fold with relief, fighting to catch my breath.

"It's okay, Zoe." The beam flashes over Sampson the shepherd. "See, it's just a dog." I can't say I blame her for her obvious state of panic. He's snarling like a sonofabitch. "Shut the fuck up, Sampson," I warn and he cowers. Turning to Zoe, I reassure, "It's just a dog, babe. He won't hurt you. You're safe."

Her head spins in my direction. "A dog? He could be mad, Jesse. Be careful. He looks about to attack." In the beam of light her skin is pale, her eyes like midnight blue saucers. I watch her lips tremble, and I want to hold her. A crazy thought flashes through my overcharged brain: she looks like someone just dragged her from the sea. Her hair is damp and stringy, almost covering her face. She's hunched over, hugging herself like a shipwrecked survivor in need of a blanket.

"He's not mad, he's spooked. Go back to the house. I'll take care of him." The damn dog won't shut up, so I yell to Zoe. "Can you find your way back?"

"I think so," her voice vibrates with fear. "Are you sure, Jesse?" Her shoulders lift and she inches away. The flashlight illuminates the path back to the cabin. "The floods are on, babe. Just follow the lights to the cabin."

Her voice begins to fade. "Should I call the animal warden? The police? Be careful, Jesse. He's vicious."

"No," I yell above the agitated dog. "Don't call anyone. Just get back to the cabin."

The light washes over Sampson and when I pet him, he calms. "Come on boy, I'll take you home." Along the way I talk to myself; how the hell will Zoe and I straighten this shit out? Then my thoughts turn to Sampson, who's panting worse than I am, because I'm sprinting through the woods like a maniac with him trying to keep up with me.

The neighbor's house squats in shadows. They probably don't even know their dog almost gave a poor girl heart failure. "You don't take to strangers, do you pup." I soothe, patting his head. Looking up at me with shining eyes, he wags his tail. "You bastard," I whisper. "Typical male. Scaring the shit out of girls. In you go, boy, and stay this time." I shove him into his oversized doghouse, leave the yard and snap the gate shut, like the idiot neighbor should have done.

I return to the cabin to find Zoe pacing in the great room, tears streaming down her face.

"Jesse," she sobs and falls into my arms. "I thought you were dead."

I cock my head ready to chuckle, but from the look on her face she's serious, so I'm serious. "I'm fine. It's the neighbor's dog. He gets loose sometimes and likes to hunt in the forest."

She gazes up with a combination of fear, relief and embarrassment. Add annoyance when I shrug my shoulders and grin.

Her fingers inch through her tangled hair. "And he was hunting *me*." She breaks into a bout laughter which I'm afraid could lead to hysteria. I recall her words when we left her place: I'm balanced. I don't think so, sweetheart.

I lead her to a chair and tuck a quilt around her. "You need a shot of booze or hot chocolate."

"Hot chocolate sounds great." Her eyes coast over me, then her gaze shifts to her dirt-caked feet peeking from beneath the quilt. "Maybe showers first?"

I feel like I've just come in out of the rain; damp and chilled. "Wouldn't be a bad idea." I nod. "I worked up an appetite, too. How about you?"

"Pancakes?" She grins.

After showering, I throw on sweats. Zoe strolls out of the bathroom wearing a bulky robe and some kind of matching turban on her head. Her face is scrubbed clean and I swear, she doesn't look a day over twelve. If she intended to *not* seduce me, she's doing a great job.

We pig out on pancakes with butter and warm syrup.

"I'll clean up," Zoe says.

"Hell no. Leave it till the morning. You must be exhausted. But I do believe we both could use a nightcap."

"I won't argue with that." She yawns and grabs a bottle and two glasses.

I light a fire and we snuggle on the rug, watching the flames spit, enjoying the peace. We don't talk, we just hug. Now and then I kiss her cheek, then I fall into thought. I think about Jamie and Claudette, wondering what awaits me when I return home. In a selfish way, I'll be sad when Claudette leaves.

I was getting used to the idea of being a stand-in dad for her baby. I need someplace to put my love. Someone to shower with affection. I've been striking out with girls my entire life, starting with a grade school teacher who made me face the corner for cursing. The only girls I've known have been the whores Jamie's brought home, and those I picked up along the way. And now I sit beside Zoe. I wonder if she'd care if she knew my past. Would she charge out of the house again?

My arm tightens around her shoulder, our heads rest together.

No one is like Zoe. Innocent. Intelligent. Talented. Kind. Everything opposite from self-centered Claudette.

"Do you feel better?" I ask.

"Yes. You?"

"I'm good."

"Jesse?"

"Yes?"

Zoe draws her legs to her chest, hugging her knees. "I want to tell you something," she whispers.

My body stiffens. "Okay babe, I'm listening."

After a few minutes of silence, I say, "We need to talk." I squeeze her shoulders and take her hand.

She doesn't remove her eyes from the fire. "I know."

She's so solemn, dread courses through my body. "Hey." I bring her face around, waiting for an explanation.

Finding You

Zoe

While waiting, I worry the animal has ripped Jesse apart. I'm consumed by guilt. You've done it again, Zoe. Fucked things up like you always do. You were on your way to making love with Jesse, about to break your curse … and you ran. He'll probably tell me to pack my bag, and we'll head for home in the morning. What guy in his right mind would want to be with a psycho chick?

I stand in the great room, warming myself before the fire, thinking about the baseball bat strangled by Jesse's fist. Whatever is out there is going to attack him. I just know it. I grab my cell, ready to dial 911, then remember his words. "Go back to the cabin. I'll handle it. It's just the neighbor's dog."

"Nice pet," I exaggerate, my voice quivering. I strain to see out the window, but beyond the floodlights is only darkness. No sky. No stars. Just slivers of moon in the distance, accompanied by lightning strikes. I worry Jesse will be caught in the approaching storm.

My heart's pounding, I'm trembling, pacing as I wait for his return. I keep checking the clock, which doesn't seem to want to move. With each passing moment I grow more and more frantic, and after fifteen minutes have elapsed, I'm in a state of distress. It's my fault. I killed my parents and now I've killed the only guy I could ever love. What's wrong with me?

Grow up, Zoe. Get over yourself. Get over the past. Move on you foolish girl. You have to learn to trust again, open your heart, risk your soul. Jesse won't hurt you.

I'm convincing myself of these things when I hear the door fly open and slam shut. I whirl, and my heart leaps to my throat. There stands Jesse, back pressed to the door, catching his breath.

"Is it raining?" He's dripping wet. I study his face. Is he angry or just exhausted?

His chuckle is tinged with sarcasm. "It's sweat." For a moment, he stares. Pensive. "Are you okay?"

"Me?" I gulp. "Are you? What was it? A wolf? Did you kill it or chase it away? Oh my God you were so long." I fall into his arms. Ready to make my confession, I sob.

He remains at the door, afraid to approach, or not wanting to.

Wringing my hands, I take a step forward. "I'm sorry, Jesse."

His shoulders shrug then square. "This time I'll accept a sorry. What's going on?"

I drop onto the braided rug before the fire, motioning for him to sit beside me.

I burst into tears. It's now or never. Jesse is a great guy and it's time to open up to him if we're going to have any kind of relationship. If he runs, he's not worth it, but I have a feeling Jesse won't bolt.

Finding You

Jesse

Knees drawn to her chest, Zoe sits before the fire; flames cast shadows over the room, dancing across her face. The brilliance surrounding her is striking. *She's* striking. I capture this moment in memory, which one day I'll paint.

I study the tight jaw of the beautiful girl I'd give my life for. What's happening to her? I lost her once, it can't happen again. We don't seem to be communicating as I hoped. And there's definitely something chewing her up inside.

"Are you ready to talk to me?" I ask, feeling the wane of my patience.

She nods and gracefully rises from the floor.

Her mood is dark. Concerned she may bolt into darkness again, I'm up on my feet beside her. This girl is giving me one hell of a workout. Only not the kind I expected. I'm emotionally tapped, which is beginning to affect me physically.

"Convince me with your voice, Zoe." Taking her shoulders, I turn her to face me. "Not with a head nod." I feel the gritting of my teeth, which naturally occurs when I struggle for control.

Zoe's ice-blue eyes could crack granite. Her stare cuts into mine, then she buries her face in her hands and throws herself against my chest.

I hold her, listening to her sob. Feeling so inadequate. "What's wrong?" My palm feels the tension in her back as I gently stroke lines and circles. "It can't be all that bad. You can talk to me."

Devastating silence. How can I reach her?

My heart is in my throat; I'm almost afraid to hear her response, but desperate to know. "Is it me? Is it something I've said? Done?" I draw a deep breath. "If it's because I came on too strong–"

With a whimper, she shakes her head which rests beside mine. She's sucking in air and letting out sobs. I feel helpless.

My arm falls lightly around her shoulders. She doesn't pull away, but she's stone. I feel her shiver. Then she lifts her head and looks up at me with sad, tear-drenched eyes, and my heart feels torn from my chest.

"It's not you, Jesse. You're the only good thing that's happened to me in years."

"Honey." I pull her closer. "What is it? You know you can tell me anything."

Her lids lower, shading her red-rimmed eyes. I lift her chin, bringing her face to mine. "If we're going to have what I'd like to have – what I hope you want to share with me – then we can't have secrets. I can't take much more of you falling apart in front of me. I can't walk away, either. You've got me in limbo here, wondering what's tearing you up like this. It's not fair to either of us. I love you, Zoe."

"Oh God, Jesse. Why?" She sounds so broken.

"Why do I love you?" My head snaps back and I drop my arms.

"No, not that. Why did it have to happen? Things could have been so different. You and I had that amazing connection in school. We could have been together. My parents would have been alive today if it hadn't been for him."

The pain on her face is unbearable. I drop kisses on her forehead, hopefully letting her know nothing will keep us apart. "Everything will be okay, baby. What happened the night of the crash? Why was your dad so angry with me?"

"It wasn't you, Jesse. It was because I'd been acting so crazy. I *was* crazy."

She takes a deep breath, stiffens, and looks me square in the eye. "I was raped." Her voice is as cold as the chill of disbelief that washes over me.

I think she's just slammed me in the head with a sack of bricks. "Christ, Zoe. No, babe." I don't want the gory details, yet I need all the facts so I can find the fuck and kill him. But I don't show her my anger. She's just opening up to me and the last thing I want to do is shove her back into silence, or the past which is obviously threatening her sanity.

Her shoulders slump. "Yes. I'm sorry to say."

"Now I know the reason for all the sorrys, babe." I wipe her tears with the pads of my thumbs and cradle her face with my palms. "You have nothing to be sorry about. He does," I growl. "Who was it?"

"I don't know," her voice quivers and she shrugs. "It happened in school."

Now I lose it. My fists ball and I slam the wall. "It happened at school?"

My mind races back to identify every dude I've ever known, trying to figure out who did this to her. Blood races to my temples, pulsing till they feel ready to burst. If it takes forever, I'll find him.

"Why didn't you tell me this before? I would have understood."

"It's not my favorite topic of conversation," she snaps. Drawing away she runs her hands up and down her arms then folds them across her chest. "I'm trying to deal."

"That's why you disappeared for a week? Holy fuck." I drag my hands through my hair and down my face. Suddenly things fall into place. A fucking shitty place.

She nods, and in broken, quivering sentences, tells me what happened, sparing the heartbreaking details no guy wants to hear. Because visualizing what this fuck did to her will haunt me until I find him. Snap his neck.

Fuming, I pace back and forth across the room stopping only long enough to slam the wall. "I want to get my hands on that fuck. Tear him to pieces." I stop to haul in a gulp of air. Facing her, I'm dead-serious blunt. "I'm going to kill him, Zoe."

Her eyes are wide. Her fingers rake through her hair and are caught in the tangles. "Stop it, Jesse. Stop yelling. You're beet red and scaring the hell out of me." She presses her brows with the heels of her hands.

I know I'm scaring her but I can't stop slamming through the house.

Zoe is also out of control. I can't blame her. I want to help her but don't know how, other than by using force. My force against the animal that raped her.

"I'll handle it." Zoe falls eerily calm, her cold eyes narrow. She speaks with guttural frankness. "I want to rip his heart out, Jesse. I want to be the butcher who guts him like a pig." Evil shadows her sweet face and it scares the fuck out of me. This girl's going to get even. One way or another. I'm worried she might get in over her head. I'm worried she might shut me out of her life … permanently.

I take a bottle of scotch from a cabinet, grab two glasses, push the sofa close to the fireplace, and drop down before the burning embers that have replaced the earlier flames.

"Sit by me, honey." I pat the cushion beside me.

Zoe settles like a feather, taking the glass I offer. I pour the scotch then examine the bottle, planning on finishing it before the night ends … hoping there's enough to last that long.

Zoe's body is wracked with frightening intervals of tremors; every few seconds her teeth chatter and her limbs seize.

I bring her hand to her lips. "Drink, hon. Let the booze relax you."

Watching me, with both hands she sips the scotch and makes a bitter face when she swallows.

"I'm relieved it's out, Jesse. But now," she takes another swig and levels her pain-filled eyes at me, "what does this do to us?"

My head snaps back. "If you think I wouldn't care about you because you were … because of what you've been through, you're so wrong." I shake my head, press my fingertips against my forehead so hard, I'm almost crushing my skull. "Don't you trust me by now?"

Zoe's face is bloodless, but a rosy blush colors her chest and spreads to the base of her neck. "I do. I don't trust me, that's the problem. I don't know what kind of partner I could be." She downs her scotch and I pour more. "You deserve so much–" Her head turns away, denying me the right to hear her.

I whip her face around as gently as possible with hands that tremble. "So do you." My fingers weave through her hair while I search her eyes, attempting to reach her soul. "I love you. I'm ready for commitment. I've never felt as ready as I do now." I shake my head. "I may sound like a dumbass, but you ground me, Zoe. I was out there flying like an unmanned jet." I take a thoughtful breath. "I need you, baby."

She watches me cautiously, unblinking, eyes glistening. "You settle me, Jesse – the chaos inside me," she whispers and my heart leaps to my throat because we're not running anymore, we're confessing.

"You brought me home, babe." My words shudder with the emotion I'm finally permitting to release.

Her head tilts. A smile plays across her lips. I watch the breakdown of anger as her face melts back to angelic.

I lean forward, sipping booze and breathing. "I know we have this connection, this need we fill in each other, but …Do you love me, Zoe?" The question is torn from my heart.

Her eyes close, then open. "I've loved you forever, Jesse." Her gaze follows the gentle sweep of her fingers as they slip across my cheek, trace my chin, and linger on my throat as I swallow. She lifts her face and whispers. "I've looked into eyes filled with hatred, soulless, dead eyes, but yours Jesse, they're so different. So filled with–"

"What do you see in my eyes, Zoe?" I'm mesmerized by her tone, the meaning of her words. At this moment, we're almost one person.

"Right now," she wets her lips with the tip of her tongue, "I think we're all made up of things we love." She studies me. I mean, really studies, her eyes digging into mine, firing off passion. "What's in your eyes? Your art. I saw the way you looked at the canvases we moved to the gallery."

I've never witnessed such a warm smile as the one that spreads across Zoe's beautiful face.

"What do you see in mine?" A brow arches as she lets her head fall to the side.

"Danger," with caution, I grin, "turbulence." The tip of my finger runs from her cheek to her brow. "I've seen flowing blue seas in your eyes," I tap the tip of her nose, "but a few minutes ago, your seas weren't calm. I felt I was watching a solar explosion, and you scared the hell out of me."

Her pale cheeks grow pink, then her head drops lightly onto my shoulder and she sighs. "When I told you about the attack, yours were like an eclipse. It broke my heart to have to tell you, Jesse." She takes my hand, presses my fingers to my heart. "I feel this beating, hear it when you hold me." She lifts her face to mine.

"Have I told you I love when you hold me?" Her entire face smiles. "Your heart beats different, like now, as we talk about our feelings, it's faster. And now your eyes are gemstones," she takes my hand to her lips. "Right now, your eyes aren't just brown, they're champagne, gold and glittery like topaz, sparkling with life."

"With love," I drop a kiss on her mouth, rest my hand on her heart, "your war drums are violins again, thank God."

Zoe's lids keep closing. A gentle yawn escapes her lips.

"It's been a hell of a night. You need sleep, babe. Come on. I'll tuck you in." Taking her hand, I lead her to the bedroom.

"What about you?"

"I'm still wound up–"

Her hand runs up my arm, her fingers dig into my bicep. "Anything I should worry about?"

My arms encircle her. "You never have to worry again." I nibble her ear. "When man feels agitated, man must paint," I grunt.

She giggles. "Okay caveman. I trust you won't disappear into the forest and leave me alone."

"I'm just going to mess around in there," I motion to the spare room with the closed door. "Right next to you."

"Painting?"

"I think I might."

"I know how you feel. If I wasn't exhausted, I'd be composing."

I pull down the spread, lift Zoe into my arms, squeeze her until she squeals, set her down and tuck the covers around her.

"I could get used to this." She covers a yawn with her hand.

"Get used to it." I brush her hair back and kiss her forehead. "I won't be long. I'll sneak in so I don't wake you, okay? So I'll say goodnight now."

When our lips meet, Zoe's eyes close, and as I peel my lips away, they remain shut. I pause at the doorway, watching the rise and fall of her chest, thanking God she's back in my life.

I'm filled with emotions I can't vent. Frustration. Angst. So I haul my ass into the spare room. Quietly, I rummage through the closet, searching for my art supplies. After wading through Jamie's swim trunks, fins and mask, I toss a snorkel aside and pull out my sketch pad and pencils. From beneath yellowing pages, I find brushes and jars. I set up my easel and in dim light I paint. Mindless, the brush finds its way.

The blank canvas takes shape without thought: passion spreads. I see with my heart, the touch of the brush. Then I step back to study the reds and purples, orange and blues, and this abstract conglomeration is me. I realize this has all been buried inside me. I dip the brush and the tip finds its own way. Lines, streaks, vivid sunsets. Geometric designs. It spells out Jesse Sinclair. The guy who never wanted much other than someone to care for. To love. To believe in. I'm covered with goosebumps; she's in the next room, fast asleep. Burdened by some bastard who forced himself on her. My teeth clench, I shake off a shudder.

Stepping back, I study my anger, longing, Zoe's loss. The picture is a figure, hooded in black, shoulders hunched. From behind it another is rising, shimmering gold outlines. Forests, rivers, but only I would know this because the canvas is covered with life before Zoe.

Finding You

Zoe

My eyes snap open, and I inhale the breathtaking morning, for a moment unaware of my surroundings. Then the prior night lights like a dragonfly on a boulder. Although bright rays of sun ripple with the curtains, I'm gripped by a shudder. Last night I shared with Jesse the darkest part of me, the agony buried deep in my soul.

Jesse pledged his love, despite everything I've put him through, everything that I've gone through. Snuggling beneath the covers I smile, not because I'm trying to, but because I can't stop the curl of my lips. Smiling is a natural reaction to the relief of overwhelming stress I've been carrying for years.

The window is open high and close to the bed. Jesse was right about the breeze blowing across a body. The magic of nature lulled me into a dreamless sleep that lasted all night. The backyard sounds like a bird sanctuary, with chatter so furious, I chuckle. Who couldn't love life on a morning like this? With Jesse … where is Jesse? I run a hand over the bed beside me. The sheet is cool, the pillow fluffed. Jesse didn't sleep here last night. With a start, I hop out of bed. I'm not sure why I'm so worried. He wouldn't leave me here alone. But is he okay? I visit the attached powder room, brush my teeth and smooth out twisted locks of my hair.

My oversized sweatshirt drapes my thighs, concealing my silky sleep shorts. Pulling my hair into a ponytail, I fasten it with my wristband, and wander into the kitchen.

Jesse stands before the window, drinking a mug of coffee. He wears jeans and a wife beater. The back of his head is a mass of tousled waves, so he must have slept someplace, just not with me.

"Hey," I say, my voice testing as I pad to his side.

Turning, he smiles. "Hey sleepyhead." His gaze coasts over me. "I was just about to wake you for breakfast. How did you sleep?"

"Like a rock. And you were right about the breeze. Beautiful." I take his coffee, set it on the counter, and put myself in his arms.

"Mmm," he moans, "it's beautiful now that you're here." His palms cross my spine, settle on my hips.

"Funny, I thought the same." The tip of my nose slides up his neck. "You smell good."

The flat of his hands stroke comforting paths in my back. "Could it be the eggs and toast?"

I wrinkle my nose. "I'm hungry, but not for eggs." I run my fingers through his tousled waves. "Did you sleep last night?" I ask, although he looks bedhead, well-rested gorgeous.

"Ah ha."

"Where?"

He shrugs his head toward the hallway. "In the spare room."

"Why?" I'm taken aback. "Did you think I needed space?" I thought we'd moved beyond that. I would have welcomed his approach last night, but would never tell him.

"It was late. I didn't want to wake you." Our lips touch for our first kiss of the day.

His mouth slides from mine and I pout. "I feel like we had our first fight."

Throwing his head back, he laughs. "I'd never want to tangle with you, tiger." He tugs my ponytail. "I've seen you in action."

"Oh and when was that?" I gleam up at him.

"The first night ... after dinner ... when you refused to let me drive you home. You can sure punch." Teasingly, he rubs his jaw, then taps my butt. "Eat your eggs, which are probably cold. I'll be right back. He disappears into the spare room which wasn't part of my tour, so I have no idea of its contents. I'm guessing it must have a bed, if that's where he slept.

I sample a forkful of eggs and yuck, they're cold. So I scrape them into the trash, but nibble on lightly buttered toast; cold but tasty.

The wood floor creaks across the room, and lifting my head I watch Jesse approach, a package tucked under his arm. My gaze sweeps his wife-beater, which conceals most of his chest. Tattoos stretch from his shoulders to his forearms, but he doesn't have the Richie Santana cartoon character appearance.

"What's that?" I lock my wrists behind my back and shoot him a crumb-licking grin.

"I'll never tell." He sweeps the wrapped package under my nose. "You'll have to open it to find out."

Unlocking my hands, I accept the gift. My fingers work carefully to loosen the ribbon without tearing it.

"I'll take that," Jesse says, stripping the red satin from my grasp. He ties it around my ponytail. "There. You look like ... who is it now? Little Red Riding Hood?"

Reaching up, my fingers close around a huge bow. "You just made me look like Minnie Mouse." I scrunch my mouth. "Someone mixed up your fairytales."

He watches me with big brown eyes, but not like a wolf. Like an anxious kid at Christmas. "Come on, Zoe. Open it."

Slowly, I tear the paper, revealing a binder which I press to my chest. "Mysterious," I whisper. "Your diary?"

"Are you kidding me?" He laughs. "Stop guessing and open the damn thing, will you?" He stands before me, hands on hips, face a picture of delight.

"Don't rush me," I tease, "I haven't received a wrapped gift in …" My eyes want to water, but I let my tears burn dry as Jesse watches me with compassion. "No one's given me a gift like this in years. I'm enjoying myself. Savoring the moment."

His coffee scented lips press my forehead. "Savor away." He backs against the counter and crosses his arms. But his eyes never leave me.

After examining the matte back cover, I carefully lift the front cover inscribed Jesse Sinclair. "Your sketchbook?" I gasp not only because Jesse is sharing with me his private moments and thoughts, but because the first page my eyes drop onto displays a charcoal drawing of me, on stage, holding my guitar. Slowly, the tips of my fingers grasp and flip each page.

Hands now stuffed in the pockets of his jeans, Jesse watches intently and nods. I linger on every page filled with pencil sketches and my heart sings. The entire book contains drawings of me in different positions and places. The facial expressions I know all too well. He's captured my every mood with perfection.

"You sketched me." Now my eyes really become misty. "You did these in school?"

His cheeks are pinker than usual. Again he nods. He pulls a hand from a pocket and massages the back of his neck; a habit which drives me insane … a tantalizing insane.

"And afterwards…" He grips the bottom of his shirt, pulls it over his head, and with the flick of his wrist the wife beater dangles on the back of a chair. Then he taps his left pec, close to his heart. His finger rests on a tattoo of a curb chain wrapping around a dangling Z, like the one I wear around my neck. "I got this because …" he looks suddenly insecure, "you made such an impression on me."

Jesse did that for me? I'm floored, but I match him by flipping my ponytail over a shoulder, baring the back of my neck. "I got this after..." My finger flicks over my nightingale. "No one ever got to call me Nightingale but you." I remember Denny, and grin at Jesse. "Although someone tried once." My brows arch. "But caught hell for it and never tried again."

Jesse's finger traces my tattoo. "I've seen it, but didn't think you…"

"Got it for you?" My palms run up and over his shoulders to lock around his neck.

Jesse

"I'm sorry to say the hot tub is drained." I share a pout with Zoe. "Jamie never does anything my dad asks, but this time." I run a hand over my beard. "Of course. Anything to screw me over." Grimacing, I shake my head. My brother would do anything to piss me off, but since he's in Texas, I have to give him a pass and blame fate for this one.

We sit side by side at the kitchen counter, drinking coffee. The book I gave Zoe is inches from her fingertips.

"I'm sure we can find other stuff to do." Consoling, she rubs my back. "Like running through the woods," She elbows my ribs and giggles.

"Sounds great. We can pick Sampson up along the way. I'm sure he'd love you in daylight." I chuckle.

She fakes a shudder. "No thanks. I like dogs better as puppies. Or at least ones that aren't taller than I am. With big red mean eyes."

"Oh come on. Sampson's a pushover. Like me." My arm drapes her shoulders. "How about we pack lunch and head to the lake. Bring your guitar and I'll bring my sketch pad."

"I'm in." She drains her cup and places it in the sink, then turns to me. "Pushover, you're not."

As if the lake and a blanket isn't risky enough, I think of Zoe in a bikini and every nerve in my body burns. "Let's get banging," I say, shoving her toward the bedroom, while I scoot into the spare room.

I strip down in seconds, slip into board shorts, and grab some towels. Shoulder resting against the cabin's front door, I'm anxious as a dog waiting to be let out to pee. Sitting beside me is a cooler packed with snacks and soda. A bag with my pencils and a pad.

I tap my knuckles on the wood frame and idly hum a random song.

Zoe finally steps from the bedroom, cloaked to the ankles by a tent-like robe, and I have to stifle a chuckle. I guess I imagined a string bikini and sexy scarf tied around her hips. Well, terrycloth it is. At least she's not wearing the turban, I muse.

She slings her guitar case over her back, her satchel over a shoulder. My arms are full, so she locks the door.

We follow the narrow path, which is out-of-control overgrown, which leads to Zoe's long string of complaints.

"Thank goodness for this robe or my legs would be gnawed by gnats or demolished by these bristles." She snorts at the bushes and swats bugs with her satchel.

"Are you always this grumpy?" I tease.

"I'm feisty. There's a difference," she huffs.

"I see," I patronize. "Why don't you let me carry that guitar that's beating your back every time you swing your bag? You'll be battered and bruised and complaining more than you are now."

The toss of her head whacks me with her ponytail, then she sucks in a breath.

Graced by the sun, the lake appears as endless strands of shimmering beads rippling with the currents. We're surrounded by forest, and where it's been cleared, meadows have replaced pines.

"What do you think?" I drop my gear at the shore and stretch out my arms. "Gorgeous and bugless."

She breathes a, "Wow. It's spectacular." Her head tilts. "Yeah. No gnats. How come?"

"They like to hang in the thickets with the hounds." I grip the band on her ponytail and free her hair.

"What are you doing?" she yelps, tossing her spilling locks from her face to cascade over her shoulders.

"I want to see your hair in sunlight." I'm seriously thinking art now. "I want to see if I can capture everything exactly the way you look right now." My brow lifts. "Without the robe."

I spread a blanket on the sandy shore, and Zoe sets down her guitar and satchel.

Finding You

Zoe

The sun beats down on my robe and I feel as though I'm cocooned by an electric blanket dialed to high. The development of moisture between my boobs makes the lake look more enticing. Talk about enticing. Jesse's body is still bronzed by summer and in sunlight, his smooth skin glistens.

"Swim before lunch?" he asks. "Or …"

I don't want lunch yet, and am definitely not ready for the '*or*', whatever that is. "Eh. I'm still full from breakfast."

"What breakfast? I saw it in the trash," he chuckles, "you're like the little kid who feeds his green beans to the dog under the table, huh?" His arms wrap and swing me in an arc. "Is that what you did when you were little?" Beaming down at me, he looks so happy.

"I sang." A giggle follows my wry reply.

He pokes my nose. "What did you sing?"

"I used to make up songs. My mom sang, too." Odd, I can talk about my mom and although I miss her, my heart no longer breaks. "What about you? Did you play with little cars and trucks?" I press my temples. "Wait. Don't tell me. You painted."

His lips spread into a grin that says, "I've been snagged," and he bites his lip which makes him innocent but charming. "Of course. I finger painted everything in the house. My mom had to follow me around with a bottle of Clorox and a rag." His laugh explodes with what must be wonderful memories.

"Tell me about your parents." I drop onto the blanket, tugging him down beside me.

"Twenty-two years of stories. Where do I begin?" His sigh is light. "I had a great time growing up, despite the fact that my brother Jamie was always around."

I smack his arm. "Aww. That's mean."

Jesse's eyes bulge. "*He's* mean. You should have seen the shit he pulled on me when we were little. And still tries to."

I pinch his cheek. "But now you're big enough to kick his butt."

He grabs my pinching finger and kisses it. "We tore up the house, that's for sure." He opens the cooler and pulls out a Coke. "What about you? No bratty sisters? Overprotective brothers?" His full lips purse into an O.

"Nope." I shake my head. Fiddle with the buttons on my robe. "Small family. Just the three of us." I roll my lips tight and they smack. "My parents were great. I have a lot of fantastic memories."

"Then there were those crazy cousins you mentioned, huh?"

I laugh. "In retrospect, the past few years weren't all that bad. Quite interesting, actually."

"You'll have to tell me all about it sometime."

"I wrote you a song." Pops out of my mouth. Maybe a deflection from my past.

His face goes soft. "Really?"

"Yup." I grin. "Want to hear it?"

"Hear it? Hell, I want to record it. No one's ever done that for me."

"No one's ever done what you've done for me."

"What's that?" he whispers to my back, which I've turned as I hop up to reach for my guitar case.

I begin to bend to unsnap it, when Jesse's strong arms stop me. Lift me. He stands behind me, pressing close, and I'm caught in his arms. I feel his lips push my hair away and he starts kissing my neck, moaning, "Mmm. You taste like strawberries."

"Shower gel—"

His hands wander to my hips, fingers gripping, and I brace myself, worrying what my reaction will be when he slips a hand under my robe and touches my skin. Will I scream? Faint? My mind has long ago buried the rape, and I refuse to let a monster control the rest of my life. So I fight. I fight off memories, demons, the urge to run. I'm filled with emotions, both good and troubling. I want to be with him so desperately, but can I? Will I scream when he tries to remove my swimsuit? I'll close my eyes when he kisses me, but what will I see in the darkness beneath my lids? Will it be Moody's face? Oh my God. I can't do that to Jesse.

Jesse spins me in his arms. His eyes are hungry, his breath comes short. He brushes the side of my face with his lips, burying them in my hair. "Are we good?" his whisper is husky, setting off a tingle deep inside me.

"Yes." My ears detect the rasp of my voice, so similar to his.

He takes me with him as he drops to the blanket, settles beside me and props on an elbow. He sifts my hair with his fingers, staring down at me with determination.

"I don't plan on losing you again."

"That's not going to happen." Beneath his gaze, I go breathless.

"You take the lead. I'm all yours," his grin is sexy, "do with me what you wish."

I study Jesse's eyes and they tell me everything I need to know. I'm safe and he cares deeply. I want to tell him how much

I love him, but I'm speechless.

I'm a manikin and his eyes are pulling the strings. I feel my smile spread clear across my face;

when I look into his eyes I see myself. Yes. His eyes mirror my emotion. So much emotion. The way I feel about him this very moment, the way I've felt about him from the first day I gazed into his big, golden brown eyes.

I must be gazing too long, for he says, "You're not falling asleep on me I hope."

My lips purse. "Not a chance."

I love his lopsided grin and the sparks of fire in his topaz stare.

"Where are you right now, Zoe Channing? What's going on inside that gorgeous blonde head of yours?"

"Just thinking." I sigh, reaching up to twirl a lock of his long dark waves.

His finger plays across my forehead, tangling in my hair. "About what?"

"About you. About me."

"And?" His eyes search mine. "Are your thoughts all warm and fuzzy?" Half of his mouth grins.

The slide of his hand from my chin, to my neck, to my robe, is persuasive.

One by one I feel his fingers open buttons while I freeze. But I don't flinch. His fingertips are mere inches from my breasts, and when he stops, before parting the front of my robe, he looks deep into my eyes. The softness could still my heart. There's passion, but it's accompanied by tenderness – convincing me I have nothing to fear. I imagine a glimmer of anticipation in his eyes – along with longing.

I feel the coolness of the breeze graze my bare skin. Then the heat of Jesse's fingers touch me.

His face moves closer, lips parted. Then he whispers: "Not

Finding You

until you are entirely sure. Completely ready. I don't want to cause you any stress. Any pain."

My writhing body screams, "Don't stop."

His fingers skim my breast, still covered by the slinky fabric of my suit, while the other wedges between my thighs, fingers igniting a fire I'd never felt before.

"I was thinking," my gasp is uncontrolled, "maybe a quick swim?" I cup his face with my hands.

He scrunches his mouth, then smiles. "As I said, you're the boss."

He gets to his feet dragging me with him. When we stand, his eyes rake over me.

He lets out a low wolf whistle. "I was expecting a string bikini, but damn, you look totally hot in whatever it is you call what you're wearing."

"It's retro." I wrinkle my nose. "You like it?"

"I love it," pausing, he adds, "you *are* a mystery." His arm slides around my waist. "Come on. Last one in is a …"

"What?" I'm breathless as we dash to the dock.

"I'll let you know when I think of it." He laughs, and again, he's like a little kid during his first day at the beach. Excitement grips his voice.

I plop onto the graying slats of wood. "Let's dangle our legs first. Eeek it's cold."

Pretending to push me in, he laughs. "It's easier to jump right in."

"Don't–" I laugh out. "It's now or never, I guess." I slide into the freezing lake, screeching, "Oh my God. It's so cold!"

Jesse dives in beside me, surfacing with his drenched hair dripping water down his face. He slicks it back with a swipe of his hand, then runs his fingers across his closed eyes. "Slightly frigid, yes. Guess I should have warned you."

His fingers dig into my abs. "Tickle torture." He laughs. "Hold your breath."

"Don't dunk me…" Too late, I'm underwater, and so is he, and he's kissing me!

We come up gasping for air. Wrapped in each other's arms, our slippery bodies slide. I feel the swell of his manhood, surprised the cold water hasn't affected him.

"That was nice," he says, "want to do it again?"

I twist in his arms, slip from his grasp and his palms graze my breasts, lingering on my hardened nipples. He appears stunned, more so than me by the intimacy of his touch. I watch his eyes cloud over, not with lake water, with desire. I feel the response of his need press firmly against my thighs, and I wonder if he'll attempt to tear my suit from my body this very moment.

"No," I screech, "quickly swimming beyond his reach, "I'm getting out before my bones crack."

Finding You

Jesse

I climb onto the pier and grabbing Zoe's hands, tow her up beside me. Like two wet ducks, we shake off lake water, swiping our hair from our faces, water from our eyes, our arms.

"Christ, your lips are blue. We better get you back into your towel sack." I grab her hand and run beside her back to the blanket.

The sprint has warmed her. And she's warmed me. She's tossing her head, laughing. In sunlight, Zoe's bright blue eyes are dazzling, or maybe it's her secret blend of magic, fueled by happiness.

"Turn around," I say spinning her.

I run my fingers through her damp hair, separate and braid the back of her head.

She lifts a hand and feels around. "A French braid? How'd you learn how to do that?"

"In the garage, when …" Oh shit.

Her brows lift above her devilish eyes. "I never knew a girl could get her hair done in a service station. I'll have to book me an appointment." Her fist pummels my abs, each jab pushing me backward.

I laugh so hard I'm too weak to fend her off.

So, she gets up in my face. To see this petite beauty stand up to me is a riot. I can't stop laughing

"Who taught you?" Stone-faced she persists.

"If I tell you, promise you'll stop attacking me?" I choke out.

"Ah ha." Her fingers sink deep into my ribcage. "Maybe."

"Okay. I give, I give. Dee."

"Dee? I didn't know she was a hair stylist." Her hands plop on her hips.

"She's not."

"Oh and this gets better and better. Did you and Dee have a thing going on?"

"No, after you left, she was crushed babe. She had no one."

"So she hung at the station, and to console her, you did her hair? Or she did yours?"

She's flinging here arms around, fingers pointing, jabbing me.

I pin her arms, kiss her, and stand at arm's length. "Dee and Claudette hung out in the back room. Doing makeup and hair. That's all." My sides literally ache from laughter.

Zoe screams with anger, and my breath hitches, ready for a first argument.

Then she folds with laughter. "Gotcha. Didn't I?" She's smug.

"You little rat."

She takes off but I chase her down before the shore turns to forest, and insects.

I capture her in my arms. Swing her into the air. "I'll get even."

Laughing, she slides down my chest. "I'm always on guard."

I believe she's serious.

"I'm taking you to dinner tonight. There's an epic bar and grill in town."

"Epic huh?" She cups my face and grins.

"Yes, epic." I roll my eyes, then squint. "Are you legal yet?"

"I will be soon, but I–"

"Let me guess," I cover her lips with mine and let them slide, "you have a fake ID."

"Of course." She gives me a nose-wrinkling grin.

With towels slung over our shoulders, sitting across from one another, we eat peanut butter sandwiches and share a Coke. Gusting breezes ruffle threads of Zoe's hair which have slipped from her braid. She keeps swiping at her nose.

"Tickling?"

"Torture." She grimaces. "I hope you don't mind if I remove your handiwork."

I nod. "Have at it."

She undoes her braid. I watch the movement of her arms lift her breasts. She wears a plunging top, and her breasts are tantalizingly plump. I find removing my eyes impossible. At the thought of sliding that fabric off, I feel the jerk of my dick.

When she finishes unbraiding, she runs her fingers through her still damp hair, attempting to shake the long tresses dry.

I cock my head, glancing at her sideways. "Your hair must be something to wash."

"It is. It takes forever to dry."

Zoe sits crossed legged. Using my butt muscles, I do an ass-crawl and stretch out a leg on either side of her, so that she's sitting in the V between my thighs. I grab her ankles and stretch her legs over mine, running my fingers over her smooth skin.

"Another bird," I muse, circling a hummingbird tattoo on her ankle with the pads of my fingers.

Her lips curl with satisfaction. "Everything on me has wings."

"You do too." Leaning forward, I push her hair off her shoulders. The tips of my fingers run over strap of her swimsuit, which ties around her neck.

"What do you call this?" I pluck the silky strap.

She tilts her head, giving me a puzzled look. "A strap?"

"Yes, but there's a name for this style."

"Oh. A halter top, is that what you mean?"

"Ah. Right." My fingers continue to play. Sliding under the strap, they slip around the back.

"I didn't know you were into fashion," one side of her mouth pulls up in a sly half grin, "along with doing hair." Then she chuckles.

My brows shrug. "I'm showing my feminine side and you think it's funny?"

"Sorry." She giggles.

"I thought we weren't using that word anymore." I close one eye and widen the other.

"Oh, sorry." She bursts out laughing. "I forgot. I won't do it again, I promise."

As we banter, my fingers find the clasp. Experienced fingers I might add because in seconds her top is unhooked as expertly as I undid her bra with two fingers last night. I hope today doesn't result in the same catastrophe, however. But hell, as I'm a dude, I was born to push the envelope.

"What are you doing?" Lifting a brow, she asks. Her head does a mild recoil.

"Just wondering how this thing works. Do you mind?"

"I appreciate you asking … after the fact." Her hand goes to the back of her neck, covering my fingers, which she doesn't remove. "Now that you found out–" Her grin is sly. "Suppose someone sees–"

"There's no one within miles of this place. You're embedded in a bunker."

"What about Sampson … your neighbors?"

"They're over two miles away, as I'm sure you guessed by the length of time it took me to get back to the cabin last night."

I'm droll but teasing.

She doesn't appear convinced, so I add, "They're an older couple. They come up from Manhattan for peace and quiet. Lock themselves in and don't come out till it's time to go home." I pluck her nose. "Don't worry, we're alone. But if you'd rather wait ... go back to the cabin–"

"No, I like it here. The sun feels good, and the breeze, well you know all about the breeze." She lifts a brow and her sweet lips slide into a smirk. "Okay, I take you at your word with the neighbors, but what about hunters?"

"I'll take the bullet." I grin. My fingertips skim her neck. "Don't worry. We're alone."

Her eyes go from bright to glazed, and I watch the muscles of her face slacken. While this all goes down, my hard-on grows at a disturbingly rapid rate. Disturbing because if she turns me down, I'll have to stagger behind a tree and jack off, or dive back into the lake. I don't think my body can take much more.

"So ... Can I?" My brows hold their arch.

"Remove my top?"

I nod.

The sparks of electricity flowing between us could start a forest fire.

Nodding, she releases my fingers and bites her bottom lip. Her hands drop to her sides and with them goes the top, which glides to the blanket.

I'm about to burst, and emit a, "Phew." Managing to restrain the 'holy fuck'.

Her luscious breasts don't move, but my eyes sure as hell do, up and down from her face to her chest. Reaching out, I run my fingers from her cheek to her neck, sliding down the tantalizing slope. My heart is pounding so hard, I lose my breath.

"Stop me now, Zoe."

"Suppose I don't want to." She appears as breathless as I am.

On my knees, I crawl behind her, place a hand on one shoulder, and nibble the other. My fingers dribble down her neck, cross her chest, and close in to cup her breasts.

Zoe throws her head back, while mine comes around to watch her profile.

A moan slips through her parting lips. "Kiss me." Her whisper is barely audible.

"Are you sure about this?" I breathe into her ear.

"We have to add 'are you sure' to the 'sorry list'," she pants and tries to drag my head around by pulling my earlobe.

"I'll be gentle."

"Just 'be' for god's sake, Jesse."

Easing her onto the blanket, I lie beside her, and as she wanted, I bring my mouth to hers. Her arms go around my neck, and our kiss is fueled with such passion, our teeth clash.

My mouth slides from hers to kiss my way down her slender torso. When I linger on her breasts, she grips my head, pulls my hair. I feel the movement of her hips. Her moans are like nothing I've ever heard. She's driving me into the animal I promised to never be.

Working my way to her tummy, I hook my thumbs in the waist of her swimsuit bottoms and draw them down to her ankles. She kicks free of the damp fabric.

I work my way across her torso, and before using my tongue, whisper, "Are you okay?"

"Yes." She doesn't stiffen.

I use my tongue and she moans and rocks her hips so desperately, I believe she's about to come. I taste her orgasm, and work my way up her overheated body.

"Should I–"

"Stop asking and do it," her soft moan hums. "Don't forget a condom," she groans.

"Done."

I bring my face to hers, my arms supporting my upper body. Slowly, I lower myself onto Zoe until my chest is crushed against her breasts, and my dick finds its place.

Over and over we roll, hips rocking, lips clutching.

Zoe doesn't bolt. She whispers, "I love you, Jesse."

Zoe

Jesse and I picnic at the lake.

"I love it here," I say.

"Beautiful, it is. Peaceful." He lifts his head to the sky and I watch his chest inflate with fresh air which he slowly releases.

"Freedom," I also look to the sky.

"Complaining about work already?"

I'm not sure which ruffles my hair, Jesse's fingertips or the wind, because the touch is light and my eyes are closed.

"Life." I sigh.

A fleeting thought of Nina invades my mind. I have no clue why I'd be thinking of Nina while anticipating intimacy with Jesse. Perhaps I wonder what Nina would say if she saw her nerdy, frigid cousin now. Nina bragged about her relationships, conquests, proclivity for bondage. I would never be subservient to anyone, not for love or money.

My concentration skips back to Jesse. I wouldn't wear a blindfold; I barely close my eyes which intend to devour my lover in the throes of passion, at his moment of release. My hands won't be bound; I want freedom to drag my fingers through his hair, grip his shoulders, rake my fingernails down his back. Which I do.

His face moves closer to mine, lips parted. Then he whispers, "Not until you are entirely sure. Completely ready. I don't want to cause you any stress. Any pain."

My body language says, "Don't stop," which my whisper confirms.

He grips my thighs, brings my hips up to meet him and I'm so wet I feel no pain. Every nerve in my body responds, firing off, sending messages to my aching breasts, every part of my throbbing body.

He pumps, driving deeper and I'm sure I'll explode. I clutch his spine, drawing him close; we're so close yet not close enough.

I want to be swallowed, be inside him deeper than he is in me.

I want nothing between us other than our moist skins which are sliding.

I want to be part of him always.

My moans drift into his mouth, and I kiss my name from his lips.

When I touch Jesse he groans. Our bodies move in a timed dance, slowly waltzing, revving with rapid thrusts. Until the moment arrives, one which I've never experienced before. And the tingling sensation that begins with an ache deep in my tummy, spreads and erupts with unimaginable fury. Then I'm spent. My breath slowly returns to normal.

Jesse's kiss endures as he has plunged deep inside me, seeking his own satisfaction. The heaviness of his breath increases to a groan, his body jerks and he collapses and rolls onto his back. Moaning even after ecstasy has released the beast in him. Then he props on an elbow and stares down at me with such love in his eyes I could cry.

Then his lips come down on mine, he positions his body, and

wraps me in his arms.

Reaching up, my fingers slide across his forehead, combing back his love-worn hair. My heart races, and my tummy tightens, but not from fear. I want him with every part of my being and I'm suddenly set free. Beneath his gaze, my mind, my soul, is at peace and at this moment, I know the past is nothing more than a book of burned pages, and Jesse's love is the wind with the strength to blow that old, disgusting book back to hell. When I close my eyes, the door to the past slams shut. And when I open them, my future smiles down at me with eyes filled with trust and love.

Finding You

Jesse

After dinner, we light a fire. Sit side by side and watch the flames. I feel the heat of Zoe's stare and the moment I turn my head her eyes reach into mine.

"It's over." She sighs and my heart skips a beat.

"What?" I choke. "What's over?"

Her entire face melts; the contented smile she gives tells me it's all good. "My nightmare."

"Oh baby." With a sigh of relief, I pull her against me. "You had me scared there for a minute."

"I'm sorry."

"No,"

"I know. I'm not sorry," her laugh is light. "I'm still learning things you've probably known since birth."

I chuckle. "Really? You could've fooled me back there at the lake."

She buries her face in my chest, then comes up for a breath. Her cheeks are rosy.

Lips curling, she inhales. "I feel amazing."

"You are amazing. I've never loved anyone, Zoe. Not even a

little. I think I waited for you. I knew it the first time I set eyes on you. That day our fingers brushed on the stage. When I handed you the wand.

"You remember?" She sounds amazed.

My eyes haven't burned this bad since Mom died. "Do I remember?" Through the lump in my throat I try to laugh. "Do I know my name?"

I laugh and squeeze her tight. "I love your name. I love your dimples. Your heart. Your soul. I love everything about you Zoe Channing. You're mine. Only mine. And I'm yours for as long as you'll have me. If this afternoon was just passion. I mean," I clear my throat and take a breath, "I understand. And if you don't want me right now, then I'll hang around and haunt you until you have no choice but to love me back, as much as I love you. That's the only way I'll ever stop haunting you."

She tilts her head. Tears streak her cheeks. "Haunt me, Jesse. Don't ever stop." She smiles.

The flames paint shadows across Zoe's face; I bask in the aftermath of this afternoon, when we made love, but mostly when she confirmed she loves me.

"I promise I've never loved anyone but you, babe," I say with an exhale.

"It wasn't a question of waiting for you either. My heart, my mind, my body," her swallow is deep, "they left me no choice."

I leave her for a moment. Crossing the room, I return with her guitar and I strum.

"I didn't know you could play," she gasps.

Her blue eyes widen with awe, which makes me feel amazing. I want to bring every emotion to Zoe, give her everything she's ever longed for. Feelings. I want to be the first to bring her love. True love.

"I didn't know it either." I tease, handing the guitar to her. "Here. You're the pro. Play something for me." I raise a brow, narrow one eye. "Hey. You never did play my song."

"Um. I remember being sidetracked." She grins and takes my hand. "By these." She sifts through my fingers.

Lifting off the floor, she tiptoes to the chair, positions the guitar in her lap and says, "This one's for you."

I watch her fingers work and life lights her eyes. She strums and her tone is whisper soft. Beautifully tuned as she sings.

Walking thru the raindrops
I'll find you again
Wandering in night mist
I'll wait till you're mine

Watching cloudy skies
Lost vision from my eyes
Searched but you were gone
From sight but not my heart

Mingling with twilight
I'll wait for a sign
Screaming out in silence
You'll hear me this time

"I think I heard you," I whisper. "My little nightingale."

She can't finish her song because our eyes meet, I step to the chair, remove the guitar and pull her up into my arms.

Our weekend at the lake flew faster than a falcon on speed and is now like a dream. A beautiful dream my mind could never have conjured. My fears are gone. I feel alive. The burden I've carried for so long has been lifted. Jesse knows my tragic story and he loves me. I'm healing; healed actually because Jesse and I made passionate love and I didn't see a madman, I saw only Jesse's face. With each touch, soft or fierce, I felt his love.

Tonight I'm excited. Excited for Jesse. It's a showcase of his art! His first exhibition, and what a rocking gallery to be part of. It's a collective show, but I know *he'll* be a sellout. He's amazing. Tonight will be the start of the career he's always dreamed of.

I've been at Jesse's house all day, helping him prepare for tonight. I hear him clunking around in his upstairs bedroom. I'm not sure if he's feeling overwhelmed, or maybe it's the outfit I laid out for him to wear. He had wanted to wear ripped jeans and t-shit, but I convinced him his rugged biker look was better left for me and the salon, and that classy would make a more striking impression. I hope I'm right. I offered to 'man-bun' his hair, but his response was a bout of laughter followed by a scowl.

Finding You

We rehearsed his speech and responses to questions he might be asked. He'll have to explain his inspiration, artistic influences, and reveal his personal side, which he isn't looking forward to. I know he'll be well-received if he'd just relax! I should talk, I'm a nervous wreck … for him.

He plods down the stairs, looking handsome and chic in black dress pants and blousy white silk shirt I picked out for him. But he looks so pathetically uncomfortable, tugging and smoothing.

"Are you sure about this outfit? I feel like Zorro." A side of his mouth turns down.

I can't control my hysterical laugh. "You look hot and sexy," I wiggle my brows. "In fact, maybe you shouldn't wear this. Girls will be all over you." My eyes narrow.

His hands grip my shoulders. "You're the only girl for me. Even though you dress me funny."

"Wait till you see what I have planned for you on Halloween." I wink.

"Remind me to tell you I'll be busy that night." He fusses with the hem of his shirt. "Should I tuck this in or–"

"Leave it out. You look like a temperamental artist." I let out a "Squee. I'm so happy for you!" I kiss his cheek, then undo the top four buttons of his shirt. "There. You're not too formal, and half buttoned, you're totally Hollywood."

"Thanks babe. I have to admit, I'm a bit on edge."

"What? No edges here. Smooth stretches and round corners."

He laughs and kisses the top of my head. "You're too much."

"So are you. And I'm so proud of you." I smooth his dark hair which falls in loose waves behind his ears. Accented by his perfect five-o'clock shadow, he looks like a hot model.

When we enter the gallery, I'm awed by the enormity of the place. Sterile but classic. Like a scene from an award winning movie. Everything is crystal and white. I'm wearing my slinky black dress, a V neck sheath, and relieved to fit right in with the hipster crowd. Before I can utter a breathless "Wow", the art on one wall catches my eye. "Striking!" I whisper.

"Thank you." Jesse smiles. His hands go from his pockets to his sides. His arms go from crossed to dangling, as we wait for an onslaught of admirers and prospective buyers.

I turn to him and crane my neck. Even with four inch heels, he towers over me. "Yours"? I know I sound amazed and hope he's not insulted by my reaction.

"I'm going to take that as a compliment." When he winks, he's so damn handsome I lose another breath. Much more of this and I'll be laid out on the floor. I manage a slight giggle and elbow him in the ribs.

"Of course, I know they're yours. They're just so ... so incredible, Jesse. I'm beyond impressed."

"I'll take that as another compliment." He grins, and his lips touch my piled-up hair. "You're incredible," his whisper is so sexy, my heart begins to throb.

The effect he has on me is better than any drug I've ever ingested, which sounds absurd, I know, but nothing could ever get me as high as being with Jesse Sinclair. He wipes my mind clean of stress, of worry, of any negative part of this world. Jesse makes life beautiful, and it shows in his art.

His arm slides around my waist, and I feel warm and secure.

"Come on, beautiful," his fingers tighten then come to rest on my hip, "I'll show you around. And did I tell you I like your hair up like that?"

"Thanks." I tug at the tendrils draping my ears, showing off just enough sparkle from my tiny diamond studs.

As he leads me through the gallery, I'm filled with all kinds of emotion ranging from pride to joy.

I notice a poster on the wall with Jesse's name splashed across it.

"This is big time." My smile is so broad, my mouth hurts. "I see commissions and solo exhibitions in your future."

"I see stars in your eyes." He kisses the tip of my nose. "Come back down to earth, Nightingale. You're the success story. I'm the struggling starving artist. Remember?" He slings an arm over my shoulder and starts walking me around and together we check out his paintings hanging on the walls, pinned to easels.

He's not the only artist. There are four in total, but the majority of the guests are clustered around Jesse's amazing art. We pause before a painting. It's a muted dark background, and the sky is midnight blue, dotted with twinkling stars.

"What's this?" Tilting my head, I point to the spray of glittering paint. "I haven't seen any others like this."

His lips form a shy curve. "Fairy dust."

When I notice the face of a girl in the center, I suck in a breath. You can barely see her because she's hidden by a night sky and trees. Her long hair is caught up in a breeze.

"She's beautiful, Jesse. Unique."

His head lowers, his lips sweep my cheek, and into my ear he whispers, "She's you."

I throw my arms around this guy who has quickly become the center of my universe. I've finally begun to let go of the horrors of the past and believe in magic again. Believe in second chances. Mine. And most of all, I have faith in Jesse who I believe is as unique as his paintings. I slide my hands over his hair, smoothing, caressing his neck, gripping his shoulders. His lips come down on mine and my legs go weak.

"Hey, don't faint on me," he teases in my ear.

I stare up at him with eyes I know must be overflowing with emotion. Mirroring his. We can't get close enough. I want him to crawl inside me. Me inside him. Be one as we were at the lake.

When I lift my eyes, I happen to notice a figure standing to my left. What catches my attention most is he seems to be staring at Jesse and me then turns his back so quickly, I don't have a chance to see his face. For a moment, I'm embarrassed because we've been kissing. I'm flushing, feeling the heat rise from my chest to my cheeks. Jesse and I were steps away from making love, right in the middle of his exhibition. This is the effect we have on one another.

His lips land on my forehead and his warm palm slides down my back. He shucks his head toward the stranger's profile and whispers, "That's the gallery owner. I should go and cozy up to him. He's the reason for my big break." His entire face lights up.

"I'll be right here waiting for you." I put a kiss on his cheek and watch him walk away.

My heart is bursting with love. He's so handsome. So talented. He's my wonderful everything. And I can't believe he's mine.

Dee clomps over wearing designer jeans and wedge heeled sandals. Grinning, she elbow's me. "Stop eating him alive, girlfriend. Save it for after the event. You two can have your own private celebration." She squeezes my arm. "This is one rocking opening. I'm so happy for Jesse. For both of you."

"Celebrate?" I inhale and blow out a breath. Just the thought of making love with Jesse sends chills down my spine. I never dreamed I could feel this way.

Dee's hand is still on my arm. She begins to tug me along the wall so we can study Jesse's artwork. As we mosey, her fingers tighten so, they actually dig into my flesh. "Hey," I cry, swinging my head to hers, "you're hurting me." My gaze then swings from the look of horror on her face to the figure standing not more than ten feet away. I might not have recognized his profile, but when he turns – I'm met with his face – it's the devil himself. My legs threaten to cave. My heart pounds so hard, my breath is fast and labored.

Jesse is now talking to some buyers across the room. This is his night and I'm thrilled for him. I can't blow it for him, for me.

My head is spinning with confusion, guilt, but mostly I'm trying to control my rage. Jesse turns to wave me over to join him, and I try to smile but my face feels like molded plastic. I shake my head, mouthing, "No," trying to blow him a kiss with ice cold lips.

He mouths, "Are you okay?" And watches me cautiously. By the look on his face I can read his mind: "Do you feel okay? You're not sick? ..."

No Jesse, I'm not sick, the boogieman just stepped out of my nightmares.

The stranger walks toward me, watching my exchange with Jesse. My focus sharpens, and I find myself starting into Moody's hollow black eyes. My jaw drops, along with my stomach, and I want to vomit. His eyes search my face quizzically, as if he's trying to remember where he's seen me before. I don't have to think. This monster has branded me with a permanent impression. The boiler room. The foul breath. The hands on my body. The fists knocking me to the floor.

I'm not sure Moody realizes it's me. He's deciding. I don't look like the same fifteen year old girl. Nor do I feel like it. From time to time, his eyes narrow. With the tips of his fingers he grooms his goatee, dark eyes shifting. Following a look of surprise, his sinister grin spreads like lava. Pressure builds in my head. My mind races. I can't let on to Jesse, so I swallow my shock, try to calm my heart which is threatening to leap from my throat.

I try to keep my face from contorting with the rise of fear. With hatred that has brewed for four miserable years. I never wanted to see this monster again, but in a way, I did. I've dreamed so many nights of plunging a knife into his heart. And now here he is. Right in front of me. His eyes shift from side to side, to the ceiling, back to me. Hands slip into pockets. I take him in from head to toe. The same dark hair, slick back ponytail at the nape of his neck. Broad shoulders, only now his broad shoulders are stuffed into an expensive suit jacket, not work clothes. And his boots are shiny designers, not dusty and worn.

Dee, frozen in her own private space, turns to watch the look on my face. We share something in common: She looks as disoriented as I feel. Her placid expression is lost; her cheeks turn beet red, and she gasps.

The three of us share stares, mine cutting from Dee's overheating cocoa eyes to Moody's evil squint.

"Dee," I whisper. "I don't feel good. My head is about to explode."

"Zoe?" She throws her arms around me before my body slumps.

My chin digs into her shoulder. "It's him," I manage before my throat seizes.

I'm out of my coma of shock, and tears trickle from my eyes.

"Come on, hon." She pulls me into the restroom and locks the door. "Oh God, Zoe. I'm so sorry. I had no idea he was back in town." She shakes her head, mumbling, "He was supposed to be in Peru or fuck knows where. I'd never have let you come here if I knew."

I'm dazed, shaking confusion from my cotton candy head. "Knew what?" I don't wait for a reply. The wheels are rolling over my brain. "Wait. Back up. How do you know he was in Peru? Coming here? You know him?"

If Dee's head dropped any further, it would snap off her body. She speaks to the floor. "I should be dead for what I let happen to you. I couldn't tell you. He would have killed me. My family."

"What the fuck are you talking about?" I suck in a breath. "He did that to you too? What he did to me?" I can't say the word. I'm still fumbling with confusion.

Dee finally raises her eyes to mine and gives me a series of desperate nods. "Every fucking time he was in town, for as long as I can remember. I dreaded Uncle Cisco's visits."

"What?" I almost lose my eyeballs. Not to mention my dinner. "You knew he was a rapist? You didn't help me catch him?" My fist hits the wall. "We could have nailed him, Dee. Together, we had proof. Now we have nothing. Too much time has passed."

"He threatened me Zoe, the same as you. I was gonna tell you. I wanted to." She squints, deflecting my glare, but the more her eyes narrow, the more tears are squeezed out. "That day I came to the hospital, I wanted to tell you, but I just couldn't. You were in such bad shape. I didn't ... I couldn't face it. Face you."

"Face me?" I find myself repeating because my brain is so numb I can barely think independently, no less rationally.

"I had no idea he'd ever do this to someone outside the family," she sobs.

"This is so sick, Dee." Turning away I stare into the mirror. Other than mascara-smeared eyes, I look the same. But I'm not the same. Old wounds have been ripped open. And now I can't run from them because Dee knows this man. I can finally face my demon. But how?

Dee is shaking so badly, I aim her at the wall so she can steady herself. I don't want to hug her, or support her. When I needed her, she failed me.

"I want to kill myself. I'm so so so sorry, Zoe."

I grab a handful of paper towels and fling them at her. "Wipe your nose. We're going to work this out."

"I'm not good at facing things, Zoe. You know me, take the high road. Low road. Whatever. Please don't make me..."

I permit myself to relive the past and it all makes sense now. Dee's outrage the day I told her. Her mood change. "Family first," is what you said. That's why you couldn't stay with me when I needed you. Why you couldn't come to the clinic with me." I glare. "Who the fuck is he? What hold did he ... does he have over you?

"He's someone we've always called uncle."

"What? And you knew he was ... is a pedophile?"

"He did it to my cousin too. None of us told." Her head hangs in shame.

"And you let him get away with it." My voice falls with disgust.

"You have no idea what my family is like. They all knew. We had to keep quiet or he'd– he threatened us. Right after he attacked–"

"No! Raped!" I scream, slamming my forehead with my fists.

"I was going to tell, I swear, but the next day he went to Venezuela. There was nothing anyone could have done. God, Zoe. If I could have changed it, could change it now, I would. I'd cut off my arm to have it be me instead."

Tears wet the front of her red silk shirt. "He's part of a drug cartel, Zoe. You don't mess with people like that."

"So it's drug money that runs this place? That's giving Jesse his big break?"

"No," her full lips pull into a tight grimace, "he owns the building but ... Jesse sold the garage. He put up his own money to host his exhibit."

"And the tattoo shop? Is that your uncle's?"

"No! It's my money. I sold my ass for that place." She gasps for air. "I had no idea he'd even have the nerve to show his face here. He stopped coming around a couple years ago. When I was old enough and smart enough to land a boyfriend in the police force."

I grab her arms and shake her like a toy. "Will you turn him in? Have your boyfriend arrest him?"

"No. I can't. It would kill my mother, my aunt. I don't want anyone to know. I can't tell on him."

"Oh God, you disgust me."

"I let you down. I'm so sorry." She sobs.

"Not as sorry as I am." My head is throbbing. My heart

pounding. I run cold water over my wrists because a migraine is setting in.

My eyes narrow at her. "If he has money, what the fuck was he doing working as a school janitor." I gasp. "Oh my God. He just wanted to be close to kids. Holy shit, Dee. You knew this?" My new world is suddenly falling apart. I don't feel like I'm dying, but I'm ceasing to exist. My brain is disconnecting from reality.

I grab Dee's arms and shake her until I lose focus. Then I roll up a fist and I slug her, like the girl in the alley at PS 243. It takes every ounce of restraint not to wrap my hands around Dee's neck and squeeze.

"You knew who he was, what he was, and you protected him." I'm still trying to digest the demented reality of it all. "You could have helped me. God knows how many others. And you didn't. You lied to me."

"I didn't lie. I couldn't–"

"If it wasn't for your fucking family, mine would still be alive." My fingers bite into her shoulders. "You could have helped me from going through hell all these years."

Another wave of agony hits me and I'm afraid, I'm angry, I'm filled with rage. I want to tackle Dee, smash her head in the mirror. I want to march out there and kick Moody in the balls, knock him to the ground, pound his skull into the cement floor, but I can't act out of emotion, or haste. And most of all, I can't involve Jesse. Not here. Not tonight. He'd kill Moody on the spot.

Retribution has to be mine, and it has to be perfectly planned.

Jesse is cracking his knuckles. Slamming his fists into the plum accent wall in my living room.

"Take a deep breath," I plead. "You're going to have a stroke for God's sake."

"I'm sorry if I'm upset because my girlfriend just told me

she was brutalized by some fucking monster that owns me. The gallery filled with my art." His palms slam his head.

He can't say rape either. I shake my head. Turn to the window. Stare out at people walking on the sidewalk below. Normal people. Not like us. Fighting, raging, desperate to escape the inevitable.

"It's my problem. I'll work it out." I know I sound defeated, but I better kick my ass into gear because I'm just getting started.

Jesse is at my side, taking my arm, trying to turn me around, but I won't let him. "No. You're not doing this alone," he says, voice softer now.

I sound dead. I feel dead. Not only does Jesse now know everything about me, but he's witnessed, first hand, the worst of me. I'm ashamed. Embarrassed. I know I shouldn't be, but I can't help it. "It's my problem. I'm not involving you."

He places himself between me and the window. He has a hand on each of my arms, pinning me. I guess he's afraid I'll either slam him or run, one of my trademark reactions.

"Whatever involves you involves me." His voice is so desperate, if I closed my eyes I think I'd see the agony in his.

"I won't let him ruin our lives, not any more than he already has." I feel the twitch of my bottom lip, and Jesse's fingertip as he soothes it.

He slips his arms around me. My head falls to his chest. I feel the beat of his heart against my cheek. My arms go around him; my palms run up and down his strong back but I'm not comforted. I'm agitated. My mind is whirling with diabolical methods of evening the score with a rapist. Then it hits me. The perfect solution.

At first, Jesse stares with shock. For a few moments, he doesn't speak. He paces. Stops long enough to slam a wall. He falls deathly still, thoughtful. With a heaving chest, he palms his temples. "I know what we can do to pull this off." Before he stops speaking, he's slipping his cell from his pocket.

"Who are you calling? I don't want anyone else to know this, Jesse." I make a grab for the phone, but he spins so abruptly the momentum causes me to stumble. I bounce onto the sofa.

He mouths, "I'm sorry, baby," while lifting a hand to silence me. "I'm calling a friend. Alana. She's been on both sides of the law. Trust me, you'll want her on your side."

"Put her on speaker … please … so I can hear."

The phone rings. Jesse clears his throat. My pulse races. A woman's voice says, "Jesse?"

"Alana. Yeah, it's me."

"Christ. Please tell me you're not still fucking around with that bimbo in Florida."

Jesse shoots me a sheepish look. His neck has been flushed for the past half hour, so it has nothing to do with me hearing about another girl; a bimbo actually. But the look in his eyes is a dead giveaway.

"No. I need a favor. A serious favor … for my girl."

Alana's chuckle is throaty. "There are clinics, Jesse. Abortion is legal–"

I'm starting to wonder what kind of relationship Jesse had with this woman, and with others. But this isn't a time for jealousy or doubt.

"This is about Zoe."

Silence, then Alana's hoarse whisper. "Zoe your high school sweetheart? The girl you said you'd never forget?"

Her squeal almost breaks my eardrum.

"Alana. We have a big problem. We need to discuss this in person. What are you doing tomorrow?"

"I guess I'm coming to New York, huh?"

Jesse disconnects and I'm all over him for information.

"Who is she?"

"An attorney."

Legal drifts through my mind, and I'm not sure if I feel more confident or panicky.

"How well do you know her? Is she trustworthy? What exactly can she do?"

I fire questions faster than he can answer.

"How is she going to find someone in South America? And most of all, can we trust her?"

We sit on my sofa, slugging Jack Daniels, and we talk. Jesse tells me how he met Alana, how he helped her out of a jam, how she repaid the debt in Florida. Hearing Jesse's stories make me feel better. I'm not the only fuckup. He's done his share as well.

"It's late," Jesse says. "You should get some rest. Alana will be here in the morning."

"Stay with me?" My eyes pierce his.

His arms go around me. "Of course, babe. I'm in this with you all the way."

"All the way to the slammer if we get caught." My body shivers. "I have such mixed emotions about this. I've dreamed of revenge for so long, but now that it's near–"

"I see that look in your eyes," he cups my face with his palms and drops a quick kiss on my lips, "don't freak out on me. That's all I ask."

We climb into my bed, our limbs tangle, but we don't make love. We hold each other until the sun comes up and the phone rings.

Alana calls from the airport. Jesse offers to pick her up, but she already has a ride, which tells me she's not coming alone.

With much silence, we fill the morning with toast and coffee and showers. We stare at the TV until Alana knocks on the door. From the sound of her voice on the phone, let's say, I wasn't sure what to expect, but certainly not the woman standing in my doorway, tote over a shoulder.

Alana is a busty long-legged woman. Her skin is dewy, and

her long dark hair shimmers with caramel highlights. Shit, she looks like a model. I wonder what she and Jesse have ... had in the past which makes her she's so willing to *fly to New York to help me.*

"Hi Alana. I'm Zoe. Thank you for coming." I'm polite yet stiff as I step aside to permit her entry into my apartment, my life.

Her open stare derails me. I watch her eyes slide over me, unsure of her perception of me, as she wears little expression. The crow's feet beside her eyes don't detract from her beauty. She's a strong, confident woman, which makes me feel like I'm back in elementary school, ready to call her ma'am.

"Jesse," she calls out.

"Hey, hon," he replies, opening his arms to her. "Good to see you. Wish it was under different circumstances."

Talk about feeling like a fifth wheel.

"We'll catch up later," she runs her hand over the side of his hair with affection, "after we discuss why I'm here."

Shit. Am I invisible?

Jesse finally emerges from his Alana trance and comes to my side. "Alana, this is Zoe." His arm goes around my waist.

"We met," she smiles, "at the door."

Jesse takes her bag, and I offer her a seat and a drink. The seat she accepts, the drink she refuses.

"What's the dilemma, Jesse?"

Dilemma? This should be fun. I wonder if she plans on billing me.

We sit at my kitchen table, drinking coffee. Jesse fills her in on my plan, sparing the details of why I came up with the plan in the first place.

I just listen. And the more I listen, the sicker I feel. What am I getting myself into? Should I turn him into the police? Ha. What would that accomplish?

"Jesse's told me a lot about you, Zoe. You write lyrics, but this plan honey, this is Screen Guild bestselling script writing. You're very creative, to say the least. From one blue eyed gal to another, what did this freak do to make you want to castrate him?" Her navy eyes bore into mine.

"He's a pedophile." I rasp. "He preys on little girls." My voice cracks and I'm pissed at myself for showing emotion when she's a piece of stone. However, she reaches across the table, snatches my hand, and gives me a warm smile that tells me she understands. With a lump in my throat, I blurt out the entire story. No wonder Jesse cares for her. She makes it easy … when she wants to.

Alana is a typical, unpredictable woman. Okay, unpredictable yes, typical, no.

"You know what he deserves?" Her mouth twists. "Incarceration. Prisoners hate child molesters." She turns to Jesse. "Do you have anything stronger than this?" She slides her cup which collides with his.

I bring the bottle of Jack from the bedroom and pour three drinks.

With revenge looming near, my breath is short. "Yeah but we have no evidence. He'll walk. Then if anything happens to him, we're suspects." I slug my drink and pour another.

"He deserves to have his dick cut off and stuffed down his throat," Jesse snarls. "Lock him in a cage with a horny bear. Or gorilla. I hear they don't discriminate."

I watch Jesse's neck go red, so I stand behind him, massaging his shoulders.

"Can you help us?" I ask, well aware my eyes plead even though my voice does not.

Alana nods. "Honey, I'm from D.C."

"How can you do this? I mean, who's going to do this for us … for me?" My fingers tighten on the back of Jesse's neck.

"You'd be surprised." She winks. "How do you think

politicians climb up to their thrones?"

Speechless, I stare.

Her smile is sly. "Because they know people, and so do I. There's nothing more rewarding than rubbing elbows with reliable people," she smirks at Jesse, "who don't mind having their backs rubbed in return for favors."

Jesse and Alana are obviously tight, sharing some sort of past. I'll pump him later. Right now, I need to concentrate on carrying out my plan.

Jesse drains his glass and slams it down on the table. He locks my wrists around his neck. "I'll be in the alley. Not, Zoe."

"Jesse, you stay out of this." Alana is forceful. "I've seen you in action."

"Exactly what don't I know about you, Jesse?" I whisper into his ear.

"He's a good man." Alana's hand comes down on his.

"This freak is a Columbian drug lord." Her voice is so controlled, I wonder what she has been through to make her so impenetrable. "You know he's got enemies who'd love to extinguish their competition. We'll find them." She slides her glass to Jesse for a refill.

Jesse pulls me onto his lap, and together we plot.

"We can't wait too long," I worry, "Dee says he comes and goes and is sometimes gone for months."

"How is she?" Jesse asks. "You two really went at it last night."

"Well, she's not in the hospital," I smirk, "that much I can say."

Jesse rolls his eyes. Opens his mouth, about to speak, but says nothing. Perhaps he's thought better than to get into the middle of my argument with Dee.

"Yes, Jesse. I know she's been through a lot. I'll patch things up with her … after this is over. And she can never ever know."

My eyes shoot daggers at him. "You have to promise."

Jesse leans back in his chair, slams a palm on his chest. "Christ. Do you think I'm crazy? This stays between the three of us."

"It absolutely has to," Alana warns.

As comrades, we lift our glasses in toast.

"I don't know about this Alana. I want to kill the mother fucker." Jesse's hand comes down on the table, churning the booze in our glasses.

"Cool it, Jesse, or we'll leave you home." She winks at me.

"You'd have ten minutes of satisfaction and spend the rest of your life in prison." I run my hand over his hair, feeling the rising heat of anger. "That's not going to happen."

"This is turning into a bad scene. You don't have to do this, Alana." I've dragged others into this and guilt eats me alive.

"Yes I do," she nods, "Jesse bailed me out twice. This will even the score."

I stare into her navy blue eyes which mirror my stubbornness and determination.

"I think we've covered everything." Alana stands to leave. "I'll be in touch to finalize the time."

"Alana," I throw my arms around her. "How can I ever thank you?"

"Just keep this guy out of trouble." She grins. "And you rest. You have darker circles than I do. You've been through enough. Let me handle the rest. We'll have a van waiting in the alley, with two delivery men. A private plane waiting at the airport."

"Christ," Jesse moans, burying his head in his hands.

"All you have to do, Zoe, is get him into that alley without anyone seeing you."

I remember how he snatched me in the deserted hallway and I shudder. "I don't think that will be a problem."

She reaches into her tote and hands me a Taser. "Will this

help calm your nerves, Jesse?" She nips his chin with her fingertips. "Remember. You cannot do to this freak what you did to Peter."

"Peter?" I tilt my head.

"Long story for another time." She grins and turns to Jesse. "He's paying the piper, Jess. They all do … eventually."

"Good to hear," Jesse replies, and I realize there was another man in Alana's life. "You look fantastic. You have that glow." Jesse grins.

"Life is good," she pitches a hip, "and yours will be as well." She taps her fingertip on his temple. "Restraint Jesse. Brains get you more places than brawn ... although sometimes excessive force is a necessity." She shoots Jesse a knowing wink.

My hands shake as I dress. I'm not sure I can pull this off, but I have to. The plans are in place, there's no turning back now. Jesse will be nearby. Jesse will be nearby. I repeat over and over. He'd never let anything happen to me.

My cell rings. "Speak of the devil," I control the fear in my voice, trying for light, strong, fearless, like Alana.

"Hey, sweetheart." Jesse is not his usual carefree self. He's also feeling the effects of what we'll be facing tonight. "How are you holding up?"

I draw in a long breath. "I'm good. Just can't wait for this to be over."

"It will be soon, honey. I hate that you have to go through this. I wish there was another way." His voice builds with tension. "There must be–"

"No." I'm forceful. "This is the only way, Jesse. The plans are in motion. We have no choice."

"I could beat him. Leave him in the alley. Leave you out of it." His voice is almost a whisper. "I'd do anything for you, Zoe. Anything."

"Then be strong for me, Jesse. I need you to be so I will be."

"I'll be in the car, right across the street the entire time. Just remember that okay? And if anything goes wrong, you put those beautiful lungs of yours to use. Scream, baby. Scream your head off."

"Okay," I say, my voice weak because I'm imagining what could go wrong, dreading having to confront a monster … again."

"Promise me, Zoe." Jesse's voice cracks.

"I promise." The LCD clock is flashing the time. "I better go, Jesse. I have to get dressed. It's almost time."

"I don't want to hang up, babe. Put me on speaker, let's talk while you get ready."

Despite the evening ahead of us, I laugh. "You always make me feel better."

"That's why I'm here. That and because–"

"Because you're amazing." I stop him. I know what he's about to say, and I can't deal with it. If he tells me he loves me, I'll have to confess I'll never be able to have a normal relationship until this is over. "I appreciate everything you're doing for me."

"You don't have to thank me. You know I'd do anything for you." I visualize his pout.

"I know. I'm sorry. I'm just really stressed out."

"Of course you are."

"So, I'll text you when I get to the gallery. Before my dirty deed." My chuckle emerges with a tremor.

Finding You

Jesse

Eyes glued to the clock, I pace. I'm dying for a beer or a joint, but I can't. I need a clear head, have to be top notch to carry out this fucking mission. For the fifth time, I check the battery life on my cell phone. Imagining running out of battery, my stomach sinks. My hands are trembling. Stop! I tell myself. You won't be any good to her if you're a nervous fuck up.

I decide to check in with Alana, make sure everything is perfect on her end. She's not answering her phone. This raises my heart rate. I know she'll be there, she'd never let me down, so I manage to calm myself, convincing myself she's out of range or her cell is buried in her purse and she'll get me back.

Sure enough, my cell rings. "Jesse?"

"Alana, thank Christ. How is everything?"

"Fine. Stop worrying. This is going to go off without a hitch. Leave it to me."

"You can't expect a control freak to fall for that line."

"Take some deep breaths. The troops are on the way."

Through static I hear a man's voice. Horns blowing. Traffic. Christ. "Where are you?"

"Just coming over the bridge and onto the Deegan. All is well. Listen, I have to go. I don't want to use up all my battery."

"Didn't you charge your fucking phone?" I snap.

"Yes I did, but if you keep bothering me." Pause. "How's Zoe holding up?" Alana sounds cautious.

My face is flushed. I've never felt so stressed in my fucking life. I check the time. "She should be on her way. She'll text me when she gets to the gallery. Then it's too late to turn back."

"We're not turning back, Jesse. Stop obsessing."

"I can't believe you're calling this obsession," I snap, then blow out a breath. "Okay. See you soon."

I hop into the Stang and light her up. I tap my jacket pocket for my cell, which I know is there, but I'm falling into a state of OCD. I might not wait in the car. I might wait around the corner, just in case. But then, if he sees me, it's off. I can't fuck this shit up.

Finding You

Zoe

My heart is pounding, my hairline damp. I welcome the breeze that's cooling my burning face. My satchel is slung over my shoulder and I'm hugging the faux leather bag for dear life. I wish I had a gun and not just a Taser and a roll of duct tape. The evening is dark. Anyone, anything, could leap out in front of me. The monster I'm on my way to lure into an alley could be lurking behind me. I start, my head whips around. My pulse is so fast, I can barely breathe. *If you don't stop this shit, you'll blow it. Imagine if you fucked up and he raped you again?* This sets off a panic attack. I'm transported back to the school bathroom, exiting into the dimly lit hallway. I feel the hand come up behind me, I actually feel his presence. *Stop it! He's not here. What you need to worry about more are the cars passing by, because no one can see you lure him into that alley.* That will bring our plan to a screeching halt.

Walking close to the building, skulking actually, I hear the echo of my stilettos clicking with each anxious step. The gallery is just a few doors away. I pause in front of the frosted glass, pretending to search through my bag for the key. I have to act nonchalant, like someone who's about to let themselves into a building. We disabled the floodlights, along with the cameras, so no one will ever know.

Since that night at the gallery Moody's been calling me, breathing into the phone, fucking with me, following me. But I've never been alone. Not like tonight. So I don't doubt he'll be here. I just have to keep fumbling in my bag for the key. I can't let myself in because he'd follow me. I'd be stuck inside this dark, ominous building with a monster. Jesse wouldn't hear my screams through these brick walls. I trust Jesse. In my heart I know he's right across the street, hiding, waiting, but I need to text him. Contact. I need contact! I pull out my phone and tap: Hey. Are you here?

Immediately my screen lights up: I'm right across the street, babe. Watching you.

I can't see you.

That's good. He won't either.

Is Alana here?

I'm texting her right now to tell her you're here.

Finding You

Jesse

All I can make out of Zoe are some strands of blonde hair that haven't been tucked into her hat. Like tinsel, they glisten in moonlight. We disabled the safety night lights on the building, so she's an easy target. At this hour, traffic is light. Now and then a car speeds by, oblivious I hope, to Zoe and me. She's wearing black, so she blends with the night.

I punch out a text to Alana. No ringing phones. Rule #1, cells on vibrate. This is why I wear a pocket t-shirt, so I can feel the vibration. I hate pocket t-shirts. I hate what we're doing.

"Come on," I whisper to the Stang's dark interior. "Pick up your fucking phone, Alana. I hope to hell you feel the vibration of your phone, of the fear I'm mentally transmitting to you. Come on. Pick up. Pick up!" I start to panic.

Zoe's still waiting in front of the gallery. I could blow the entire plan by trying to sneak into the alley. I could spook him, which is something I'm considering because I can't take much more of this fucking tension. My gut is in knots. Alana is in that alley, with her men, waiting. I tell myself. She has to be. She would have let me know if something went wrong.

While I'm arguing with myself, I see him skulk along the building. The husky figure moves slowly, carefully, like a stalking cat about to pounce on a mouse. His intentions are evident. It takes every ounce of self-control to not jump out of this car and kick every last ounce of air out of his lungs, permanently.

He's beside her, reaching out, she's backing away. Close, closer, almost to the alley, which I'm sure

fucking delights the fuck. The perfect place to trap his victim. His sweet, young victim.

I refuse to take my eyes away, but my cell is vibrating against my heart. My pounding heart.

"Jesse. Stop her, Jesse," Alana screams in my ear.

"What the fuck?"

"We're hung up on bridge construction. We won't be there for at least ten minutes."

I don't respond. I drop the phone, yank the door open, and charge across the street. Zoe's not screaming, my mind reasons. She's handling it. She's okay.

Finding You

Zoe

I feel him before he speaks. Before he traps my body against the door with his. *Tonight his breath isn't foul,* shoots through my brain. I'm comparing tonight with the real attack, the one I couldn't stop. Tonight Moody is the victim, and I'm suddenly courageous because Alana is waiting in the alley with her men, and Jesse is just across the street.

"Fancy meeting you here," he blows into my ear. Reaching out he tugs on of the tendrils hanging from my hat. His nose is at my neck and he's sniffing me like a he's a dog and I'm a piece of meat. "Mmm. You smell delicious. You weren't wearing perfume that day. Just sweet innocent soap."

"What arc you doing here?" I control my voice that longs to break into a frantic scream. "Why are you following me?"

His body presses close and I feel the lump in his crotch. My stomach lurches and I think I'm about to vomit. But I have a job to do. Calm, I need to remain calm. Get him into the alley. That's where they're waiting.

"You flaunted yourself enough. You're the one calling and hanging up on me. I'm not that stupid. So you liked it, huh? And now you're back for more." His laugh is evil, like sandpaper coats his throat. "They always come back for more."

"You do," I snap. "I hate you. I hate what you did to me. To Dee." I yank away. I'm older now. Stronger. He's not expecting this. Managing to untangle my body from his, I edge toward the alley. Moody permits this because this is his building. He knows it well. He knows there's no camera. He knows there's a dead end alley I'm edging toward. He thinks he'll trap me. That I won't be able to escape. Hah, I want to laugh in his face. Spit in his face. He's got another think coming.

I edge along the building, my hand sliding along the uneven bricks. A ragged edge cuts me and I feel the sticky blood in my palm. With each step I take, he follows. We're like two magnets. And I can't believe it's working. He's not at all suspicious. He's following along.

"Where are you taking me? Into the shadows, so we can be alone?"

"Why don't you fuck off?" I'm so brave, which probably excites him.

"Fuck yes, off no. You want this. You know you do." He reaches out for my arm, but I yank it away and I run. Deep into the alley, but it's so dark I can't see the van, and a monster is on my heels.

"You've got nowhere to run, girly."

Momentum slams me into the wall and it knocks the wind out of me. My mind races. Where's the van? There's no van! Just a wall? What the fuck? Before I can scream for Jesse, Moody pins me to the wall, one hand around my throat, the other securing one of my arms. I flail, kick, thrash, but his hold on my neck is suffocating me. I believe he's crushing my windpipe. Is he going to kill me? Jesse, my mind screams. Jesse! But I'm not really screaming, so Jesse isn't about to rescue me. It's my plot, my deal, so I bring up a knee and land a blow to Moody's bulging crotch. His excitement is a great target.

"Ugh," he grunts and folds.

I've disabled him long enough to grab the strap of my bag and swing it full force at his head. The bag connects with a smack, disorienting him. I use this opportunity to run! But Moody grabs my arm, whirls me around and slams me against the wall. "Bitch." His hand goes to my throat again.

Jesse

The alley is dark, but I hear the scuffling. I don't have to sneak up on them because Zoe is struggling like a wildcat, trying to free herself, and has him completely occupied. Body and mind, I believe. In moments, I make out their outlines, throw myself against his back and hook my arm around his throat. I have to get him off Zoe, so she can breathe. I'm afraid he's about to strangle her.

The grip of my arm cripples him. His arms drop to his sides then snap. His fingers dig into my bicep as he attempts to pry my arm from his throat, but it's not happening. I'm holding on for dear life.

"Run Zoe. Get the hell out of here."

Zoe's bent over, trying to catch her breath. I want to go to her, comfort her, but I can't let him go. I jam a knee into his spine, and his body is arched. I know I can't strangle him, so I yell to Zoe. "The tape. Give me the tape."

Moody might overpower little girls, but he's shit against me. I pull him to the ground and smash his face into the pavement. He's grunting, I'm panting. I have a knee on his back, holding him in place, so I can twist his arms around his back.

"Tape his wrists," I yell to Zoe. "Then his feet."

Within minutes, he's hogtied and I can release my hold, leap to my feet and pull Zoe into my arms.

"We did it baby," I almost cry into the side of her face. In the struggle, her hat was ripped off and her hair falls past her shoulders. She smells so sweet. I brush a hand through her hair, and this calms me.

Headlights slide down the alley, heading straight for us. The van creeps and when it stops, the lights fade. Alana hops out of the passenger side door, breathless.

"Are you two okay?" She stutters, "I'm so sorry Jesse. We got hung up on the bridge." She hugs herself, like she's feeling a chill. "I couldn't believe it. I almost had a heart attack." Her head rocks.

"I think we all need to chill, take some deep breaths," I say.

"We need to get going," a deep voice grunts when two human tanks slide out of the van and come up beside us.

"Everything cool?" the other asks.

"Looks like you've got it under control. Step aside. We can take over," the first hulk cuts in. "Get a move on."

Moody is on his stomach, struggling in vain. He's letting out a series of groaning, "What the fuck is going on?"

Ignoring him, Zoe, Alana and I remain in our huddle. The two delivery men, as Alana refers to them, hoist Moody off the pavement like he's a sack of flour. He grunts and struggles but he's no match for any of us. They toss him into the van, rolling him onto his back.

"You're gonna be fucking sorry for this," he threatens. "You have no idea who you're fucking with."

"Yeah. I think we do, you piece of shit," Alana snaps, then pulls Zoe in for a hug. "Go for it girl, you earned it."

Zoe is eerily calm.

"You did great, honey." My words are choked because I'm holding back tears. "I still can't believe we pulled this off." I run my hand over my head again and again.

But Zoe is in a world of her own. "Get in, Jesse," she says climbing into the back of the van.

Alana and the men hop into the front.

Zoe kneels beside Moody, dangerously close, surprisingly close.

When I try to pull her away, she shrugs me off. She's in high gear and is driven by intent.

Zoe

I'm in a state of shock, suffering a depersonalization similar to the night my parents were killed. Surreal. This is too surreal. Pull yourself together, girl, my mind alerts. So I spring into action.

Kneeling beside Moody, I stare at the sight of this weak man, hatred pouring from my lips. "How does it feel?" I'm sarcastic.

The men have loaded Moody into the back of the van like cargo. We're backing out of the alley, and the movement almost causes me to fall onto him, I'm hovering that close. But Jesse's arm shoots out to steady me. I give him a smile. Trembling, but it's still a smile.

"You tell me," Moody slurs, arrogant. "How did it feel?"

"I want to kick you in your ugly face, cut your balls off, you know that? But ... no marks, remember? No bruises. No one can ever know what went on here tonight." I snarl. "Tell anyone, and I'll kill you ... and your family." I stop to study the shock that tightens his face.

"Look. That was a long time ago. Bygones, you know?" His body rolls side to side as we pull out onto the road. "Let me go and you'll never hear from me again. I'm a rich man. I'll even pay you. All of you." He yells so the others in front can hear.

I gather a mouthful of saliva and aim it square at his face. "Pervert."

Moody's beginning to freak. I believe he realizes this is not a joke. Or a bad dream. "What are you gonna do, kill me?" A tinge of forced bravado clings to his words, but he's also beet red, sweat pouring over his face, mixing with my saliva, indicating he's more worried than he lets on.

"No. I'm not going to kill you." My head swings to Jesse and I grin. "Neither will he." The chill down my spine turns from apprehension to pleasure. I could permit myself to feel like a monster, but I'm justified. My focus returns to Moody. "For once in your life you're going to do something for someone else," my teeth clench so tight I don't feel any movement of my lips.

"What are you talking about? If it's money, I told you. Whatever charity you pick, I'll donate."

"You're gonna donate, alright, but not money."

"What the fuck are you talking about, bitch."

"Shut your mouth," Jesse snarls, and his boot slams Moody's side.

"You're going on a little trip. Back to your homeland. You're about to be an organ donor. Give back to the community." I backhand him. "This is for all the little girls you took everything from."

"You can't prove anything."

"I don't need to."

"So you're out for revenge." He tries to laugh but sounds pathetic.

"You have no clue what I have in mind or you wouldn't be smirking. You'd be shitting your pants."

This seems to do the job because his lips tremble, followed by his limbs.

"Not revenge, justice. Stop struggling. We need to deliver a perfectly healthy donor." I turn to Jesse. "No more kicking, babe. We can't damage any of his internals."

"What the fuck?" Moody sounds frantic. "You can't do this." His eyes go wild darting from Jesse to me.

"Watch me." My grating voice tears my throat.

"You're gonna kill me?"

"I already told you, I would never kill you. What you're about to do is quite noble, actually. You'll be helping other people, good people. And they're waiting for you...as we speak."

Moody is nonstop struggling, trembling, crying and pleading. "Don't do this. I have money. I can do things for you–"

"You've already done things ... to me ... things I have to live with for the rest of my life."

"When this is all over, when I get back, I'll report you," he threatens in a quivering voice.

I laugh so hard, I can barely stop. I know it's not because I think any of this is funny; it's relief. It's finally over.

"You're not coming back. You signed yourself away as a permanent donor. Organs, blood, whatever is needed. Oh, and after you wake up in a hospital bed, you'll be transferred to a wheel chair, where you'll spend the rest of your life. Every day will be a surprise. Every day ... payback. As they say, it's a bitch, isn't it?"

Epilogue

Zoe

We ride to the Jersey shore, sit at the water's edge, side by side, Jesse's arm around me, my head on his shoulder. Denny's song – technically my song, wafts through the air.

"Hear that?" I ask Jesse, who seems to be in another place, daydreaming.

"The ocean?" His finger traces a heart in the sand.

"No, the song playing on the boardwalk loudspeakers."

He cocks an ear. "Yeah. Why?"

"Comatose. It was mine."

"Was?"

"Yup." I nod. "And I gave it to someone very special."

"Great song." With a sigh, Jesse gazes out over the ocean.

I bring his face around. "A dear friend. Someone who believed in me enough to give me a start. To tell me when it was time to finish."

Denny has made it. I'm happy for him. Thrilled for myself. I have everything I need sitting right beside me.

"Watching the sunset over the ocean is amazing," Jesse says.

"I sense some artwork," I chuckle.

"Maybe." His arm brings me close. "You know me too well." He inhales ocean air. "I could live here. It's so tranquil."

"I know what you mean." I run my palm up and down his thigh. "When I was little, my parents brought me to the Connecticut shore. We'd get there early, Mom would grab a table under the trees," I take a moment to think, "Maybe it was Sherwood Island? Anyway, Dad would light the charcoal and get the briquettes red and ready to cook." I sigh. "Some things stick with you. I can still smell the aroma."

"Ah. Charcoal burgers. We went to Sherwood, too. Jamie and I would stay in the water all day, until we pruned." He chuckles. "But we ate sandwiches, potato salad, pickles. I'm getting hungry."

"Me too. Mom said she couldn't keep me out of the water." I giggle.

"Small world." Jesse's arm tightens. "Why didn't we meet sooner? We could have saved ourselves a lot of grief." He nuzzles my neck. "You must have been an adorable toddler." His fingers drag over my head.

My giggle leads into a sigh. "Fate has her reasons, Jesse."

"Yeah. Guess you're right." Sand sifts through his fingers.

I rest my head on his shoulder. "Sometimes I wonder what it all means."

"What, babe?"

"Life."

He leans in for a kiss. Taking my hand, he traces my palm. "I see a long and meaningful life, not to mention, fruitful."

"A few years ago, I wouldn't have agreed. But now I hope it's long and even though I like surprises, a little more predictable." I slide a finger over his throat and feel his slow and even pulse. "And very fruitful."

"That's nice to know. I'm tired of chasing you." He chuckles and plays with my hoop earring.

"It's been a long haul. We've both been through so much. But in a way, I think adversity makes you a better person. Like when everything isn't handed to you, and you have to fight your way up from hell, it makes you appreciate what you have ... what *we* have. Do you know what I mean?"

His beautiful eyes look deep into my soul. "What do we have?" I haven't seen him this serious since the wolf attack that turned out to be a dog. Or the night my dad almost chewed his head off.

"Each other?" My eyes question. Please let the answer be yes. Let the conversation be leading in the right direction. Please, for once in my life make something be easy.

He smiles. His finger circles my lips. "From now on things are going to get easier ... because we have each other." After a kiss, he whispers, "We have a lot to do."

"And all the time in the world." I'm lazy, reflective.

"Yup, we've come full circle, Zoe." His lips brush my hair. "If you could go anywhere in the world, where would it be?"

"Oh, wow, I've never really thought about it." I tilt my head, tucking my windblown hair behind my ears. "But I guess I'd love to visit Hawaii. Maybe Ireland. Or Tuscany. Yes! Tuscany."

Jesse laughs. "Whoa. Pick one."

"Tuscany. Why?" I grin up at him. "Are you going to paint it for me?" I giggle.

"The gallery is doing well. My paintings are selling. I think it's time to get away for a while. Think about the future."

"The future?" I'm grateful my hard swallow is silent.

"I love you, Zoe. I have for a long time. It took for what feels like forever to find you again." Every muscle in his face tightens. "I don't ever want to go through that again. I never want to lose you." Taking my hand, he caresses my fingers.

"Jesse. The entire time, there was never anyone else in my heart. And there never will be."

Finding You

Our lips meet and I press his possessively, breaking only to whisper, "I'll never let you go."

Jesse caresses my ring finger. I hold my hand up to see the braided band he's tattooed. I lift his hand and kiss his matching braided finger.

"You like?" he says.

"I love."

"Someday I'll put the real thing on your finger."

My heart is about to burst ... but now, with nothing other than love.

Jesse eases me onto my back. He slips a hand under my shirt, and I feel his fingers on my tummy.

"You're tickling me." I squirm.

"Will you please sit still for a minute, you little control freak."

I feel the slide of something cold, then a gentle pressure on my skin.

"Seriously?"

"What?"

"You're writing on my stomach?"

He laughs. "Keep still. You're ruining my artwork."

"What? What are you drawing?" I strain to lift my head but as he leans over me, his broad shoulder blocks my view.

"This better be water based." I threaten.

"Mmm. Let's take a taste and see." His lips play on my tummy for what feels like a full five minutes. And while he nibbles, I giggle. "Yep. Tastes like Crayola to me."

"You're tickling me. What are you doing down there, Jesse?"

"Doodling." With that he lifts his head. A splotch of black marker dots the tip of his nose.

"You look like a puppy." I burst into laughter and grab a handful of his hair.

He licks my neck and pants in my ear.

Suddenly serious, I gaze into his magical brown eyes. "I never laugh so much as when I'm with you."

He frowns. "It's a good thing, right?"

"It's wonderful."

I stretch out and watch clouds sail across the swirling blue sky, thinking about Mom and Dad. Recalling the tangled mess of a life that feels so far away. The beauty of it now. I owe a lot of my happiness to Jesse, but in my heart, I know I was on the right road before he came back into my life. I can definitely make it on my own. But I'd much rather walk through the next door of life with Jesse at my side.

I'm powerful. I'm healed. This doesn't mean I'll ever forget the nightmare past, but I've learned to let it go. It's part of my life. I own it. I own me. I like being me. And since this is my one and only life, I have promised to make the most of it.

"I feel like I've lived a thousand years," I say, sighing with contentment.

"Maybe you've lived a thousand years, but I've loved you forever, Zoe Channing."

"I love you more than anything, Jesse Sinclair. Now let me see what you drew on my belly."

I gaze down to see fairies, butterflies, and two doves nesting beak to beak. I gaze up at him and lift a brow.

Then we laugh. We laugh, and tears roll down our cheeks.

Finding You

Jesse

Zoe is sitting on my lap, arms draping my shoulders. At my insistence, she's singing *Comatose*, while I rock her in my arms.

> *I never knew it could be this way*
> *I never knew I could love so much*
> *Rainbows on your fingertips*
> *Burn when they brush my lips*

"You should be singing your song on the radio. Not some dude."

"Nah. Denny's got a rocking voice. And I have other plans."

"You do, huh?" The wind's whipping up. I pull strands of hair from her face.

Her brows crease. "Environmental justice. Alana is an inspiration. I can't wait to get into a courtroom."

"She's a cool chick."

"She is. And I want to be strong, Jesse. Be my own person."

My brow lifts. "Keeping it all to yourself, huh?" I tease, hugging her tight.

"And you." She sinks a finger into my abs. "I want to send a message, Jesse." Her eyes are fierce.

"I get your signals all the time, baby." I nuzzle her neck. She's still warm, although the sun is sinking like a road flare over the horizon.

"Not that kind." I take a punch to the gut. "Women can wage wars too. That's my message."

I bury my face in her boobs. "Don't I know it."

"Thank God for Alana." The sigh she heaves lifts my head.

"True that. And the sun is now the moon. Guess we should get going." I slide her from my lap to the blanket beside me.

Zoe scrubs marker off the tip of my nose, then kisses it. "Yeah, my tummy's growling. Who's cooking tonight?"

"The Colonel," I laugh. "Maybe Stouffers. Have you ever been to Texas?" My question comes out of left field.

"Been there, sang there. How about you?" She stretches her legs, her toes digging into sand.

"Been there, lived there." I tug her earlobe. "I plan on calling my dad."

Her cheek rests on my chest. "Nice."

I smooth her hair. "Very nice. Tell him I want to show him what a good woman I have."

Her head whips up. "You want to go to Texas? With me?"

"Ah ha." My lips briefly touch hers.

"Florida. Texas." Closing her eyes, she lifts her face to the breeze. "So you've been around a lot, huh?"

"Pretty much." I ruffle her hair.

"With a lot of women?"

"My share, I guess. I'm human." I spill sand on her bare legs.

"And you? Been with many dudes? Or..." I palm my face. "You don't have to answer that. In fact, don't answer that."

Visions of Zoe have been locked in my head since day

one; she's pure; not that I'm a chauvinist, but dudes can be sluts, not girlfriends. I want my woman to be a slut in my bed and a lady outside. If I told this to Zoe, she'd beat me to a pulp. I hold in a chuckle.

She brings her face to mine. "No it's okay. I've been with a few guys." Her fingers slip over my beard, tracing my frown.

"Not like that, Jesse. I've never met anyone I wanted to give myself to." She takes a deep breath. "I believe in fairytales."

"Do you–" I tweak her nose.

"Yup. And in princes."

Jesse

Our flight lands in Dallas. We grab our bags and pick up a compact rental.

Zoe and I drive out to Dad's ranch, and I brief her on what we might be walking into. "Anything is possible when you're with the Sinclairs. So be prepared." I grin, but my fingers grip the wheel tighter. I haven't spoken to Claudette or my brother in a while, and I'm hoping Jamie has worked out his wild.

Zoe chuckles. "Your family can't be any worse than the Romanos." She pats my thigh. "Everything works out in the end. Even the Romanos." She's wistful.

I sneak a glance. Zoe is gazing out the window, her face tipped up to the sky.

"You look hot, babe."

"I am. It must be a hundred degrees."

I reach across the seat and squeeze her shoulder. "Who didn't want the A/C? Who wanted fresh country air?" I chuckle. "And I wasn't referring to the heat."

"Sinclair & Sons," she says excitedly as we approach the shingle hanging on the signpost. Her hand comes up to cover mine. "Look at the cows grazing in the field ... I love farms. No wait, they have horns." She gasps. "Cattle."

"Texas Longhorns," I chuckle, "we'll make a cowgirl out of you yet." Thinking of Zoe dressed in a sexy little cowgirl outfit raises my pulse.

In the driveway is a double cab truck and a brand new Cadillac. Out in a field is a tractor. The driveway is gravel. Our tires crunch to a halt.

"Wow, this is a big house, Jesse." Zoe marvels, her neck stretching out the window of our car. "A real ranch."

I chuckle. "That's my dad. Go big, like Texas. He knows us, Jamie actually. And that he'll probably be stuck with him for a long time."

I think back to the phone call I received from my brother after I bought Claudette a one-way ticket to Dallas and drove her to the airport.

"Are you telling me this is on me?" His astounded voice choked through the phone line. "I own this?" I never heard Jamie so panic-stricken. "This is not on my shoulders, bro. I can't own this one, bro." His groan sounded so pathetic, a laugh of satisfaction froze in my throat.

"Can't she stay up there, Jess?"

My brother stopped calling me Jess when I was old enough to fight back. After that I was dickface or douchebag. "This is not on me, bro." I fired back. "She's all yours, dude. Get used to being called Daddy."

"Fuck you, douchebag." Click and he was gone.

I park beside Colton's truck. Zoe hops out first, dragging her bag from the back seat.

Music emanates from behind the house and with it comes a cowboy. With long strides, Colton is at our side, throwing an arm around me, then he opens his arms to Zoe.

"Hey kid, is this the little lady I heard big things about?" The deep creases around his mouth disappear with his smile. "She's a willowy little thing, but quite a bundle." He winks at me and I hold my breath, wondering what will come out of his mouth next. "No wonder you were so damn smitten."

Zoe beams up at him, fingers calming her long hair which is swirling in the wind.

Zoe's smile is warm and content. "You must be Colton."

Chewing a toothpick, he nods. "Don't pay attention to any of those rumors you might have heard." Chuckling, he lays his arm lightly around her shoulders. "Come on, kids, everyone's out back, waiting on you. You're just in time for barbeque."

Following Colton around the house, the aroma of steaks on a grill fills the air. Picking up the scent of corn, I remember shucking and figure I'll be doing a lot more in the coming days.

Chase toddles toward us, assisted by Dad. I scoop him up with a hug. "Zoe, I'd like you to meet Chase Sinclair." I put his small hand in hers.

"Hello Chase. You're cuter than your pictures." She nuzzles his hand and plucks his little chin.

"Chase, how's my little man? Give me five buddy. Where's your daddy?" I search the yard, ready for a confrontation with Jamie.

Colton yells, "Kids are here," at the top of his lungs, and Jamie and Claudette walk out the back door and stroll across the yard. Claudette's smiling, Jamie's carrying an armload of beers. They don't wear wedding bands but they're doing a hell of a job raising their son.

I gaze down at Chase: he has Jamie's eyes. My eyes? Family eyes.

Colton strides to Chickie, picks her up and swings her in the air. Yep, should have known by the Cadillac Chickie was here. She lassoed Colton. I chuckle.

"Nice wheels, Chickie," I call out.

"You know me, Jess. Only the best." Colton takes her punch to his chest.

Calling out to Colton, I chuckle. "Don't let her corrupt you, bro. And whatever you do, don't go into a bar with her or you'll be leaving with two black eyes."

Chickie hangs on Colton's arm. "Look at how this cowboy fills out his jeans." She pats his ass.

Chase is handed over to Claudette, who gives us a brief smile then saunters off.

"Dad, this is Zoe." I slide my arm around my girl.

He lifts her with a bear hug. "It's wonderful to finally meet you, Zoe," he says, then whispers in her ear. "You picked the right one."

I laugh as Dad sets my girlfriend down, then I take her in my arms. "Yep. She's the keeper."

Jamie, forever the ball buster, shuffles to my side carrying two beers. "How about us studs take a ride into town ... get a few drinks at the Barn. I was kinda thinking about Twilight." He grins.

I know he's referring to Twilight the singer, not the end of day.

"No thanks," my arm tightens around Zoe. "I have everything I need right here," I squeeze her tight and kiss her cheek, "in this yard and Dad's barn looks good to me."

Dad drops Chase into Jamie's arms. "Almost time to chow down, boys."

Claudette and Colton load the table with enough food to feed an entire crew of ranch hands.

Jamie ruffles Chase's dark hair with his lips. "Hey little man. One of these days, Daddy's gonna take you to the Barn." He grins at me. I think back to my mom saying, "Like father, like son," many years ago.

My horny brother is honorable after all. I hope he stays that way, honorable, not horny.

I breathe a sigh of relief and slap him on the back.

Jamie is taking good care of his boy.

Here we stand, three generations of Sinclairs. I get misty, thinking I wish Mom was here to see this, then I look at the sky and believe she's smiling down at us all.

Finding You

Zoe

I like the ranch. The sounds, the smells, the love that surrounds me.

Over dinner, one by one, I study the faces. The women are loved, but the Sinclair men have secrets.

"How about the barn and twilight?" Jamie's smirk is directed at Jesse.

Jamie is the catalyst, but the others fold over in laughter.

"What happened in the barn?" I ask Jesse, curiosity killing me.

Jamie snickers and Colton shoves an elbow into his ribs.

Jesse squeezes my hand, whispering, "I'll tell you all about it someday."

"I'll definitely need to know about twilight and the barn," with a nudge of my elbow, I whisper back.

"We're setting up a stage for you, Zoe," Colton's baritone silences the chatter. "I'm up for dancin' with my gal." He's out of his seat, pulling Chickie into his arms.

I smile. "I only sing lullabies now."

Chase is playing with the butterfly charm dangling from the

belt of my shorts. I lift him onto my lap and cuddle him. Hum the same song I sang to Angelina, who Jesse will be meeting one day … soon, I hope.

The glow on Jesse's face says he's happy, he's home. He has everything his heart has ever longed for: family, art exhibits, me.

I listen to laugher, take part in the passion, and something tells me, Jesse and I have both come full circle. No one could ever replace my mom and dad, but being welcomed into the Sinclair family sure is a good start.

In my heart, I'm home.

Finding You

Finding You

About The Author

I'm Victoria (January) Valentine, a New York writer and indie book publisher. I've been writing for most of my life in one form or another: poetry, short stories, song lyrics, children's books, adult novels. *Agony of Being Me* & *Finding You* are her latest.

My favorite genres to read and write are horror, thrillers, and contemporary romance. Besides being inspired by my family, I owe a shout out to Robert C. Wilson, author of *Crooked Tree*, and Robert McCammon, author of *They Thirst* and other fabulous books. The moment I read their novels, I knew I wanted to write horror.

Besides writing and publishing for others, I blog and when time permits, I host Away With Words on Blogtalkradio on Wednesdays @ 6:00 PM EST USA, where I pimp indie and traditionally published authors and their amazing books and careers. Our gabfests are a blast.

Thank you for reading *Agony of Being Me duo*. A writer would be nowhere without the support of readers and fans. I treasure each and every one of you and would love to hear from you!

Indie publishing is not always easy, but it's a blessing. Dear readers ... Thank you from the bottom of my heart for supporting me and my efforts. Right after I started Agony, my husband was diagnosed with incurable sarcoma. He passed away on May 6th 2015. Agony has had as many ups and downs as its author. During the writing process, the manuscript grew so long, I felt splitting it into two books would be best. There is so much to digest in the lives of these characters, and you may need a breather! I sure do.

For me, writing Agony has been exhausting. I've relived some of the past, some good, some not, but in the end it all turned out as God planned. Tom went home, and I finished my story.